KT-451-014

Praise for the GONE series

'I really can't give enough praise to this book . . . I had that feeling I had when I was reading THE HUNGER GAMES . . . that I had come across something rare and brilliant!' *Winged Reviews, Amazon.co.uk*

'Exciting, high-tension story told in a driving, torrential narrative that never lets up. This is great fiction. I love these books.' *Stephen King*

'An excellent mystery, boldly conceived.' *The Bookseller*

'I just couldn't put it down! Last night I picked it up, intending to read a chapter or two . . . Instead, I read two hundred pages.' *Teen review on Amazon.com*

'A chilling portrayal of a world without rules.' *Reading Zone*

'GONE covers all the bases . . . horror, suspense, superheroes and supervillains.' *Waterstone's Book Quarterly*

'Levels of nastiness almost worthy of Dante.' *Guardian*

'Gripping from the first moment on . . . a brilliantly plotted fantasy.' *Lovereading*

'If Stephen King had written LORD OF THE FLIES, it might have been a little like this.' *Voice of Youth Advocates (VOYA)*

MICHAEL GRANT

Agent Orange lyrics used by permission.
'A Cry For Help In A World Gone Mad,'
written by Michael A. Palm, courtesy of Covina High Music

First published in Great Britain 2009
by Egmont UK Limited
This edition first published in 2012
by Electric Monkey, an imprint of Egmont UK Limited
The Yellow Building, 1 Nicholas Road, London W11 4AN
First published in the USA 2008
by HarperTeen

Published by arrangement with HarperTeen
a division of HarperCollins Publishers, Inc.
1350 Avenue of the Americas, New York,
New York 10019, USA

Text copyright © 2008 Michael Grant

The moral rights of the author have been asserted

ISBN 978 1 4052 4235 6

15

www.electricmonkeybooks.co.uk

A CIP catalogue record for this title is available from the British Library

Typeset by Avon DataSet Ltd, Bidford on Avon, Warwickshire
Printed and bound in Great Britain by Clays Ltd, St Ives plc

45875/22

MIX
Paper
FSC FSC® C018306

EGMONT

Our story began over a century ago, when seventeen-year-old Egmont Harald Petersen found a coin in the street. He was on his way to buy a flyswatter, a small hand-operated printing machine that he then set up in his tiny apartment.

The coin brought him such good luck that today Egmont has offices in over 30 countries around the world. And that lucky coin is still kept at the company's head offices in Denmark.

For Katherine, Jake, and Julia

Michael Grant has always been fast paced. He's lived in almost 50 different homes in 14 US states, and moved in with his wife, Katherine Applegate, after knowing her for less than 24 hours. His long list of previous occupations includes cartoonist, waiter, law librarian, bowling alley mechanic, restaurant reviewer, documentary film producer and political media consultant.

Michael and Katherine have co-authored more than 150 books, including the massive hit series Animorphs, which has sold more than 35 million copies. Working solo, Michael is the author of the internationally bestselling series GONE and the groundbreaking transmedia trilogy BZRK.

Michael, Katherine and their two children live in the San Francisco Bay Area, not far from Silicon Valley. Michael can be contacted on Twitter (@thefayz), Facebook (authormichaelgrant), and via good, old-fashioned email (Michael@themichaelgrant.com).

ONE

ONE MINUTE THE teacher was talking about the Civil War. And the next minute he was gone.

There.

Gone.

No 'poof'. No flash of light. No explosion.

Sam Temple was sitting in third-period history class staring blankly at the blackboard, but far away in his head. In his head he was down at the beach, he and Quinn. Down at the beach with their boards, yelling, bracing for that first plunge into cold Pacific water.

For a moment he thought he had imagined it, the teacher disappearing. For a moment he thought he'd slipped into a daydream.

Sam turned to Mary Terrafino, who sat just to his left. 'You saw that, right?'

Mary was staring hard at the place where the teacher had been.

'Um, where's Mr Trentlake?' It was Quinn Gaither, Sam's best, maybe only, friend. Quinn sat right behind Sam. The two of them favoured window seats because sometimes, if you caught just the right angle, you could actually see a tiny sliver of sparkling water

1

between the school buildings and the homes beyond.

'He must have left,' Mary said, not sounding like she believed it.

Edilio, a new kid Sam found potentially interesting, said, 'No, man. Poof.' He did a thing with his fingers that was a pretty good illustration of the concept.

Kids were staring at one another, craning their necks this way and that, giggling nervously. No one was scared. No one was crying. The whole thing seemed kind of funny.

'Mr Trentlake poofed?' said Quinn, with a suppressed giggle in his voice.

'Hey,' someone said, 'where's Josh?'

Heads turned to look.

'Was he here today?'

'Yes, he was here. He was right here next to me.' Sam recognised the voice. Bette. Bouncing Bette.

'He just, you know, disappeared,' Bette said. 'Just like Mr Trentlake.'

The door to the hallway opened. Every eye locked on it. Mr Trentlake was going to step in, maybe with Josh, and explain how he had pulled off this magic trick, and then get back to talking in his excited, strained voice about the Civil War nobody cared about.

But it wasn't Mr Trentlake. It was Astrid Ellison, known as Astrid the Genius, because she was . . . well, she was a genius. Astrid was in all the AP classes the school had. In some subjects she was taking online courses from the university.

Astrid had shoulder-length blonde hair, and liked to wear starched white short-sleeved blouses that never failed to catch Sam's eye. Astrid was out of his league, Sam knew that. But there was no law against thinking about her.

'Where's your teacher?' Astrid asked.

There was a collective shrug. 'He poofed,' Quinn said, like maybe it was funny.

'Isn't he out in the hallway?' Mary asked.

Astrid shook her head. 'Something weird is happening. My math study group . . . there were just three of us, plus the teacher. They all just disappeared.'

'What?' Sam said.

Astrid looked right at him. He couldn't look away like he normally would, because her gaze wasn't challenging, sceptical like it usually was: it was scared. Her normally sharp, discerning blue eyes were wide, with way too much white showing. 'They're gone. They all just . . . disappeared.'

'What about your teacher?' Edilio said.

'She's gone, too,' Astrid said.

'Gone?'

'Poof,' Quinn said, not giggling so much now, starting to think maybe it wasn't a joke after all.

Sam noticed a sound. More than one, really. Distant car alarms, coming from town. He stood up, feeling self-conscious, like it wasn't really his place to do so, and walked on stiff legs to the door. Astrid moved away so he could step past her. He could smell her shampoo as he went by.

Sam looked left, down towards room 211, the room where Astrid's math wonks met. The next door down, 213, a kid stuck out his head. He had a half-scared, half-giddy expression, like someone buckling into a roller-coaster.

The other direction, down at 207, kids were laughing too loud. Freaky loud. Fifth-graders. Across the hall, room 208, three sixth-graders suddenly burst out into the hallway and stopped dead. They stared at Sam, like he might yell at them.

Perdido Beach School was a small-town school, with everyone from kindergarten to ninth grade all in one building, elementary and middle school together. High school was an hour's drive away in San Luis.

Sam walked towards Astrid's classroom. She and Quinn were right behind him.

The classroom was empty. Desk chairs, the teacher's chair, all empty. Math books lay open on three of the desks. Notebooks, too. The computers, a row of six aged Macs, all showed flickering blank screens.

On the chalkboard you could quite clearly see 'Polyn'.

'She was writing the word "polynomial"', Astrid said in a church-voice whisper.

'Yeah, I was going to guess that,' Sam said drily.

'I had a polynomial once,' Quinn said. 'My doctor removed it.'

Astrid ignored the weak attempt at humour. 'She disappeared in the middle of writing the "o". I was looking right at her.'

Sam made a slight motion, pointing. A piece of chalk lay on the floor, right where it would have fallen if someone were

4

writing the word 'polynomial' – whatever that meant – and had disappeared before rounding off the 'o'.

'This is not normal,' Quinn said. Quinn was taller than Sam, stronger than Sam, at least as good a surfer. But Quinn, with his half-crazy half-smile and tendency to dress in what could only be called a costume – today it was baggy shorts, army-surplus desert boots, a pink golf shirt, and a grey fedora he'd found in his grandfather's attic – put out a weird-guy vibe that alienated some and scared others. Quinn was his own clique, which was maybe why he and Sam clicked.

Sam Temple kept a lower profile. He stuck to jeans and understated T-shirts, nothing that drew attention to himself. He had spent most of his life in Perdido Beach, attending this school, and everybody knew who he was, but few people were quite sure what he was. He was a surfer who didn't hang out with surfers. He was bright, but not a brain. He was good-looking, but not so that girls thought of him as a hottie.

The one thing most kids knew about Sam Temple was that he was School Bus Sam. He'd earned the nickname when he was in seventh grade. The class had been on the way to a field trip when the bus driver had suffered a heart attack. They'd been driving down Highway 1. Sam had pulled the man out of his seat, steered the bus on to the shoulder of the road, brought it safely to a stop, and calmly dialled 911 on the driver's cell phone.

If he had hesitated for even a second, the bus would have plunged off a cliff and into the ocean.

His picture had been in the paper.

'The other two kids, plus the teacher, are gone. All except Astrid,' Sam said. 'That's definitely not normal.' He tried not to trip over her name when he said it but failed. She had that effect on him.

'Yeah. Kind of quiet in here, brah,' Quinn said. 'OK, I'm ready to wake up now.' For once, Quinn was not kidding.

Someone screamed.

The three of them stumbled into the hall, which was now full of kids. A sixth-grader named Becka was the one screaming. She was holding her cell phone. 'There's no answer. There's no answer,' she cried. 'There's nothing.'

For two seconds everyone froze. Then a rustle and a clatter, followed by the sound of dozens of fingers punching dozens of keypads.

'It's not doing anything.'

'My mom would be home, she would answer. It's not even ringing.'

'Oh, my God: there's no Internet, either. I have a signal, but there's nothing.'

'I have three bars.'

'Me too, but it's not there.'

Someone started wailing, a creepy, flesh-crawly sound. Everybody talked at once, the chatter escalating to yelling.

'Try 911,' a scared voice demanded.

'Who do you think I called, numbnuts?'

'There's no 911?'

'There's nothing. I've gone through half my speed dials, and there's not anything.'

The hall was as full of kids as it would have been during a class change. But people weren't rushing to their next class, or playing around, or spinning the locks on their lockers. There was no direction. People just stood there, like a herd of cattle waiting to stampede.

The alarm bell rang, as loud as an explosion. People flinched, like they'd never heard it before.

'What do we do?' more than one voice asked.

'There must be someone in the office,' a voice cried out. 'The bell went off.'

'It's on a timer, moron.' This from Howard. Howard was a little worm, but he was Orc's number-one toady, and Orc was a glowering thug of an eighth-grader, a mountain of fat and muscle who scared even ninth-graders. No one called Howard out. Any insult to Howard was an attack on Orc.

'They have a TV in the teachers' lounge,' Astrid said.

Sam and Astrid, with Quinn racing after them, pelted towards the lounge. They flew down the stairs, down to the bottom floor, where there were fewer classrooms, fewer kids. Sam's hand on the door of the teachers' lounge, they froze.

'We're not supposed to go in there,' Astrid said.

'You care?' Quinn said.

Sam pushed the door open. The teachers had a refrigerator. It was open. A carton of Dannon blueberry yogurt was on the floor, gooey contents spilled on to the ratty carpet. The TV was on, with no picture, just static.

Sam searched for the remote. Where was the remote?

Quinn found it. He started running through the channels. Nothing and nothing and nothing.

'Cable's out,' Sam said, aware it was kind of a stupid thing to say.

Astrid reached behind the set and unscrewed the coaxial cable. The screen flickered and the quality of the static changed a little, but as Quinn ran the channels there was still nothing and nothing and nothing.

'You can always get channel nine,' Quinn said. 'Even without cable.'

Astrid said, 'Teachers, some of the kids, cable, broadcast, cell phones, all gone at the same time?' She frowned, trying to work it out. Sam and Quinn waited, like she might have an answer. Like she might say, 'Oh, sure, now I understand.' She was Astrid the Genius, after all. But all she said was, 'It doesn't make any sense.'

Sam lifted the receiver on the wall phone, a landline. 'No dial tone. Is there a radio in here?'

There wasn't. The door slammed open and in rushed two kids, fifth-grade boys, their faces wild, excited. 'We own the school!' one yelled, and the other gave an answering hoot.

'We're going to bust open the candy machine,' the first one announced.

'That's maybe not a good idea,' Sam said.

'You can't tell us what to do.' Belligerent, but not sure of himself, not sure he was right.

'You're right, little dude. But look, how about we all try and keep it together till we figure out what's going on?' Sam said.

'You keep it together,' the kid yelled. The other one hooted again, and off they went.

'I guess it would be wrong to ask them to bring me a Twix,' Sam muttered.

'Fifteen,' Astrid said.

'No, man, they were, like, ten,' Quinn said.

'Not them. The kids in my class. Jink and Michael. They were both math whizzes, better than me, but they had LDs – learning disabilities, dyslexia – that kept them back. They were both a little older. I was the only fourteen-year-old.'

'I think maybe Josh was fifteen, in our class,' Sam said.

'So?'

'So he was fifteen, Quinn. He just . . . just disappeared. Blink and he was gone.'

'No way,' Quinn said, shaking his head. 'Every adult and older kid in the whole school just disappears? That makes no sense.'

'It's not just the school,' Astrid said.

'What?' Quinn snapped at her.

'The phones and the TV?' Astrid said.

'No, no, no, no, no,' Quinn said. He was shaking his head, half smiling, like he'd been told a bad joke.

'My mom,' Sam said.

'Man, stop this,' Quinn said. 'All right? It's not funny.'

For the first time Sam felt the edge of panic, like a tingling at the base of his spine. His heart was thumping in his chest, labouring as if he'd been running.

Sam swallowed hard. He sucked at the air, unable to take more than shallow breaths. He looked at his friend's face. He'd never seen Quinn so scared. Quinn's eyes were behind shades, but his mouth quivered, and a pink stain was creeping up his neck. Astrid was still calm, though, frowning, concentrating, trying to make sense of it all.

'We have to check it out,' Sam said.

Quinn let loose a sort of sobbing breath. He was already moving, turning away. Sam grabbed his shoulder.

'Get off me, brah,' Quinn snapped. 'I have to go home. I have to see.'

'We all have to go see,' Sam said. 'But let's go together.'

Quinn started to pull away, but Sam tightened his grip. 'Quinn. Together. Come on, man, it's like a wipeout, you know? You get launched, what do you do?'

'You try not to get worked up,' Quinn muttered.

'That's right. You keep your head straight through the spin cycle. Right? Then swim towards daylight.'

'Surfing metaphor?' Astrid asked.

Quinn stopped resisting. He let go of a shuddering breath. 'OK, yeah. You're right. Together. But my house first. This is messed up. This is so messed up.'

'Astrid?' Sam asked, not sure of her, not sure at all if she wanted to go with him and Quinn. It felt presumptuous to ask her, and wrong not to ask.

She looked at Sam, looked like she was hoping to find something in his face. Sam suddenly realised that Astrid the Genius didn't know what to do, or where to go, any better than he did. That seemed impossible.

From the hallway they heard a rising cacophony of voices. Loud, scared, some babbling, as if it would be OK as long as they didn't stop talking. Some voices were just wild.

It wasn't a good sound. It was frightening all by itself, that sound.

'Come with us, Astrid, OK?' Sam said. 'We'll be safer together.'

Astrid flinched at the word 'safer'. But she nodded.

This school was dangerous now. Scared people did scary things sometimes, even kids. Sam knew that from personal experience. Fear could be dangerous. Fear could get people hurt. And there was nothing but fear running crazy through the school.

Life in Perdido Beach had changed. Something big and terrible had happened.

Sam hoped he was not the cause.

TWO

KIDS POURED OUT of the school, alone or in small groups. Some of the girls walked in threes, hugging each other, tears streaming down their faces. Some boys walked hunched over, cringing as if the sky might fall on them, not hugging anyone. A lot of them were crying, too.

Sam flashed on news videos he'd seen of school shootings. It had that kind of feel to it. Kids were bewildered, scared, hysterical, or hiding hysteria beneath laughter and bold displays of rowdiness.

Brothers and sisters were together. Friends were together. Some of the really little kids, the kindergarteners, the first-graders, were wandering on the grounds, not really going anywhere. They weren't old enough to know their way home.

Preschoolers in Perdido Beach mostly went to Barbara's Day Care, a downtown building decorated with faded appliqués of cartoon characters. It was next to the Ace hardware store and across the plaza from the McDonald's.

Sam wondered if they were OK, the littles down at Barbara's. Probably. Not his responsibility. But he had to say something.

'What about all these little kids?' Sam said. 'They'll wander into the street and get run over.'

Quinn stopped and stared. Not at the little kids, but down the street. 'You see any cars moving?'

The stoplight changed from red to green. There were no cars waiting to go. The sound of car alarms was louder now, maybe three or four different alarms. Maybe more.

'First we see about our parents,' Astrid said. 'It's not like there aren't any adults anywhere.' She didn't seem sure of that, so she amended it. 'I mean, it's unlikely there are no adults.'

'Yeah,' Sam agreed. 'There must be adults. Right?'

'My mom will most likely either be home or playing tennis,' Astrid said. 'Unless she has an appointment or something. My mom or dad will have my little brother. My dad's at work. He works at PBNP.'

PBNP was Perdido Beach Nuclear Power. The power plant was just ten miles from the school. No one in the town thought about it much any more, but a long time ago, in the nineties, there had been an accident. A freak accident, they called it. A once-in-a-million-years coincidence. Nothing to worry about.

People said that's why Perdido Beach was still a small town, why it hadn't ever gotten really big like Santa Barbara down the coast. The nickname for Perdido Beach was Fallout Alley. Not very many people wanted to move to a place called Fallout Alley, even though all the radioactive fallout had been cleaned up.

The three of them, with Quinn a few steps ahead, walking

fast on his long legs, headed down Sheridan Avenue and turned right on Alameda.

At the corner of Sheridan Avenue and Alameda Avenue was a car with the engine running. The car had smashed into a parked SUV, a Toyota. The Toyota's alarm came and went, screeching one minute, then falling silent.

The air bags in the Toyota had deployed: limp, deflated white balloons drooped from the steering wheel and the dashboard.

No one was in the SUV. Steam came from beneath the crumpled hood.

Sam noticed something, but he didn't want to say it out loud.

Astrid said it: 'The doors are still locked. See the knobs? If anyone had been inside and gotten out, the doors would be unlocked.'

'Someone was driving and blinked out,' Quinn said. He wasn't saying it like it was supposed to be funny. Funny was over.

Quinn's house was just about two blocks down Alameda. Quinn was trying to maintain, trying to stay nonchalant. Trying to keep acting like cool Quinn. But all of a sudden, Quinn started running.

Sam and Astrid ran too, but Quinn was faster. His hat fell off his head. Sam bent and scooped it up.

By the time they caught up, Quinn had thrown open his front door and was inside. Sam and Astrid went as far as the kitchen and stopped.

'Mom. Dad. Mom. Hey!'

Quinn was upstairs, yelling. His voice got louder each time

he yelled. Louder and faster, and the sob was clearer, harder for Sam and Astrid to pretend not to hear.

Quinn came pelting down the stairs, still yelling for his family, getting only silence in return.

He still had his shades on, so Sam couldn't see his friend's eyes. But tears were running down Quinn's cheeks, and tears were in his ragged voice, and Sam could practically feel the lump in Quinn's throat because the same lump was in his own throat. He didn't know what to do to help.

Sam set Quinn's fedora down on the counter.

Quinn stopped in the kitchen. He was breathing hard. 'She's not here, man. She's not here. The phones are dead. Did she leave a note or anything? Do you see a note? Look for a note.'

Astrid flicked a light switch. 'The power is still on.'

'What if they're dead?' Quinn asked. 'This can't be happening. This is just some kind of nightmare or something. This . . . this isn't even possible.' Quinn picked up the phone, punched the talk button, and listened. He punched the button again and put the phone to his ear again, then dialled, stabbing at buttons with his index finger and babbling the whole time.

Finally, he put the phone down and stared at it. Stared at the phone like he expected it to start ringing any second.

Sam was desperate to get to his own house. Desperate and afraid, wanting to know and dreading knowing. But he couldn't rush Quinn. If he made his friend leave the house now, it would be like telling Quinn to give up, that his parents were gone.

'I had a fight with my dad last night,' Quinn said.

'Don't start thinking that way,' Astrid said. 'One thing we know: *you* didn't cause this. None of us caused this.'

She put her hand on Quinn's shoulder, and it was as if that was the signal for him to finally fall apart. He sobbed openly, pulled his shades off, and dropped them on the tile floor.

'It's going to be OK,' Astrid said. She sounded like she was trying to convince Quinn, but also herself.

'Yeah,' Sam said, not believing it. 'Of course it is. This is just some . . .' He couldn't think of how to finish the sentence.

'Maybe it was God,' Quinn said, looking up, suddenly hopeful. His eyes were red and he stared with sudden, manic energy. 'It was God.'

'Maybe,' Sam said.

'What else could it be, right? S-so – so – so –' Quinn caught himself, choked down the panicked stutter. 'So it'll be OK.' The thought of some explanation, any explanation, no matter how weak, seemed to help. 'Duh, of course it will be OK. It'll totally be OK.'

'Astrid's house next,' Sam said. 'She's closest.'

'You know where I live?' Astrid asked.

This would not be a good time to admit that he had followed her home once, intending to try to talk to her, maybe ask her to go to a movie, but had lost his nerve. Sam shrugged. 'I probably saw you some time.'

It was a ten-minute walk to Astrid's home, a two-storey, kind-of-new house with a pool in the back. Astrid wasn't rich, but her house was much nicer than Sam's. It reminded Sam of the house he used to live in before his stepfather left. His stepfather hadn't been rich, either, but he'd had a good job.

Sam felt weird being in Astrid's home. Everything in it seemed nice and a little fancy. But everything was put away. There was nothing out that could be broken. The tables had little plastic cushions on the corners. The electrical sockets had childproof covers. In the kitchen the knives were in a glass-front cupboard with a childproof lock on the handle. There were kid-proof knobs on the stove.

Astrid noticed him noticing. 'It's not for me,' she said snippily. 'It's for Little Pete.'

'I know. He's . . .' He didn't know the right word.

'He's autistic,' Astrid said, very breezy, like it was no big thing. 'Well, no one here,' she announced. Her tone said she'd expected it, and it was fine.

'Where's your brother?' Sam asked.

Astrid yelled then, something he hadn't known she could do. 'I don't know, all right? I don't know where he is.' She covered her mouth with one hand.

'Call to him,' Quinn suggested in a strange, carefully enunciated, formal voice. He was embarrassed by his freak-out. But at the same time, he wasn't quite done freaking out.

'Call to him? He won't answer,' Astrid said through gritted teeth. 'He's autistic. Severely. He doesn't . . . he doesn't relate. He won't answer, all right? I can yell his name all day.'

'It's OK, Astrid. We're going to make sure,' Sam said. 'If he's here, we'll find him.'

Astrid nodded and fought back tears.

They searched the house inch by inch. Under the beds. In the closets.

They went across the street to the home of a lady who sometimes took care of Little Pete. There was no one home there, either. They searched every room. Sam felt like a burglar.

'He must be with my mom, or maybe my dad took him to the plant with him. He does that when there's no one else to babysit.' Sam heard desperation in her voice.

Maybe half an hour had passed since the sudden disappearance. Quinn was still weird. Astrid seemed about to fall apart. It wasn't even lunchtime but already Sam was wondering about night. The days were short, it was November 10, almost Thanksgiving. Short days, long nights.

'Let's keep moving,' Sam said. 'Don't worry about Little Pete. We'll find him.'

'Is that meant to be a pro forma reassurance or a specific commitment?' Astrid asked.

'Sorry?'

'No, I'm sorry. I meant, you'll help me find Petey?' Astrid asked.

'Sure.' Sam wanted to add that he would help her anywhere, any time, forever, but that was just his own fear talking, making him want to babble. Instead, he started towards his own house, knowing now beyond doubt what he would find, but needing to check anyway, and to check something else, too. Needing to see if he was crazy.

Needing to see if it was still there.

The Chumash

GONE

This was all crazy. But for Sam, the crazy had started long before.

For the hundredth time Lana craned her head to look back and check on her dog.

'He's fine. Stop fretting,' Grandpa Luke said.

'He could jump out.'

'He's dumb, all right. But I don't think he'll jump out.'

'He's not dumb. He's a very smart dog.' Lana Arwen Lazar was in the front seat of her grandfather's battered, once-red pickup truck. Patrick, her yellow Labrador, was in the back, ears streaming in the breeze, tongue hanging out.

Patrick was named for Patrick Star, the not-very-bright character on *SpongeBob*. She wanted him up front with her. Grandpa Luke had refused.

Her grandfather turned on the radio. Country music.

He was old, Grandpa Luke. Lots of kids had kind of young grandparents. In fact, Lana's other grandparents, her Las Vegas grandparents, were much younger. But Grandpa Luke was old in that wrinkled-up-leather kind of way. His face and hands were dark brown, partly from the sun, partly because he was Chumash Indian. He wore a sweat-stained straw cowboy hat and dark sunglasses.

'What am I supposed to do the rest of the day?' Lana asked.

Grandpa Luke swerved to avoid a pothole. 'Do whatever you want.'

'You don't have a TV or a DVD or Internet or anything.'

Grandpa Luke's so-called ranch was so isolated, and the old man himself was so cheap, his one piece of technology was an ancient radio that only seemed to pick up a religious station.

'You brought some books, didn't you? Or you can muck out the stable. Or climb up the hill.' He pointed with his chin towards the hills. 'Nice views up there.'

'I saw a coyote up the hill.'

'Coyote's harmless. Mostly. Old brother coyote's too smart to go messing with humans.' He pronounced coyote 'kie-oat'.

'I've been stuck here a week,' Lana said. 'Isn't that long enough? How long am I supposed to stay here? I want to go home.'

The old man didn't even glance at her. 'Your dad caught you sneaking vodka out of the house for some punk.'

'Tony is not a punk,' Lana shot back.

Grandpa Luke turned the radio off and switched to his lecturing voice. 'A boy who uses a girl that way, gets her in the middle of his mess, that's a punk.'

'If I didn't get it for him, he would have tried to use a fake ID and maybe have gotten in trouble.'

'No maybe about it. Fifteen-year-old boy drinking booze, he's going to find trouble. I started drinking when I was your age, fourteen. Thirty years of my life I wasted on the bottle. Sober now for thirty-one years, six months, five days, thank God above and your grandmother, rest her soul.' He turned the radio back on.

'Plus, the nearest liquor store's ten miles away in Perdido Beach.'

Grandpa Luke laughed. 'Yeah. That helps, too.'

At least he had a sense of humour.

The truck was bouncing crazily along the edge of a dry gulch that went down a hundred feet, down to more sand and sagebrush, stunted pine trees, dogwoods, and dry grasses. A few times a year, Grandpa Luke had told her, it rained, and then the water would go rushing down the gulch, sometimes in a sudden torrent.

It was hard to imagine that as she gazed blankly down the long slope.

Then, without warning, the truck veered off the road.

Lana stared at the empty seat where her grandfather had been a split second earlier.

He was gone.

The truck was going straight down. Lana lurched against the seat belt.

The truck picked up speed. It slammed hard into a sapling and snapped it.

Down the truck went in a cloud of dust, bouncing so hard, Lana slammed against the headliner, her shoulders beaten against the window. Her teeth rattled. She grabbed for the wheel, but it was jerking insanely and suddenly the truck rolled over.

Over and over and over.

She was out of her seat belt, tossing around helplessly inside the cabin. The steering wheel was beating her like an agitator in a washing machine. The windshield smashed her shoulder, the gearshift was like a club across her face, the rear-view mirror shattered on the back of her head.

21

The truck came to a stop.

Lana lay face down, her body twisted impossibly, legs and arms everywhere. Dust choked her lungs. Her mouth was full of blood. One of her eyes was blocked, unable to see.

What she could see with her one good eye was impossible to make sense of at first. She was upside down, looking at a patch of low cactus that seemed to be growing at right angles to her.

She had to get out. She oriented as best she could and reached for the door.

Her right arm would not move.

She looked at it and screamed. Her right forearm, from elbow to wrist, no longer formed a straight line. It was twisted into an angle like a flattened 'V'. It was rotated so that her palm faced out. The jagged ends of broken bones threatened to poke through her flesh.

She thrashed in panic.

The pain was so terrible, her eyes rolled up in her head and she passed out.

But not for long. Not long enough.

When she woke up, the pain in her arm and left leg and back and head and neck made her stomach rise. She threw up over what had been the tattered headliner of the truck.

'Help me,' she croaked. 'Help. Someone help!'

But even in her agony she knew there was no one to help. They were miles from Perdido Beach, where she'd lived until a year ago when her folks moved to Las Vegas. This road led nowhere except to the ranch. Maybe once a week someone else would come down this road, a lost backpacker or the old woman who played checkers with Grandpa Luke.

'I'm going to die,' Lana said to no one.

But she wasn't dead yet, and the pain wasn't going away. She had to get out of this truck.

Patrick. What had happened to Patrick?

She croaked his name, but there was nothing.

The windshield was starred and crumpled, but she couldn't kick it out with her one good leg.

The only way was the driver's side window, which was behind her. She knew that the mere act of turning around would be excruciating.

Then, there was Patrick, poking his black nose in at her, panting, whimpering, anxious.

'Good boy,' she said.

Patrick wagged his tail.

Patrick was not some fantasy dog that suddenly learned to be smart and heroic. He did not pull Lana from the steaming wreckage. But he stayed with her as she spent an hour of hell crawling out on to the sand.

She rested with her head shaded by a sagebrush. Patrick licked blood from her face.

With her good hand Lana detailed her injuries. One eye was covered in blood from a gash on her forehead. One leg was broken, or at least twisted beyond use. Something hurt inside her lower back, down where her kidneys were. Her upper lip was numb. She spit out a bloody piece of broken tooth.

The worst by far was the horrifying mess of her right arm. She couldn't bear to look at it. An attempt to lift it was immediately abandoned: the pain could not be endured.

She passed out again and came to much later. The sun was remorseless. Patrick lay curled beside her. And in the sky above, a half-dozen vultures, their black wings spread wide, circled, waiting.

THREE

'**THAT** TRUCK,' SAM said, pointing. 'Another crash.' A FedEx truck had ploughed through a hedge and slammed an elm tree in somebody's front yard. The engine was idling.

They ran into two kids, a fourth-grader and his little sister, playing a half-hearted game of catch on their front lawn. 'Our mom's not home,' the older one said. 'I'm supposed to go to my piano class this afternoon. But I don't know how to go there.'

'And I have tap dance. We're getting our costumes for the recital,' the younger one said. 'I'm going to be a ladybug.'

'You know how to get to the plaza? You know, in town?' Sam said.

'I guess so.'

'You should go there.'

'I'm not supposed to leave the house,' the little one said.

'Our grandma lives in Laguna Beach,' the fourth-grader said. 'She could come get us. But we can't get her on the phone. The phone doesn't work.'

'I know. Maybe go wait down at the plaza, right?' When the kid just stared at him, Sam said, 'Hey, don't get too upset, OK? You have any cookies or ice cream in the house?'

25

'I guess so.'

'Well, there's no one telling you not to eat a cookie, is there? Your folks will show up soon, I think. But in the meantime have a cookie, then come down to the plaza.'

'That's your solution? Have a cookie?' Astrid asked.

'No, my solution is to run down to the beach and hide out until this is all over,' Sam said. 'But a cookie never hurts.'

They kept moving, Sam and Quinn and Astrid. Sam's home was east of downtown. He and his mom shared a small, squashed-looking one-storey house with a tiny, fenced backyard and no real front yard, just a sidewalk. Sam's mother didn't make much money working as a night nurse up at Coates Academy. Sam's dad was out of the picture, always had been. He was a mystery in Sam's life. And last year his step-father had left, too.

'This is it,' Sam said. 'We don't believe in showing off with a big house and all.'

'Well, you live near Town Beach,' Astrid said, pointing to the only advantage of this house or this neighbourhood.

'Yeah. Two-minute walk. Less if I cut through the yard of the house where the biker gang lives.'

'Biker gang?' Astrid said.

'Not the whole gang, really, just Killer and his girlfriend Accomplice.' Astrid frowned, and Sam said, 'Sorry. Bad joke. It's not a great neighbourhood.'

Now that he was here, Sam didn't want to go in. His mother would not be there.

And there was something in his house maybe Quinn, and especially Astrid, shouldn't see.

He led the way up the three sun-faded, grey-painted wooden steps that creaked when you stepped on them. The porch was narrow, and a couple of months ago someone had stolen the rocking chair his mom had put out there so she could sit and rock in the evening before she went to work. Now they just had to drag out kitchen chairs.

That was always the best time of day for them, the beginning of his mother's workday, the end of Sam's. Sam would be home from school, and his mom would be awake, having slept most of the day. She would have a cup of tea, and Sam would have a soda or maybe a juice. She would ask him how school had gone that day, and he wouldn't really tell her very much, but it was nice to think about how he could tell her if he wanted to.

Sam opened the door. It was quiet inside, except for the refrigerator. The compressor on it was old and noisy. The last time they'd talked out on the porch, feet up on the railing, his mom had wondered whether they should get the compressor fixed, or whether it would be cheaper just to get a second-hand refrigerator. And how would they get it home without a truck.

'Mom?' Sam said to the emptiness of the family room.

There was no answer.

'Maybe she's up the hill,' Quinn said. 'Up the hill' was the townie phrase for Coates Academy, the private boarding school. The hill was more like a mountain.

'No,' Sam said. 'She's gone like all the others.'

The stove was on. A frying pan had burned black. There was nothing in the pan. Sam turned off the cooktop.

'This is going to be a problem all over town,' he said.

Astrid said, 'Yeah, stoves left on, cars running. Somebody needs to go around and make sure things are off and the little kids are with someone. And there's pills, and alcohol, and some people probably have guns.'

'In this neighbourhood some people have artillery,' Sam said.

'It has to be God,' Quinn said. 'I mean, how else, right? No one else could do this. Just make all the adults disappear?'

'Everyone fifteen or over,' Astrid corrected. 'Fifteen isn't an adult. Trust me, I was in class with them.' She wandered tentatively through the living room, like she was looking for something. 'Can I use the bathroom, Sam?'

He nodded reluctantly. He was mortified to have her here. Neither Sam nor his mother was really into housekeeping. The place was more or less clean, but not like Astrid's house.

Astrid closed the bathroom door. Sam heard the sound of running water.

'What did we do?' Quinn asked. 'That's what I don't get. What did we do to piss God off?'

Sam opened the refrigerator. He stared at the food there. Milk. A couple of sodas. Half of a small watermelon placed cut side down on a plate. Eggs. Apples. And lemons for his mom's tea. The usual.

'I mean, we did something to deserve this, right?' Quinn said. 'God doesn't do things like this for no reason.'

'I don't think it was God,' Sam said.

'Dude. Had to be.'

Astrid was back. 'Maybe Quinn's right. There's nothing, you know, normal, that can do this,' she said. 'Is there? It doesn't make any sense. It's not possible and yet it happened.'

'Sometimes impossible things happen,' Sam said.

'No, they don't,' Astrid argued. 'The universe has laws. All the stuff we learn in science class. You know, like the laws of motion, or that nothing can go as fast as the speed of light. Or gravity. Impossible things don't happen. That's what impossible means.' Astrid bit her lip. 'Sorry. It's not really the time for me to be lecturing, is it?'

Sam hesitated. If he showed them, crossed this line, he wouldn't be able to make them forget it. They would keep at him till he told them everything.

They would look at him differently. They would be freaked, like he was.

'I'm going to change my shirt, OK? In my room. I'll be right back. There's stuff to drink in the fridge. Go ahead.'

He closed the door to his room behind him.

He hated his room. The window opened on to an alley and the glass was that translucent kind you couldn't really see out of. The room was gloomy even on a sunny day. At night it was so dark.

Sam hated the dark.

His mom made him lock up the house at night when she was at work. 'You're the man of the house now,' she would say, 'but still, I'd feel better if I knew you had the door locked.'

He didn't like it when she said that, about him being the man of the house. The man of the house now.

Now.

Maybe she didn't really mean anything by it. But how could she not? It was eight months since his stepfather had fled their old house. Six months since Sam and his mother had moved to this shabby bungalow in this decrepit neighbourhood and his mother had been forced to take the low-paying job with the lousy hours.

Two nights ago there had been a thunderstorm and the lights had gone out for a while. He'd been in total darkness, except for faint flashes of lightning that turned the familiar things in his room eerie.

He'd managed to fall asleep for a while, but a huge crack of thunder had awakened him. He'd come out of a terrifying nightmare to total darkness in an empty house.

The combination had been too much. He'd cried out for his mother. A big, tough kid like him, fourteen, almost fifteen, yelling 'Mom' in the darkness. He had reached out his hand, pushing at the darkness.

And then . . . light.

It had appeared not quite all the way inside his closet. He could kind of hide it by closing the closet door. But when he'd tried to close the door all the way, the light had simply passed right through it. Like the door wasn't even there. So the door was kind of closed, not all the way. He had hung some shirts casually over the top of the door to block most of the light, but

30

that lame deception wasn't going to last long. Eventually his mom would see . . . well, when she came back, she would.

He pulled the closet door open. The camouflage fell away.

It was still there.

The light was small, but piercing. And it hovered there, unmoving, unattached to anything, no strings. Not a lamp or a light bulb, just a tiny ball of pure light.

It was impossible. It was something that could not exist. And yet there it was. The light that had simply appeared when Sam had needed it, and had not gone away.

He touched it, but not really. His fingers just went through it, feeling only a warm glow, no hotter than bathwater.

'Yes, Sam,' he whispered to himself, 'still there.'

Astrid and Quinn thought today was the beginning, but Sam knew better. Normal life had started coming apart eight months ago. Then, normalcy again. And then, this light.

Fourteen years of normal for Sam. Then normal had started to slip off its track.

Today, normal had crashed and burned.

'Sam?'

It was Astrid calling from the living room. He glanced at the doorway, anxious lest she come in and see. He did his hurried best to hide the light again, and went back to his companions.

'Your mom was writing on her laptop,' Astrid said.

'Probably checking email.' But when he sat down at the table and looked at the screen, it was open to a Word document, not a browser.

It was a diary. Just three paragraphs on the page.

It happened again last night. I wish I could take this to G. But she'll think I'm crazy. I could lose my job. She'll think I'm on drugs. If I had a way to put cameras all over, I could get some proof. But I have no proof, and C's 'mother' is rich and generous to CA. I'd be out the door. Even if I tell someone the whole truth, they'll just put me down as an overwrought mother.

Sooner or later, C or one of the others will do something serious. Someone will get hurt. Just like S with T.

Maybe I'll confront C. I don't think he'll confess. Would it make any difference if he knew everything?

Sam stared at the page. It hadn't been saved. Sam hunted around on the computer's desktop and found the folder labelled 'Journal'. He clicked on it. It was password-protected. If his mother had saved this final page, it too would have been under a password.

'CA' was easy. Coates Academy. And 'G' was probably the head of the school, Grace. 'S', too, was easy: Sam. But who was 'C'?

One line seemed to vibrate as he stared at it: 'Just like S with T.'

Astrid was reading over his shoulder. She was trying to be subtle, but she was definitely peeking. He closed the laptop.

'Let's go.'

'Where?' Quinn asked.

'Anywhere but here,' Sam said.

FOUR

'**LET'S** HEAD FOR the plaza,' Sam said. He closed the door of his home behind him, locked it, and stuck the key in his jeans.

'Why?' Quinn asked.

'It's where people will probably go,' Astrid said. 'There's nowhere else, is there? Unless they go back to the school. If anyone knows anything, or if there are any adults, that's where they'd be.'

Perdido Beach occupied a headland south-west of the coastal highway. On the north side of the highway the hills rose sharply, dry brown and patchy green, and formed a series of ridges that ran into the sea north-west and south-east of town, limiting the town to just this space, confining it to just this bulge.

There were just over three thousand residents in Perdido Beach – far fewer now. The nearest mall was in San Luis. The nearest major shopping centre was down the coast twenty miles. North, up the coast, the mountains pressed so close to the sea that there was no space for building, except for the narrow strip where the nuclear power plant sat. Beyond that was national parkland, a forest of ancient redwoods.

33

Perdido Beach had remained a sleepy little town of straight, tree-lined streets and mostly older, Spanish-style stucco bungalows with sloped orange tile roofs or old-style flat roofs. Most people had a lawn they kept well trimmed and green. Most people had a fenced backyard. In the tiny downtown, ringing the plaza, there were palm trees and plenty of angled parking spaces.

Perdido Beach had a resort hotel south of town, and Coates Academy up in the hills, and the power plant, but aside from that, only a smattering of businesses: the Ace hardware, the McDonald's, a coffee shop called Bean There, a Subway sandwich shop, a couple of convenience stores, one grocery store, and a Chevron station on the highway.

The closer Sam and Astrid and Quinn got, the more kids they encountered walking towards the plaza. It was like somehow all the kids in town had figured out that they wanted to be together. Strength in numbers. Or maybe it was just the crushing loneliness of homes that were suddenly not homey any more.

Half a block away, Sam smelled smoke and saw kids running.

The plaza was a small open space, a sort of park with patches of grass and a fountain in the middle that almost never worked. There were benches and brick sidewalks and trash cans. At the top of the square the modest town hall and a church sat side by side. Stores ringed the plaza, some of them closed up forever. Above some of the stores were apartments. Smoke was pouring from a second-storey window of an apartment above an out-of-business flower shop and a seedy insurance agency. As Sam came to a panting stop, a jet of orange flame burst from a high window.

Several dozen kids were standing, watching. A crowd that struck Sam as very strange, until he realised why it was strange: there were no adults, just kids.

'Is anyone in there?' Astrid called out. No one answered.

'It could spread,' Sam said.

'There's no 911,' someone pointed out.

'If it spreads, it could burn down half the town.'

'You see a fireman anywhere?' A helpless shrug.

The day care shared a wall with the hardware store, and both were only a narrow alley away from the burning building. Sam figured they had time to get the kids out of the day care if they acted fast, but the hardware store was something they could not afford to lose.

There had to be forty kids just standing there gawking. No one seemed about to start doing anything.

'Great,' Sam said. He grabbed two kids he sort of knew. 'You guys, go to the day care. Tell them to get the littles out of there.'

The kids stared at him without moving.

'Now. Go. Do it!' he said, and they took off running.

Sam pointed at two other kids. 'You and you. Go into the hardware store, get the longest hose you can find. Get a spray nozzle, too. I think there's a spigot in that alley. Start spraying water on the side of the hardware store and up on the roof.'

These two also stared blankly. 'Dudes: not tomorrow.

Now. Now. Go! Quinn? You better go with them. We want to wet down the hardware – that's where the wind will take the fire next.'

Quinn hesitated.

People were not getting this. How could they not see that they had to do something, not just stand around?

Sam pushed to the front of the crowd and in a loud voice said, 'Hey, listen up, this isn't the Disney Channel. We can't just watch this happen. There are no adults. There's no fire department. *We* are the fire department.'

Edilio was there. He said, 'Sam's right. What do you need, Sam? I'm with you.'

'OK. Quinn? The hoses from the hardware store. Edilio? Let's get the big hoses from the fire station, hook 'em up to the hydrant.'

'They'll be heavy. I'll need some strong guys.'

'You, you, you, you.' Sam grabbed each person's shoulder, shaking each one, pushing them into motion. 'Come on. You. You. Let's go!'

And then came the wailing.

Sam froze.

'There's someone in there,' a girl moaned.

'Quiet,' Sam hissed, and everyone fell silent, listening to the roar and crackle of the fire, the distant car alarms, and then, a cry: 'Mommy.'

Again. 'Mommy.'

Someone mocked the voice in falsetto. 'Mommy, I'm scared.'

It was Orc, actually finding the situation funny. Kids drew away from him.

'What?' he demanded.

Howard, never far away from Orc, sneered. 'Don't worry, School Bus Sam will save us all, won't you, Sam?'

'Edilio. Go,' Sam said quietly. 'Bring everything you can.'

'Man, you can't go up in there,' Edilio said. 'They'll have air tanks and stuff at the fire station. Wait, I'll bring it all.' He was already running, shepherding his crew of strong kids ahead of him.

'Hey, up there,' Sam yelled. 'Kid. Can you get to the door or the window?'

He stared up, craning his neck. There were six windows on the front of the building upstairs, one in the alley. The far left window was where the fire was, but now smoke was drifting out of the second window, too. The fire was spreading.

'Mommy!' the voice cried. It was a clear voice, not choking from the smoke. Not yet.

'If you're going in there, wrap this around your face.' Somehow Astrid had come up with a wet cloth, borrowed from someone and soaked.

'Did I say I was going in there?' Sam asked.

'Don't get hurt,' Astrid said.

'Good advice,' Sam said drily, and wrapped the wet fabric around his head, over his mouth and nose.

She grabbed his arm. 'Look, Sam, it's not fire that kills

people, it's smoke. If you get too much smoke, your lungs will swell up, they'll fill with fluid.'

'How much is too much?' he asked, his voice muffled by the cloth.

Astrid smiled. 'I don't know everything, Sam.'

Sam wanted to take her hand. He was scared. He needed someone to lend him some courage. He wanted to take her hand. But this wasn't the time. So he managed a shaky smile and said, 'Here goes.'

'Go for it, Sam,' a voice yelled in encouragement. There was a ragged chorus of cheers from the crowd.

The entrance to the building was unlocked. Inside were mailboxes, a back door to the flower shop, a dark, narrow stairway heading up.

Sam almost made it to the top of the stairs before he ran into an opaque wall of swirling smoke. The wet cloth did nothing. One breath and he was on his knees, choking and gagging. Tears filled his stinging eyes.

He crouched low and found more air. 'Kid, can you hear me?' he rasped. 'Yell, I need to hear you.'

The 'Mommy' was faint this time, from down the hall to the left, halfway to the other side of the building. Maybe the kid would jump out the window into someone's arms, Sam told himself. It would be stupid to get himself killed if the kid could just jump.

The stink of the smoke was intolerable, awful, everywhere. It had a sourness to it, like smoke plus curdled milk.

Sam stayed on his knees and crawled down the hallway. It was strange. Eerie. The ratty hall runner below him seemed so normal: faded Oriental pattern, frayed edges, a few crumbs, and a dead roach. An overhead light bulb was on, filtering pale light down through the ominous grey.

The smoke was swirling slowly lower, pressing down on him, forcing him lower and lower to find air.

There had to be six or seven apartments. No way to know which was the right one, the kid wasn't yelling any more. But the apartment on fire was probably the one just to his right. Smoke was shooting out from below that door, thick, fast, and furious as a mountain stream. He had seconds, not minutes.

He rolled on to his back. The smoke pouring from under the door was like a waterfall in reverse, falling upwards in a cascade. He kicked at the door, but it was no good. The lock was higher up; all his kick did was rattle the door. To break it open he would have to stand up, straight into that killing smoke.

He was scared. And he was mad, too. Where were the people who were supposed to do this? Where were the adults? Why was this up to him? He was just a kid. And why hadn't anyone else been crazy enough, stupid enough to rush into a burning building?

He was mad at all of them and, if Quinn was right and this was something God had done, then he was mad at God, too.

But if Sam had done this . . . if Sam had made all this happen . . . then there was no one to be mad at but himself.

He took in all the breath he could manage, jumped to his

feet, and slammed against the door all in one frantic motion.

Nothing.

And slammed again.

Nothing.

And again, and he had to breathe now, he had to, but the smoke was everywhere, in his nose, his eyes, blinding him. Again and the door opened and he fell in and hit the floor, face down.

The smoke trapped in the room erupted into the hallway, exploded out like a lion escaping its cage. For a few seconds there was a layer of breathable air at floor level and Sam took in a breath. He had to fight to keep from coughing it back out. If he did that, he was going to die, he knew it.

And for just a second it was partly clear in the apartment. Like a break in the clouds that gives you a little tease of clear blue sky before drawing the dark curtain once more.

The kid was on the floor, gagging, coughing, just a little kid, a girl, maybe five at most.

'I'm here,' Sam said in his strangled voice.

He must have looked terrifying. A big shape wreathed in smoke, face covered, black soot in his hair, smearing his skin.

He must have looked like a monster. That was the only explanation. Because the little girl, the terrified, panicky little girl, raised both of her hands, palms out, and from those chubby little hands came a blast, an explosion, jets of pure flame.

Flame. Shooting out of her tiny hands.

Flame!

Aimed at him.

The blast narrowly missed Sam. It passed his head with a whoosh and hit the wall behind him. It was like napalm, jellied gasoline, liquid fire that stuck to the wall where it hit and burned with mad intensity.

For a second he could only stare, frozen in amazement.

Insane.

Impossible.

The little girl cried out in terror and raised her hands again. This time she wouldn't miss.

This time she would kill him.

Not thinking, just reacting, Sam extended his arm, palm out. There was a flash of light, bright as an exploding star.

The kid fell on her back.

Sam crawled to her, shaking, stomach clenched, wanting to scream, thinking, no, no, no, no.

He scooped the kid into his arms, afraid she would wake up, and afraid that she wouldn't. He stood up.

The wall to his right fell in with a sound like ripping cardboard. Plaster was falling away, revealing the wall's structure, the lathe boards and two-by-fours. The fire was inside the wall.

A blast of heat, like opening an oven, staggered Sam. Astrid had said it wasn't the fire that killed you. Well, she hadn't seen this fire, or guessed that a little kid could shoot flame from her hands.

Sam held the child in his arms. Fire to his back and to his right, crisping his eyelashes, baking his flesh.

41

A window straight ahead.

He stumbled forwards. He dropped the kid like a sack of dirt and slammed the window up with both hands. Smoke roiled around him, the fire chasing it towards this fresh source of oxygen.

Sam felt in the gloom for the child and found her. He lifted her, and there, miraculously, was a pair of hands waiting to take the kid. Hands reaching through the smoke, seeming almost supernatural.

Sam collapsed against the sill, half hanging out of the window, and someone grabbed him, and dragged and slid him down the aluminium ladder. His head smacked the rungs and he did not mind one tiny bit because out here was light and air and through squinting, weeping eyes he could see the blue sky.

Edilio and a kid named Joel manhandled Sam down to the sidewalk.

Someone sprayed him with a hose. Did they think he was on fire?

Was he on fire?

He opened his mouth and gulped greedily at the cold water. It washed over his face.

But he couldn't hold on to consciousness. He floated away. Floated on his back on gentle surf.

His mother was there. She was sitting on the water just beside him. Her chin rested on her knees. She wasn't looking at him.

'What?' he said to her.

'It smelled like fried chicken,' she said.

'What?' he said.

His mother reached over and slapped him hard across the face. His eyes flew open.

'Sorry,' Astrid said. 'I needed to wake you up.'

She knelt beside him and placed something against his mouth. A plastic mask. Oxygen.

He coughed, and breathed. He pulled the mask away and threw up, right on the sidewalk, doubled over like a drunk in an alleyway.

Astrid looked away discreetly. Later he would be embarrassed. Right now he was just glad to be able to throw up.

He breathed more oxygen.

Quinn was holding the garden hose. Edilio was racing to hook one of the bigger fire hoses up to the hydrant. There was a trickle, then, as Edilio worked the long-handled wrench and opened the hydrant all the way, a gusher. The kids on the other end had to wrestle the hose like they were fighting a python. It would have been funny some other time.

Sam sat up. He still couldn't talk.

He nodded to where half a dozen kids knelt around the little fire-starter. She was black, black by race and from the coating of soot. Her hair was gone on one side, burned away. On the other side she had a little girl's pigtail held with a pink scrunchy.

Sam knew from the reverential way the kids knelt there. He knew, but he had to ask, anyway. His voice was a soft croak.

Astrid shook her head. 'I'm sorry, Sam,' she said.

Sam nodded.

'Her parents probably had the stove on when they disappeared,' Astrid said. 'That's most likely what caused the fire. Or maybe a cigarette.'

No, Sam thought. No, that wasn't it.

The little girl had the power. She had the power Sam had, at least something like it.

The power he had used in panic to create an impossible light.

The power he had used once and almost killed someone with.

The power he had just used again, dooming the very person he was trying so hard to save.

He was not the only one. He was not the only freak. There was – or had been – at least one other.

Somehow, that realisation was not comforting.

FIVE

291 HOURS 07 MINUTES

NIGHT CAME TO Perdido Beach.

The street lights turned on automatically, doing little to push back the darkness, doing a lot to cast deep shadows on frightened faces.

Close to a hundred kids milled around the plaza. Everyone seemed to have a candy bar and a soda. The little store, the one that sold mostly beer and corn chips, had been looted. Sam had snagged a PayDay and a Dr Pepper. The Reese's and Twix and Snickers were all gone by the time he got there. He'd left two dollars on the counter as payment. The money was gone within seconds.

The apartment building had burned half away before the fire had run out of energy. The roof had collapsed. Half the upper floor was gone. The ground floor looked like it would survive, though the shop windows were smoke-blackened on the inside. Smoke rose now in tendrils, not billows, and the stench was everywhere.

But the hardware store and the day care had been saved.

The body of the little girl still lay on the sidewalk. Someone had put a blanket over her. Sam was grateful for that.

45

Sam and Quinn sat on the grass, towards the centre of the plaza, near the dead fountain. Quinn rocked back and forth, hugging his knees.

Bouncing Bette came over and stood awkwardly in front of Sam. She had her little brother with her. 'Sam, do you think it's safe to go to my house? We have to get something.'

Sam shrugged. 'Bette, I don't know any more than you do.'

Bette nodded, hesitated, and walked away.

All the park benches were taken. Some little family units draped sheets over the few benches, making limp pup tents. Many kids went home to their empty houses, but others needed people around them. Some found comfort in the crowd. Some just needed to see what was going on.

Two kids Sam didn't know, probably fifth-graders, came up and said, 'Do you know what's going to happen?'

Sam shook his head. 'No, guys, I don't.'

'Well, what should we do?'

'I guess just hang out for a while, you know?'

'Hang out here, you mean?'

'Or else go to your house. Sleep in your own bed. Whatever feels right.'

'We're not scared or anything.'

'You're not?' Sam asked dubiously. 'I'm so scared, I wet myself.'

One kid grinned. 'No, you didn't.'

'Nah. You're right. But it's OK to be scared, man. Every single person here is scared.'

It was happening a lot. Kids coming to Sam, asking him questions for which he had no answers.

He wished they would stop.

Orc and his friends dragged lawn chairs out of the hardware store and set themselves up right in the middle of what had once been Perdido Beach's busiest intersection. They were just beneath the stoplight, which continued changing from green to yellow to red.

Howard was berating some lower-ranking toady who had lit a Prest-O log and was trying to get it to grow into a bonfire. Orc's crew brought a couple of wood axe handles and wooden baseball bats out of the hardware store and tried unsuccessfully to burn them.

They also carried metal bats and small sledgehammers from the hardware store. Those they kept.

Sam didn't bring up the little girl, the way she was just lying there. If he brought it up, then it would become his job to do something. To dig a grave and bury her. To read the Bible or say words. He didn't even know her name. No one seemed to.

'I can't find him.' It was Astrid, reappearing after an absence of at least an hour. She had gone to hunt for her little brother. 'Petey's not here. Nobody has seen him.'

Sam handed her a soda. 'Here. I paid for it. Tried to, anyway.'

'I don't usually drink this stuff.'

'You see any "usually" around here?' Quinn snapped.

Quinn didn't look at her. His eyes were restless, going from person to person, thing to thing, like a nervous bird, never making direct eye contact. He looked strangely naked without his shades and fedora.

Sam was worried about him. Of the two of them, it was Sam who was usually too serious.

Astrid let Quinn's rudeness slide and said, 'Thanks, Sam.' She drank half the can but didn't sit down. 'Kids are saying it's some military thing gone wrong. Or else terrorists. Or aliens. Or God. Lots of theories. No answers.'

'Do you even believe in God?' Quinn demanded. He was looking for an argument.

'Yes, I do,' Astrid said. 'I just don't believe in the kind of God who disappears people for no reason. God is supposed to be love. This doesn't look like love.'

'It looks like the world's worst picnic,' Sam said.

'I believe that's what's called gallows humour,' Astrid said. Noticing Sam and Quinn's blank looks, she said, 'Sorry. I have this annoying tendency to analyse what people say. You'll either get used to it or decide you can't stand me.'

'I'm leaning towards the second choice,' Quinn muttered.

Sam said, 'What's gallows humour?'

'Gallows, as in what they hang people from. Sometimes when people are nervous or afraid, they make jokes.' Then she added, a bit ruefully, 'Of course, some people, when they're nervous or afraid, turn pedantic. And if you don't know what pedantic means, here's a clue: in the dictionary, I'm the illustration they use.'

Sam laughed.

A little boy no more than five years old and carrying a sad-eyed grey teddy bear came over. 'Do you know where my mom is?'

'No, little man, I'm sorry,' Sam said.

'Can you call her on the telephone?' His voice trembled.

'The phones don't work,' Sam said.

'Nothing works,' Quinn snapped. 'Nothing works and we're all alone here.'

'You know what I bet?' Sam asked the boy. 'I'll bet they have cookies at the day care. It's right across the street. See?'

'I'm not supposed to cross the street.'

'It's OK. I'll watch while you do, OK?'

The little boy stifled a sob, then walked off towards the day care, clutching his bear.

Astrid said, 'Kids come to you, Sam. They're looking to you to do something.'

'Do what? All I can do is suggest they eat a cookie,' Sam said, with too much heat in his tone.

'Save them, Sam,' Quinn said bitterly. 'Save them all.'

'They're all scared, like us,' Astrid said. 'There's no one in charge, no one telling people what to do. They sense you're a leader, Sam. They look to you.'

'I'm not a leader of anything. I'm as scared as they are. I'm as lost as they are.'

'You knew what to do when the apartment was burning,' Astrid said.

Sam jumped to his feet. It was just nervous energy, but the

49

movement drew the gaze of dozens of kids nearby. All looking at him like he was going to do something. Sam felt a knot in his stomach. Even Quinn was looking at him expectantly.

Sam cursed under his breath. Then, in a voice just loud enough to carry a few feet, he said, 'Look, all we have to do is hang tight. Someone is going to figure out what's happened and come find us, OK? So everyone just chill, don't do anything crazy, help each other out and try to be brave.'

To Sam's amazement he heard a ripple of voices repeating what he'd said, passing it on like it was some brilliant remark.

'The only thing we have to fear is fear itself,' Astrid whispered.

'What?'

'It's what President Roosevelt said when the whole country was scared because of the Great Depression,' Astrid explained.

'You know,' Quinn said, 'the one good thing about this was that I got away from history class. Now history class is following me.'

Sam laughed. Not much, but it was a relief to hear that Quinn still had a sense of humour.

'I have to find my brother,' Astrid said.

'Where else could he be?' Sam asked.

Astrid shrugged helplessly. She looked cold in her thin blouse. Sam wished he had a jacket to offer her. 'With my parents somewhere. The most likely places are where my dad works or else where my mom plays tennis. Clifftop.'

Clifftop was the resort hotel just above Sam's favourite

surfing beach. He'd never been inside or even on the grounds.

'I guess Clifftop is more likely,' Astrid said. 'I hate to ask, but will you guys go with me?'

'Now?' Quinn asked, incredulous. 'At night?'

Sam shrugged. 'Better than sitting here, Quinn. Maybe they have TV there.'

Quinn sighed. 'I hear the food's great at Clifftop. Top-notch service.' He stuck a hand out and Sam hauled him to his feet.

They passed through the huddled crowd. Kids would call out to Sam to ask him what was going on, ask him what they should do. And he would say things like, 'Hang in. It's going to be OK. Just enjoy the vacation, man. Enjoy your candy bars while you can. Your parents will be back soon and take it all away.'

And kids would nod or laugh or even say, 'Thanks,' as if he had given them something.

He heard his name being repeated. Heard snatches of conversation. 'I was on the bus that time.' Or, 'Dude, he ran right into that building.' Or, 'See, he said it would be OK.'

The knot in his stomach was growing more painful. It would be a relief to walk out into the night. He wanted to get away from all those frightened faces looking to him, expecting something from him.

They walked close to Orc's intersection encampment. The lame fire was sputtering, melting the tarmac beneath the embers. A six-pack of Coors beer rested in an ice-filled cooler. One of Orc's friends, a big baby-faced lump called Cookie, was looking green and woozy.

'Hey. Where do you guys think you're going?' Howard demanded as they approached.

'For a walk,' Sam said.

'Two dumb surfers and a genius?'

'That's right. We're going to teach Astrid how to surf. You have a problem with that?'

Howard laughed and looked Sam up and down. 'You think you're the man, don't you, Sam? School Bus Sam. Big deal. You don't impress me.'

'That's a shame, because I live my entire life in hopes of impressing you, Howard,' Sam said.

Howard's face grew shrewd. 'You need to bring us back something.'

'What are you talking about?'

'I don't want Orc's feelings to be hurt,' Howard said. 'I think whatever you're going to get, you should bring him back some.'

Orc was sprawled in a looted chair, legs spread, paying only slight attention. His never-very-focused eyes were wandering. But he grunted, 'Yeah.' The moment he spoke, several of his crew discovered an interest in Sam's group. One, a tall, skinny kid nicknamed Panda because of his dark-ringed eyes, tapped his metal bat on the blacktop menacingly.

'So you're a big hero or something, huh?' Panda said.

'You're wearing that line out,' Sam said.

'No, no, not Sammy, he doesn't think he's better than the rest of us,' Howard sneered. He did a rough parody of Sam at the fire. 'You get a hose, you get the kids, do this, do that,

I'm in charge here, I'm . . . Sam Sam the Surfer Man.'

'We're going to go now,' Sam said.

'Ah ah ah,' Howard said, and pointed upwards with a flourish to the stoplight. 'Wait till it turns green.'

For a tense few seconds Sam considered whether he should have this fight now, or avoid it. Then the light changed and Howard laughed and waved them past.

SIX

NO ONE SPOKE for several blocks.

The streets grew emptier and darker as they joined the beach road.

'The surf sounds strange,' Quinn observed.

'Flat,' Sam agreed. He felt like eyes were following him, even though he was out of sight of the plaza.

'Fo-flat, brah,' Quinn said. 'Glassy. But there's a low-pressure front just out there. Supposed to be a long period swell. Instead it sounds like a lake.'

'Weatherman isn't always right,' Sam said. He listened carefully. Quinn was better at reading the conditions. Something sounded like it might be strange in the rhythm, but Sam wasn't sure.

Lights twinkled here and there, from houses off to the left, from street lights, but it was far darker than normal. It was still early evening, barely dinnertime. Houses should have been lit up. Instead, the only lights were those on timers or those left on throughout the day. In one house, blue TV light flickered. When Sam peeked in the window he saw two kids eating chips and staring at the static.

All the little background noises, all the little sounds you barely registered – phones ringing, car engines, voices – were gone. They could hear each footstep they made. Each breath they took. When a dog erupted in frenzied barking, they all jumped.

'Who's going to feed that dog?' Quinn wondered.

No one had an answer for that. There would be dogs and cats all over town. And there were almost certainly babies in empty homes right now, too. It was all too much. Too much to think about.

Sam peered towards the hills, squinted to shut out the lights of town. Sometimes, if they had the stadium lights of the athletic field turned on, you could see a distant twinkle of light from Coates Academy. But not tonight. Just darkness from that direction.

A part of Sam denied that his mother was gone. A part of him wanted to believe she was up there, at work, like any other night.

'The stars are still there,' Astrid said. Then she said, 'Wait. No. The stars are up, but not the ones just above the horizon. I think Venus should be almost setting. It's not there.'

The three of them stopped and stared out over the ocean. Standing still, all they heard was the odd, placid, metronomic regularity of the lapping waves.

'This sounds bizarre, but the horizon looks higher than it should be,' Astrid said.

'Did anyone watch the sun go down?' Sam asked.

No one had.

'Let's keep moving,' Sam said. 'We should have brought bikes or skateboards.'

'Why not a car?' Quinn asked.

'You know how to drive?' Sam asked.

'I've seen it done.'

'I've seen heart surgery performed on TV, too,' Astrid said. 'That doesn't mean I'm going to try it.'

Quinn said, 'You watch heart surgery on TV? That explains a lot, Astrid.'

The road wound away from the shore and up to Clifftop. The resort's understated neon sign, nestled roadside between carefully trimmed hedges, was lit. The grand front entrance was lit up like it was Christmas – the resort had strung strands of twinkling white lights early.

A car sat empty, one door open, trunk popped up, suitcases on a bellman's trolley nearby.

When they approached, the automatic doors of the hotel swung wide.

The lobby was open and airy, with a polished blond wood counter that curved for about thirty feet, a bright tile floor, gleaming brass accents leading towards a more shadowy bar. At the bank of elevators, one stood open, waiting.

'I don't see anyone,' Quinn said in a subdued whisper.

'No,' Sam agreed. There was a TV in the bar with nothing on. No one at the front desk or the concierge desk, no one in the lobby, no one in the bar. Their footsteps echoed on the tile.

'The tennis courts are this way,' Astrid said, and led them

away. 'That's where my mom and Little Pete would have been.'

The tennis courts were lit up. No sound of balls being whacked by rackets. No sound at all.

They all saw it at the same time.

Cutting straight across the farthest tennis court, slicing through well-tended landscaping, cutting through the swimming pool, was a barrier.

A wall.

It shimmered ever so slightly.

It did not look opaque, but whatever light came through it was milky, indistinct, and no brighter than their surroundings. The wall was slightly reflective, like looking into a frosted-glass window. It made no sound. It did not vibrate. It seemed almost to swallow sound.

It could be just a membrane, Sam thought. Just a millimetre thick. Something he could poke with a finger and pop like a balloon. It might even be nothing more than an illusion. But his instinct, his fear, the feeling in the pit of his stomach, told him he was looking at a wall. No illusion, no curtain, but a wall.

The barrier went up and up, but faded against the background of the night sky. It extended as far as they could see to the left and right. No stars shone through it, but eventually, farther up, the stars reappeared.

'What is it?' Quinn asked. There was awe in his tone.

Astrid just shook her head.

'What is it?' Quinn repeated more urgently.

They approached the barrier with slow steps, ready to run away, but needing to get closer.

They entered the chain-link enclosure and crossed the tennis court. The barrier cut right through the net. The net started from a vertical pole and ended in the shimmering blankness of the barrier.

Sam pulled on the net. It stayed firmly in place. No matter how much he yanked, no more net came through the barrier.

'Careful,' Astrid whispered.

Quinn dropped back, letting Sam take the lead. 'She's right, brah, careful.'

Sam was just a few feet away from the barrier, hand outstretched. He hesitated. He spotted a green tennis ball on the ground and picked it up.

He tossed it towards the barrier.

It bounced back.

He caught the ball on the bounce and looked at it. No marks. No sign it had done anything but bounce.

He took the last three steps and, this time, without hesitating, pressed his fingertips against the barrier.

'Aaah.' He yanked his hand away and looked at it.

'What?' Quinn yelled.

'It burned. Oh, man. That hurt.' Sam shook his hand to throw off the pain.

'Let me look at it,' Astrid said.

Sam extended his hand. 'It feels OK now.'

'I don't see any burn mark,' Astrid said, turning his hand with hers.

'No,' Sam agreed. 'But, trust me, you don't want to touch that thing.'

Even now, even with all that was happening, he registered her touch like a very different sort of electric shock. Her hand was cold. He liked that.

Quinn picked up a chair that sat on one of the sidelines. It was a substantial wrought-iron chair. Quinn lifted it high, held it in front of him, and slammed the legs into the barrier.

The barrier did not yield.

Quinn hit it again, even harder, hard enough that the recoil spun him back.

The barrier did not yield.

Suddenly Quinn was screaming, cursing, slamming the chair wildly again and again against the barrier.

Sam couldn't step close enough to stop him without getting hit. He placed a restraining hand on Astrid's arm. 'Let him get it out.'

Again and again Quinn hurled the chair against the barrier. It left no mark.

Finally Quinn dropped the chair, sat down on the tarmac, put his head in his hands, and howled.

The lights were burning bright inside the McDonald's when Albert Hillsborough walked in. A smoke alarm was blaring. A separate beep, beep, beep called urgently for attention between the louder, angrier bleats of the alarm.

Kids had gone behind the counter and taken the cookies and Danish pastries from the display case. A box of Happy Meal toys, tie-ins to a movie Albert hadn't seen yet, was open, the toys scattered. There were no fries in the bin but plenty were on the floor.

Feeling self-conscious, Albert walked around to the kitchen door and tried to open it. It was locked. He went back and hopped the counter.

It felt illegal somehow, being on the far side of the counter.

A basket of burned, black fries sat resting in the hot oil. Albert found a towel, grabbed the basket handle, and lifted it out of the oil. He hooked it in place so that the oil drained properly. The fries had been cooking since that morning.

'I guess those are about done,' Albert said to himself.

The fry timer continued to beep. It took him a second, but he found the right button and pushed it. That killed one noise.

Three tiny, black cookies were on the grill. Hamburgers that, like the fries, were about ten hours past done.

Albert found a spatula, scooped up the burgers, and tossed them into the trash. The burgers had long since stopped smoking, but no one had been around to reset the smoke alarm. It took Albert a few minutes to figure out how to climb up without landing on the searing-hot grill so he could push the reset.

The silence was a physical relief.

'That's better.' Albert climbed down. He wondered if he should turn off the fryers and the grill. That would be the safest thing to do. Turn everything off and go outside. Out into the dark of the plaza, where kids were gathering, scared, looking for a rescue that was very late in coming. But he didn't really know anyone out there.

Albert was fourteen, the youngest of six kids. The smallest, too. His three brothers and two sisters ranged in age from fifteen to twenty-seven. Albert had already checked his home: none of them were there. His mother's wheelchair was empty. The couch where she would normally be lying and watching TV and eating and complaining about the pain in her back was abandoned. Her blanket was there, nothing else.

It was weird to be alone, even for a while. Weird not to have some bossy sibling telling him what to do. He couldn't remember a time when he wasn't being bossed around.

Now Albert walked the McDonald's kitchen more alone than he could ever have imagined being.

He found the walk-in freezer. He yanked on the big chrome handle and the steel door opened with a gasp and a breath of cold steam.

Inside were metal racks and box upon box of clearly labelled hamburgers, big plastic bags of chicken nuggets, chicken strips, fries. A smaller number of boxes of sausage patties. But mostly, lots of burgers.

He moved on to the walk-in refrigerator, not so cold and pristine, more interesting. There were plastic-covered trays of sliced tomato, bags of shredded lettuce, big plastic tubs of Big Mac sauce and mayonnaise and ketchup, blocks and blocks of sliced yellow cheese.

He found a tiny break room festooned with posters about safety and the Heimlich manoeuvre, all in both English and Spanish. The dry goods were stacked against the walls of the break room: giant boxes of paper cups and boxes of waxed-paper wraps. Dull metal cylinders loaded with Coca-Cola syrup.

In the back, near the rear door, were tall, wheeled racks of buns and muffins.

Everything had a place. Everything was organised. Everything was clean, albeit with a sheen of grease.

At some point, and he hadn't really noticed the exact moment, Albert had stopped just seeing it all as interesting and started seeing it as inventory. He was mentally translating the separate ingredients into Big Macs, chicken sandwiches, Egg McMuffins.

Albert's oldest sister Rowena had taught him to cook. With their mom incapacitated, the kids had always had to fend for themselves. Rowena had been the unofficial cook until Albert hit his twelfth birthday and then part of the kitchen duties had devolved to him.

He could make red beans and rice, his mother's favourite dish. He could make hot dogs. He could make French toast and bacon. He had never admitted it to Rowena, but Albert enjoyed cooking. It was a lot better than just doing the clean-up, which, unfortunately, he still had to do even though he was now responsible for the evening meal on Fridays and Sundays.

The manager had a tiny office. The door was ajar. Inside was a cramped desk, a locked safe, a phone, a computer, and a wall shelf straining under the weight of several thick operator's manuals.

He heard sound: voices, and someone banging into a straw dispenser, then apologising. Two seventh-graders were leaning on the counter, staring up at the overhead menu like they were waiting to order.

Albert hesitated, but not for long. He could do it, he told himself, almost surprised by the thought.

'Welcome to McDonald's,' Albert said. 'May I help you?'

'Are you open?'

'What would you like?'

The kids shrugged. 'Two number-one combos?'

Albert stared at the computer console. It was a maze of colour-coded buttons. That would have to wait.

'What kind of drink? I mean beverage?'

'Orange soda?'

'Coming right up,' Albert said. He found burger patties in a refrigerator drawer below the grill. They made a satisfying sound as he slapped them on to the grill.

He spotted a paper hat resting on a shelf. He put it on.

While the burger patties sizzled, he opened the thick manual and searched the index for French fries.

SEVEN

LANA LAY IN the dark, staring up at the stars.

She couldn't see the vultures any more, but they weren't far off. Several had tried to land nearby, and Patrick had scared them off. But she knew they were still out there.

She was scared. Scared of dying. Scared of never seeing her mom and dad again. Her mom and dad, who probably didn't even know she was missing. They called Grandpa Luke every night and talked to her, told her they loved her . . . and refused to let her come home.

'We want you to have a break from the city, sweetheart,' her mother would say. 'We want you to have some time to think and clear your head.'

Lana burned with fury at her parents. Especially her mother. If she let it, the anger could burn so hot, it almost blanked out her pain.

But not quite. Not really. Not for long. The pain was her whole world now. Pain and fear.

She wondered what she looked like right now. She had never been pretty, really – her eyes, she felt, were too small, her dark hair too lank to do more with than let hang there. But now, with her face a mass of bruises, cuts, and caked-on blood, she probably looked like something from a horror movie.

Where was Grandpa Luke? She only half remembered the seconds before the crash, and the crash itself was just a blur, fractured images of space twirling around her as her body was bludgeoned.

It was confusing. Made no sense. Her grandfather had simply disappeared from the truck: one minute there, and the next not there. She had no memory of the truck door opening or closing, and why would the old man have jumped out?

Crazy.

Impossible.

She was sure of one thing: there had been no word of warning from her grandfather. In a heartbeat he was gone and she was plunging down the ravine.

Lana was desperately thirsty. The closest place she knew where she could get a drink was the ranch. It was probably no more than a mile away. If she could somehow get up to the road ... but even in daylight, even healthy, the climb would have been nearly impossible.

She raised her throbbing head a little and twisted till she saw the truck. It was just a few feet away, wheels up, silhouetted against the stars.

Something scuttled across her neck. Patrick sat up, focused on the faint sound.

'Don't let anything get me, boy,' she begged.

Patrick woofed, the way he did when he wanted to play.

'I don't have any food for you, boy,' she said. 'I don't know what's going to happen to us.'

Patrick settled back down, head on paws.

'I guess Mom will be happy,' Lana said. 'I guess she'll be really happy she made me come here.'

She would not have noticed the eyes glittering in the dark, except that Patrick was up all at once, bristling and growling like nothing she had ever heard before.

'What is it, boy?'

Green eyes, hovering, disembodied. Staring straight at her. The eyes blinked at a lazy speed, opened again.

Patrick was barking like crazy now, prancing back and forth.

The mountain lion roared. It was a hoarse, deep-throated, snarling sound.

Lana yelled, 'Go away! Leave me alone!' Her voice was pathetic – weak, and aware of its own weakness.

Patrick ran back to Lana, then turned, finding his courage again, and faced the mountain lion.

In a flash, battle was joined, an explosion of snarling, canine and feline, deep, terrible sounds. In half a minute it was over and the mountain lion's glittering eyes reappeared farther away. They blinked once, stared, then were gone.

Patrick came back slowly. He slouched heavily beside Lana.

'Good boy, good boy,' Lana cooed. 'You scared off that old lion, didn't you, boy? Oh, my good dog. Good boy.'

Patrick wagged his tail weakly.

'Did he hurt you, boy? Did he hurt you, my good boy?'

She ran her one usable hand over her dog. His ruff was wet, slick to the touch. It could only be blood. She probed, and Patrick whimpered in pain.

Then she felt the flow. There was a deep cut in Patrick's neck. The blood was pumping out, surging with each heartbeat, draining the dog's life away.

'No, no, no,' Lana cried. 'You can't die. You can't die.'

If he died, she would be alone in the desert, unable to move. Alone.

The mountain lion would come back.

Then the vultures.

No. No. That wasn't going to happen.

No.

The fear was too much to contain, it couldn't be reasoned with, it couldn't be resisted. Lana cried out in terror, 'Mommy. Mommy. Mommy. I want my mom! Help me, someone help me! Mommy, I'm sorry, I'm sorry, I want to go home, I want to go home.'

She sobbed and babbled, and the pain of loneliness and fear felt even greater than the agony of her battered body. It choked the air from her lungs.

She was alone. Alone with pain. And soon the mountain lion's teeth . . .

Patrick had to live. He had to live. He was all she had.

She cuddled her dog as close as she could without her own pain obliterating consciousness. She placed her palm over his wound, pressing as hard as she dared.

She would stop the blood.

She would hold him and stop his life from escaping.

She would hold life inside him and he wouldn't die.

But blood still drained through her fingers.

She held on and focused all her will on staying awake to hold the wound, to keep her friend alive.

'Good boy,' she whispered through parched lips.

She fought to stay awake. But thirst and hunger, pain and fear, loneliness and horror were too much for her. After a long while Lana fell asleep.

And her hand slipped from the dog's neck.

Sam, Quinn, and Astrid spent much of the night searching the hotel for Little Pete. Astrid figured out how to access the hotel's security system and make a plastic pass key that worked on all doors.

They checked each room. They did not find Astrid's brother, or anyone else.

They came to an exhausted halt in the last room. The barrier cut right through it. It was as if someone had put up a wall in the middle of the room.

'It cuts right through the TV,' Quinn said. He picked up a remote control and punched the red power button. Nothing.

Astrid said, 'I'd love to know what it looks like on the other side of the barrier. Did someone's half a TV just turn on over there?'

'If so, maybe they could tell me if the Lakers won,' Quinn

GONE

said, but no one, including him, was in the mood to laugh.

'Your brother is probably safely on the other side, Astrid,' Sam said, then added, 'with your mom, probably.'

'I don't know that,' Astrid snapped. 'I have to assume that he's alone and helpless and that I'm the only one who can do anything to help him.'

She crossed her arms over her chest and hugged herself tightly. Then, 'I'm sorry. That sounded like I was mad at you.'

'No. You just sounded mad. Not at me,' Sam said. 'We can't do any more tonight. It's almost midnight. I think we should go back to that big room we saw.'

Astrid could only nod, and Quinn looked about ready to crash. They found the suite. It had a huge balcony that over-looked the ocean far below. To the left the barrier blocked the view. It travelled far out over the ocean, as far as they could see. It was like a wall extending out from the hotel itself, an endless wall.

The suite had a room with a king-size bed and a room with two queens, all very plush. There was a minibar fridge containing liquor, beer, soda, nuts, a Snickers, a Toblerone bar, and a few other snacks.

'Boys' room,' Quinn said, then flopped on to one of the two queens, face down. Within seconds he was asleep.

Sam and Astrid stood together for a while on the balcony, splitting the Toblerone. Neither of them said anything for a long time.

'What do you think this is?' Sam asked finally. He didn't need to explain what he meant by 'this'.

69

'Sometimes I think it's a dream,' Astrid said. 'It's so strange that no one has shown up. I mean, the place should be crawling with soldiers and scientists and reporters. Suddenly a wall just appears out of nowhere, most of the people in town disappear, and yet there aren't any network satellite trucks?'

Sam had already reached a grim conclusion about that. He wondered if Astrid had, too.

She had. 'I don't think it's just a straight wall cutting us off from the south, you know? I think it may be a circle. It may go all the way around us. We may be cut off in every direction. In fact, since no one has come to rescue us, I think that's pretty likely. Don't you?'

'Yeah. We're in a trap. But why? And why disappear everyone over the age of fourteen?'

'I don't know.'

Sam let the silence linger, not wanting to ask the next question on his mind, not sure he wanted the answer. Finally, 'What happens when kids turn fifteen?'

Astrid turned her blue eyes on him, and he met her gaze. 'When is your birthday, Sam?'

'November twenty-second,' he said. 'Just five days before Thanksgiving. Twelve days from now. No, just eleven days now, since it's after midnight. You?'

'Not till March.'

'I like March better. Or July, or August. First time I ever wished I was younger.'

So that she wouldn't keep looking at him the way she was

70

looking at him and feeling sorry for him, he said, 'You think they're all still alive somewhere?'

'Yes.'

'You think that because you really think so, or because you just want them to be alive?'

'Yes,' she said, and smiled. 'Sam?'

'Yeah.'

'I was on the school bus that day. Remember?'

'Vaguely,' he said, and laughed. 'My fifteen minutes of fame.'

'You were the bravest, coolest person I'd ever known. Everyone thought so. You were the hero of the whole school. And then, I don't know. It was like you kind of just . . . faded.'

He resented that a little. He hadn't faded. Had he? 'Well, most days the bus driver doesn't have a heart attack,' Sam said.

Astrid laughed. 'You're one of those people, I think. You go along in your life just sort of living. And then something goes wrong and there you are. You step up and do what you have to do. Like today, the fire.'

'Yeah, well, to tell you the truth, I kind of prefer the other part. The part where I just live my life.'

Astrid nodded like she understood, but then she said, 'That's not going to happen this time.'

Sam hung his head and looked down at the lawn below. A lizard scampered across a stone walkway. Quick, slow, quick, then it disappeared. 'Look, don't expect too much from me, OK?'

'OK, Sam.' She said it, but not like she meant it. 'Tomorrow we're going to figure this all out.'

'And find your brother.'

'And find my brother.'

She turned away. Sam stayed on the balcony. He couldn't hear the surf. There was very little breeze. But he could smell flowers from the grounds below. And the salt smell of the Pacific hadn't changed.

He had told Astrid he was scared, and he was. But there were other feelings, too. The emptiness of the too-quiet night seeped into him. He was alone. Even with Astrid and Quinn, he was alone. He knew what they did not.

The change was so big that he couldn't get his mind to take it all in.

It was all connected, he was sure of that. What he had done to his stepfather, what he had done in his room, what had happened with the little pigtailed flamethrower, the disappearance of everyone over the age of fourteen, and this impermeable, impossible barrier – all were pieces of the same puzzle.

And his mother's diary, that too.

He was scared, overwhelmed, lonely. But less lonely in one way than he had been these last months. The little fire-starter proved that he was not the only one with power.

He was not the only freak.

He held up his hands and looked at his palms. Pink skin, calluses from waxing his surfboard, a life line, a fate line. Just a palm.

How? How did it happen?

What did it mean?

And if he was not the only freak, did that mean he was not responsible for this catastrophe?

He extended his hands, palms out, towards the barrier as if to touch it.

In a panic he could make light.

In a panic he could burn a man's hand off.

But surely he could not have done this.

That brought him a sense of relief. No, he had not done this.

And yet someone or something had.

EIGHT

'**SIT** STILL, I'M trying to change your diaper,' Mary Terrafino said to the toddler.

'It's not a diaper,' the little girl said. 'Diapers are for babies. It's my trainee pants.'

'Oh, sorry,' Mary said. 'I didn't know.'

She finished pulling the training pants up and smiled, but the little girl collapsed in tears.

'My mommy always puts my trainee pants on.'

'I know, sweetie,' Mary said. 'But tonight I'm doing it, OK?'

Mary wanted to cry herself. She had never wanted to cry more. Night had fallen. She and her nine-year-old brother, John, had handed out the last of the Cheddar-flavoured Goldfish. They had handed out all the juice boxes. They were almost out of diapers. Barbara's Day Care wasn't set up for overnight care. They only had a limited supply of diapers on hand.

There were twenty-eight kids in the larger of the two rooms. Watching over them were Mary and John and a ten-year-old girl named Eloise, like in the books, who mostly kept an eye on her four-year-old brother. Eloise was one of the fairly responsible ones. A couple of other kids, overwhelmed, not knowing how to

74

cope, had just dropped off siblings and made no attempt to stay and help.

Mary and John had prepared formula and filled bottles. They'd made 'meals' of whatever was in the day care and whatever John managed to scrounge up. They had read picture books aloud. They had played the Raffi CDs over and over again.

Mary had said the words 'Don't worry, it's going to be all right' a million times. She had hugged every kid again and again, so that it seemed like she was on a factory assembly line handing out hugs.

Still, the kids cried for their mothers. Still, they asked, 'When is my mommy coming? Why isn't she here? Where is she?' They demanded in petulant, scared voices, 'I want my mom. I want to go home. Now.'

Mary was shaking with exhaustion.

She fell into the rocking chair and just stared at the room. Cribs. Mats on the floor. Tiny bodies curled this way and that. Most asleep. Except for the two-year-old girl who would not stop crying. And the baby who wandered in and out of wailing fits.

Her brother, John, was fighting sleep, his curls bouncing as he jerked his head up only to have it drift lower . . . lower. He was slumped in a chair across the room, rocking a makeshift bassinet that was really just a long plastic planter liberated from the hardware store. She caught his eye and said, 'I am so proud of you, John.'

He smiled his sweet smile, and Mary almost fell apart. Her

lip quivered. Tears welled in her eyes. There was a lump in her throat and a pain in her chest.

'I have to go pee,' a voice called.

Mary located the source. 'Come on, Cassie, let's go,' she said. The bathroom was just outside the main room. She led the way, then she waited, leaning against the wall. Afterwards, she wiped the little girl's bottom.

'My mommy always does that,' Cassie said.

'I know, sweetheart.'

'My mommy always calls me that.'

'Sweetheart? Oh. Would you like me to call you something else?'

'No. But I just want to know when my mommy is coming. I miss her. I always hug her and she kisses me.'

'I know. But until she comes back, can I give you a kiss?'

'No. Only my mommy.'

'OK, sweetheart. Let's go back to bed.'

Back in the main room Mary went to John. 'Hey, brother.' She ruffled his red curls. 'We're running out of stuff. We'll have a problem in the morning. I have to go see what I can round up. Can you hang in here for a while?'

'Yeah. I can wipe butts.'

Mary went out into the night on to the mostly quiet plaza. Some kids were sleeping on benches. Some huddled in little groups around flashlights. She spotted Howard walking along with a Mountain Dew in one hand and a baseball bat in the other.

'Have you seen Sam?' Mary asked.

'What do you want with Sam?'

'I can't take care of all those littles with just John to help me.'

Howard shrugged. 'Who asked you to?'

That was too much. Mary was tall and strong. Howard, though a boy, was smaller. Mary took two steps towards him, pushing her face right into his. 'Listen, you little worm. If I don't take care of those kids, they'll die. Do you understand that? There are babies in there who need to be fed and need to be changed, and I seem to be the only one who realises it. And there are probably more little kids still in their homes, all alone, not knowing what's happening, not knowing how to feed themselves, scared to death.'

Howard took a step back, tentatively lifted the bat, then let it fall. 'What am I supposed to do?' he whined.

'You? Nothing. Where's Sam?'

'He took off.'

'What do you mean, he took off?'

'I mean him and Quinn and Astrid took off.'

Mary blinked, feeling stupid and slow. 'Who's in charge?'

'You think just because Sam likes to play the big hero every couple years that makes him the guy in charge?'

Mary had been on the bus two years ago when the driver, Mr Colombo, had had his heart attack. She'd had her head in a book, not paying attention, but she had looked up when she felt the bus swerve. By the time she had focused, Sam was guiding the bus on to the shoulder of the road.

In the two years that followed, Sam had been so quiet and so modest and so not involved in the social life of the school that Mary had sort of forgotten that moment of heroism. Most people had.

And yet she hadn't even been surprised when it was Sam who had stepped up during the fire. And she had somehow assumed that if anyone was going to be in charge, it would be Sam. She found herself angry with him for not being here now: she needed help.

'Go get Orc,' Mary said.

'I don't tell Orc what to do, bitch.'

'Excuse me?' she snapped. 'What did you just call me?'

Howard gulped. 'Didn't mean nothing, Mary.'

'Where is Orc?'

'I think he's sleeping.'

'Wake him up. I need some help. I can't stay awake any longer. I need at least two kids who have experience babysitting. And then I need diapers and bottles and nipples and Cheerios and lots of milk.'

'Why am I going to do all that?'

Mary didn't have an answer. 'I don't know, Howard,' she said. 'Maybe because you're really not a complete jerk? Maybe you're really a decent human being?'

That earned her a sceptical look and a derisive snort.

'Look, kids will do what Orc says,' Mary said. 'They're scared of him. All I'm asking is for Orc to act like Orc.'

Howard thought this over. Mary could almost see the wheels spinning in his head.

'Forget it,' she said. 'I'll talk to Sam when he gets back.'

'Yeah, he's the big hero, isn't he?' Howard said, dripping sarcasm. 'But hey, where is he? You see him around? I don't see him around.'

'Are you going to help or not? I have to get back.'

'All right. I'll get your stuff, Mary. But you better remember who helped you. You're working for Orc and me.'

'I'm taking care of little kids,' Mary said. 'If I'm working for anyone, it's for them.'

'Like I say, you remember who was there when you needed them.' Howard turned on his heel and swaggered away.

'Two babysitters and food,' Mary called after him.

Mary returned to the day care. Three kids were crying, and it was spreading. John was staggering from crib to floor mat.

'I'm back,' Mary said. 'Get some sleep, John.'

John simply crumpled. He was snoring before he hit the floor.

'It's OK,' Mary told the first crying child. 'It's going to be all right.'

SAM SLEPT IN his clothes and woke too early.

He had spent the night on the couch in the large main room of the hotel suite. He knew from camp-outs on the beach that Quinn talked in his sleep.

He blinked and saw Astrid, a slender shadow against the sun. She was standing in front of the window but looking at him. He quickly wiped his mouth on the pillow.

'Sorry, sleep drool.'

'I didn't mean to wake you up, but look at this.'

The morning sun had come up behind the town, up from behind the ridge. Rays of sunlight that sparkled and danced on the water seemed unable to touch the grey blankness of the barrier. It curved far out to sea, a wall rising from the ocean.

'How high is it?' Sam wondered aloud.

Astrid said, 'I should be to able to calculate it. You measure from the base of the wall to a point, then you figure the angle and . . . never mind. It has to be at least a couple hundred feet high. We're three storys up and we're nowhere near the top. If there is a top.'

'What do you mean if there is a top?'

'I'm not sure. Don't take anything I say too seriously: I'm just thinking out loud.'

'So think out loud enough for me to hear,' Sam said.

Astrid shrugged. 'OK. There may not be a top. It may not be a wall, it may be a dome.'

'But I see the sky,' Sam argued. 'I see clouds. They're moving.'

'Right. Well, imagine this: you're holding a piece of black glass in your hand. Like a really big, really dark sunglasses lens. You tilt it one way, it's opaque. You tilt it another way, it's reflective. You squint real hard straight into it and you almost think you can see some light coming through. It all depends on the angle and the –'

'You hear that?' Quinn asked. He had arrived unnoticed, scratching himself indiscreetly.

Sam listened hard. 'An engine. Not far away, either.'

They ran from the room, pelted down the stairs, and burst through double doors on to the hotel grounds. Around the corner, back to the tennis courts.

'It's Edilio. The new kid,' Sam said.

Edilio Escobar was seated in the open cage of a small yellow backhoe. As they watched, he manoeuvred close to the barrier and lowered the shovel. It bit through grass and came up with a shovelful of dirt.

'He's trying to dig his way out,' Quinn said. He broke into a run and leaped up impulsively on to the backhoe beside Edilio. Edilio jumped about a foot in the air, but came down grinning.

Edilio killed the engine. 'Hey, guys. I guess you kinda noticed this, huh?' He jerked a thumb at the barrier. 'By the way, don't touch it.'

Sam nodded ruefully. 'Yeah. We figured that out.'

Edilio revved the engine and dug three more scoops. Then he hopped down, picked up a shovel, and prised away the last few inches of dirt between the hole and the barrier.

The barrier continued, even underground.

Working together, Edilio, Sam, and Quinn dug five feet down with backhoe and shovel. They found no bottom to the barrier.

But Sam did not want to stop. There had to be a bottom. There had to be. He was hitting rock, unable to get the shovel to bite deep. Each spadeful was lighter than the one before.

'Maybe a jackhammer. Or at least some picks to break it up down here.' Only then, hearing no response, did he realise he was the only one still digging. The others were standing, looking down at him.

'Yeah, maybe,' Edilio said finally. He bent down to give Sam a hand up out of the hole.

Sam clambered up, tossed his shovel aside, and beat the dirt from his jeans. 'It was a good idea, Edilio.'

'Like what you did at the fire, man,' Edilio said. 'You saved the hardware and the day care.'

Sam didn't want to think about what he had saved or not saved. 'Wouldn't have saved anything, including my own butt, without you, Edilio. And Quinn and Astrid,' he added as an afterthought.

Quinn shot a hard look at Edilio. 'So why are you here?' he asked.

Edilio sighed and propped his shovel against the barrier. He wiped sweat from his face and looked around at the well-tended grounds. 'My mom works here,' Edilio said.

Quinn smirked a little. 'Is she, like, the manager?'

'She's in housekeeping,' Edilio said evenly.

'Yeah? Where do you live?' Quinn asked.

Edilio pointed at the barrier. 'Over there. About two miles down the highway. We have a trailer. My dad, my two little brothers. They had a bug, so my mom kept them home. Alvaro, my big brother, he's in Afghanistan.'

'He's in the army?'

'Special Forces,' Edilio grinned. 'The elite.'

He wasn't a big kid, but he stood so straight, he didn't seem short. His eyes were dark, seeming almost without whites, gentle but not fearful. He had rough, scarred hands that looked like they belonged on another body. He held his arms slightly out from his trunk, hands turned palm forwards just a bit, like he was getting ready to catch something. He seemed both completely still and yet ready to jump into action.

'This is stupid when you think about it. People on the other side of the barrier, they know what's happened,' Quinn said. 'I mean, it's not like they haven't noticed that we're behind this wall all of a sudden.'

'So?' Sam asked.

'So they have better equipment and stuff than we do, right? They can dig a lot deeper, get under the barrier. Or go around it. Or fly over it. This is a waste of time here.'

'We don't know how far down or high up the barrier extends,' Astrid said. 'It looks like it stops a couple hundred feet up, but maybe that's an optical illusion.'

'Over, under, around, or through,' Edilio said. 'There's got to be a way.'

'Kind of like when your folks came over the border from Mexico, huh?' Quinn said.

Sam and Astrid both aimed shocked looks at Quinn.

Edilio stood even straighter and, despite being six inches shorter than Quinn, seemed to be looking down at him. In a calm, quiet voice Edilio said, 'Honduras is where my folks are from. They had to come all the way through Mexico before they even reached the border. My mom works as a maid. My father is a farmhand. We live in a trailer and drive an old beater. I still have a little accent because I learned Spanish before I learned English. Anything else you need to know, man?'

Quinn said, 'I wasn't trying to start anything, amigo.'

'That's good,' Edilio said.

It wasn't a threat, not really. And in any case, Quinn had twenty pounds on Edilio. But it was Quinn who took a step back.

'We have to go,' Sam said. To Edilio, he explained, 'We're looking for Astrid's little brother. He's . . . he needs someone to look after him. Astrid thinks he may be up at the power plant.'

'My father's an engineer there,' Astrid explained. 'But it's about ten miles from here.'

Sam hesitated before asking Edilio to join them. It would annoy Quinn. Quinn wasn't acting like himself, which wasn't really strange, given what was going on, but Sam found it unsettling. Edilio, on the other hand, had kept his head together at the fire. He'd stepped up.

Astrid made the decision for him. 'Edilio? Would you like to come with us?'

Now Sam was a little peeved. Did Astrid think Sam couldn't take care of things? She needed Edilio?

Astrid rolled her eyes at Sam. 'I thought I would cut to the chase and avoid more male posturing.'

'I wasn't posturing,' Sam grumbled.

'How are you going to travel?' Edilio asked.

'I don't think we should try to drive a car, if that's what you mean,' Sam said.

'I maybe got something. Not a car, but better than walking ten miles.' Edilio led them to a garage door hidden away around the back of the pool changing room. He raised the garage door, revealing two golf carts with the logo of Clifftop Resort on the sides. 'The groundskeepers and the security guys use them to get around and go over to the golf course on the other side of the highway.'

'Have you driven one of these before?' Sam asked.

'Yeah. My dad picks up a shift sometimes at the golf course. Groundskeeping. I go with him, help out.'

That simplified the decision. Even Quinn had to see the logic. 'OK,' Quinn said grudgingly. 'You drive.'

Sam said, 'We can try the direct road to the highway. It's the first right.'

'You're avoiding downtown,' Astrid said. 'You don't want kids coming up to you, asking you what they should do.'

'You want to get to PBNP?' Sam asked. 'Or do you want to watch me stand around telling people they have nothing to fear but fear itself?'

Astrid laughed, and it was, in Sam's opinion, probably the sweetest sound he had ever heard.

'You remember,' Astrid said.

'Yeah. I remember. Roosevelt. The Great Depression. Sometimes, if I really strain my brain, I can even do multiplication.'

'Defensive humour,' Astrid teased.

They motored across the parking lot and on to the road. There they took a sharp cut-back right turn on to a narrow, newly paved section. The golf cart slowed going uphill to barely better than walking speed. They soon saw that the road dead-ended into the barrier. They stopped and stared solemnly at the abrupt end of the pavement.

'It's like a *Road Runner* cartoon,' Quinn said. 'If you go paint a tunnel on to it, we can go through, but Wile E. Coyote will smash into it.'

'OK. Back down to the cliff road then, but cut through the back streets to the highway – don't go near the plaza,' Sam said. 'We need to find Little Pete already. I don't want to have to stop and talk to a bunch of kids.'

'Yeah, plus we don't want anyone stealing the cart,' Edilio said.

'Yeah. There's that,' Sam admitted.

'Stop,' Astrid yelled, and Edilio slammed on the brakes.

Astrid jumped off her seat and trotted back to something white by the roadside. She knelt down and picked up a twig.

'It's a seagull,' Sam said, puzzled that Astrid should care. 'Maybe bashed into the barrier, huh?'

'Maybe. But look at this.' She poked the bird's foot with the twig, lifting it up.

'Yeah?'

'It's webbed, of course. Like it should be. But look at the way the toes extend out. Look at the nails. They're talons. Like a bird of prey. Like a hawk or an eagle.'

'You sure it's a regular seagull?'

'I like birds,' she explained. 'This is not normal. Seagulls don't need talons. So they don't have talons.'

'So it's a bird freak,' Quinn said. 'Can we move on now?'

Astrid stood up. 'It's not normal.'

Quinn barked a laugh. 'Astrid, we're not even in the same time zone as normal. This is what you're worrying about? Bird toes?'

'This bird is either a solitary freak, a random mutation,' Astrid said, 'or it's a whole new species that suddenly appeared. Evolved.'

'Again I have to go with "so what?"' Quinn said.

Astrid was on the verge of saying something. Then she shook her head a little, telling herself no. 'Never mind, Quinn. Like you said, we're a long way from normal.'

They loaded up again and took off at twelve miles an hour. They turned on Third and cut back, distancing themselves from town, and ran up Fourth, which was a quiet, shady, decidedly shabby, older residential street close by Sam's house.

The only cars they saw were parked or crashed. The only people they saw were a couple of kids crossing the street behind them. They heard TV sounds coming from one house, but quickly determined that it was a DVD.

'At least the electricity is still on,' Quinn said. 'They haven't taken away our DVDs. MP3s will still work, too, even without web access. We'll still have tunes.'

'They,' Astrid noted. 'We've moved on from "God" to "they".'

They reached the highway and stopped.

'Well. That's creepy,' Quinn said.

In the middle of the highway was a UPS tractor-trailer. The trailer had broken free and was on its side, like a discarded toy. The tractor, the truck part, was still upright, but off to the side of the road. There was a Sebring convertible smashed against the front. The convertible had not fared well. The impact was head-on. The car was crumpled to about half its usual length. And it had burned.

'The drivers poofed, car driver and truck driver,' Quinn said.

'At least no one got hurt,' Edilio said.

'Unless there was a kid in the car,' Astrid pointed out.

No one suggested checking. Nothing had survived that crash or the subsequent fire. None of them wanted to see if there was a small body in the back seat.

The highway was four lanes, two going each way, not divided, but with a turning lane in the middle. There was always traffic.

Even in the middle of the night there was traffic. Now, only silence and emptiness.

Edilio laughed a little shakily. 'I'm still expecting some big old truck to come barrelling down on us, run us over.'

'It would almost be a relief,' Quinn muttered.

Edilio stepped on the pedal, the electric motor whirred, and they eased out on to the highway, skirting around the overturned UPS trailer.

It was an eerie experience. They were going slower than a strong cyclist on a highway where no one ever travelled at less than sixty miles an hour. They crept past a muffler shop and the Jiffy Lube, past a squat office building that housed a lawyer and an accountant. In several places cars from the highway had ploughed into parked cars. A convertible was all the way inside the dry-cleaner's. It had taken out the plate-glass window. Clothing in plastic wrap lay strewn across the car's hood and into the passenger compartment.

There was a graveyard silence as they drove. The only sound came from the soft rubber tyres and the strained whirring of the electric motor.

The town lay to their left. To the right the land rose sharply to a high ridge. The ridge loomed above Perdido Beach, its own sort of wall. The thought had never occurred to Sam so forcefully before that Perdido Beach was already bounded by barriers, by mountains on the north and east, by ocean to the south and west. This road, this silent, empty road, was just about the only way in or out.

Ahead was the Chevron station. Sam thought he saw movement there.

'What do you guys think?' he asked.

'Maybe they have food. It's a mini-mart, right?' Quinn said. 'I'm hungry.'

'We should keep going,' Astrid said.

'Edilio?' Sam pressed.

He shrugged. 'I don't want to be paranoid. But, man, who knows?'

Sam said, 'I guess I vote for keeping going.'

Edilio nodded and eased the golf cart to the left side of the road.

'If there are kids there, we smile and wave and say we're in a hurry,' Sam said.

'Yes, sir,' Quinn said.

'Don't pull that, brah. We took a vote,' Sam said.

'Yeah. Right.'

There were clearly people at the Chevron station. A slight breeze carried a torn Doritos bag down the highway towards them, a red and gold tumbleweed.

As the golf cart approached, one kid, then another, stepped out into the road. Cookie was the first. The second kid Sam didn't recognise.

'T'sup, Cookie,' Sam called out as they drew within twenty yards.

'T'sup, Sam?' Cookie replied.

'Looking for Astrid's little brother, man.'

'Hold up,' Cookie said. He was carrying a metal baseball bat. The other kid beside him had a croquet mallet with green stripes.

'Nah, man, we're on a mission, we'll catch you later,' Sam said. He waved, and Edilio kept his foot on the pedal. They were within a couple of feet and would soon be past.

'Stop them,' a voice yelled from the Chevron station. Howard was running and, behind him, Orc. Cookie stepped in front of the cart.

'Don't stop,' Sam hissed.

'Man, look out,' Edilio warned Cookie.

Cookie jumped aside at the last second. The other kid swung his mallet hard. The wood shaft hit the steel pole that supported the cart's awning. The mallet head snapped off and narrowly missed Quinn's head.

Then they were past and Quinn yelled back, 'Hey, you almost knocked my head in, jerkwad.'

They were maybe thirty feet on and pulling away when Orc yelled, 'Catch them, you morons.'

Cookie was a big kid, not fast. But the other kid, the one holding the broken mallet, was smaller and quicker. He broke into a sprint. Howard and Orc were farther back, running full out, but Orc was heavy and slow and Howard pulled away from him.

The kid with the mallet caught up to them. 'You better stop,' he said, panting, running alongside.

'I don't think so,' Sam said.

'Dude, I'll stab you with this stick,' the kid threatened, but he was panting harder. He made a weak stab with the shattered end of the mallet.

Sam caught it and twisted it out of his hands. The kid tripped and sprawled. Sam tossed the stick aside contemptuously.

Howard was almost in range, coming up directly behind the cart. Astrid and Quinn watched calmly as Howard pumped hard, skinny arms windmilling. He threw a glance back and realised Orc wasn't going to catch up.

'Howard, what do you think you're doing, man?' Quinn asked in a perfectly reasonable voice. 'You're like a dog chasing a truck. What are you going to do if you catch us?'

Howard got the point and slowed down.

Edilio said, 'It's a low-speed chase, man. Maybe we'll be on the news.'

That got a nervous laugh.

Five minutes later, no one was laughing. 'There's a truck coming up fast,' Astrid said. 'We need to pull over.'

'They won't run us down,' Quinn said. 'Even Orc's not that crazy.'

'They may or may not want to run us down,' Astrid said, 'but that's a fourteen-year-old driving a Hummer. You really want to be on the road?'

Quinn nodded. 'We're in for a pounding.'

THE HUMMER WEAVED back and forth across the road, but there was no way to pretend it wasn't going to catch them.

'Keep going or pull off?' Edilio asked. His hands were white-knuckled on the wheel.

'They're going to kick our butts now,' Quinn yelled. 'We should have just stopped. I told you we should have just stopped, but no.'

The Hummer closed the distance with shocking speed.

'They're going to hit us,' Astrid yelled.

Quinn jumped off the cart and ran. The Hummer shuddered to a stop. Cookie and the Mallet Kid piled out and went after Quinn.

'Pull over,' Sam said. He jumped off and ran to Quinn's aid.

Quinn tried to leap the ditch beside the road, but landed badly. The two thugs were on him before he could recover. Cookie pounded him in the back with his fist.

Sam made a flying leap at Cookie. He grabbed Cookie in the crook of one arm and yanked him forwards with his momentum.

Cookie landed hard on his belly, and Sam rolled free. Cookie had dropped his bat to pound Quinn with his fists, and Sam dived for it. Mallet, Edilio, and Quinn had a brief but violent tussle that left Edilio and Quinn standing and the other kid down. But it had given Orc and Howard time to climb down from the truck.

Orc swung his bat and caught Edilio behind the knees. Edilio dropped like a sack of cement.

Gripping Cookie's bat, Sam raced to get between Orc and Edilio.

'I don't want to fight you,' Sam shouted.

'I know you don't want to fight me,' Orc said confidently. 'Nobody wants to be fighting me.'

Astrid came striding up. 'All of you stop it,' she yelled. Her fists were balled up. There were tears in her eyes. But she was angry, not sad. 'We don't need this crap.'

Howard slid between Orc and Astrid. 'Step off, Astrid, my man Orc has to teach this punk a lesson.'

'Step off?' Astrid shot back. 'You don't tell me to step off you . . . you invertebrate.'

'Astrid, stay out of this, I got this,' Sam said. Edilio tried to stand firm, but he could barely stand at all.

Surprisingly, Orc said, 'Hey. Let Astrid talk.'

Pumped on adrenaline, Sam almost didn't hear him. But then he processed what Orc had said and kept his mouth shut.

Astrid took a deep breath. Her hair was flying wild. Her face was red. Finally, struggling for calm, she said, 'We're not looking for a fight.'

'Speak for yourself,' Cookie muttered.

'This is crazy,' Astrid said. 'We're just looking for my brother.'

Orc's slit eyes narrowed further. 'The retard?'

'He's autistic,' Astrid snapped.

'Yeah. Little Pe-tard,' Orc sneered, but he didn't push it.

'You should have stopped, Sammy.' Howard made a *tsk-tsk* sound, shaking his head regretfully.

'That's what I said, and I'm the one who ends up getting pounded?' Quinn gestured wildly, angry at Sam.

Howard nodded towards Quinn, amused. 'You should have listened to your bro there, Sam. I told you last night, you need to take care of my man Orc.'

'Take care of him? What does that mean?' Astrid demanded.

Howard turned cold eyes on her. 'You have to show Captain Orc some respect, that's what I mean.'

'Captain?' Sam resisted the urge to laugh.

Howard stepped close, brave with Orc standing right behind him. 'Yeah. Captain. Someone had to step up and take charge, right? You were busy, I guess, maybe surfing or whatever, so Captain Orc volunteered to be in charge.'

'In charge of what?' Quinn asked.

'Stopping everybody running crazy, that's what.'

'Yeah,' Orc agreed.

'Kids were busting everything up, taking anything they wanted,' Howard went on.

'Yeah.'

'And all those booger-eaters, all those little kids running

around, no one to even stop them crying or change their diapers. Orc made sure they were taken care of.' Howard grinned a huge grin. 'He comforted them. Or at least made sure someone did.'

'That's right,' Orc said, as if it was the first time he'd heard it put that way.

'No one else wanted to get things under control, so Orc did,' Howard said. 'And so he is the Captain now, until the adults come back.'

'Only they ain't coming back,' Orc said.

'That's totally right,' Howard said. 'What the Captain said.'

Sam glanced at Astrid. The truth was, someone needed to get people to stop acting crazy. Orc would not have been Sam's choice for that job. But he didn't want to do it himself.

The fight had mostly gone out of the situation. And now that the two sides were lined up face-to-face, there was no question who would win if it started up again. It was four to four, but the four bullies included Orc, and he counted for three at least.

'We just want to go look for Little Pete,' Sam said finally, swallowing his anger.

'Yeah? If you're looking for something, it's best if you go kind of slow,' Howard said with a smirk.

'You want the golf cart,' Sam said.

'That's what I'm talking about, Sammy,' Howard said, spreading his hands wide in a gesture of conciliation.

'It's, like, people pay taxes, right?' Mallet said.

'Exactly,' Howard agreed. 'It's a tax.'

'Who are you, anyway?' Astrid challenged Mallet. 'I've never seen you at school.'

'I go to Coates Academy.'

Sam said, 'My mom's the night nurse up there.'

'Not any more,' the kid said.

'Why are you down here?' Astrid again.

'I didn't get along with the kids up there.' Mallet tried to toss the line off like it was a joke, but the effect was undermined by the fear in his eyes.

'Are there any adults up there?' Sam asked hopefully.

'Aw,' Howard said. 'Sammy wants his mommy.'

'Take the golf cart,' Sam said.

'Don't waste your time trying to look all bad at me. See, I know you, man,' Howard said. 'School Bus Sam. Mr Fireman. You go all heroic, but then you disappear. Don't you? It kind of comes and goes with you. Everyone last night is all, "Where's Sam? Where's Sam?" And I had to say, "Well, kids, Sam is off with Astrid the Genius because Sam can't be hanging out with regular people like us. Sam has to go off with his hot blonde girlfriend."'

'She's not my girlfriend,' Sam said, and instantly regretted it.

Howard laughed, delighted to have provoked him. 'See, Sam, you always got to be in your own little world, too good for everyone, while me and Captain Orc and our boys here, we're always going to be around. You step away, and we step up.'

Sam could feel Astrid and Quinn watching, waiting for him to deny what Howard was saying. But what was the point? Sam had felt the expectations of so many kids in the plaza, kids waiting for him to step up, like Howard said. And all he had wanted to do was run away. He had jumped at the chance to go off with Astrid.

'I'm bored with this,' Orc grunted.

Howard grinned. 'OK, Sam. You can go find Little Pe-tard, but when you come back, you better have a nice present for the Captain. Captain runs the FAYZ, man.'

'The what?' Astrid asked.

Howard was clearly pleased to be asked. 'I came up with that myself. FAYZ. Spelled F-A-Y-Z. It stands for Fallout Alley Youth Zone. Fallout Alley, and nothing but kids.'

Howard laughed his mean laugh. 'Don't worry, Astrid, it's just a FAYZ. Get it? It's just a FAYZ.'

The sun was hot on her face. Lana opened her eyes. Ominous winged shapes floated above her, crossed the sun, floated back. The vultures watched her and waited, confident of a meal.

Her tongue was swollen so that it filled her mouth, almost gagging her. Her lips were cracked. She was dying.

She looked around for the body of her poor dog. He should have been right there beside her. But there was no body.

She heard a familiar bark.

'Patrick?'

He came bounding over to her, excited, urging her to come and play.

She lifted her one good arm and touched Patrick's neck. His

fur was matted with dried blood. She probed where the fatal bite had been. The wound was closed. There was still a scab on the site, but it was no longer bleeding, and judging from Patrick's behaviour, he had never felt better.

Had she dreamed it all? No, the dried blood was proof.

She strained to recall her last conscious moments from the night. Had she prayed? Was that it, a miracle? She didn't remember doing that, she wasn't a person who thought about prayer.

Had she caused this? Had she somehow healed Patrick?

She almost laughed. She was getting delirious. She was losing her mind. Imagining things.

Crazy from the pain and thirst and hunger.

Crazy.

She smelled something foul. Sickly sweet and foul.

She looked at her shattered right arm. The flesh, especially the taut, stretched flesh that barely contained her shattered arm bones, was dark, black edging towards green. The smell was awful.

Lana took several deep breaths, shaky, fighting the upsurge of terror. She'd heard of gangrene. It was what happened when flesh died or circulation was cut off. Her arm was dying. The smell was the odour of rotting human flesh.

A vulture fluttered to a landing just a few feet away. It stared at her with beady eyes and bobbed its featherless neck. The vulture knew that smell, too.

Patrick came bounding back, barking, and the vulture reluctantly flapped away.

'Not getting me,' Lana croaked, but the weakness of her own voice just scared her further. The vultures were going to get her. They were.

But there was Patrick, healed after a seemingly fatal wound.

Lana laid her left hand on the flesh just below the bone on her right arm. The flesh was hot to the touch. It felt puffy beneath the crust of dried blood.

She closed her eyes and thought, whatever did it, however it happened for Patrick, I want it now for me. I don't want to die. I don't want to die.

She drifted off then, thinking of home. Of her room. Posters on the walls, a dreamcatcher hanging in front of one window, forgotten stuffed animals in a wicker basket, a closet bursting with clothing, her collection of Asian fans, which everyone thought was weird.

She wasn't mad at her parents any more. She just missed them. She wanted her mother more than anything. And her dad, too. He would know how to save her.

She dreamed feverish dreams, images that made her gasp and pant and caused her heart to beat like a jackhammer.

She felt herself floating on a thin crust of land. The land was like the skin of a balloon. Below, an open space full of swirling clouds and sudden jets of flame. And farther down still, a monster, something out of her childhood, the monster that had often startled her from sleep.

It was chiselled of living stone, a rough, slow-moving, cunning beast with burning black eyes.

And within that terrible beast, a heart. Only this heart glowed green, not red. And this heart was like an egg, cracked open so that brilliant, painful light escaped.

She woke with a start from the sound of her own cry.

She sat up, as she always did when waking from a nightmare in her own bed.

She sat up.

The pain was terrible. Her head pounded, her back, her . . . She stared at her right arm.

For a while she forgot to breathe. Forgot even the pain in her head and back and leg. Forgot them all. Because the pain in her arm was gone.

Her arm was straight. From elbow to wrist it formed a straight line again.

The gangrene was gone as well. The smell of death was gone.

Her arm was still crusted in dried blood but it was nothing, nothing at all compared with what had been there, nothing like what it had been.

Trembling, she lifted her right arm.

It moved.

Slowly she clenched her right fist.

The fingers came together.

It was not possible. It was not possible. What she was seeing could not be.

But pain didn't lie. And the searing pain in her arm was now no more than a dull throb.

Lana placed her left hand on her broken leg.

It wasn't quick. It took a long time and she was terribly weak from thirst and hunger. But she kept her hand there until, an hour later, she did what she had feared she would never do again: Lana Arwen Lazar stood up.

Two vultures sat perched atop the overturned pickup truck.

Lana said, 'Guess you waited for nothing.'

ELEVEN

SAM, QUINN, EDILIO, and Astrid moved off on foot, insults and laughter following them.

'Quinn, Edilio, are you guys OK?' Astrid asked.

'Aside from the big bruise I'll probably have in the middle of my back?' Quinn answered. 'Sure. Aside from the fact that I got pounded on for no reason, I'm perfect. Great plan, brah. Worked out well. We gave away the golf cart, and we got beat up and humiliated.'

Sam bit back a desire to yell at his friend. Quinn wasn't wrong. Sam had voted to ignore the roadblock, and they had paid a price.

Howard's words stung. It was like the little worm had peeled back his skin and shown the world what Sam was really like. Not about thinking he was too good for everyone, that was wrong, but about him not wanting to step up. Sam had his reasons, but right now they didn't matter as much as the burning feeling that he was shamed in front of his friends.

'I'll be fine, no big thing,' Edilio said to Astrid. 'If I keep walking, it'll go away.'

'Oh yeah, great, be a big man, Edilio.' Quinn sneered. 'Maybe you enjoy getting pounded on. Me, no. I do not enjoy getting pounded on. And now we're supposed to walk all the way to the power plant? Why, so we can look for some little kid who probably doesn't even know he's missing?'

Again Sam resisted the surge of anger. As mildly as he could he said, 'Brother, nobody is making you come.'

'You saying I shouldn't?' Quinn took two quick steps and grabbed Sam's shoulder. 'You saying you want me to leave, brah?'

'No, man. You're my best friend.'

'Your only friend.'

'Yeah. That's right,' Sam admitted.

'All I'm saying is, who died and made you king?' Quinn asked. 'You're acting like you're the boss here. How did that happen? How come I'm taking orders from you?'

'You're not taking orders,' Sam said angrily. 'I don't want anyone taking orders from me. If I wanted people taking orders from me, all I had to do was stay in town and start telling people what to do.' In a quieter voice Sam said, 'You can be in charge, Quinn.'

'I never said I wanted to be in charge,' Quinn huffed. But he was running out of resentment. He shot a dark look at Edilio, a wary look at Astrid. 'It's just weird, brah. Used to be it was you and me, right?'

'Yeah,' Sam agreed.

In a whining voice Quinn said, 'I just want to get our boards and head for the beach. I want everything to go back to how it was.' Then in a startling shout he cried, 'Where is everyone?

Why haven't they come for us? Where. Are. My. Parents?'

They began walking again, Edilio hobbling a little, Quinn falling behind and muttering. Sam walked beside Astrid, still self-conscious in her presence.

'You handled Orc back there,' he said. 'Thanks.'

'I tutored him through remedial math.' She made a wry smile. 'He's a little intimidated by me. We can't count much on that, though.'

They walked down the middle of the highway. It was strange to see the yellow line under their feet, strange.

'Fallout Alley Youth Zone,' Astrid said.

'Yeah. I guess that will stick, huh?'

'Maybe it's not just a joke,' Astrid said. 'Maybe this is about Fallout Alley?'

Sam looked sharply at her. 'You mean maybe an accident at the nuclear plant?'

She shrugged. 'I'm not sure I mean anything.'

'But you think it could be connected? Like the plant blew up or something?'

'The power is still on. Perdido Beach gets all its power from the plant. The lights are still on. So one way or the other, the plant is still running.'

Edilio stopped. 'Hey, guys. Why are we walking?'

'Because that jerk Orc and that tool Howard stole our golf cart,' Quinn said.

'Dude,' Edilio said, and pointed at a car that had plunged off the road and come to a stop in the drainage ditch. There were two bikes mounted on a trunk-top bike rack.

'I feel bad taking someone's bike,' Astrid said.

'Get over it,' Quinn said. 'Haven't you noticed? It's a whole new world. It's the FAYZ.'

Astrid peered up at a seagull floating not far above them. 'Yes, Quinn. I did notice.'

They took the two bikes and rode two-on, Quinn perched on Edilio's handlebars, Astrid on Sam's. Her hair blew in his face, stinging him a little. Sam was sorry when they located two more bikes.

The highway did not go to the power plant. They had to turn on to a side road. There was an impressive stone guardhouse at the turn-off, and a red-striped gate, like the ones at a railroad crossing. It was lowered to bar the way. They pedalled around it.

The road wound through hillsides carpeted in desiccated grass and wilting yellow wild flowers. There were no homes or businesses near the plant. It was surrounded by hundreds of acres of emptiness in all directions. Steep hillsides and infrequent stands of trees, meadows and dry creeks.

Eventually the road veered down to the tumbled rock shoreline. The view was stunning, but the surf, normally explosive, was gentle, tamed. The road rose and fell, wound back on itself a couple of times, hid behind hills, and then opened on a new panorama of the ocean.

'There's another security gate up ahead,' Astrid said.

'If there's a guard there, I'll kiss him,' Quinn said.

'This is all constantly watched and patrolled,' Astrid said.

'They have almost a private army that protects the plant.'

'Not any more,' Sam said.

They came to a chain-link fence topped with razor wire. The fence extended down to the rocks on the left, and disappeared up into the hills on the right. There was a much more serious guardhouse here, almost a fortress. It looked like it could handle a major attack. The gate was a tall section of chain link that could roll back and forth at the push of a button.

They stopped pedalling and stood looking up at the obstacle.

'How do we get in?' Astrid wondered.

'Someone climbs the gate,' Sam said. 'Rock, paper, scissors?'

The three boys did rock, paper, scissors, and Sam lost.

'Dude. Paper? Come on,' Quinn teased. 'Everybody knows you go with scissors on the first round.'

Sam scaled the chain link quickly, but the razor wire gave him pause. He took off his shirt and wrapped it around the most troublesome strand of wire. He carefully swung a leg over and yelped as the wire nicked his thigh. Then he was over. He dropped to the ground, leaving his shirt behind on the wire.

He entered the guardhouse. The air-conditioning was on full blast, making him instantly regret the loss of his shirt.

A bank of colour monitors showed the road they had just come down, as well as a rotating array of outdoor scenes: ocean and rock and mountain. It also showed several passcard-protected doors to the plant.

In the restroom he spotted an electronic passcard on a lanyard, hanging from a hook. Some guy had been using the can when he disappeared. Sam hung the lanyard around his neck.

In a closet off the main room he found a grey-green military-style uniform shirt, many sizes too large. Against the wall was a locked rack of automatic weapons, machine pistols. The room smelled of oil and sulphur.

He looked for a long time at the guns. Automatic weapons versus baseball bats.

'Don't go down that road,' Sam muttered.

He left the gun closet and closed the door firmly. But his hand rested on the knob awhile. Then he shook his head. No. It had not gotten to that point.

Not yet.

The force of the temptation made him queasy. What was the matter with him that he had even considered it for a second?

He pushed the button to open the gate.

'What took you so long?' Quinn asked suspiciously.

'I was looking around for a shirt.'

The power plant stood in perfect isolation, a vast, imposing complex of warehouse-like buildings dominated by two immense, concrete bell-jar domes.

All his life Sam had heard about the power plant. It seemed like half the people in Perdido Beach worked here. Growing up, he had heard the recited reassurances. And he wasn't afraid of nuclear power, really. But now, seeing the actual plant – a bright, bristling beast crouched above the sea and beneath the mountains – it made him nervous.

'You could pile every house in Perdido Beach into this

place,' Sam said. 'I've never seen it up close. It's big.'

'It kind of reminds me of when I was in Rome and saw St Peter's, this really big cathedral,' Quinn said. 'It's, like, you know, you feel small looking at it. Like maybe you should kneel down, just to be on the safe side.'

'Stupid question, right, but we aren't going to get radioactive, are we?' Edilio asked.

'This isn't Chernobyl,' Astrid said tartly. 'They didn't even have containment towers there. That's what the two big domes are. The actual reactors are under the containment domes so if anything does happen, the radioactive gas or steam is contained inside.'

Quinn slapped Edilio on the back, fake friendly. 'And that's why there's nothing to worry about. Except, huh, they call this area Fallout Alley. I wonder why? What with everything being totally safe and all.'

Quinn and Sam knew the story, but for Edilio's benefit, Astrid pointed at the more distant of the two domes. 'See how the colour is different, the one dome looks newer? The dome over there was hit by a meteorite. Almost fifteen years ago. But what are the odds of that ever happening again?'

'What were the odds of it happening once?' Quinn muttered.

'A meteorite?' Edilio echoed, and he glanced up at the sky. The sun was well past its high point and settling towards the water.

'A small meteorite moving at high speed,' Astrid said. 'It hit the containment vessel and blew it up. Vaporised it. It hit the reactor and just kept going. Actually, it was good it was moving so fast.'

Sam saw the picture in his head. He could imagine the big space rock hurtling down at impossible speed, trailing fire, blowing the concrete dome apart.

'Why is it good that it was so fast?' Sam asked.

'Because it drilled into the earth and carried ninety per cent of the uranium fuel down with it into the crater. It pushed it almost a hundred feet down. So they basically just filled in the hole, paved it over, and rebuilt the reactor.'

'I heard a guy was killed,' Sam said.

Astrid nodded. 'One of the engineers. I guess he was working in the reactor area.'

'You telling me there's a bunch of uranium under the ground and no one is supposed to think that's dangerous?' Edilio said sceptically.

'A bunch of uranium and one dude's bones,' Quinn said. 'Welcome to Perdido Beach, where our slogan is "Radiation? What radiation?"'

Astrid led the way. She had visited the plant many times with her father. She found an unmarked, unremarkable door in the slab side of the turbine building. Sam swiped the passcard in the slot, and the door clicked open.

Inside they found a cavernous space with a high ceiling of interlaced I beams and a painted concrete floor. There were four massive engines, each bigger than a locomotive. The noise was incredible.

'These are the turbines,' Astrid shouted over the hurricane howl. 'The uranium creates a reaction that heats up water, which makes steam, which comes here, spins the turbines, and generates electricity.'

'So, you're saying it doesn't involve giant hamsters on a wheel?' Quinn yelled. 'I was misinformed.'

'I guess we better look here first,' Sam shouted. He looked at Quinn.

Quinn performed a languid, mocking salute.

They spread out through the turbine room. Astrid reminded them that Little Pete usually wouldn't come when called. The only way to find him was to look in every corner, every space where a little kid could possibly stand, sit, or hide.

Little Pete was not in the turbine room.

Astrid finally signalled them to move on. After passing through two sets of doors, they could hear normal speech again.

'Let's go to the control room,' Astrid suggested, and led the way down a gloomy corridor and into a dated-looking control room. It looked like a set from a NASA space launch, with old-school computers, flickering monitors, and way too many panels with way too many glowing lights, switches, and ancient data ports.

There, sitting on the control room floor, rocking slightly back and forth, playing a muted hand-held video game, was Little Pete.

Astrid did not run to him. She stared with what looked to Sam like something close to disappointment. She seemed almost to shrink down a little.

But then she forced a smile and went to him.

'Petey,' Astrid said in a calm voice. Like he had never been missing, like they'd been together all along and there was nothing weird about seeing him alone in the middle of a nuclear plant control room playing Pokémon on a Game Boy.

'Thank God he wasn't in with the reactors,' Quinn said. 'I was going to say a big N-O to searching that.'

Edilio nodded agreement.

Little Pete was four years old, blond like his big sister, but freckled and almost girlish, he was so pretty. He didn't look at all slow or stupid; in fact, if you didn't know better, you'd have thought he was a normal, probably smart, kid.

But when Astrid hugged him, he seemed barely to notice. Only after almost a minute did he lift one hand from the video game control and touch her hair in an abstracted way.

'Have you had anything to eat?' Astrid asked. Then she revised the question. 'Hungry?'

She had a particular way of talking to Little Pete when she wanted his attention. She held his face in her hands, carefully blocking his peripheral vision, half covering his ears. She put her face close to his and spoke calmly but with slow, careful enunciation.

'Hungry?' she repeated slowly but firmly.

Little Pete's eyes flickered. He nodded yes.

'OK,' Astrid said.

Edilio was inspecting the dated-looking electronics that covered most of one wall. He frowned and wrinkled his brow. 'Everything looks like it's normal,' he reported.

Quinn scoffed. 'I'm sorry, are you a nuclear engineer as well as a golf cart driver?'

'I'm just looking at the readouts, man. I figure green is good, right?' He moved to a low, curved table supporting three computer monitors before three battered swivel chairs.

'I can't even read this stuff,' Edilio admitted, peering closely at one monitor. 'It's all numbers and symbols.'

'I'm going to the break room to find some food for Petey,' Astrid announced. She started to move away, but Little Pete began to whimper. It was the sound a puppy makes when it wants something.

Astrid looked pleadingly at Sam. 'Most of the time he doesn't realise I'm around. I hate to leave him when he's relating.'

'I'll get the food.' Sam said. 'What does he like?'

'Chocolate is never refused. He . . .' She started to say more but stopped herself.

'I'll get him something,' Sam said.

Edilio had moved on to what seemed to be the most up-to-date piece of equipment in the room, a plasma screen mounted on the wall.

Quinn was looking up at the screen as well, rotating slowly in one of the engineer's chairs. 'See if you can get another channel, that one's boring.'

'It's a map,' Edilio said. 'There's Perdido Beach. There's some little towns back in the hills. It goes all the way to San Luis.'

The map glowed pale blue, white, and pink, with a red bull's-eye in the centre.

'The pink is the fallout pattern in case there is ever a release,' Astrid said. 'The red is the immediate area where the radiation would be intense. It gets data on wind patterns, the contours of the land, the jet stream, all that, and adjusts it.'

'The red and the pink, that's the danger?' Edilio asked.

'Yes. That's the plume where the fallout would be above acceptable levels.'

'That's a lot of land,' Edilio said.

'But it's weird,' Astrid said. She guided Little Pete to his feet and went closer to the map. 'I've never seen it look like that. Usually the plume goes inland, you know, from the prevailing winds coming off the ocean. Sometimes the plume stretches all the way down to Santa Barbara. Or else up across the national park, depending on weather.'

The pink pattern was a perfect circle. The red zone was like a bull's-eye inside that outer circle.

'The computer's not getting satellite weather data,' Astrid said. 'So it must have reverted to its default setting, which is this red circle with a ten-mile radius, and a pink circle with a hundred-mile radius.'

Sam peered at the map, unable at first to make sense of it. Then he began to locate the town, beaches he knew, other features.

'The whole town's inside the red zone,' Sam said.

Astrid nodded.

'The red zone goes right to the far south end of town.'

'Yes.'

Sam glanced at her to discover whether she saw what he saw. 'It runs right through Clifftop.'

'Yes,' she said slowly. 'It does.'

'Are you thinking . . .'

'Yes,' Astrid said. 'I'm thinking it's a pretty amazing coincidence that the barrier seems to line up with the edge of the danger zone.' Then she added, 'At least what we know of the barrier. We don't know that it includes the entire red spot.'

'Does this mean there's been some kind of radiation leak?'

Astrid shook her head. 'I don't think so. There'd be radiation alarms going off all over the place. But what's weird is, it's like cause and effect, only backwards. The FAYZ is what cut off the weather data, which caused the computer to default. FAYZ first, then the map goes to default. So why would the FAYZ barrier be following a map whose lines it caused?'

Sam shook his head and smiled a little ruefully. 'I must be tired. You lost me. I'll go find some food.' He headed down the hall in the direction Astrid had indicated.

When he looked back she was standing, staring up at the map, a tight, grim expression on her face.

She noticed Sam watching her. Their eyes locked. She flinched, like he had caught her at something. She put one protective arm around Little Pete, who had buried his face back in his game. Astrid blinked, looked down, took a deep shaky breath, and deliberately turned away.

TWELVE

272 HOURS 47 MINUTES

'COFFEE.' MARY SAID the word like it might be magic. 'Coffee. That's what I need.'

She was in the cramped, narrow teachers' room at Barbara's Day Care, searching the refrigerator for something, anything, to feed a little girl who refused to eat. She had almost fallen into the refrigerator, she was so tired, and then she spotted the coffeemaker.

It's what her mother did when she was tired. It's what everyone did when they were tired.

In response to Mary's desperate, late-night plea for help, Howard had supplied the day care with a single box of diapers. They were Huggies for newborns. Useless. He had sent over two gallons of milk and half a dozen bags of chips and Goldfish. And he had sent Panda, who proved to be worse than useless. Mary had overheard him threatening to smack a crying three-year-old and had shooed him out of the building.

But the twins, Anna and Emma, had come on their own to help out. It wasn't enough people, not by a long shot, but Mary had been able to get two full hours of sleep.

But then, when she woke that morning – no, it was

116

afternoon, wasn't it, she had lost track. She was so groggy, she not only had no idea what time it was, for the first few seconds she had no idea where she was.

Mary had never made coffee before, but she had seen it done. With bleary eyes she tried to figure it out. There was a scoop. There were filters.

Her first effort was a long wait for nothing. Only after sitting and staring in a coma-like state for ten minutes did she realise she had forgotten to put water in the machine. When she did put the water in, it erupted in a spout of steam. But after five minutes more she had a fragrant pot of coffee.

She poured a cup and took a tentative sip. It was very hot and very bitter. She had no milk to spare, but she did still have some sugar. She started off with two big spoonfuls.

That was better.

Not good, but better.

She carried the cup back into the main room. At least six kids were crying. Diapers needed changing. The youngest kids needed feeding. Again.

A three-year-old girl with wispy blonde hair spotted Mary and came running. Without thinking, Mary reached down. The coffee spilled on to the child's neck and shoulder.

The girl screamed.

Mary shouted in fear. 'Oh, God.'

John came running. 'What happened?'

The little girl howled.

Mary froze.

'What should we do?' John cried.

Anna came running, a baby in her arms. 'Oh, my God, what happened?'

The little girl screamed and screamed.

Mary carefully sat the coffee cup on the counter. Then she ran from the room and from the school.

She ran weeping to her home two blocks away. She fumbled the door open. She could barely see through her tears. Deep sobs racked her whole body.

It was cool and silent inside. Everything just like it always was. Only so quiet, so quiet that her sobs sounded like harsh, animal sounds.

Mary soothed herself. 'It'll be all right, it'll be all right.' The same lie she'd been telling the kids. She quieted the racking sobs.

Mary sat at the kitchen table. She laid her head on her arms, intending to cry some more, quietly. But the time for tears was past.

For a while she just listened to the sound of her own breathing. She stared at the wood grain of the table. Exhaustion made it swirl.

It was impossible to believe that her mother and father were not home.

Where were they? Where were they all?

Her bedroom, her bed were just up the stairs.

She couldn't do it. She couldn't go to sleep. If she did, she wouldn't wake up for hours and hours.

The kids needed her. Her brother, poor John, coping while she freaked out.

Mary opened the freezer. Ben & Jerry's fudge brownie ice cream. DoveBars. She could eat them and then she would feel better.

She could eat them and then she would feel worse.

If she started, she wouldn't stop. If she started eating when she felt like this, she wouldn't stop until the shame became so great, she would force herself to vomit it all back up.

Mary had suffered from bulimia since she was ten. Binge eating followed by purging, again and again in a quickening cycle of diminishing returns that had left her forty pounds overweight at one point, and her teeth rough and discoloured from the stomach acid.

She'd been clever enough to conceal it for a long time, but her parents had found out eventually. Then had come therapists and a special camp and, when none of that really helped, medication. Speaking of which, Mary reminded herself, she needed to get the bottle from her medicine cabinet.

She was better now with the Prozac. Her eating was under control. She didn't purge any more. She had lost some of the extra weight.

But why not eat now? Why not?

The cold air of the freezer wafted over her. The ice cream, the chocolate, there it was. It wouldn't hurt. Not just once. Not now when she was scared to death and alone and so tired.

Just one DoveBar.

She pulled it out of the box and with fumbling, anxious fingers tore open the wrapper. It was in her mouth in a flash, so good, so cold, the chocolate slick and greasy as it melted on her tongue. The crunch of the shell as she bit into it, the soft luscious vanilla ice cream inside.

She ate it all. She ate like a wolf.

Mary grabbed the Ben & Jerry's, and now she was beginning to cry again as she put it into the microwave and softened it for twenty seconds. She wanted it runny, she wanted it to be like cold chocolate soup. She wanted to slurp it down.

The microwave dinged.

She grabbed a spoon, a big one, a soup spoon. She prised the lid from the ice cream and half spooned, half poured the pint of rich chocolate down her throat, barely tasting it in her eagerness.

She was weeping and eating, licking her hands, shaking the spoon.

She licked the lid.

Enough, she told herself.

She pulled out two large plastic garbage bags, the big black ones. Systematically she filled one with anything she could feed to the children: saltines, peanut butter, honey, Rice Chex, Nutri-Grain bars, cashews.

The second bag she carried upstairs. She piled in pillowcases and sheets, toilet paper, towels – especially towels because they could be substituted for diapers.

She found the bottle of Prozac. She opened it and tipped it

into her hand. The pills were green and orange, oblong. She popped one and swallowed it by cupping water from the faucet with her hand.

There were only two pills left.

She dragged the two bags to the front door.

Then she went back upstairs to her bathroom. She carefully locked the door behind her.

She knelt in front of the toilet, raised the lid, and stuck her finger down her throat until the gag reflex forced the food from her stomach.

When she was done she brushed her teeth. She went back downstairs. Took hold of the bags and began dragging them to the day care.

'I'm guessing Little Pete can't balance on bike handlebars,' Sam said to Astrid.

'No, he can't,' Astrid confirmed.

'OK, then, we'll be on foot. It's what, like, four o'clock? Maybe we better stay here the night, start out in the morning.' Self-conscious about Quinn's earlier complaints, Sam said, 'What do you think, Quinn? Stay or go for it?'

Quinn shrugged. 'I'm beat. Besides, they have a candy machine.'

The plant manager's office had a couch, which Astrid could share with Little Pete. She offered a still-stiff Edilio the back cushions. They pushed the couch into the control room.

Sam and Quinn searched the facility until they happened

upon the infirmary. There were gurneys there, hospital beds on wheels.

Quinn laughed. 'Surf's up, brah.'

Sam hesitated. But then Quinn took off running, got the gurney up to speed, jumped aboard, and even managed to stand up before slamming into a wall.

'OK,' Sam said. 'I can do that.'

They had a few minutes of gurney surfing through the abandoned hallways. And Sam discovered he could still laugh. It seemed like a million years since Sam had surfed with Quinn. A million years.

Sam and Quinn parked their gurneys in the control room. None of them really understood any of the controls, but it felt like the place to be.

They found that Edilio had rounded up five radiation suits, almost like space suits, each with a hood, a gas mask, and a small oxygen bottle.

'Nice, Edilio,' Quinn said. 'Just in case?'

Edilio looked uncomfortable. 'Yeah, just in case.'

When Quinn smirked, Edilio said, 'You don't think all that has happened is because of this place? Look at that map, man. Red bull's-eye that just happens to go right where the barrier goes? Maybe that Howard guy had it right, you know? Fallout Alley Youth Zone? It's a pretty big coincidence.'

Astrid, weary, said, 'Radiation doesn't cause barriers to appear or people to disappear.'

'It's deadly stuff, right?' Edilio pressed.

Quinn sighed and pushed his gurney towards a dark corner, bored by the discussion. Sam waited to hear Astrid's answer.

'Radiation can kill you,' Astrid agreed. 'It can kill you quickly, it can kill you slowly, it can give you cancer, it can just make you sick, or it can do nothing. And it can cause mutations.'

'Mutation like a seagull that suddenly has a hawk's talons?' Edilio asked pointedly.

'Yes, but only over a long, long time. Not overnight.' She stood up and took Little Pete's hand. 'I have to get him to bed.' Over her shoulder she said, 'Don't worry, you won't mutate in the night, Edilio.'

Sam stretched out on his gurney. The control room had muted lighting that went almost but not quite to dark once Astrid found the switches. The computer monitors and the LCD readouts glowed.

Sam might have chosen to leave more of the lights on. He doubted he would be able to sleep.

He lay remembering the last time he'd gone surfing with Quinn. Day after Halloween. It had only been early November sun, but in memory it was very bright, every rock and pebble and sand crab outlined in gold. In his memory the waves were wondrous, almost living things, blue and green and white, calling to him, challenging him to leave his worries behind and come out and play.

Then the scene shifted and his mother was at the top of the cliff, smiling and waving down to him. He remembered that day. She was almost always asleep during the morning hours when he surfed. But this day she came to watch.

She'd been wearing her blue and white flowery wraparound skirt and a white blouse. Her hair, much lighter than his own, blew in the stiff breeze, and she seemed frail and vulnerable up there. He wanted to yell to her to step back from the edge.

But she couldn't hear him.

He yelled up to her, but she couldn't hear him.

He woke suddenly from the memory that had become a dream. There were no windows, no way to see if it was day or night outside. But no one else was awake.

He slid off the gurney and stood up, careful to make no sound. One by one he checked on the others. Quinn silent for once, no sleep-talking; Edilio snoring on the cushions Astrid had given him; Astrid curled on one end of the couch in the office; and Little Pete asleep at the other end.

Their second night without parents. That first night in a hotel, and now here, in this nuclear power plant.

Where tomorrow night?

Sam did not want to go back to living in his home. He wanted his mother back, but not their home.

On the desk in the plant manager's office Sam spotted an iPod. He wasn't optimistic about the musical taste of the manager, who, judging by the family photo on his desk, was about sixty years old. But he didn't think he could go back to sleep.

He crept as silently as he could across the office, almost brushing Astrid's hand. Around the desk, shifting the chair ever so slightly, leaning carefully away from a shelf of trophies – golf, mostly.

A sudden movement at his feet, a rat. He jumped back and slammed into the glass-shelf trophy display.

There was a tremendous crash.

Little Pete's eyes flew open.

'Sorry,' Sam said, but before he could speak another syllable, Little Pete began to screech. It was a primitive sound. An ear-splitting, insistent, repetitive, panicky-baboon sound.

'It's OK,' Sam said. 'It's –'

His throat seized and choked off any sound. He couldn't speak.

He couldn't breathe.

Sam clutched at his throat. He felt invisible hands wrapped around his neck, steel fingers choking off his air. He slapped and prised at the fingers, and all the while Little Pete screeched and flapped his arms like a bird trying to fly.

Little Pete shrieked.

Edilio and Quinn were up and running.

Sam felt blood in his eyes, darkening his vision. His heart pounded. His lungs convulsed, sucking on nothing.

'Petey, Petey, it's all right,' Astrid said, soothing her brother, stroking his head, cuddling him against her. Her eyes were desperate with fear. 'Window seat, Petey. Window seat, window seat, window seat.'

Sam staggered into the desk.

Astrid fumbled for Little Pete's Game Boy. She turned it on.

'What's happening?' Quinn yelled.

'He heard a loud noise,' Astrid yelled. 'It startled him. When he's scared, he freaks. It's OK, Petey, it's OK, I'm here. Here's your game.'

Sam wanted to yell that it was not OK, that he was choking, but he couldn't make a sound. His head was swimming.

'Hey, Sam, what are you doing?' Quinn demanded.

'He's choking!' Edilio said.

'Can't you shut that stupid kid up?' Quinn yelled.

'He won't stop until everyone is calm,' Astrid said through gritted teeth. 'Window seat, Petey, go to your window seat.'

Sam fell to one knee.

This was crazy.

He was going to die.

Fear took hold of him.

His world was going black.

His hands, palm out, pushed at nothing.

Suddenly there was a brilliant flash of light.

It was as if a small star had gone supernova in the plant manager's office.

Sam fell, unconscious.

He was conscious again ten seconds later, on his back, the scared faces of Quinn and Edilio staring down at him.

Little Pete was silent. His too-pretty eyes were glued to his video game.

'Is he alive?' Quinn asked in a faraway voice.

Sam breathed in, sharp and sudden. Then another breath.

'I'm OK,' he rasped.

'Is he OK?' Astrid asked in a voice edged with panic, but controlled to avoid setting Little Pete off again.

'Where did that light come from?' Edilio demanded. 'Did you guys see that?'

'Dude: they saw that on the moon.' Quinn's eyes were wide.

'We are out of this place,' Edilio said.

'Where can we –' Astrid said.

Edilio cut her off. 'I don't care. Out of this place.'

'You got that right,' Quinn said. He reached down and yanked Sam to his feet.

Sam's head was still spinning, his legs wobbly. No point in resisting, the panic was in every face around him. This wasn't the time to argue or explain.

He didn't trust himself to speak, just pointed towards the door and nodded.

They ran.

THIRTEEN

THEY TOOK NOTHING with them, just ran, with Quinn in the lead and Edilio bunched with Astrid and Little Pete, and Sam woozing along behind.

They ran until they were past the main gate. They stopped, panting, bent over, resting hands on knees. It was very dark. The power plant seemed even more of a living, breathing thing at night. It was illuminated by a hundred spotlights, which just made the hills looming above them darker.

'OK, what was that?' Quinn demanded to know. 'What was that?'

'Petey just panicked,' Astrid said.

'Yeah, I get that part,' Quinn said. 'What about that light that went off?'

'I don't know,' Sam managed to rasp.

'What were you choking on, brah?'

'I was just choking,' Sam said.

'Just choking? Just choking on air?'

'I don't know, maybe . . . maybe I was sleepwalking or something and grabbed something to eat and choked on it.'

It was weak, and Quinn's disbelieving look, mirrored by Edilio, said they weren't buying it.

'That's probably it,' Astrid said.

It was so unexpected, even Sam couldn't hide a look of surprise.

'What else could have caused him to choke?' Astrid asked. 'And the light must have been some internal alarm system going off.'

'No offence, Astrid, but no way,' Edilio said. He put his hands on his hips, squared himself up to Sam, and said, 'Man, it's time you started telling us the truth. I respect you, man. But how am I going to respect you if you lie to me?'

Sam was caught off guard. It was the first time he, or any of them, had seen Edilio angry.

'What do you mean?' Sam stalled.

'There's something going on, man, and it's about you, all right?' Edilio said. 'That light just now? I saw that light before. I saw it just before I pulled you out that window from that burning building.'

Quinn's head snapped around. 'What? What are you saying?'

Edilio said, 'The wall and the disappearing people, that's not all of it. There's some other strange thing going on. Something is going on with you, Sam. And Astrid too, since she was pretty quick to try to cover for you just now.'

Sam was surprised to realise that Edilio was right: Astrid knew something, too. He wasn't the only one keeping secrets. He felt a wave of relief. He didn't have to be alone on this.

'OK.' Sam took a deep breath and tried to organise his thoughts before he started blurting it all out.

'First, I don't know what it is, all right?' Sam said quietly. 'I don't know where it comes from. I don't know how it happens. I don't know anything about it except that sometimes . . . it's this . . . there's this light.'

'What are you talking about, brah?' Quinn demanded.

Sam held up his hands, turning his palms towards his friend. 'I can . . . Dude, I know it sounds like I'm crazy, but sometimes this light just comes shooting out of my hands.'

Quinn barked a laugh. 'No, man, that doesn't sound crazy. Crazy is you saying you're better than me at riding a curl. This is mentally ill. This is off the hook. Let me see you do it.'

'I don't know how,' Sam confessed. 'It's happened four times, but I can't just make it happen.'

'Four times you shot lasers out of your hands.' Quinn was on the line between laughing and yelling. 'I've known you, like, half your life, and now you're the Green Lantern? Right.'

'It's true,' Astrid said.

'Bull. If it's true, then do it. Show me.'

Sam said, 'I'm trying to tell you, it only happens when I'm panicked or whatever. I don't make it happen, it just happens.'

Edilio said, 'Just now you said four times. I saw the flash at the fire. I saw it just now. What's the other two times?'

'The time before was at my house. It made . . . I mean, I made . . . this light. Like a light bulb kind of. It was dark. I had a nightmare.' He met Astrid's steady gaze and suddenly a different light bulb went off. 'You saw it,' he accused her. 'You saw the light in my room. You've known all along.'

'Yes,' Astrid admitted. 'I've known since that first day. And I've known about Petey for longer.'

Edilio still wanted the basics laid out. 'The fire, here, this light bulb thing, that's three.'

'First time was Tom,' Sam said. The name meant nothing to Edilio, but it did to Quinn.

'Your stepfather?' Quinn demanded sharply. 'Ex-stepfather, I mean.'

'Yeah.'

Quinn was staring hard at Sam. 'Brah, you aren't saying what you sound like you're saying, right?'

'I thought he was trying to hurt my mom,' Sam said. 'I thought . . . I was asleep, I woke up, I come down the stairs, they're both in the kitchen yelling, I see Tom with a knife, and there's this flash of light shooting out of my hands.'

Sam felt tears stinging his eyes. It surprised him. He didn't feel sad. If anything, he felt relieved. He hadn't told anyone about this before. This was a weight coming off his shoulders. But at the same time, he registered the way Quinn drew back a step, putting distance between them.

'My mom knew, of course. She covered at the emergency room. Tom was yelling that I had shot him. The doctors saw a burn, so they knew it wasn't a gunshot. My mom told some lie about Tom falling against the stove.'

'She had to choose between protecting you or supporting her husband,' Astrid said.

'Yeah. And Tom realised, once the pain was under control, he realised he would end up in the psychiatric ward if he kept talking about his stepson shooting beams of light at him.'

'You burned your stepfather's hand off?' Quinn asked, his tone shrill.

'Whoa, back up. Did what?' Edilio demanded. It was his turn to be surprised.

Quinn said, 'His stepfather ended up with a hook, man. They had to cut his hand off, like, right here.' He made a chopping motion on his forearm. 'I saw him, like, a week ago, over in San Luis. He's got one of those hooks now, you know, with, like, two pincers or whatever? He was buying cigarettes and handing the clerk money with his hook.' He pantomimed it, using two fingers for the pincers of the prosthetic arm.

'So you're some kind of freak?' Quinn asked. He still seemed undecided whether he was mad or found it funny.

'I'm not the only one,' Sam said defensively. 'That girl in the fire. I think she started that fire. When she saw me, she panicked. It was like liquid fire came out of her hands.'

Edilio said, 'So you shot back. You did your thing at her.' Sam could see only the outline of his face in the darkness. 'That's what's been dogging you. You think you hurt her.'

'I don't know how to control it. I don't ask for it to come. I don't know how to make it go away. I'm just glad I didn't hurt Little Pete. I was choking.'

132

Quinn and Edilio turned their attention to the little boy now. Little Pete rubbed sleep from his eyes and stared past them, indifferent to them, maybe not even aware that they existed. Maybe wondering why he was standing in the damp night air outside a nuclear power plant. Maybe not wondering anything.

'He's one, too,' Quinn accused. 'A freak.'

'He doesn't know what he's doing,' Astrid said.

'That's not exactly reassuring,' Quinn snapped. 'What's his trick? He shoot missiles out of his butt or something?'

Astrid smoothed her brother's hair down with her hand and let her fingers trace the side of his face. 'Window seat,' she whispered. Then, to the others, '"Window seat" is a trigger phrase. It helps him find a calm place. It's the window seat in my room.'

'Window seat,' Little Pete said unexpectedly.

'He talks,' Edilio said.

'He can,' Astrid said. 'But he doesn't much.'

'He talks. Great. What else does he do?' Quinn demanded pointedly.

'He seems able to do a lot of things. Mostly we're good, the two of us. Mostly he doesn't really notice me. But once, I was doing his therapy, working with this picture book we work on sometimes. I show him a picture and try to get him to say the word and, I don't know, I guess I was in a bad mood that day. I guess I was too rough taking his hand and putting his finger on the picture like you're supposed to do. He got mad. And then, I wasn't there any more. One second I was in his room, and then all of a sudden I was in my room.'

There was a dead silence as the four of them stared at Little Pete.

'Then maybe he can zap us out of the FAYZ and back to our folks,' Quinn said finally.

Silence fell again. The five of them stood in the middle of the road, the humming, bright-lit power plant behind them, a dark road descending ahead.

'I keep waiting for you to laugh, Sam,' Quinn said to Sam. 'You know: say "gotcha". Tell me it's all some trick. Tell me you're just goofing on me.'

'We're in a new world,' Astrid said. 'Look, I've known about Petey for a while. I tried to believe it was some kind of miracle. Like you, Quinn, I wanted to believe it was God doing it.'

'What is doing it?' Edilio asked. 'I mean, you're saying this stuff was happening before the FAYZ.'

'Look, I'm supposedly smart, but that doesn't mean I understand any of this,' Astrid admitted. 'All I know is that under the laws of biology and physics, none of this is possible. The human body has no organ that generates light. And what Petey did, the ability to move things from one place to another? Scientists have figured out how to do it with a couple of atoms. Not entire human beings. It would take more energy than the entire power plant produces, which means that, basically, the laws of physics would have to be rewritten.'

'How do you rewrite the laws of physics?' Sam wondered.

Astrid threw up her hands. 'I can just about, barely, follow AP physics. To understand this, you'd have to be Einstein or

Heisenberg or Feynman, on that level. I just know that impossible things don't happen. So either this isn't happening, or somehow the rules have been changed.'

'Like someone hacked the universe,' Quinn said.

'Exactly,' Astrid said, surprised that Quinn had gotten it. 'Like someone hacked the universe and rewrote the software.'

'Nothing but kids left, there's some big wall, and my best friend is magic boy all of a sudden,' Quinn said. 'I figured, OK, at least whatever else, I still have my brah, I still have my best friend.'

Sam said, 'I'm still your friend, Quinn.'

Quinn sighed. 'Yeah. Well, it isn't exactly the same, is it?'

'There are probably others,' Astrid said. 'Others like Sam and Petey. And the little girl who died.'

'We have to keep this quiet,' Edilio said. 'We can't be telling anyone. People don't like people they think are better than they are. If regular kids find out about this, it's going to be trouble.'

'Maybe not,' Astrid said hopefully.

'You're smart, Astrid, but if you think people are going to be happy about this, you don't know people,' Edilio said.

'Well, I won't be the one blabbing about it,' Quinn said.

Astrid said, 'OK, I think probably Edilio's right. At least for now. And especially we can't let anyone find out about Petey.'

'I'm not saying anything,' Edilio confirmed.

'You guys know. That's enough,' Sam said.

They started walking together towards the distant town. They walked in silence. At first, bunched together. Then Quinn moved out in front. And Edilio drifted to one side. Astrid was with Little Pete.

Sam let himself fall behind. He wanted quiet. He wanted privacy. Part of him would have liked to drift farther and farther back until he was left behind, forgotten by the others.

But he was tied to these four people now. They knew what he was. They knew his secret. And they had not turned against him.

The sound of Quinn singing 'Three Little Birds' came drifting back. Sam quickened his pace to catch up with his friends.

SAM, ASTRID, QUINN, and Edilio flopped on the grass of the plaza, exhausted. Little Pete remained standing, playing his game, oblivious, as though an all-night, ten-mile walk were just a stroll. The rising sun silhouetted the mountains behind them and lit the too-calm ocean.

The grass was wet with dew that soaked straight through Sam's shirt. He thought, I'll never be able to sleep here. And then he was asleep.

He woke up with sun in his eyes. He blinked and sat up. The dew had burned off, and now the grass was crisping in the heat. There were a lot of kids around. But he didn't see his friends. Maybe they had gone looking for food. He was hungry himself.

When he stood up he noticed that the crowd was moving, all in one direction, towards the church.

He joined the movement. A girl he knew walked by. He asked what was going on.

She shrugged. 'I'm just following everyone else.'

Sam kept moving till the crowd began to congeal. Then he hopped up on the back of a park bench, balancing precariously but able to see over everyone's head.

Four cars were making their way down Alameda Avenue. They drove at a stately pace, like a parade. Adding to that impression, the third car in line was a convertible with the top down. All four cars were dark, powerful, and expensive vehicles. The last car in line was a black SUV. They drove with their lights on.

'Is it someone coming to rescue us?' a fifth-grader called up to Sam.

'I don't see any police cars, so I doubt it. You might want to hang back, man.'

'Is it the aliens?'

'I think if it was aliens, we'd be seeing spaceships, not BMWs.'

The procession or parade or convoy or whatever it was drove up alongside the kerb at the top of the plaza, just across the street from the town hall, and stopped.

Kids climbed out of each car. They wore black slacks and white shirts. Girls wore pleated black skirts and matching knee-high socks. Both boys and girls had on blazers in a subdued shade of red, with a large crest sewn over the heart. Boys and girls alike wore striped ties of red, black, and gold.

The crest featured ornate letters 'C' and 'A' in gold thread over a background that showed a golden eagle and a mountain lion. Beneath the crest was the Latin motto of Coates Academy: *Ad augusta, per angusta.* To high places by narrow roads.

'They're all Coates kids.' It was Astrid. She and Little Pete stood with Edilio and Quinn. Sam jumped down to be beside them.

'A well-rehearsed display,' Astrid said, as though reading Sam's mind.

As the Coates kids climbed out of the cars, the crowd actually drew back a step. There had always been a rivalry between the kids in town, who thought of themselves as normal kids, and the Coates kids, who tended to be wealthy and, although the Academy tried to disguise the fact, strange.

Coates was the place your rich parents sent you when other schools found you 'difficult'.

The Coates kids lined up, not quite a drill team in their order and precision, but like they had practised it.

'Quasi-military,' Astrid said in a low, discreet voice.

Then one boy, wearing a bright yellow V-necked sweater instead of his blazer, stood up in the convertible. He grinned sheepishly and climbed nimbly from the back seat on to the trunk. He gave a little self-deprecating wave, as if to say he couldn't believe what he was doing.

He was handsome, even Sam noticed that. He had dark hair and dark eyes, not much different from Sam himself. But this boy's face seemed to glow with an inner light. He radiated confidence, but without arrogance or condescension. In fact, he managed to seem genuinely humble even while standing alone, looking out over everyone else.

'Hi, everyone,' he said. 'I'm Caine Soren. You probably figured out that I . . . we . . . are from Coates Academy. Either that or we all just have the same bad taste in clothing.'

There was a bit of a laugh from the crowd.

'A self-deprecating joke to loosen us up,' Astrid said, continuing her whispered commentary.

Out of the corner of his eye, Sam noticed Mallet. The boy was turning away, crouching down, acting like he was trying to hide. Mallet was a Coates kid. What was it he'd said? That he didn't get along with the kids at Coates? Something like that.

'I know there's a tradition of rivalry between the kids of Coates Academy and the kids of Perdido Beach,' Caine said. 'Well, that was the old days. It looks to me like we're all in this together. We all have the same problems now. And we should work together to deal with our problems, don't you think?'

Heads were nodding in response.

His voice was clear and just a little higher, maybe, than Sam's, but strong and determined. He had a way of looking at the crowd before him that made it seem he was meeting every person's eye, seeing every person as an individual.

'Do you know what happened?' a voice asked.

Caine shook his head. 'No. I don't think we probably know any more than you. Everyone fifteen and over disappeared. And there's the wall, the barrier.'

'We call it the FAYZ,' Howard said loudly.

'The phase?' Caine appeared interested.

'F-A-Y-Z. Fallout Alley Youth Zone.'

Caine considered that for a moment, then laughed. 'That's excellent. Did you come up with that?'

'Yeah.'

'It's vital to keep a sense of humour when the world seems to have suddenly become a very strange place. What's your name?'

'Howard. I'm the Captain's number-one guy. Captain Orc.'

An uneasy ripple moved through the crowd. Caine read it instantly. 'I hope you and Captain Orc will join me and anyone else who wants to sit down and talk about our plans for the future. Because we do have a plan for the future.' He emphasised this last sentence with a chopping motion, like he was cutting away the past.

'I want my mom,' a little boy cried out suddenly.

Every voice fell silent. The boy had said what they were all feeling.

Caine hopped down from the car and went to the boy. He knelt down and took the boy's hands in his own. He asked the boy's name, and reintroduced himself. 'We all want our parents back,' he said gently, but loudly enough to be overheard clearly by those nearest. 'We all want that. And I believe that will happen. I believe we will see our moms and dads, and older brothers and sisters, and even our teachers again. I believe that. Do you believe it, too?'

'Yes.' The little boy sobbed.

Caine wrapped him in a hug and said, 'Be strong. Be your mommy's strong little boy.'

'He's good,' Astrid said. 'He's beyond good.'

Then Caine stood up. People had formed a circle around him, close but respectful. 'We all have to be strong. We all have to get through this. If we work together to choose good leaders and do the right thing, we will make it.'

The entire crowd of kids seemed to stand a little taller. There were determined looks on faces that had been weary and frightened.

Sam was mesmerised by the performance. In just a few minutes' time, Caine had infused hope into a very frightened, dispirited bunch of kids.

Astrid seemed mesmerised too, though Sam thought he detected the cool glint of scepticism in her eyes.

Sam was sceptical himself. He distrusted rehearsed displays. He distrusted charm. But it was hard not to think that Caine was at least trying to reach out to the Perdido Beach kids. It was hard not to believe in him, at least a little. And if Caine really did have a plan, wouldn't that be a good thing? No one else seemed to have a clue.

Caine raised his voice again. 'If it's OK with everyone here, I would like to borrow your church. I would like to sit down with your leaders, in the presence of our Lord, and discuss my plan, and any changes you want to make. Are there maybe, oh, a dozen people who could speak for you?'

'Me,' Orc said, shouldering his way forwards. He still carried his aluminium baseball bat. And he had acquired a policeman's helmet, one of the black plastic helmets the Perdido Beach cops used when they patrolled on bicycles.

Caine fixed the thug with a penetrating stare. 'You must be Captain Orc.'

'Yeah. That's me.'

Caine stuck out his hand. 'I'm honoured to meet you, Captain.'

Orc's mouth dropped open. He hesitated. Sam thought it was probably the first time in Orc's turbulent life that anyone had said they were honoured to meet him. And probably the first time anyone had offered to shake his hand. Orc was clearly confused. He glanced at Howard.

Howard was looking from Orc to Caine, sizing up the situation. 'He's paying you props, Captain,' Howard said.

Orc grunted, shifted the bat from right hand to left, and stuck out his thick paw. Caine grabbed it with both his hands and solemnly looked Orc in the eye as they shook hands.

'Smooth,' Astrid said under her breath.

Still holding Orc's hand in his, Caine challenged, 'Now, who else speaks for Perdido Beach?'

Bouncing Bette said, 'Sam Temple here went into a burning building to rescue a little girl. He can speak for me, anyway.'

There was a murmur of agreement.

'Yeah, Sam is a hero for real,' a voice said.

'He could have died,' another voice seconded.

'Yeah, Sam's the guy.'

Caine's smile came and disappeared so quickly, Sam wasn't sure it had happened. For that millisecond it was a look of triumph. Caine walked straight up to Sam, open and forthright, hand extended.

'There are probably better people than me,' Sam said, backing away.

But Caine grabbed his elbow and manoeuvred him into a handshake. 'Sam, is it? It sounds like you truly are a hero.

Are you related to our school nurse, Connie Temple?'

'She's my mother.'

'I'm not surprised that she would have a brave son,' Caine said with deep feeling. 'She's a very good woman. I see you're humble as well as brave, Sam, but I . . . I'm asking for your help. I need your help.'

With the mention of his mother, everything fell into place. Caine. 'C'. What were the odds that 'C' was some other kid from Coates?

Sooner or later, C or one of the others will do something serious. Someone will get hurt. Just like S with T.

'OK,' Sam said. 'If that's what people want.'

A few other names were mentioned, and Sam half-heartedly, but loyally, named Quinn.

Caine's eyes flickered from Sam to Quinn, and for just a millisecond there flashed a cynical, knowing look. But it was gone in a heartbeat, replaced by Caine's practised expression of humility and resolve.

'Then let's go in together,' Caine said. He turned and marched purposefully up the church steps. The rest of the chosen fell in behind him.

One of the Coates kids, a dark-eyed, very beautiful girl, waylaid Sam and held out her hand. Sam took it.

'I'm Diana,' she said, not letting his hand go. 'Diana Ladris.'

'Sam Temple.'

Her midnight eyes met his and he wanted to look away, feeling awkward, but somehow could not.

'Ah,' she said, as if someone had told her something fascinating. Then she let him go and smirked. 'Well, well. I guess we'd better go in. We don't want to leave Fearless Leader without followers.'

It was a Catholic church, built a hundred years earlier by the rich man who had owned the cannery that now lay rusting and abandoned, a tin-plated eyesore by the marina.

With soaring arches, half a dozen statues of saints, and wonderful well-worn wooden pews, the church was much grander than the small town of Perdido Beach probably deserved. Of the six tall, peaked windows, three retained their original stained-glass representations of Jesus in various parables. The other three had been lost over time to vandals or weather or earthquakes and had been replaced with cheaper, abstract-patterned stained glass.

When Astrid entered the church she dipped to one knee and made the sign of the cross while looking up at the intimidatingly large crucifix above the altar.

'Is this where you go to church?' Sam asked in a whisper.

'Yes. You?'

He shook his head. It was Sam's first time inside. His mother was a non-observant Jew, no one spoke about what his father was, and Sam himself had only a vague interest in religion. The church made him feel small and definitely out of place.

Caine had moved confidently towards the altar. The altar

itself was not very grand, just a pale marble rectangle up three maroon-carpeted steps. Caine did not go to the old-fashioned raised pulpit, but stood on the second of the three steps.

In all, fifteen kids were there, including Sam Temple, Quinn, Astrid and Little Pete, Albert Hillsborough, and Mary Terrafino; Elwood Booker, the best ninth-grade athlete, and his girlfriend, Dahra Baidoo; Orc, whose real name was rumoured to be Charles Merriman; Howard Bassem; and Cookie, whose real name was Tony Gilder.

From Coates Academy, in addition to Caine Soren, there was Drake Merwin, a smiling, playful, mean-eyed kid with shaggy, sandy-coloured hair; Diana Ladris; and a lost-looking fifth-grader with big glasses and a blond bed-head introduced by Caine as Computer Jack.

All of the Perdido Beach kids sat in pews, with Orc and his crew sprawling across the front pew. Computer Jack sat down as far to one side as he could. Drake Merwin stood smirking, arms across his chest, on Caine's left, and Diana Ladris watched the crowd from Caine's right.

It was again brought home to Sam that the Coates kids had rehearsed everything about this morning, from the staged motorcade – which must have taken hours of driving practice to master – to this presentation. They must have started planning and practising right after the FAYZ came.

That was a troubling thought.

After all the introductions were done, Caine moved briskly to explain his plan.

'We need to work together,' he announced. 'I think we should organise so that things aren't destroyed, and problems can be handled. I think our goal should be to maintain. So that once the barrier comes down, and once the disappeared people come back, they will find that we've done a pretty darn good job of keeping things together.'

'The Captain is already maintaining,' Howard said.

'He's obviously done an excellent job,' Caine allowed, walking down the steps and towards Orc as he spoke. 'But it's a burden. Why should Captain Orc have to do all the work? I think we need a system, and I think we need a plan. Captain Orc,' he addressed the thug directly, 'I'm sure you don't want to have to allocate food and care for the sick and keep the day care functioning, and read all the things you'd have to read, and write all the things you'd have to write, in order to establish a system here in Perdido Beach.'

Astrid whispered, 'He's guessed that Orc is nearly illiterate.'

Orc glanced at Howard, who seemed mesmerised by Caine. Orc shrugged. As Astrid said, the mention of reading and writing made him uncomfortable.

'Exactly,' Caine said, as though Orc's shrug signified agreement. He returned to centre stage and addressed the entire group. 'We seem to have a reliable source of electricity. But communication is down. My friend Computer Jack thinks we can get the cell phones up and running.' There was an excited murmur, and Caine raised his hands. 'I don't mean that we'll be able to call anyone outside of . . . what was

Howard's brilliant term? The FAYZ? But we would at least be able to communicate among ourselves.'

Eyes swivelled to Computer Jack, who gulped and bobbed his head yes and pushed his glasses up and blushed.

'It will take time, but together we can do it,' Caine said. He emphasised his certainty by smacking his closed right fist into his left palm. 'In addition to a sheriff to sort of make sure the rules are being followed, a job that I think Drake Merwin is qualified to do since his father is a Highway Patrol lieutenant, we'll need a fire chief to handle emergencies, and I nominate Sam Temple. Based on what people said earlier about his brave action in that fire, I think he's an obvious choice, don't you?'

There were nodded heads and murmurs of agreement.

'He's co-opting you,' Astrid whispered. 'He knows you're his competition.'

'You don't trust him,' Sam whispered back. It was not a question.

'He's a manipulator,' Astrid said. 'Doesn't mean he's bad. He may be OK.'

Mary said, 'Sam saved the hardware store and the day care. And he almost saved that little girl. Speaking of which, someone needs to bury her.'

'Exactly,' Caine said. 'God willing, we won't have to face that need again, but someone has to bury the dead. Just as someone needs to help people who get sick or hurt. And someone needs to take care of the little children.'

Dahra Baidoo spoke up and said, 'Mary has totally been

taking care of the prees – I mean, pre-schoolers,' she explained. 'Her and her brother, John.'

'But we need help,' Mary said quickly. 'We're not getting any sleep. We're out of diapers and food and' – she sighed – 'everything. John and I know the kids now, and we can keep running things, but we need help. We need a lot of help.'

Caine seemed to mist up, almost as if he might shed a tear. He walked quickly to Mary, drew her to her feet, and put his arm around her. 'What a noble person you are, Mary. You and your brother will be given the power to draft . . . How many people will it take to care for the prees?'

Mary calculated in her head. 'The two of us and four others, maybe,' she said. Then, gaining confidence, she said, 'Actually, we need four in the morning and four in the afternoon and four at night. And we need diapers and formula. And we need to be able to ask people to get us stuff, like food.'

Caine nodded. 'The young ones are our greatest responsibility. Mary and John, you have absolute authority to draft whatever people you need, and demand whatever supplies you need. If anyone argues, Drake and his people, including Captain Orc, will make sure you get what you need.'

Mary looked overwhelmed and grateful.

Howard did not.

'Say what, now? I let it go by before, but are you saying Orc works for this guy?' He jerked a thumb at Drake, who just smiled like a shark. 'We don't work for anyone. Captain Orc doesn't work for anyone, or under anyone, or follow anyone's orders.'

Sam saw a coldly furious expression appear on Caine's handsome face, then disappear as swiftly as it had come.

Orc must have seen it too, because he stood up, and Cookie along with him. Both clutched bats. Drake, still smiling, stepped between them and Caine. A fight was coming, sudden as a tornado.

Diana Ladris, oddly, was eyeing Sam closely, as if unconcerned by Orc.

Caine sighed, raised his hands, and used both palms to smooth back his hair.

There came a rumble, up through the floor and the pews. A small earthquake, minor, nothing that Sam, like most Californians, hadn't felt before.

Everyone jumped to their feet, everyone knew what you did in an earthquake.

But then came a rending sound, steel and wood twisting, and the crucifix separated from the wall. It ripped free of the bolts holding it in place, like an invisible giant had yanked it away.

No one moved.

A shower of plaster and pebbles fell on the altar.

The crucifix toppled forwards. It fell like a chainsawed tree.

As it fell, Caine dropped his hands to his sides. His face was grim, hard, and angry.

The crucifix, at least a dozen foot tall, slammed with shocking force down on to the front-row pew. The impact was as loud and sudden as a car wreck.

Orc and Howard jumped aside. Cookie was too slow. The

horizontal bar of the cross caught his right shoulder.

He was on the ground and a red stain was spreading.

It all happened in the space of a few heartbeats. So fast that the kids who'd leaped to their feet didn't have the chance to bolt.

'Help me, help me!' Cookie cried.

He lay bellowing on the floor. Blood was seeping through the fabric of his T-shirt. It pooled on the tiles.

Elwood shoved the cross off him, and Cookie screamed.

Caine had not moved. Drake Merwin kept his cold gaze on Orc, his arms still crossed, seemingly indifferent.

Diana Ladris maintained her focus on Sam. The knowing smirk on her face didn't waver.

Astrid grabbed Sam's arm and whispered, 'Let's get out of here. We have to talk.'

Diana saw that as well.

'Ahhh, ahhhh, help me, oh man, I'm hurt!' Cookie cried.

Orc and Howard made no move to help their fallen comrade.

Caine, perfectly calm, said, 'This is terrible. Does anyone know first aid? Sam? Your mother was a nurse.'

Little Pete, who had sat silent and still as a stone, began to rock faster and faster. His hands flapped as if he were warding off an attack of bees.

'I have to get him out of here, he's spiralling,' Astrid said, and bundled Little Pete away. 'Window seat, Petey, window seat.'

'I'm not a nurse,' Sam blurted. 'I don't know . . .'

It was Dahra Baidoo who broke from her stunned trance to kneel beside the thrashing, bellowing Cookie. 'I know some first aid. Elwood, help me.'

'I guess we have our new nurse,' Caine said, sounding no more agitated or concerned than the school principal announcing a name for the honour roll.

Diana turned away, drifted past Caine, and whispered something in his ear. Caine's dark eyes swept across the shocked kids, seeming to size them up in turn. He formed a bare smile, and nodded imperceptibly to Diana.

'This meeting is adjourned till we can help our wounded friend . . . what is his name? Cookie?'

Cookie's voice was even more urgent, demanding help, edging towards hysteria. 'It really hurts, it really hurts bad, oh, God.'

Caine led Drake and Diana down the aisle, past Sam, following Astrid and Little Pete from the church.

Drake paused halfway, turned back, and spoke for the first time. In an amused voice he said, 'Oh, um, Captain Orc? Have your people – the ones who aren't injured – line up outside. We'll work out your . . . um, duties.'

With a grin that was almost a snarl, Drake added a cheerful, 'Later.'

FIFTEEN

251 HOURS 32 MINUTES

JACK WAS SLOW to realise that he should follow Caine and the rest out of the church. He jumped up too suddenly and banged into the pew, making a noise that drew the attention of the quiet boy Caine had called a hero.

'Sorry,' Jack said.

Jack walked quickly outside. At first he couldn't see any of the other Coates kids. A lot of people were outside the church, milling around, talking about what had happened inside. Cookie's cries of pain were only slightly muffled.

Jack spotted the tall blonde girl he'd seen inside, and her little brother.

'Excuse me, do you know where Caine and everybody went?'

The girl, he didn't remember her name, looked him in the eye. 'He's in the town hall. Where else would our new leader be?'

Jack often missed nuance when people talked. But he didn't miss her cold sarcasm.

'Sorry to bother you.' He pushed his glasses back up on his nose and tried to smile at the same time. He bobbed his head and looked around for the town hall.

'It's right there.' The girl pointed. Then she said, 'My name is

Astrid. Do you really think you can get the phones working?'

'Sure. It will take time, though. Right now the signal goes from your phone to the tower, right?' His tone was condescending and he formed his hands into a schematic of a tower with beams radiating towards it. 'Then it gets sent on to a satellite, then down to a router. But we can't send signals to the satellite now, so –'

He was interrupted by a shockingly loud cry of pain from inside the church. It made him flinch.

'How do you know we can't reach a satellite?' Astrid asked.

He blinked in surprise and made the smug face he made whenever someone questioned his technological expertise. 'I doubt you would understand.'

Astrid said, 'Try me, kid.'

To Jack's surprise, she seemed to follow everything he said. So he went on to explain how he could reprogram a few good desktop computers to serve as a primitive router for the phone system. 'It wouldn't be fast. I mean, it couldn't handle more than, say, a dozen calls simultaneously, but it should work at a basic level.'

Astrid's little brother seemed to be staring at Jack's hands, which he was now twisting nervously. Jack was anxious being away from Caine. Before they had come down from Coates Academy, Drake Merwin had warned everyone that they should keep talk with the Perdido Beach kids to a minimum.

A warning from Drake was serious.

'Well, I better go,' Jack said.

Astrid stopped him. 'So you're into computers.'

'Yeah. I'm kind of a tech guy.'

'How old are you?'

'Twelve.'

'That's young to have those skills.'

He laughed dismissively. 'Nothing I've been talking about is hard to do. It's not something most people could do, but it's not hard for me.'

Jack had never been shy when it came to his tech skills. He'd gotten his first real computer for his fourth Christmas. His parents still told the story of how he had spent fourteen hours on the machine that first day, pausing only for Nutri-Grain bars and juice boxes.

By the time he was five he could easily install programs and navigate the web. By age six his parents were turning to him for computer help. By eight he had his own website and was acting as his school's unofficial tech support.

At nine, Jack had hacked into the computer system of his local police department to erase a speeding ticket for a friend's father.

His own parents found out and panicked. The next semester he was at Coates Academy, which was known as a place to send smart, difficult children.

But Jack wasn't difficult, and he resented it. In any case, it didn't help him stay out of trouble. On the contrary, there were kids at Coates whom Jack's parents would have called bad influences. Some of them, very bad influences.

And some were just bad.

'So, what would be hard for you, Jack?' Astrid asked.

'Almost nothing,' he answered truthfully. 'But what I would like to do is get some kind of Internet working. Here in the . . . in whatever this is.'

'It seems we're calling it the FAYZ.'

'Yeah. Here in the FAYZ. I mean, I'd estimate there are two hundred and twenty-five or so decent computers, based on the number of homes and businesses. The land area is pretty small, so it would be fairly simple to set up Wi-Fi. That's easy. And if I had even a pair of old G5s to work with, I think I could stand up a limited local system.'

He smiled happily at the thought.

'That would be great. So, tell me, Comp – should I really call you Computer Jack?'

'That's what everyone calls me. Or sometimes just Jack.'

'OK, Jack. What is Caine up to?'

Jack was caught off guard. 'What?'

'What's he up to? You're a smart kid, you have some idea.'

Jack wanted to leave, but he couldn't figure out how to do it. Astrid moved in and put her hand on his arm. He stared down at the hand.

'I know he's up to something,' Astrid said. Her little brother trained his big, vacant saucer eyes on Jack. 'You know what I think?'

Jack shook his head slowly.

'I think you're a nice person,' Astrid said. 'I think you're very smart, so people don't always treat you very well. They're scared of your talent. And they try to use you.'

Jack caught himself nodding in agreement.

'But I don't think that kid Drake is a nice person. He's not, is he?'

Jack held very still. He didn't want to give anything away. He was not as quick at understanding people as he was machines. Mostly people weren't that interesting.

'He's a bully, isn't he? Drake, I mean.'

Jack shrugged.

'I thought so. And Caine?'

When Jack didn't answer, Astrid let the question hang there. Jack swallowed and tried to look away, but it wasn't easy.

'Caine,' Astrid repeated. 'There's something wrong with him, isn't there?'

Computer Jack's resistance crumbled, but not his caution. He lowered his voice to a whisper. 'He can do things,' Jack said. 'He can –'

'Jack. There you are.'

Jack and Astrid both jumped. It was Diana Ladris. She nodded cordially at Astrid. 'I hope your little brother is all right. The way you rushed out of there, I thought maybe he was sick.'

'No. No, he's fine.'

'He's lucky to have you,' Diana said. As she said it, she took Astrid's hand in hers, like she was determined to shake hands. But Jack knew better.

Astrid pulled her hand away.

Diana had a nice smile, but she didn't use it now. Jack wondered if Diana had been able to finish with Astrid. Probably not; it usually took her longer to read a person's power level.

The mood of confrontation was broken by the sound of a diesel engine. It was a kid who looked like he might be Mexican, driving a backhoe down the street.

'Who is that?' Diana asked.

'Edilio,' Astrid said.

'What's he doing?'

The boy on the backhoe began to dig a trench, right in the grass of the plaza, close to the sidewalk where the little girl's body lay under its blanket, avoided by all.

'What's he doing?' Diana repeated.

'I think he's burying the dead,' Astrid said softly.

Diana frowned. 'Caine didn't tell him to do that.'

'What does it matter?' Astrid asked. 'It needed to be done. In fact, I think I'll go and see if I can help. You know, if you think that would be OK with Caine.'

Diana didn't smile. She didn't snarl, either, and Jack had seen her do that on more than one occasion. 'You seem like a nice girl, Astrid,' Diana said. 'I'll bet you're one of those brainy, Lisa Simpson types, all full of great ideas and worried about saving the planet or whatever. But things have changed. This isn't your old life any more. It's like . . . you know what it's like? It's like you used to live in a really nice neighbourhood, and now you live in a really tough neighbourhood. You don't look tough, Astrid.'

'What caused it? The FAYZ. Do you know?' Astrid demanded, refusing to be intimidated.

Diana laughed. 'Aliens. God. A sudden shift in the space–time continuum. I heard someone call you Astrid the Genius, so you've probably thought of explanations I can't even guess at. It doesn't matter. It's happened. Here we are.'

'What does Caine want?' Astrid asked.

Jack could not believe Astrid hadn't withered in the face of Diana's confidence. Most people did. Most people couldn't stand up to her. If they did, they were sorry.

Jack thought he saw a flicker of appreciation spark Diana's dark eyes.

'What does Caine want? He wants what he wants. And he'll get it,' Diana said. 'Now, run off to the funeral over there. Stay out of my way. And take care of your little brother. Jack?'

The sound of his own name snapped Jack out of his trance. 'Yes.'

'Come.'

Jack fell into step behind Diana, ashamed of his instant, dog-like obedience.

They marched up the steps of the town hall. Caine, to the surprise of no one who knew him, had taken over the mayor's office. He was behind a massive mahogany desk, rocking slowly from side to side in a too-big maroon leather chair.

'Where did you go?' Caine asked.

'I went to get Jack.'

Caine's eyes flickered. 'And where was Computer Jack?'

Diana said, 'Nowhere. He was just wandering, lost.'

She was covering for him, Jack realised with a shock.

'I ran into that girl,' Diana said. 'The blonde with the strange brother.'

'Yes?'

'They call her Astrid the Genius. I think she's involved with that kid, the fire kid.'

'His name is Sam,' Caine reminded her.

'I think Astrid's someone we need to keep an eye on.'

'Did you read her?' Caine asked.

'I got a partial read, so I'm not sure.'

Caine spread his hands in exasperation. 'Why am I begging for information here? Just tell me.'

'She's on about two bars.'

'Any idea what her powers may be? Lighter? Speeder? Chameleon? Not another Dekka, I hope. She was difficult. And hopefully not a Reader like you, Diana.'

Diana shook her head. 'No idea. I'm not even sure she's two bars.'

Caine nodded. Then he sighed as if the weight of the world were on his shoulders. 'Put her on the list, Jack. Astrid the Genius: two bars. With a question mark.'

Jack pulled out his PDA. It no longer got internet, of course, but its other functions still worked. He punched in the security code and opened the file.

The list opened. There were twenty-eight names on it, all Coates kids. In the column after each name was a number:

one, two, or three. Only one name had a four after it: Caine Soren.

Jack focused on thumbing in the information.

Astrid. Two bars. Question mark.

He tried not to think about what it meant for the pretty blonde girl.

'That went better than I hoped,' Caine said to Diana. 'I predicted there'd be some local bully we'd have to deal with. And I said there would be a natural leader. We get the bully working for us, and we keep an eye on the leader until we're ready to deal with him.'

'I'll keep an eye on him,' Diana said. 'He's cute.'

'Did you get a reading on him?'

Jack had seen Diana take Sam's hand. So he was amazed when Diana said, 'No. I didn't have a chance.'

Jack frowned, uncertain if he should remind Diana. But that was stupid. Of course Diana would know if she'd read Sam or not.

'Do it as soon as you can,' Caine said. 'You saw the way everyone looked at him? And when I asked for nominations, his was the first name mentioned. I don't like it, his being Nurse Temple's son. That's a bad coincidence. Get a read on him. If he has the power, we may not be able to wait to deal with him.'

Lana was healed.

But she was weak. Hungry. Thirsty.

The thirst was the worst thing. She wasn't sure she could stand it.

But she had been through hell and survived. And that gave her some reason for hope.

The sun was up but not yet touching her with its rays. The gulch was in the shade. Lana knew that her best chance was to make it back to the ranch before the ground grew as hot as a pie fresh from the oven.

'Don't start thinking about food,' she rasped. She was heartened to discover that she still had a voice.

She tried to climb straight back up to the road, but two skinned knees and two abraded palms later she admitted that wasn't happening. Even Patrick couldn't make the climb. It was just too steep.

That left following the ravine until, hopefully, it came out somewhere. It wasn't an easy walk. In most places the ground was hard, but in other places it shifted and slid and landed her on hands and knees.

Each time she fell, it was harder to get back up. Patrick was panting hard, plodding rather than bounding, just as tired and footsore as she was.

'We're in this together, right, boy?' she said.

Brush tore at her legs, rocks bruised her feet. In places there were thickets of thornbush that had to be bypassed. In one place the thorns couldn't be avoided, and she had to work her way through with time-wasting caution, accumulating scratches that burned like fire on her bare legs.

But once through she laid her hand on the scratches, and the pain ebbed. After ten minutes or so, there was no sign of the scratches.

It was miraculous. Lana was convinced of that. She knew she didn't personally have the power to heal dogs or people. She'd never done it before. But how the miracle came about, she did not know. Her mind was on more pressing issues: how to scale this sudden rise, or skirt that bramble patch, or where, where, where in this parched landscape she could find water and food.

She wished she'd paid a lot more attention to the lie of the land while driving to and from the ranch. Did this gulch head for the ranch, or did it veer past? Was she almost there? Was she now wandering blindly towards the true desert? Was anyone looking for her?

The walls of the ravine weren't as tall any more, but they were just as steep, and closer. The gulch was narrowing. That had to be good news. If it was narrowing and becoming shallower, didn't that mean she must be nearing the end?

She had her eyes down on the ground, watching out for snakes, when Patrick stopped stock-still.

'What is it, boy?' But she saw what it was. There was a wall across the gulch. The wall rose impossibly tall, far higher than the gulch itself, a barrier made of . . . of nothing she had ever seen before.

Its sheer size, combined with its utter strangeness in this place, struck fear into her. But it didn't seem to be doing anything. It was just a wall. It was translucent, like watery milk.

It shimmered just slightly, as if it might be a video effect. It was absurd. Impossible. A wall where no wall had any business being.

She edged closer, but Patrick refused to come along.

'We have to go see what it is, boy,' she urged.

Patrick disagreed. He had no interest in seeing what it was.

Up close she could make out a faint reflection of herself.

'Probably a good thing I can't see myself any better,' she muttered. Her hair was stiff with dried blood. She knew she was filthy. She could see that her clothing was ripped, and not in an artistic, trendy way, just ripped to ribbons in places.

Lana covered the last few feet to the barrier and touched it with one finger.

'Ahh!'

She yelped and pulled her finger away. Before the crash she would have described the pain as searing. Now she had higher standards for what counted as real pain. But she wouldn't be touching the wall again.

'Some kind of electric fence?' she asked Patrick. 'What is it doing here?'

There was no choice now but to try to scale the side of the gulch. The problem was that Lana was pretty sure the ranch lay to her left, and that side was impossible to climb. She would have needed a rope and pitons.

She figured she could make it up the right side, pushing from tumbled boulder to crumbling ledge. But then, unless she was totally turned around, she'd be placing the gulch between herself and the ranch.

The remaining alternative was to head back the way she came. It had taken half the day to get this far. The day would be over before she made it back to her starting point. She would die back where she started.

'Come on, Patrick. Let's get out of here.'

It took what felt like an hour to climb the right-hand slope. All the while under the silent, baleful stare of the wall that Lana had come to think of as a living thing, a vast malevolent force determined to stop her.

When she finally reached the top, she blinked and shaded her eyes and scanned left to right, all the way. That's when she almost fell apart. There was no sign of the road. No sign of the ranch. Just a sheer ridge and no more than a mile of flat land before she would have to start climbing.

And that impossible wall. That impossible, could-not-be-there wall.

One way blocked by the gulch, the other by the mountains, the third by the wall that lay across the landscape like it had been dropped out of the sky.

The only open path was back the way she had come, back along the narrow strip of flat land that followed the gulch.

She shielded her eyes and blinked in the sunlight.

'Wait,' she said to Patrick. 'There's something there.'

Nestled up against the barrier, not far from the foot of the mountains. Was it really a patch of green, shimmering in the rising heat waves? It had to be a mirage.

'What do you think, Patrick?'

Patrick was indifferent. The spirit had gone from the dog. He was in no better shape than she was herself.

'I guess a mirage is all we have,' Lana said.

They set off together. At least it was easier than the climb up out of the gulch. But the sun was like a hammer now, beating down on Lana's unprotected head. She could feel her body giving up even as her spirit was tortured by doubt. She was chasing a mirage with the last of her strength. She would die chasing a stupid mirage.

But the green patch did not disappear. It grew slowly larger as they closed the distance. Lana's consciousness was a flickering candle now. In and out. Alert for a few seconds, then lost in a formless dream.

Lana staggered, feet dragging, half blind from the relentless glare of the sun, when she realised that her foot had stepped from dust on to grass.

Her toes registered the sponginess of the grass.

It was a minuscule lawn, twelve feet by twelve feet. In the centre was a back-and-forth sprinkler. It was not turned on. But a hose led from the sprinkler. The hose led around a small, windowless wooden cabin.

It wasn't much of a cabin, no bigger than a single room. Behind the cabin was a half-tumbled wooden shack. And a windmill of sorts, really just an airplane propeller placed atop a ramshackle tower twenty feet tall.

Lana staggered along the hose, following it to its source. It came from a once-painted, now sandblasted steel tank elevated on a platform of railroad ties beneath the makeshift windmill. A rusty pipe jutted up from the ground beneath the windmill. There were valves and connecting pipes. The hose came to an end at a faucet welded into the end of the tank.

'It's a well, Patrick.'

Lana fumbled frantically with weak fingers at the hose connection.

It came off.

She twisted the knob and it turned. Water, hot and smelling of minerals and rust, came gushing.

Lana drank. Patrick drank.

She let the water flow over her face. Let it wash the blood from her face. Let it soften her crusted hair.

But she had not come this far to let her salvation drain away for a momentary pleasure. She twisted the knob shut again. The last drop quivered on the brass lip, and she took it on her fingertip and used it to clean the crust from her bloodied eye.

Then, for the first time in forever, she laughed. 'We're not dead yet, are we, Patrick?' Lana said. 'Not yet.'

SIXTEEN

'**YOU** HAVE TO boil the water first. Then you put in the pasta,' Quinn said.

'How do you know that?' Sam was frowning, turning a blue box of rotini around trying to find instructions.

'Because I've seen my mom do it, like, a million times. The water has to start boiling first.'

Sam and Quinn stared at the big pot of water on the stove.

'A watched pot never boils,' Edilio said.

Sam and Quinn both looked away. Edilio laughed. 'It's just a saying. It's not actually true.'

'I knew that,' Sam said. Then he laughed. 'OK, I didn't know it.'

'Maybe you can just zap it up with your magic hands,' Quinn suggested.

Sam ignored him. He found Quinn's teasing on that front annoying.

The firehouse was a two-storey cinder-block cube. Down below was the garage that housed the fire engine and the ambulance.

The second floor was the living area, a large room that encompassed a kitchen, an oblong dining table, and a mismatched pair of couches. A door led to a separate, narrow room lined with bunk beds, space for six people.

The main room was almost but not quite cheerful. There were photos of firefighters, some in stiff formal poses, some goofing with their buddies. There were letters of thanks from various people, including illustrated letters from the first-grade class visit that all began with 'Dear Firefighter', although the spelling was sometimes mysterious.

There was a large round table that had displayed the remains of an abruptly abandoned poker game – fallen hands of cards, chips, cigars in ashtrays – when the three of them first arrived but had since been cleaned off.

And there was a surprisingly well-stocked pantry: jars of tomato sauce, cans of soup, boxes of pasta. There was a red-lacquered can of home-made cookies, now pretty stale but not inedible if you microwaved them for fifteen seconds.

Sam had accepted the assignment as fire chief. Not because he wanted to, but because so many other people seemed to want him to. He hoped no one would call on him to actually do anything, because after three days in the firehouse the three of them still barely knew how to start the fire engine, let alone drive it anywhere or do anything with it.

The one time a kid had come rushing up yelling 'Fire,' Sam, Quinn, and Edilio had half carried, half dragged a hose and a hydrant wrench six blocks only to discover that the kid's brother had microwaved a can. The smoke was just from a burned-out microwave oven.

But, on the plus side, they knew where to find all the emergency supplies in the ambulance. And they had practised with the big hose and the hydrant outside so they could be quicker and more efficient than Edilio had been at the first fire.

And they had totally mastered the fireman's pole.

'We're out of bread,' Edilio said.

'Don't need bread if you have pasta,' Sam said. 'They're both carbs.'

'Who's talking about nutrition? You're supposed to have bread with a meal.'

'I thought your people ate tortillas,' Quinn said.

'Tortillas are bread.'

'Well, we have no bread,' Sam said. 'Not of any kind.'

'In another week or so, no one will have any bread,' Quinn pointed out. 'Bread has to be made fresh, you know. It gets mouldy after a while.'

Three days had passed since Caine and his posse had swept into town and basically taken over.

Three days with no one arriving to rescue them. Three days of deepening depression. Three days of growing acceptance that, for now, at least, this was life.

And the FAYZ itself – everyone called it that now – was five days old. Five days with no adults. Five days without mothers, fathers, big brothers and sisters, teachers, police officers, store clerks, paediatricians, clergy, dentists. Five days without television, Internet, or phones.

Caine had been welcomed at first. People wanted to know

that someone was in charge. People wanted there to be answers. People wanted rules. Caine was very good at establishing his authority. Each time Sam had dealt with him, he came away impressed at the way Caine could act with complete confidence, as if he had been born to the job.

But already, in just three days, doubts had grown, too. The doubts centred on Caine and Diana, but more still on Drake Merwin. Some kids argued you needed someone a little scary around to make sure rules were obeyed. Other kids agreed with that, but pointed out that Drake was more than a little scary.

Kids who defied Drake or any of his so-called sheriffs had been slapped, punched, pushed, knocked down or, in one case, dragged into a bathroom and given a swirlie. Fear of Drake was replacing fear of the unknown.

'I can make tortillas fresh,' Edilio said. 'I just need flour, a little shortening, salt, baking powder. We have all that here.'

'Save it for taco night,' Quinn said. He took the pasta from Sam and dumped it into the pot.

Edilio frowned. 'You hear something?'

Sam and Quinn froze. The loudest sound was the boiling water.

Then they all heard it. A voice, wailing.

Sam took three steps to the fireman's pole, wrapped his legs and arms around it, and dropped through the hole in the floor to land in the garishly lit garage below.

The garage was open to the evening air. Someone – a girl, judging by the long reddish hair – was slumped on the threshold, looking like she might be trying to crawl, moving but not really going anywhere.

Three figures advanced up the driveway from the street.

'Help me,' the girl pleaded softly.

Sam knelt beside her. He recoiled in shock. 'Bette?'

The left side of Bouncing Bette's face was covered in blood. There was a gash above her temple. She was panting, gasping, like she had collapsed after a marathon and was trying with her last ounce of energy to crawl across the finish line.

'Bette, what happened?'

'They're trying to get me,' Bette cried, and clutched at Sam's arm.

The three dark figures advanced to the edge of the circle of light. One was clearly Orc. No one else was that big. Edilio and Quinn moved into the garage doorway.

Sam disengaged from Bette and took up a position beside Edilio.

'You want me to beat on you guys, I will!' Orc yelled.

'What's going on here?' Sam demanded. He narrowed his eyes and recognized the other two boys, a kid named Karl, a seventh-grader from school, and Chaz, one of the Coates eighth-graders. All three were armed with aluminium bats.

'This isn't your business,' Chaz said. 'We're dealing with something here.'

'Dealing with what? Orc, did you hit Bette?'

'She was breaking the rules,' Orc said.

'You hit a girl, man?' Edilio said, outraged.

'Shut up, wetback,' Orc said.

'Where's Howard?' Sam asked, just to stall while he tried to figure out what to do. He'd lost one fight to Orc already.

Orc took the question as an insult. 'I don't need Howard to handle you, Sam.'

Orc marched right up to Sam, stopped a foot away, and put his bat on his shoulder like he was ready to swing for a home run. Like a batter ready for the next fastball. Only this was closer to T-ball: Sam's head was impossible to miss.

'Move, Sam,' Orc ordered.

'OK, I'm not doing this again,' Quinn said. 'Let him have her, Sam.'

'Ain't no "let me",' Orc said. 'I do what I want.'

Sam noticed movement behind Orc. There were people coming down the street, twenty or more kids. Orc noticed it too, and glanced behind him.

'They aren't going to save you,' Orc said, and swung the bat hard.

Sam ducked. The bat whooshed past his head, and Orc rotated halfway around, carried forwards by the momentum.

Sam was thrown off balance, but Edilio was ready. He let loose a roar and ploughed head first into Orc. Edilio was maybe half Orc's size, but Orc was knocked off his feet. He sprawled out on the concrete.

Chaz went after Edilio, trying to pull him off Orc.

The crowd of kids who had come running down the

street surged forwards. There were angry voices and threats, all aimed at Orc.

They yelled, Sam noted, but no one exactly jumped into the unequal fight.

A voice cut through all the noise.

'Nobody move,' Drake said.

Orc pushed Edilio off and jumped to his feet. He started kicking Edilio, landing size-eleven Nike blows into Edilio's defensive arms. Sam jumped in to help his friend, but Drake was quicker. He stepped behind Orc, grabbed him by the hair, yanked his head back, and smashed his elbow into Orc's face.

Blood poured from Orc's nose, and he howled in rage.

Drake hit him again and released Orc to fall to the concrete.

'Which part of "nobody move" did you not understand, Orc?' Drake demanded.

Orc rose to his knee and went for Drake like a linebacker. Drake stepped aside, nimble as a matador. He stuck his hand out and said to Chaz, 'Give me that.'

Chaz handed him the bat.

Drake hit Orc in the ribs with a short, sharp forwards thrust of the bat. Then again in the kidneys and again in the side of the head. Each blow was measured, accurate, effective.

Orc rolled over on to his back, helpless, exposed.

Drake pushed the thick end of the bat against Orc's throat. 'Dude. You really need to learn to listen when I talk.'

Then Drake laughed, stepped back, twirled the bat in the air, caught it, and rested it on his shoulder. He grinned at Sam.

'Now, how about you tell me what's going on, Mr Fire Chief.'

Sam had gone up against bullies before. But he'd never seen anything like Drake Merwin. Orc outweighed Drake by at least fifty pounds, but Drake had handled him like a little toy action figure.

Sam pointed at Bette, still cowering. 'I think Orc hit her.'

'Yeah? So?'

'So I wasn't going to let him do it again,' Sam said as calmly as he could.

'It didn't look to me like you were getting ready to rescue anyone. Looked to me like you were about to get your head knocked off your shoulders,' Drake said.

'Bette wasn't doing anything wrong,' a shrill young voice from the crowd yelled.

Without looking back, Drake said, 'Shut up.' He pointed at Chaz. 'You. Explain what this is about.'

Chaz was an athletic-looking kid with nearly shoulder-length blond hair and trendy glasses. He was wearing the Coates uniform, dirty and rumpled after many days' use. 'That girl was doing something.' He pointed at Bette. 'She was using the power.'

Sam felt a cold chill run up his spine.

The power, he had said. Like it was just something you mentioned in casual conversation. Like it was a common thing everyone knew about.

Drake smirked. 'Why, whatever can you possibly mean, Chaz?' The way he said it was an unmistakable threat.

'Nothing,' Chaz said quickly.

'She was doing a magic trick,' a voice yelled. 'She wasn't hurting anyone.'

'I told her to stop.' Orc was on his feet again, glaring with undisguised hatred, but also some wariness, at Drake.

'Orc is a deputy sheriff,' Drake said reasonably. 'So when he tells someone to stop doing something wrong, they have to stop. If this girl refused to obey, hey, I guess she got what she deserved.'

'You don't have the right to beat on people,' Sam said.

Drake had a shark's grin: too many teeth, too little humour. 'Someone has to make people listen to the rules. Right?'

'There are rules against doing magic tricks?' Edilio asked.

'Yes,' Drake said. 'But I guess some people didn't know that. Chaz? Give the fire chief the latest copy of the rules.'

Sam accepted a crumpled, folded piece of paper without looking at it.

'There you go,' Drake said. 'Now you know the rules.'

'No one's doing magic around here,' Quinn said, placating.

'Then my work is done,' Drake said, and laughed at his own wit. He tossed the baseball bat to Chaz. 'OK. Everyone go home.'

'Bette will stay here for a while,' Sam said.

'Whatever.'

Drake drew Orc and the others in his wake. The crowd parted for him.

Sam knelt beside Bette. 'We're going to get you bandaged up.'

'What's this about magic tricks?' Quinn asked her.

Bette shook her head. 'It was nothing.'

'She made little balls of light come out of her hands,' a young voice said. 'It was a cool trick.'

'OK, you guys heard what Drake said: everybody out of here,' Quinn said in a loud voice. 'All of you go home.'

Sam, Quinn, and Edilio half carried Bette inside and sat her in the ambulance. Edilio used the sterile wipes to clean the blood from her face, applied an antibiotic cream, and used two butterfly bandages to close the wound.

'You can spend the night here, Bette,' Sam said.

'No, I have to get home, my brother will need me,' Bette said. 'But, thanks.' She managed a smile for Edilio. 'I'm sorry I got you kicked.'

Edilio shrugged, embarrassed. 'No big thing.'

Sam left to walk Bette home. Quinn and Edilio trudged back up the stairs.

Quinn went to the pot and used the slotted spoon to drain a few pieces of rotini. He tasted one.

'It's like mush, man.'

'Overcooked,' Edilio agreed, looking over his shoulder.

Quinn said, 'Cheerios?'

He poured himself some and began humming to himself, determined not to get into a conversation with Edilio. It was getting so he could barely stand Edilio. His cheerfulness. His competence at just about everything. And just now, the way he had thrown himself against Orc like some kind of Mexican commando.

It was stupid, Quinn thought, stupid going after a guy like Orc. It was too bad what had happened to Bette, but what was the point picking a fight with someone you couldn't beat? If Drake hadn't come along, Edilio would be lucky to be walking right now.

Come to think of it . . .

Sam returned. He nodded at Edilio and barely looked at Quinn.

Quinn gritted his teeth. Perfect. Now Sam was mad at him for not getting his head beat in. Like Sam was such a big hero. Quinn could remember lots of times when Sam had wimped out on waves that Quinn jumped on. Lots of times.

'The pasta didn't survive,' Quinn said.

'I got Bette home. I hope she's OK,' Sam said. 'She said she was OK.'

'Bette's got what you have, doesn't she?' Quinn said as Sam sat down and dug into his own bowl of cereal.

'Yeah. Maybe less of it, I guess. She told me all she can do is make her hands kind of glow.'

'So she hasn't burned anyone's arm off yet, huh?' Quinn was tired of the way Sam was looking at him with a mixture of pity and contempt. He was tired of being dissed just because he had some common sense and minded his own business.

Sam looked up, eyes narrowed, like he might make an argument of it. But he pressed his lips into a grim line and pushed his food away and said nothing.

Quinn said, 'This is why you can't tell anyone. People will

think you're a freak. You see what happens to freaks.'

'Bette's not a freak,' Sam said in the forced-calm way he had, that gritted-teeth thing he did. 'She's just a girl from school.'

'Don't be stupid, Sam,' Quinn said. 'Bette, Little Pete, the girl in the fire, you. If there's four of you, there's more. Normal people aren't going to like that. Normal people are going to think you're dangerous or whatever.'

'Is that what you think, Quinn?' Sam asked in a quiet voice. But still he avoided looking Quinn in the eye.

Sam found the rules sheet in his back pocket, unfolded it and spread it on the table.

Quinn said, 'I'm just saying look around, man. Kids have enough to be scared of. How are normal people –'

'You want to stop saying "normal people" like that?' Sam snapped.

Edilio, always the peacemaker now between Sam and Quinn, said, 'Read out those rules, man.'

Sam sighed. He flattened the paper carefully, scanned down the page, and made a rude noise. 'Number one says Caine is the mayor of Perdido Beach and the whole area known as the FAYZ.'

Edilio snorted. 'Doesn't think much of himself, does he?'

'Number two, Drake is appointed sheriff and has the power to enforce the rules. Number three, I'm fire chief and responsible for responding to emergencies. Great. Lucky me.' He glanced up and added, 'Lucky us.'

'Nice of you to remember the little people,' Quinn sniped.

'Number four, no one may enter any store and remove

anything without permission from the mayor or the sheriff.'

Quinn said, 'You have a beef with that? People can't be just looting stuff all the time, grabbing whatever.'

'No beef with that,' Sam agreed reluctantly. 'Five says we all have to help Mother Mary at the day care, provide her with whatever she asks for, and help any time she says. OK. Fair enough. Six: thou shalt not kill.'

'Really?' Quinn asked.

Sam made a wan smile, the way he did when he was tired of being mad and expected everyone else to be tired of it, too. 'Kidding,' Sam said.

'OK, stop goofing and just read the thing.'

'Just trying to keep a sense of humour while the world's falling apart around us,' Sam said. 'Six: we all have to help out on jobs like searching homes or whatever. Seven: we're all supposed to pass information on any bad behaviour to Drake.'

'So we're all supposed to be informers,' Edilio said.

'Don't worry, there's no immigration cops, no Migra,' Quinn said. 'And, anyway, if someone can figure out how to send you back to Mexico, I'll go with you.'

'Honduras,' Edilio said. 'Not Mexico. For, like, the tenth time.'

'Number eight, here it is. I'll read it like it's written,' Sam said. '"People will not perform magic tricks or any other action that causes fear or worry."'

'What's that mean?' Quinn asked.

'It means Caine obviously knows about the power.'

'Big surprise.' Edilio nodded over his bowl of cereal. 'Kids talking like it was an act of God. I always said Caine had the power. People saying Caine's like a mago. You know, like a magician.'

Quinn said, 'Nah, man, if he had the power, he wouldn't be having Orc and Drake trying to stop people using it.'

'Sure he would, Quinn,' Sam said. 'If he wanted to be the only one who had it.'

'Paranoid much, brah?'

'Number nine,' Sam continued reading. '"We are in a state of emergency. During this crisis no one should criticise, ridicule, or hinder any of the people performing their official duties."'

Quinn shrugged. 'Well, we are having a crisis, right? If this isn't a crisis, I don't know what would be.'

'So we're suddenly not allowed to say anything?' Sam was shaking his head in disbelief. The moment of attempted reconciliation was over. Sam was back to being disappointed in Quinn.

'Look, it's like school, right?' Quinn argued. 'You can't diss the teachers. Not to their faces, anyway.'

'Then you'll really like number ten, Quinn: "The sheriff may decide that the above rules are insufficient to cover some emergency situations. In those cases, the sheriff may formulate whatever rules are needed to keep order and keep people safe."'

"Formulate," Quinn snorted. 'Sounds like Astrid helped them write it.'

Sam pushed the paper away. 'No. Not Astrid's style.' He

folded his hands together, placed them on the table, and announced, 'This is wrong.'

Edilio's worried look mirrored Sam's. 'Yeah, man, this ain't right. That's saying Caine and Drake can do whatever they want, any time they want.'

'That's what it comes down to,' Sam agreed. 'And he's getting people to start suspecting each other, turn against each other.'

Quinn laughed. 'You don't get it, brah. People are already suspicious. This isn't normal times, OK? We're cut off, we have no adults of any kind, no police or teachers or parents, and no offence, but we have some of us, like, mutating or whatever. You act like you expect everything to just go along like normal, like there is no FAYZ.'

Sam was done with his patient act. 'And you're acting like you think Bette deserved that beating. Why are you not pissed off, Quinn? Why are you OK with the idea that a girl we know, a girl who never hurt anyone, gets beat down by Orc?'

'Oh, that's where you're going? Like it's my fault?' Quinn stood up and shoved his chair back. 'Look, Sam, I'm not saying it's right for her to get beat on, all right? But what do you expect? I mean, kids get picked on for wearing the wrong clothes or sucking at sports or whatever. And that's when there are teachers and parents around. That's just everyday life. You think now, as messed up as everything is, kids are going to be thinking, "Oh, Sam can shoot firebolts out of his eyeballs or whatever, OK, that's cool?" No, brah, that's not the way it is.'

To Quinn's surprise, and even more to Sam's, Edilio said,

'He's right. If there's more people with, you know, like you and Bette, there's going to be trouble. Some folks with the power, some folks without. Me, I'm used to being a second-class citizen.' He shot a dark look at Quinn, which Quinn ignored. 'But other people are going to be jealous and they're going to get scared and, anyway, they're all weirded out, so they are going to be looking for someone to blame. In Spanish, we say *cabeza de turco*. It means someone you blame for all your problems.'

'Scapegoat,' Quinn translated.

Edilio nodded. 'Yeah, that's it. A scapegoat.'

Quinn spread his hands wide in an expression of aggrieved innocence. 'What have I been saying? That's the way it is: you're different, you get to be a victim. You try and act all superior, Sam, all righteous, but you haven't even figured it out yet. Worst that happened to us back then was we get in trouble, get suspended, get an "F" or whatever. Screw up now and it's a baseball bat up alongside your head. There were always bullies, but the adults were still in charge. Now? Now the bullies rule. Different game, brother, a whole different game. We play by the bully rules now.'

SEVENTEEN

169 HOURS 18 MINUTES

'I NEED MORE pills,' Cookie cried in a voice that to Dahra Baidoo's dismay never seemed to weaken or grow hoarse.

'It's too soon,' Dahra said for the millionth time in the last three days.

'Give me the pills!' Cookie bellowed. 'It hurts. It hurts so bad.'

Dahra pressed her hands over her ears and tried to make sense of the text open in front of her. It would probably have been easy to figure out what to do if she still had the Internet. Then she could have opened a Google page and punched in 'Vicodin' and 'overdose'. It was harder to get a straight answer from the thick, dog-eared *Physicians' Desk Reference* someone had brought her from the only doctor's office in Perdido Beach.

The problem, among other things, was that she was playing mix-and-match with everything from Advil to Vicodin to Tylenol with codeine. There was nothing in the book about how to control pain by mixing together a little of this and a little of that and not enough of anything.

Dahra's boyfriend, Elwood, was slumped in a chair, passed out. He had been a faithful friend, at least so far as hanging around and keeping her company. And he always helped her lift Cookie up to slide the bedpan under his butt when he needed to go.

But there were limits to what her boyfriend would do. He wouldn't clean out the bedpan. He wouldn't hold the funnel when the boy needed to pee.

Dahra had done that. In the three days since she had accidentally become the person responsible for this squalid, dark, windowless, joyless, subterranean kingdom of misery beneath the church, Dahra had done all sorts of things she never thought she could do. Things she sure didn't want to do, including giving a diabetic seven-year-old daily insulin injections.

There was a knock at the door and Dahra swivelled her chair away from the desk and the circle of light that spilled over the almost useless book.

Mary Terrafino was there with a girl who looked like she was maybe four.

'Hi, Mary,' Dahra said. 'What do we have here?'

'I'm so sorry to bother you,' Mary said. 'I know how busy you are. But she has some kind of pain in her stomach.'

The two girls hugged. They hadn't known each other well before the FAYZ, but now they were like sisters.

Dahra knelt down to eye level with the little girl. 'Hi, honey. What's your name?'

'Ashley.'

'OK, Ashley, let's get your temperature and see what's going on. Can you come over and sit on the table?'

Dahra slid the electronic thermometer into a fresh plastic cover and popped the thermometer into the little girl's mouth.

'You have the moves down,' Mary said, and smiled.

Cookie bellowed suddenly, so loudly and so obscenely that Ashley almost swallowed the thermometer.

'I'm running out of pain pills,' Dahra said. 'I don't know what to do. We've emptied out the doctor's office and sometimes we get some meds that people have found when they're doing house searches. But he's in so much pain.'

'Is it getting any better? His shoulder, I mean?'

'No,' Dahra said. 'It's not going to get better. All I can do is keep it clean.' She examined the thermometer. 'Ninety-eight point nine. That's well within the normal range. Lie back and let me check something. I'm going to push on your tummy. It might tickle a little.'

'Are you going to give me a shot?' the little girl asked.

'No, honey. I just want to push on your tummy.' Dahra pressed down with her fingertips, pressed the girl's belly pretty far down and then released suddenly. 'Did that hurt?'

'It tickled.'

'What are you checking for?' Mary asked.

'Appendicitis.' Dahra shrugged. 'It's about all I know, Mary. When I look up "stomach pain", I get everything from constipation to stomach cancer. Probably she needs to poop.' To the little girl she said, 'Have you pooped today?'

'I don't think so.'

'I'll sit her on the toilet,' Mary said.

'Make her drink some water. You know, like a couple of cups.'

Mary squeezed her hand. 'I know you're not a doctor, but it's good to have you.'

Dahra sighed. 'I'm trying to read that book. But mostly all it does is scare me. I mean, there are a million diseases I've never even heard of and I don't want to even think about.'

'Yeah. I can imagine.'

Mary was stalling. Dahra asked her if there was something else.

'Listen, um, I know this is weird and all,' Mary said, lowering her voice to a confidential level. 'But anything I tell you . . .'

'I don't talk to anyone about what goes on here,' Dahra said a little stiffly.

'I know. Sorry. It's not . . . I mean, it's something embarrassing.'

'Mary. I am so past embarrassing. I am way into humiliating and disgusting now, so nothing you tell me is going to bother me.'

Mary nodded. She twisted her fingers together and said in a rush, 'Look, I take Prozac.'

'What for?'

'Just some, you know, some issues. The thing is, I ran out. I know it's not as important as a lot of what you're doing.' She glanced at Cookie. 'It's just, when I don't have the pills, I get . . .' She sucked in sharply and let go of a sigh that was almost a sob.

'No problem,' Dahra said. She wanted to push for further information, but instinct told her to drop it. 'Let me see what I have. Do you know what strength of pill you take?'

'Forty milligrams, once a day.'

'I have to pee,' Cookie moaned pitiably.

Dahra went to the cupboard where she kept the medications. Some were in large white pharmacy bottles, some in smaller brown twist-top bottles. And she had some sample packs taken from the doctor's office.

Elwood woke up with a snort. 'Oh. Man. I fell asleep.'

'Hi, Elwood,' Mary said.

'Uh-huh,' Elwood said, and rested his head on his hand and fell back to sleep.

'He's nice to stay with you,' Mary said.

'He's useless,' Dahra said sharply. But then she relented. 'But at least he's here. I guess I can give you some twenty-milligram pills and let you take two.' She tapped the capsules into her palm. 'Here's enough for a week. Sorry, I don't have a bottle or anything.'

Mary took the pills gratefully.

'You're a good person, Dahra. When this is all over some day, you know, when we grow up, you can become a doctor.'

Dahra laughed bitterly. 'After this, Mary, that's the last thing I'd want to be.'

The doors of the hospital pushed in suddenly. Both girls turned sharply to see Bouncing Bette. She staggered in with her right hand pressed against her head. 'My head hurts,' Bette said. She was barely comprehensible. She spoke with noticeable slurring. Her left arm seemed to be lifeless, hanging limp by her side. Her left leg trailed as she took several steps closer.

Dahra ran to catch her as Bette collapsed.

'Elwood, wake up,' Dahra yelled.

Dahra, Elwood, and Mary half dragged, half carried Bette to the bed where Ashley had been examined.

'I have to poop now,' Ashley said.

'Oh, God, I need some more pills!' Cookie howled.

'Shut up!' Dahra shouted. She put her hands over her ears and squeezed her eyes shut. 'Everyone shut up.'

Bette was on the table now, whispering, 'I'm sorry.' It came out, 'Mm shrree.'

'I didn't mean you, Bette,' Dahra apologised. 'Just lie back.' Dahra looked at her face and said to Elwood, 'Get the book.'

She propped the *Physicians' Desk Reference* open on Bette's stomach and began thumbing quickly through the index.

'Mm het hur,' Bette said. She raised her good arm to touch the bloody lump on the side of her head.

'Did someone hit you, Bette?' Elwood asked.

Bette seemed confused by the question. She frowned as if the question made no sense. She moaned in pain.

'One side of her body isn't working right,' Dahra said. 'Look at the way her mouth is drooping. And her eyes. They don't match.'

'Mmm het hur bad,' Bette moaned.

'I think she's saying her head hurts,' Mary said. 'What do we do?'

'I don't know. How about if I just cut open her head and see if I can fix it?' Dahra was shrill. 'Then I'll just do some quick surgery on Cookie. No problem. I mean, I have this stupid book.' She snatched the book up and threw it across the room. It skidded across the polished linoleum floor.

Dahra tried taking several deep breaths. The little girl, Ashley, was crying. Mary was looking at Dahra like she had lost her mind. Cookie was alternating between crying for pills and crying that he needed to pee.

'Ta care mm buh er,' Bette said. She grabbed Mary's arm. 'Mmm il buh.'

Bette's face contorted in pain. And then her features relaxed.

'Bette,' Dahra said.

'Bette. Uh-uh, don't do this, Bette.'

'Bette,' Dahra whispered.

She placed two fingers against Bette's throat.

'What did she say?' Elwood asked.

Mary answered. 'I think she was asking us to take care of her brother.'

Dahra lifted her fingers from Bette's neck. She stroked the girl's face once, a lingering goodbye.

'Is she . . .' Mary couldn't finish the question.

'Yes,' Dahra whispered. 'There was probably bleeding inside her head, not just outside. Whoever hit her in the head killed her. Elwood, go find Edilio at the firehouse. Tell him we have to bury Bette.'

'She's with God now,' Mary said.

'I'm not sure there is a God in the FAYZ,' Dahra said.

*

They buried Bette next to the fire-starter in the plaza at one o'clock in the morning. There was no place to keep dead bodies, and no way to prepare the bodies for the grave.

Edilio dug the hole with his backhoe. The sound of it, the straining of the engine, the sudden jerks of the shovel, seemed horribly loud and horribly out of place.

Sam was there, along with Astrid and Little Pete; Mary; Albert, who came over from the McDonald's; Elwood, standing in for Dahra, who had to stay with Cookie; and the twins, Anna and Emma. Bette's little brother was there too, nine years old, sobbing, with Mary's arm around him. Quinn opted not to attend.

Sam and Edilio had carried Bette's body the few dozen feet from the church basement to the plaza.

They couldn't figure out a gentle or dignified way to lower Bette into the hole, so in the end they just rolled her in. She made a sound like a dropped backpack.

'We should say something,' Anna suggested. 'Maybe things we remember about Bette.'

So they did, telling what few stories they could remember. None of them had been close friends of hers.

Astrid began the Lord's Prayer. 'Our father, who art in heaven, hallowed be thy name.' Little Pete said it along with her. More words than anyone had ever heard him speak. The others, all but Sam, joined in.

Then they each shovelled a spadeful of dirt over her and stood back while Edilio used the backhoe to finish the job.

'I'll make her a cross tomorrow,' Edilio said when he was finished.

As the ceremony was breaking up, Orc and Howard appeared, ghosts in the mist, watching. No one spoke to them. They left after a few minutes.

'I shouldn't have let her go home,' Sam said to Astrid.

'You're not a doctor. There was no way you could know she had internal bleeding. And, anyway, what could you have done? The question is, what are we going to do now?'

'What do you want to do?' Sam asked.

'Orc murdered Bette,' Astrid said flatly. 'Maybe he didn't mean to, but it's still murder.'

'Yes. He killed her. So what do you want to do?'

'At least we can demand that something be done to Orc.'

'Demand of who?' Sam said. He zipped his jacket. It was chilly. 'You want to go demand justice from Caine?'

'Rhetorical question,' Astrid commented.

'Does that mean it's a question I don't expect you to be able to answer?'

Astrid nodded. Neither of them had anything to say for a while. Mary and the twins, with Bette's little brother in tow, headed back to the day care.

Elwood said, speaking to no one in particular, 'I don't know if Dahra can keep this up much longer.' Then he squared his shoulders and marched back towards the hospital.

Edilio came and stood with Sam and Astrid. 'This can't just be something that happened,' he said. 'You hear me? We let this go, where does it stop? People can't be beating each other up so bad they die.'

'You have a suggestion?' Sam asked coldly.

'Me? I'm the wetback, remember? I'm not from around here. I don't even know these people. I'm not the big genius, and I'm not the one with this power thing, man.' He kicked at the dirt, hard, like it was someone he wanted to hurt. He seemed like he might say more, but he bit his lip, spun, and strode away.

Sam said, 'Caine has Drake and Orc, Panda and Chaz, and I hear Mallet has made peace with him. And maybe a half-dozen other guys.'

'Are you afraid of them?' Astrid asked him.

'Yeah, Astrid, I am.'

'OK,' she said. 'But you were scared of going into a burning building, too.'

'You don't get this, do you?' Sam demanded with enough heat that Astrid took a step back. 'I know what you want, OK? I know what you and a bunch of other people want. You want me to be the anti-Caine. You don't like the way he's doing things and you want me to go kick him out. Well, here's what you don't know: even if I could do all that, I wouldn't be any better than him.'

'You're wrong about that, Sam. You're –'

'That night when I first used the power? When I hurt my stepfather? How do you think I felt?'

'Sad. Regretful.' Astrid looked at his face like the answer would be written there. 'Scared, probably.'

'Yeah. All that. And one more thing.' He held up his hand and inches from her nose squeezed his fingers into a tight fist. 'I also felt a rush, Astrid. A rush. I thought, oh, my God, look at the power I have. Look what I can do. A huge, crazy rush.'

'Power corrupts,' Astrid said softly.

'Yeah,' Sam said sarcastically. 'I've heard that.'

'Power corrupts, absolute power corrupts absolutely. I forget who said it.'

'I make a lot of mistakes, Astrid. I don't want to make that mistake. I don't want to be that guy. I don't want to be Caine. I want to . . .' He spread his arms wide, a gesture of helplessness. 'I just want to go surfing.'

'You won't be corrupted, Sam. You wouldn't do those things.' He had moved back. She moved to close the distance.

'How can you be so sure?'

'Well, two reasons. First, it's not your character. Of course you felt a rush from the power. Then you pushed it away. You didn't grab at it, you pushed it away. That's reason number one. You're you, you're not Caine or Drake or Orc.'

Sam wanted to agree, wanted to accept that, but he felt he knew better. 'Don't be so sure.'

'And reason number two: you have me,' Astrid said.

'Do I?'

'Yes.'

That drained the anger and frustration from him like someone had pulled a plug. For a long moment he was lost, gazing into her eyes. She was very close. His heart shifted to a deeper rhythm that vibrated his whole body.

There were just inches between them. He closed the distance by half, stopped.

'I can't kiss you with your little brother watching,' he said.

Astrid stepped back, took Little Pete by the shoulders, and turned him so he was facing away.

'How about now?'

EIGHTEEN

164 HOURS 32 MINUTES

ALBERT LEFT THE funeral ceremony and crossed the plaza towards the McDonald's. He wished he had someone to talk to. Maybe if he flipped the lights on, someone would come in for a very late burger.

But the small crowd dispersed before he could unlock the front door of the McDonald's – his McDonald's – and the plaza was left empty and silent but for a faint hum from power lines overhead.

Albert stood with his keys in one hand and his McDonald's-issue cap in his other hand – he had taken it off out of respect for the dead – and let a sense of gloom and foreboding wash over him. He was a naturally optimistic person, but a night-time funeral of a young girl murdered by bullies . . . that wasn't something that exactly perked up your mood.

Albert had enjoyed being alone since the FAYZ. He worried about his brothers and sisters. He missed his mom. But he had gone in an instant from being the youngest of six, the goat, the victim, the overworked and under-appreciated youngster, to being a responsible and respected person in this strange new community.

None of which changed the fact that right now, with the smell of fresh-turned earth in his nostrils and disquiet boring holes in his brain, he would have loved to be watching one of his mother's favourite gruesome crime shows and sneaking popcorn out of the bowl on her lap.

The big issues in the FAYZ – the what and the why and the how – didn't bother Albert much. He was a practical person, and, anyway, those were things for someone like Astrid to ponder. As for the events of this night, the killing of Bette, that was for Sam and Caine and those guys to work out.

What had Albert worried was something entirely different: no one was working. No one but Mary and Dahra and occasionally Edilio. Everyone else was moping or wandering or fighting or else just sitting around and playing video games or watching DVDs. They were all like rats living in an abandoned house: they ate what they found, messed wherever they liked, and left things dirtier and more run-down than they found them.

It couldn't last. Everyone was just killing time. But if all they did was kill time, time would end up killing them.

Albert believed that. Knew that. But he couldn't explain it to anyone and make them listen. He couldn't talk with the smooth assurance of a Caine, or the knowing detachment of an Astrid. When Albert spoke, people didn't pay attention the way they did to Sam.

He needed someone else's words to explain what his instincts told him must be true.

Albert dropped his keys into his pocket and marched up the

street with a determined stride that echoed off dark storefronts. The smart thing to do would be to head home, get a few hours of sleep. It would be dawn soon. But he wasn't going to sleep, he knew that. Sam and Caine and Astrid and Computer Jack all had their things they did, their things they knew, but this was Albert's.

'We can't be rats,' he muttered to himself. 'We have to be . . .' But even trying to explain it to himself, he didn't know the right words.

The county library branch in Perdido Beach wasn't an impressive place. It was a dusty, gloomy, low-ceilinged storefront that hit him with a whiff of mildew when he swung the door open. He had never entered the place before and was a little surprised to find it unlocked with the overhead fluorescent tubes still flickering and buzzing.

Albert looked around and laughed. 'No one's been here since the FAYZ,' he said to a rack of yellowed paperbacks.

He looked in the librarian's old oak desk. You never knew where a candy bar might be hiding. He found a can of peppermints. They looked like they'd been there quite a while, treats to be handed out to kids who never came.

He popped one in his mouth and began to walk the meagre stacks. He knew he needed to know something, but he didn't know what he needed to know. Most of the books looked like they'd been there, undisturbed, since before Albert was born.

He found a set of encyclopedias – like Wikipedia, but paper and very bulky. He plopped down on the ratty carpet and opened the first book. He didn't know what he was looking for, but he knew where to start. He slid out the volume for 'W' and turned to the entry for 'work'. There were two main entries. One had to do with work in terms of physics.

The other entry talked about work as the 'activities necessary for the survival of society'.

'Yeah,' Albert said. 'That's what I'm talking about.'

He started reading. He jumped from volume to volume, understanding only part of what he was reading, but understanding enough to follow another lead and then another. It was exactly like following hyperlinks, only slower, and with more lifting.

'Work' led to 'labour', which led him to 'productivity,' which led to someone named 'Karl Marx', which led to another old guy named 'Adam Smith'.

Albert had never been much of a serious student. But what he had learned in school had never mattered much from his point of view. This mattered. Everything mattered now.

Albert drifted slowly off to sleep and woke up with a start, feeling eyes watching him.

He spun around, jumped to his feet, and heaved a huge sigh of relief when he saw that it was just a cat. The cat was a yellow tabby, a little fat, probably old. It had a pink collar and heart-shaped brass tag. It stood with perfect confidence and self-possession in the middle of the aisle. The cat stared at him from green eyes. Its tail twitched.

'Hi, kitty,' Albert said.

The cat disappeared.

Gone.

Albert recoiled in shock, his face suddenly ablaze with pain. The cat was on him, on his face, digging razor-claws into his head. The cat hissed, needle-teeth exposed by a fierce scowl a millimetre from Albert's eyes.

Albert yelled for help, yelled at the cat. The cat dug its claws deeper. Albert still had a volume of the encyclopedia in his right hand – the 'S' book. He slammed it down on his own head.

The cat was gone. The book knocked Albert silly.

And now the cat was clear across the room, sitting calmly atop the librarian's desk.

It was impossible. Nothing moved that fast. Nothing.

Albert drew a shaky breath and began backing towards the door to the street.

Without any movement that Albert's eyes could detect, the cat went from the desk to the back of Albert's neck. It was on him like a mad thing, clawing, scratching, tearing, hissing.

Again, Albert swung the heavy book and again the blow landed on his own flesh because now the cat was perched atop a stack, peering down at Albert, mocking him with cool, green-eyed contempt.

It was going to attack him again.

Instinct made Albert swing the book up to protect his face.

He felt the book jump violently in his hands.

The cat's face, distorted by rage, was an inch from Albert's own face.

But the book was still in place.

And the cat was in the book.

No, *through* the book.

Albert stared in shock as the cat's eyes darkened and its animal soul fled.

He dropped the encyclopedia on the floor.

The book, the heavy blue leather-bound volume, bisected the cat just behind the front paws. It was as if someone had cut the cat in half and sewed it in two pieces to the book. The back of the cat stuck out from the back cover.

Albert was panting as much from terror as exertion. The thing on the floor, that thing wasn't possible. The way the cat had moved, not possible.

'Nightmare. You're having a nightmare,' he told himself.

But if it was a dream it was a dream with a lot of the texture of reality. Surely he wouldn't dream the smell of mildew. Surely he wouldn't dream the way the cat's bladder and bowels emptied messily in death.

Albert remembered seeing the librarian's large shoulder bag at her desk. With shaking hands he emptied the contents out on to the desk: lipstick, wallet, compact, a cell phone all scattered.

He picked up the encyclopedia. It was heavy. The weight of the cat added to the book had to be twenty pounds. And the cat-in-the-book was bulky, too big to fit easily into the bag.

But he had to show this to someone. This was an impossible thing. Impossible. Except that it was real. Albert needed someone else to tell him that it was real, someone to confirm that he wasn't dreaming or crazy.

Not Caine. Sam? He would be at the firehouse, but this wasn't a Sam thing, it was an Astrid thing. Two minutes later he was on Astrid's well-lit stoop.

Astrid opened her door cautiously and only after checking the peephole.

'Albert? It's the middle of the . . . oh, my God, what happened to your face?'

'I could use some Band-Aids,' Albert said. He'd forgotten what he must look like. He'd forgotten the pain. 'Yeah. I could use some help. But that's not why I came here.'

'Then . . .'

'Astrid. I need . . .' His words failed him, then. Now safe in Astrid's entryway, the fear took hold and for a minute he just could not form a word or make a sound.

Astrid drew him inside and closed the door.

'I need . . .' he began again, and again couldn't say more. In a strangled voice he said, 'Just look.'

He dumped the cat and the book on to the Oriental rug.

Astrid went completely still.

'It was so fast. It attacked me. I couldn't even see it move. It was like it was in one place, right? And then it was on me. I mean, it didn't jump, Astrid. It just . . . appeared.'

Astrid knelt to push gingerly at the book. She tried to make the book fall open, but the body of the cat went through each page and held them together. Not like the cat had made a hole; like the cat had fused together with the paper.

'What is it, Astrid?' Albert pleaded.

She said nothing, just stared. Albert could all but see the wheels turning in her brain. But she gave him no answer, and Albert accepted after a while that no answer would be forthcoming. No explanation was possible for a thing that could not be.

But she had seen the thing, the impossible thing. He wasn't crazy.

After what felt like a very long time Astrid whispered, 'Come on, Albert, let's do something with those scratches.'

Lana lay in the dark in the cabin listening to the mysterious sounds of the desert outside. Something made a soft, slithery sound like a hand stroking silk. Something else emitted rapid percussive bursts, a tiny insect drummer who slowed after a few seconds and lost his way and fell silent before starting all over again.

The windmill squeaked infuriatingly. Never for long, never in any kind of pattern. There was no real breeze, just whispers that turned the weathered wooden blades a quarter-turn . . . squeak . . . or a half-turn . . . squeak, squeak . . . or barely nudged them to produce a sound like the shrill peep of a baby bird.

Against all that was the reassuring snore from Patrick. He would snore and stop and snore again and every now and then give up a low yipping sound that Lana found endearing.

Lana's body was well. Her injuries were all miraculously

healed. She had washed away the caked-on blood. She had water and food and shelter.

But Lana's brain was an engine revved to breakneck speed. It turned over and over, swirling through memories of pain, memories of terror, flashes of her grandfather's empty seat, the tumble down the slope, the buzzards, the lion.

But as lurid as all those images were, they were just fresh paint splashed on more permanent images. The pictures that lingered were of home. School. The mall. Her dad's car and her mom's van. The community pool. The sizzling fantasy skyline of the Las Vegas strip visible from her bedroom window.

Taken all together, the pictures churning and churning in her head fed a constant slow burn of rage.

She should be home, not here. She should be in her room. She should be with her friends. Not alone.

Not alone listening to eerie noises and a squeak and a snore.

If she had been a little more careful . . . She had tried to stuff the bottle of vodka into her shoulder bag, the cute one with the beadwork she liked. The bag was too small, but the only bag big enough was her book bag and she hadn't wanted to carry it because it didn't work with her outfit.

For that, she had been caught. For a stupid question of fashion, of looking cool.

And now . . .

A tidal wave of fury at her mother swept across her. It felt like she would drown in all that rage.

Her mother, that's who she blamed. Her father just did what

her mom told him to do. He had to back her up even though he was the nicer one, not as strict or as snipey as her mother.

What was the big deal if she gave Tony a bottle of vodka? It's not like he was driving a car.

Lana's mother just didn't understand Las Vegas. Vegas wasn't Perdido Beach. There were pressures on her in Las Vegas. It was a city, not a town, and not just any city. Kids grew up faster in Vegas. Demands were made, even of seventh-graders, eighth-graders, let alone a ninth-grader like her.

Her stupid mother. Her fault.

Although it was kind of hard to blame her mother for the blank, intimidating wall in the desert. Kind of hard to blame her for that.

Maybe it was aliens and right now some creepy monsters were chasing her mother and father through the streets of Las Vegas, like in that movie, *War of the Worlds*. Maybe.

Lana found that thought strangely comforting. After all, at least she wasn't being chased by aliens in giant tripods. Maybe the wall was some kind of defence put up against the aliens. Maybe she was safe on this side of the wall.

The bottle of vodka wasn't the only time she'd snuck something for Tony. Lana had palmed some of her mother's Xanax for him. And she had shoplifted a bottle of wine once from a convenience store.

She wasn't naive: she never thought Tony loved her or anything. She knew he was using her. But she was using him too, in her own way. Tony had some status in the school, and some of that had been transferred to her.

Patrick snorted and raised his head very suddenly.

'What is it, boy?'

She rolled from the narrow cot and crouched silent and fearful in the dark cabin.

Something was outside. She could hear it moving. Faint sounds of padded feet on the ground.

Patrick stood up but in a strange, slow-motion way. His hackles were raised, the fur on his back bristling. He was staring intently at the doorway.

There was a scratching sound, exactly like a dog might make, trying to get inside.

And then Lana heard, or thought she heard, a garbled whisper. 'Come out.'

Patrick should be barking, but he wasn't. He was rigid, panting too hard, staring too fixedly.

'You're just imagining things,' Lana whispered, trying to reassure herself.

'Come out,' the gravelly whisper called again.

Lana discovered that she had to pee. Had to go very badly and there was nothing like a bathroom in the cabin.

'Is someone there?' she cried.

No answer. Maybe it had just been her imagination. Maybe it was just the wind.

She crept to the door and listened intently. Nothing. She glanced at Patrick. Her dog was still bristling, but he had relaxed a bit. The threat – whatever it had been – had moved away.

Lana opened the door a crack. Nothing. Nothing she could see, anyway, and Patrick was definitely no longer worried.

She had no choice: she had to run to the outhouse. Patrick bounded along beside her.

The outhouse was a simple vertical box, undecorated, unadorned, not overly smelly and quite clean. There was no light, of course, so she had to feel her way around, locate the seat and the toilet paper.

At one point she started giggling. It was, after all, a little funny peeing in an outhouse while her dog stood guard.

The walk back to the shack was a bit more leisurely. Lana took a moment to gaze up at the night sky. The moon was already descending towards the western horizon. The stars . . . well, the stars looked odd. But she wasn't quite sure why she thought so.

She resumed the walk back to the cabin and froze. Between her and the front door stood a coyote. But this was like none of the coyotes her grandfather had pointed out to her. None of those had been even as big as Patrick. But this shaggy yellow animal was the size of a wolf.

Patrick had not seen or heard the animal approach and now he seemed almost too shocked to react. Patrick, who had leaped to battle a mountain lion, now seemed cowed and uncertain.

Lana's grandfather had lectured her on desert animals: the coyote that was to be respected but not feared; the lizards that would startle you with their sudden bursts of speed; the deer that were more like large rats than like Bambi; the wild burros so different from their domesticated brothers; and the rattlesnakes that were no threat so long as you wore boots and kept your eyes open.

'Shoo,' Lana yelled, and waved her hands as her grandfather had taught her to do if she ever came too close to a coyote.

The coyote didn't move.

Instead it made a sharp yipping sound that caused Lana to jump back. Out of the corner of her eye she saw dark shapes rushing towards her, three or four of them, swift shadows.

Now Patrick reacted. He growled menacingly, bared his teeth and raised his hackles, but the coyote didn't move and his companions were approaching fast.

Lana had been told that coyotes were not dangerous to humans, but there was no way to believe that now. She dodged to the right, hoping to fake out the coyote, but the animal was far too quick to be fooled.

'Patrick, get him,' she urged helplessly.

But Patrick wasn't going any further than growling and putting on a show and in seconds the other coyotes would arrive and then . . . well, who knew what then?

Lana had no choice: she had to reach the cabin. She had to reach the cabin or die.

She yelled at the top of her voice and ran straight at the coyote in her path.

The animal recoiled in surprise.

There was a flash of something small and dark and the coyote yelped in pain.

Lana was past him in a heartbeat. Ten steps to the cabin door. Ten, nine, eight, seven, six . . .

Patrick ran ahead of her, panicked, and shot inside.

Lana was on his heels, spun, and slammed the door shut without even slowing down. She skidded to a stop, turned, ran back to the door, and threw herself against it.

But the coyotes did not pursue. They had other problems. She heard wild yelping, canine cries of pain and rage.

After a while the yelping slowed, slurred, and finally stopped. A new coyote voice set up a wild howling, howling at the moon.

Then silence.

In the morning, with the sun bright and all the night's terrors banished, Lana found the coyote dead, a hundred feet from her door. Still attached to its muzzle was half a snake with a broad, diamond-shaped head. Its body had been chewed in half but not before the venom had flowed into the coyote's bloodstream.

She looked for a long time at the snake's head. It was a snake without any doubt. And yet she was sure she had seen it fly.

Lana put that out of her mind. And along with it she dismissed the whisper she had heard because flying snakes and whispering coyotes the size of Great Danes, well, none of that was possible. There was a word for people who believed impossible things: crazy.

'I guess Grandpa wasn't that big an expert on desert wildlife after all,' she said to Patrick.

'**YOU** DON'T HAVE to like the dude, brah, but he's doing good stuff.' Quinn was poised to knock on the door of their third house that morning. It was Sam and Quinn and a Coates kid, a girl named Brooke. They were 'search team three'.

It was day eight of the FAYZ. The fifth day since Caine had moved in and taken over.

The second day since Sam had kissed Astrid beside a freshly dug grave.

Caine had organised ten search teams to move through the town, each covering a square block to start. The idea was to go into each house on each of the four streets that formed the block. They were to make sure the stove was off, the air-conditioning was off, the TV was off, interior lights were off, and the porch lights lit. They were to turn off automatic irrigation systems and turn off hot-water heaters.

If they couldn't figure any of that out, they would add it to a list for Edilio to follow up on. Edilio always seemed able to figure out mechanical things. He was running around Perdido Beach with a tool belt and two Coates kids as 'helpers'.

The search teams were also to search for lost kids, babies who might have been abandoned, might be trapped in cribs. And pets, too.

In each house they made a list of anything useful, like computers, and anything dangerous, like guns or drugs. They were to note how much food there was and collect all the medicines so they could be sent to Dahra. Diapers and formula went to the day care.

It was a good plan. It was a good idea.

Caine had some good ideas, no question. Caine had tasked Computer Jack to come up with an emergency communication system. Computer Jack had the idea of going old school: he'd set up short-wave radios in the town hall, the fire station, the day care, and the abandoned house Drake used for himself and some of his sheriffs.

But Caine had taken no action against Orc.

Sam had gone to him to demand action.

'What am I supposed to do?' Caine had asked reasonably. 'Bette was breaking the rules, and Orc is a sheriff. It was a tragedy for everyone involved. Orc feels very bad.'

So Orc still prowled the streets of Perdido Beach. For all Sam knew, Bette's blood was still on the bully's bat. And now the fear of the so-called sheriffs was magnified ten times over.

'Let's just get this over with,' Sam said. He wasn't going to get into a discussion of Caine in front of Brooke. He assumed the ten-year-old was a spy. In any case, he was in a foul mood because one of the houses they were to visit later was his own.

Quinn knocked. He rang the bell. 'Nada.' He tried the door. It was locked. 'Bring on the hammer,' Quinn said.

Each search team had a wagon, either taken from the hardware store or borrowed from someone's yard. They carried a heavy sledgehammer in the wagon.

It had taken them two hours to deal with the first two houses. It was going to be a while before every home in Perdido Beach had been searched and rendered safe.

'You want to do the hammer?' Sam asked, deferring to Quinn.

'I live for the hammer, brah.'

Quinn hefted the hammer and swung it against the door, just below the doorknob. The wood splintered, and Quinn pushed the door back.

The smell hit them hard.

'Oh, man, what died in here?' Quinn said, like it was a joke.

The joke fell flat.

Just inside the door, on the hardwood floor, lay a baby's pacifier. The three of them stared at it.

'No, no, no. I can't do this,' Brooke said.

The three of them stayed on the porch, no one willing to go in. But no one was willing to close the door and just walk away, either.

Brooke's hands were shaking so badly, Sam reached for them and held them in his. 'It's OK,' he said. 'You don't have to go in.'

She was chubby, freckled, with straw-dry reddish hair. She wore the Coates uniform and had seemed, up until this moment, almost a cipher. She never joked or played around, just did what she was supposed to do, following Sam's lead.

'It's just, after Coates . . .' Brooke said.

'What about Coates?' Sam asked.

Brooke flushed. 'Nothing. Just, you know, all the adults disappearing.' Then, feeling like she had to explain some more, she said, 'It's, like, I don't want to see any more creepy stuff, OK?'

Sam shot a significant look at Quinn, but Quinn just shrugged and said, 'There's, like, a dead little kid in there. We don't have to go inside to know that.'

Sam yelled, 'Is there anyone in there?' as loud as he could. Then to Quinn, 'We can't just ignore this.'

'Maybe we should report it to Caine,' Quinn said.

'I don't see him going house-to-house,' Sam snapped. 'He's sitting on his butt acting like he's the emperor of Perdido Beach.'

When no one took the bait, Sam said, 'Give me one of the big garbage bags.'

Quinn peeled one off.

Ten minutes later Sam was done. He dragged the bag with its sad contents across the carpet to the front door. He hefted it by the drawstrings and carried it out to the wagon.

'Like taking out the trash,' Sam said to no one. His hands were shaking. He felt so angry, he wanted to hurt someone. He felt angry enough that if he could have gotten his hands on whoever caused all this, he would have choked the life out of them.

Mostly Sam was angry at himself. He had never really known this family. It was a one-parent home, the mom and various boyfriends. And the little boy. The family weren't friends, or even acquaintances, but still, he should have thought to check on the baby. That should have been his first thought. He should have remembered, but he hadn't.

Without looking back at Quinn and Brooke, Sam said, 'Open some windows. Let some air in there. We can come back when it's not so . . . when the smell is gone.'

'Brah, I'm not going in there,' Quinn said.

Sam quickly closed the distance between them. Seeing his face, Quinn took a step back. 'I picked the baby up and stuffed him in a trash bag, all right? So go in there and open the windows. Do it.'

'Man, you really need to step off,' Quinn said. 'I don't take orders from you.'

'No, you take them from Caine,' Sam said.

Quinn stuck his hand out, almost taunting. 'I'm sorry, am I annoying you? Why don't you just burn my hand off, magic boy?'

Sam and Quinn had had many arguments over the years. But since the coming of the FAYZ, especially since Sam had told Quinn the truth about himself, simple disagreements had turned quickly poisonous. They were in each other's faces now like they might both start swinging. Sam was mad enough to.

Brooke said, 'I'll do it, Sam.'

Sam, his face still just inches from Quinn's, said, 'I don't want it to be this way between us.'

Quinn relaxed his muscles. He forced a grin. 'No big thing, brah.'

To Brooke, Sam said, 'Open the windows. Then go tell Edilio to dig another hole. I'll go do my house. It would be nice if you could pull the wagon downtown. But if you can't, I'll understand.'

Without another word to Quinn he stormed off but stopped short at the end of the walkway. 'Brooke, see if you can find a picture of him and his mom, OK? I don't want him to be buried alone. He should have . . .'

He couldn't say any more. Eyes half blinded by unexpected tears, he marched down the street and stumbled up the steps to his own home, the house he hated, and slammed the door behind him.

It took a while before he even noticed his mother's laptop computer was gone.

He went to the table. He touched the tabletop, right where the laptop had been, as though to reassure himself he wasn't imagining things.

Then he noticed the open drawers. The open cabinets. The food hadn't been taken, just tossed around, some of it ending up on the floor.

He bolted for his room. The light was still there. His weak attempt at camouflaging it had been torn down.

Someone knew. Someone had seen.

But it didn't stop there. In his mother's bedroom the drawers and the closet had been ransacked.

His mother kept a locked, flat, grey metal box in her closet. Sam knew because she'd pointed it out to him on more than one occasion. 'If anything ever happens to me, this is where my will is.' She was very serious, but then she'd said, 'You know, in case I get hit by a bus.'

'We don't have any buses in Perdido Beach,' he'd pointed out.

'Hmm. I guess that explains why they're never on time,' she'd said, and then laughed and hooked him in for a hug.

Holding on to him she had whispered, 'Sam, your birth certificate is in there, too.'

'OK.'

'It's up to you whether you want to see it.'

He had stiffened against her embrace. She was offering him a chance to know what it said on the birth certificate. There would be three names listed: his, his mother's, and his father's.

'Maybe. Maybe not,' he had said.

She held him tightly, but he gently disengaged and stood apart from her. He wanted then to say something. To apologise for what had happened to Tom. To ask her whether he had also, somehow, scared off his true father.

But his was a life with secrets. And even though his mother had made the offer, Sam knew she didn't want him to violate the code of secrecy.

For months Sam had known about the box. Known where he could find the key.

Now the box was gone.

He had very little doubt who had taken it, who had searched the house.

By now, Caine knew that Sam had the power.

He retrieved his bike. He wanted desperately to be with Astrid. She would make sense of everything.

Most kids got around on bikes – not always their own – or skateboards. Only the prees walked. And as he crossed through the plaza on his way to Astrid's home there was a procession of them walking right across the street. Brother John was in the lead. Mother Mary was pushing a two-seat stroller. Some girl in a Coates uniform was carrying a toddler on her hip. Two other kids, drafted for the day, were shepherding the line of some thirty or so preschoolers. They were solemn for a group of little kids but there was at least some horseplay, enough that Mary had to yell, 'Julia and Zosia, get back in line.'

The twins, Emma and Anna, brought up the rear. Sam knew them fairly well, having actually gone out with Anna on a date once. Emma had a single stroller, and Anna was pushing a Ralph's grocery store cart loaded with snacks and diapers and baby bottles.

Sam stopped and waited for them to cross the street. They stuck to the crosswalk, which, he supposed, was a good thing. Best for the prees to learn to cross the street like there might be traffic. Some kids had been doing some driving, often with bad results. Caine had the rules on that too, now: no one was allowed to drive, except for some of Caine's people and Edilio,

217

who theoretically might have to drive the ambulance or the fire truck. If he ever figured out how.

'T'sup, Anna?' Sam asked politely.

'Hi, Sam. Where have you been?'

He shrugged. 'Fire station. I kind of live there now.'

Anna pointed at the littles marching ahead of her. 'Baby duty.'

'Drag,' Sam said.

'It's OK. I don't mind it.'

'And she's great at it, too,' Mary called back encouragingly.

'I can change a diaper in under sixty seconds,' Anna said with a laugh. 'Less, if it's number one.'

'Where are you guys all going?'

'The beach. We're going on a picnic.'

'Cool. See you later,' Sam said.

Anna waved over her shoulder as she passed.

'Hey, wish Anna and me happy birthday, Sam,' Emma called back.

'Happy birthday to both of you,' Sam said. He stood up on the bike's pedals and picked up speed, heading for Astrid's.

He felt a little sad thinking back on his one date with Anna. She was a nice girl. But he wasn't all that interested in dating back then, that was the truth. He'd only gone out because he felt like it was required. He didn't want kids to think he was a dork. And his mother kept asking about whether he was going out, so he had taken Anna to a movie. He remembered the movie, in fact: *Stardust.*

His mother had driven them. It was her night off. She had dropped them at the theatre and picked them up afterwards. He and Anna had gone to the California Pizza Kitchen and split a barbecue chicken pizza.

Birthday?

Sam jerked the bike into a sharp turn and pounded the pedals back, back towards where he'd passed the prees. It didn't take long to catch them. They were just reaching the beach, all the toddlers toddling over the low seawall, laughing now as they took off their shoes and ran on to the sand, and Mother Mary, sounding just like a teacher, yelled, 'Hang on to your shoes. Don't lose your shoes. Alex, pick up your shoes and carry them.'

Anna and Emma had parked the shopping cart full of snacks and diapers and bottles. Emma was unbuckling her charge from the stroller.

'Check his diaper,' Mother Mary reminded her, and Emma did.

Sam threw his bike down and ran, breathless, to Anna.

'What's up, Sam?'

'What birthday?' he panted.

'What?'

'What birthday, Anna?'

It took a while for her to absorb his fear. It took a while for the reason for his fear to dawn on her.

'Fifteen,' Anna said in a whisper.

'What's the matter?' Emma asked, sensing her twin's mood. 'It doesn't mean anything.'

'It doesn't,' Anna whispered.

'You're probably right,' Sam said.

'Oh, my God,' Anna said. 'Are we going to disappear?'

'When were you born?' Sam asked. 'What time of day?'

The twins exchanged scared looks. 'We don't know.'

'You know what, no one has blinked out since that first day, so it's probably –'

Emma disappeared.

Anna screamed.

The other older kids took notice, the littles, too.

'Oh, my God!' Anna cried. 'Emma. Emma. Oh, God!'

She grabbed Sam's hands and he held her tight.

The prees, some of them, caught the fear. Mother Mary came over. 'What's going on? You're scaring the kids. Where's Emma?'

Anna just kept saying, 'Oh, my God,' and calling her sister's name.

'Where's Emma?' Mary demanded again. 'What's going on?'

Sam didn't want to explain. Anna was hurting him with the pressure of her fingers digging into the backs of his hands. Anna's eyes were huge, staring holes in him.

'How far apart were you born?' Sam asked.

Anna just stared in blank horror.

Sam lowered his voice to an urgent whisper. 'How far apart were you born, Anna?'

'Six minutes,' she whispered.

'Hold my hands, Sam,' she said.

'Don't let me go, Sam,' she said.

'I won't, Anna, I won't let you go,' Sam said.

'What's going to happen, Sam?'

'I don't know, Anna.'

'Will we go to where our mom and dad are?'

'I don't know, Anna.'

'Am I going to die?'

'No, Anna. You're not going to die.'

'Don't let go of me, Sam.'

Mary was there now, a baby on her hip. John was there. The prees, some of them, watched with serious, worried looks on their faces.

'I don't want to die,' Anna repeated. 'I . . . I don't know what it's like.'

'It's OK, Anna.'

Anna smiled. 'That was a nice date. When we went out.'

'It was.'

For a split second it was like Anna blurred. Too fast to be real. She blurred, and Sam could almost swear that she had smiled at him.

And his fingers squeezed on nothing.

For a terribly long time no one moved or said anything.

The littles didn't cry out. The older kids just stared.

Sam's fingertips still remembered the feel of Anna's hands. He stared at the place where her face had been. He could still see her pleading eyes.

Unable to stop himself, he reached a hand into the space she had occupied. Reaching for a face that was no longer there.

221

Someone sobbed.

Someone cried out, other voices then, the prees started crying.

Sam felt sick. When his teacher had disappeared he hadn't been expecting it. This time he had seen it coming, like a monster in a slow-motion nightmare. This time he had seen it coming, like standing rooted on the railroad tracks, unable to jump aside.

TWENTY

'IT JUST HAPPENED,' Drake announced.

Caine sat in his over-large leather chair, the one that had formerly belonged to the mayor of Perdido Beach. It made him look small. It made him look very young. And to make matters worse, he was chewing on his thumbnail, which made it almost seem that he was sucking his thumb.

Diana was on the couch, lying back reading a magazine and barely paying attention. 'What happened?'

'The two girls you had me following. They both just took the big jump. They poofed, as that idiot Quinn says.'

Caine jerked to his feet. 'Just as I predicted. Just like I said.' Caine did not seem to be happy to have been proven right. He came around from behind his desk and, to Drake's great enjoyment, snatched the magazine out of Diana's hand and threw it across the room. 'You think maybe you could pay attention?'

Diana sighed and sat up slowly, brushed a piece of lint from her blouse. 'Don't get pissy with me, Caine,' she warned. 'I'm the one who said we needed to start collecting birth certificates.'

Drake had made time to check out Diana's psych file the day

after the FAYZ came. But her file had been missing by then. In its place she had left Drake's file lying open on the doc's desk and drawn a little smiley face beside the word 'sadist'.

Drake had already hated her. But after that, hating Diana had become a full-time occupation.

To Drake's disgust, Caine accepted Diana's back talk. 'Yeah. That was a good idea,' Caine said. 'A very good idea.'

'Diana's boy Sam was there,' Drake said.

Diana did not respond to the provocation.

'He was holding the one girl's hand when she bugged,' Drake added. 'Looking right into her eyes. See, the first girl goes and they all know what's coming at that point. The second girl, she was weepy over it. I was too far off to hear what she said, but you could tell she was basically wetting herself.'

'Sadism,' Diana said. 'The enjoyment of another person's pain.'

Drake stretched his shark grin. 'Words don't scare me.'

'You wouldn't be a psychopath if they did, Drake.'

'Knock it off, you two,' Caine said. He slumped back in the over-sized chair and started biting his thumb again. 'It's November seventeenth. I have five days to figure out how to beat this.'

'Five days,' Drake echoed.

'I don't know what we'd do if you bugged out, Caine,' Drake said. He sent Diana a look that said he knew exactly what he would do if Caine wasn't around any more.

Computer Jack came bursting into the room in his usual flustered, goggle-eyed way, carrying an open laptop.

'What?' Caine snarled.

'I hacked it,' Computer Jack said proudly. When he got blank looks in reaction, he said, 'Nurse Temple's laptop.'

Caine looked nonplussed. 'What? Oh. Great. I have bigger problems. Give it to Diana. And get out.'

Computer Jack handed the laptop to Diana and scuttled from the room.

'Scared little worm, isn't he?' Drake said.

'Don't mess with him. He's useful,' Caine warned. 'Drake. What did you see exactly when the girl . . . vacated?'

'The first one, I wasn't looking right at her when it happened. The second one, I kept my eyes on her. One minute there, the next gone.'

'At one seventeen?'

Drake shrugged. 'Close enough, anyway.'

Caine slammed his hand down on the desk. 'I don't want close enough, you idiot,' he shouted. 'I'm trying to figure this out. You know, it's not just me, Drake. We all get older. You'll be there some day too, waiting to disappear.'

'April twelfth, just one minute after midnight, Drake,' Diana said. 'Not that I've memorised the exact day, hour, and minute or . . .' She fell silent, reading the computer screen.

'What?' Caine asked.

Diana ignored him but it was clear that she had found something of great interest in the diary of Connie Temple. Diana rose with swift, feline grace and yanked open the filing cabinet. She pulled the grey metal box out and placed it almost reverently on Caine's desk.

'No one's opened it yet?' she demanded.

'I was more interested in Nurse Temple's laptop,' Caine said. 'Why?'

'Be useful, Drake,' Diana ordered. 'Break this lock.'

Drake grabbed a letter opener, inserted the blade in the cheap lock, and twisted. The lock broke.

Diana opened the box. 'This looks like a will. And, ah, this is interesting, a newspaper clipping about the school bus thing we've all heard about. And . . . here it is.'

She held up a plastic folder protecting an elaborately printed birth certificate. She stared at it and started laughing.

'That's enough, Diana,' Caine warned. He jumped up and yanked the birth certificate from her hand. He stared, frowning. Then he sat down hard, like he was a marionette and someone had cut his strings.

'November twenty-second,' Diana said, grinning spitefully.

'Coincidence,' Caine said.

'He's three minutes older than you.'

'It's a coincidence. We don't look alike.'

'What's the word for twins who aren't identical?' Diana put her finger to her mouth, a parody of deep thought. 'Oh yeah, fraternal twins. Same womb, same parents, different eggs.'

Caine looked like he might faint. Drake had never seen him like that. 'It's impossible.'

'Neither of you knows your real father,' Diana said. Now she was playing nice, as close to sympathetic as she ever managed to be. 'And how many times have you told me you don't seem to be anything like your parents, Caine?'

'It makes no sense,' Caine breathed. He reached for Diana's hand and, after a hesitation, she let him take it.

'What are you two talking about?' Drake demanded. He didn't enjoy being the one person not in on the joke. But they both ignored him.

'It's in the diary, too,' Diana said. 'Nurse Temple. She knew you were a mutant. She suspected you had some kind of impossible power, and she was obviously on to some of the others, as well. She suspected you of causing half a dozen injuries where no one could ever figure out a cause.'

Drake barked a laugh, catching on. 'Are you saying Nurse Temple was Caine's mother?'

Caine's face blazed in sudden rage. 'Shut up, Drake.'

'Two little boys born on November twenty-second,' Diana said. 'One stays with his mother. One is taken away, adopted by another family.'

'She was your mother and she gave you up and kept Sam?' Drake said, laughing in his enjoyment of Caine's humiliation.

Caine swivelled away from Diana and extended his hands, palms out, towards Drake.

'Mistake,' Diana said, though whether she was talking to Drake or Caine wasn't clear.

Something slammed Drake's chest. It was like being hit by a truck. He was lifted off his feet and thrown against the wall. He smashed a pair of framed prints and fell in a heap.

He made himself shake it off. He wanted to jump up and go

for Caine, finish him quick before the freak could hit him again. But Caine was there, looming over him, face red, teeth bared, looking like a mad dog.

'Remember who's the boss, Drake,' Caine said, his voice low, guttural, like it was coming from an animal.

Drake nodded, beaten. For now.

'Get up,' Caine ordered. 'We have work to do.'

Astrid was on the front porch with Little Pete. It was the best place to get some sun. She sat in the big white wicker rocker with her feet propped up on the railing. Her bare legs were blazing white in the sunshine. She had always been pale and was never the kind of person who obsessed over a tan, but she was feeling the need for sunlight today. Days with Little Pete tended to be spent indoors. And after a couple of days of that, the house was turning into a prison.

She wondered if this was how her mother had felt. Did it explain why her mom had gone from devoting every day and every night to Little Pete to finding any excuse she could to dump him on whoever would take him?

The street Astrid lived on had changed in small ways since the FAYZ. Cars sat and never moved. There was never any traffic. The lawns were all getting shaggy. The flowers that Mr Massilio two doors down always kept so beautiful were fading, limp from lack of care. Flags were up on a couple of mailboxes, waiting for a mailman who was never coming. There was an open umbrella blowing listlessly down the street, moving an inch or two at a time. A couple of houses away some wild animal, or maybe just a hungry pet, had overturned the garbage can and spilled blackened banana peels and sodden newspapers and chicken bones down the driveway.

Astrid spotted Sam pedalling furiously on his bike. He'd said he would come by to take her to the grocery store and she had been waiting for him with an uncomfortable mix of emotions. She wanted to see him. And she was nervous about it.

The kiss had definitely been a mistake.

Unless it wasn't.

Sam threw his bike on the lawn and climbed the steps.

'Hi, Sam.' It was clear that he was upset. She lowered her legs and sat forwards.

'Anna and Emma just poofed.'

'What?'

'I was standing there. I was watching them. I was holding Anna's hand when it happened.'

Astrid rose and, without really thinking about it, wrapped her arms around Sam like she did when she was trying to comfort Little Pete.

But unlike Little Pete, Sam responded to her touch by awkwardly hugging her back. For a moment his face was in her hair and she heard his ragged breathing close to her ear. And it seemed like they might do it again, the kissing thing, but then, both at once, they pushed away.

'She was scared,' Sam said. 'Anna, I mean. She saw Emma disappear. They were born just six minutes apart. So, first

Emma. Then Anna, waiting for it. Knowing it was coming.'

'How horrible. Sam, come inside.' She glanced at her brother. He was playing his game, as usual.

Astrid led Sam to the kitchen and poured him a glass of water. He drank half of it in a single gulp.

'I have five days,' Sam fretted. 'Five. Days. Not even a week.'

'You don't know that for sure.'

'Don't, OK? Just don't. Don't tell me some story about how it's all going to be fine. It's not going to be fine.'

'OK,' Astrid said. 'You're right. Somehow, age fifteen is this line, and when you reach it, you poof out.'

That confirmation seemed to calm him down. He had just needed to have the truth set out clearly without evasions. It occurred to Astrid that this was a way she could help Sam, not just now, but in the future. If they had a future.

'I was avoiding it. Not thinking about it. I'd kind of convinced myself it wasn't going to happen.' He managed a wry grin, mostly, it seemed, for her benefit. He could see his own fear reflected in her and now he was trying to tamp it down. 'On the plus side, it means I don't have to worry about how depressing it's going to be having Thanksgiving here in the FAYZ.'

'There may be a way to beat it,' Astrid said cautiously.

He looked at her hopefully, like maybe she had an answer. She shook her head, so he said, 'No one's even looking for a way out of the FAYZ. There may be a way to escape. For all we know, there's a big, wide-open gate in the barrier. Maybe out to sea.

Maybe out in the desert or up in the national park. No one has even looked.'

Astrid resisted the urge to label that sentiment as 'grasping at straws'.

Instead, she said, 'If there was a way out there would be a way in. And the whole world must know what's happened. Perdido Beach, the power plant, the highway suddenly blocked – it's not like the world hasn't noticed. And they have more people and more resources than we do. They must have half the scientists in the world working on it. But here we are still.'

'I know. I know all that.' He was calmer now and sat on one of the bar stools that lined the kitchen counter. He ran one hand over the smooth granite surface as if appreciating the coolness of the stone. 'I've been thinking, Astrid. What about an egg?'

'Um. I'm out of eggs.'

'No, I mean, think about an egg. The baby chicken pokes his way out of the egg, right? But if you try to break into the egg, it all comes apart.' He did a crumbling thing with his fingertips to illustrate. When she didn't respond, he slumped and said, 'It made perfect sense when I was thinking about it.'

'Actually, it does make a certain amount of sense,' she said.

He was clearly taken aback. His eyes twinkled in a way she liked, and he smiled lopsidedly. 'You sound surprised,' he said.

'I am, a little. It may turn out to be an apt analogy.'

'You're only saying "apt analogy" to remind me you're smarter than I am,' he teased.

Their eyes locked. Then both looked away, smiling with embarrassment.

'I'm not sorry, you know,' he said. 'I mean, wrong time, wrong place, and all, but I'm still not sorry.'

'You mean . . .'

'Yeah.'

'No, me neither,' Astrid said. 'Um, it was my first time. You know, if you don't count when I kissed Alfredo Slavin in first grade.'

'First time?'

'Well. Yeah. You?'

He shook his head and winced regretfully. Then he said, 'But it was the first time I meant it.'

A comfortable silence fell between them.

Then Astrid said, 'Sam, the eggshell thing: what you're saying is that if people outside try to penetrate the barrier wall, it might be dangerous to us. And the people outside might have figured that out. It may be that only we can safely break the barrier and emerge. Maybe the whole world is waiting, watching, hoping we'll figure out how to hatch.' She opened the cabinet above her and produced a half-empty bag of cookies. She put them on the counter and took one for herself. 'It's a good theory, but you realise it's still not likely.'

'I know. But I don't want to just sit here and wait for the clock to tick down if there's a way out of the FAYZ.'

'What is it you want to do?'

He shrugged. He had a way of doing that that didn't express

doubt or uncertainty but was more like a person sloughing off a heavy burden, freeing himself up to act. 'I want to start by following the barrier and seeing if there just happens to be some big gate. Maybe you walk through that gate and everyone's there, you know? My mom, your parents. Anna and Emma.'

'Teachers,' Astrid supplied.

'Don't ruin a happy picture,' Sam said.

'What happens if you do find a gate, Sam? You go through it? What happens to all the kids still in the FAYZ?'

'They get out, too.'

'You won't know for sure it's a gate unless you go through it. And once you do, there may not be a way back in.'

'Astrid, in five days I vacate. I poof. I dig a hole.'

'You have to think about yourself,' Astrid said without inflection.

Sam looked stricken. 'I don't think it's fair to –'

Whatever he had been about to say was lost because at that moment there were two noises in rapid succession. The first was a thump coming from outside. The second was Little Pete's screech.

Astrid ran for the door, burst through, and found Little Pete curled into a ball, shivering, howling, ready to launch a full-scale breakdown.

There was a rock on the plank floor beside him.

And standing on the sidewalk, laughing, were Panda, a Coates kid named Chris, and Quinn. Panda and Chris held baseball bats. Chris was also carrying a white trash bag. Inside the bag, just visible, was the logo of a new-model game player.

'Did you throw a rock at my brother?' Astrid yelled, fearless in her outrage. She dropped to her knees beside Little Pete.

Sam was halfway across the lawn, moving with a purposeful stride.

'What did you do, Panda?'

'He was ignoring me,' Panda said.

'Panda was just goofing, Sam,' Quinn said. He stepped between Sam and Panda.

'Throwing a rock at a defenceless little kid is just goofing?' Sam demanded. 'And what are you doing hanging with this creep, anyway?'

'Who you calling a creep?' Panda demanded. He took a tighter grip on his baseball bat, but not really like he meant to start swinging.

'Who do I call a creep? Anyone who throws a rock at a little kid,' Sam said, not backing down.

Quinn raised his hands, playing the peacemaker. 'Look, take a breath, brah. We were just on a little mission for Mother Mary. She drafted Panda and sent him to look for some little kid's stuffed bear, OK? We were doing a good thing.'

'Doing good and stealing someone's stuff?' Sam pointed at the trash bag in Chris's grip. 'And on the way back, you figured you'd throw a rock and hit an autistic kid?'

'Hey, step off,' Quinn said. 'We're bringing the game to Mary so she has something for the kids to do.'

Little Pete was screaming in Astrid's ear now, so she couldn't hear everything that was said, just snatches of angry words between an increasingly huffy Quinn and a coldly furious Sam.

Then Sam spun on his heel and stalked back towards her and Quinn gave him the finger behind his back and sauntered off down the street with Panda and the Coates kid.

Sam threw himself violently into a porch chair. For the ten minutes it took Astrid to soothe her little brother and redirect him to his video game, Sam just seethed.

'He's becoming useless. Worse than useless,' Sam said. Then, relenting, he said, 'We'll get past it.'

'You mean you and Quinn?'

'Yeah.'

Astrid considered just keeping her mouth shut, not pushing it. But this was a talk she needed to have with Sam sooner or later. 'I don't think he's going to get over it.'

'You don't know him that well.'

'He's jealous of you.'

'Well, of course I am so terribly handsome,' Sam said, straining to make a joke of it.

'He's one kind of person, you're another. When life is going along normally, you're sort of the same. But when life turns strange and scary, when there's a crisis, suddenly you're completely different people. It's not Quinn's fault, really, but he's not brave. He's not strong. You are.'

'You still want me to be the big hero.'

'I want you to be who you are.' She remained beside Little

235

Pete but reached out to take Sam's hand. 'Sam, things are going to get worse. Right now everyone is kind of in a state of shock. They're scared. But they haven't even realised how scared they should be. Sooner or later the food supply runs out. Sooner or later the power plant fails. When we're sitting in the dark, hungry, despairing, who's going to be in charge? Caine? Orc? Drake?'

'Well,' he said drily, 'you make it all sound like a lot of fun.'

'OK, I'll stop nagging you,' Astrid said, sensing that she needed to back off. She was asking the impossible of this boy she barely knew. But she knew it was the right thing to do.

She believed in him. She knew he had a destiny.

She wondered why. It wasn't logical, really. She didn't believe in destiny. All her life Astrid had relied on her brain, on her grasp of facts. Now some part of her she barely knew existed, some buried, neglected part of her mind, was urging her on – no good reasons, just an instinct that kept pushing her to push him.

But she was sure.

Sure.

Astrid turned towards Little Pete so that Sam wouldn't see the frown of worry on her face, but she didn't release his hand.

She was sure. Like she was answering two plus two. That sure.

She let go of his hand. She took a deep, shaky breath. And now she was not sure at all. Her frown deepened. 'Let's go get the groceries,' Astrid said.

He was elsewhere, preoccupied, so he didn't notice the way

Astrid stared at her own hands, face screwed up in concentration.
She wiped her palms on her shorts.

'Yeah,' he said. 'Better go while we still can.'

TWENTY ONE

'**SHOW** ME YOUR list,' Howard demanded. He was outside the front door of Ralph's grocery, seated in a lawn chair, with his feet propped up on a second chair. He had a small combo TV/DVD playing *Spider-Man 3*. He barely looked up as they approached.

'I don't have a list,' Astrid said.

Howard shrugged. 'You need a list. No one goes in without a list.'

Sam said, 'OK, do you have a piece of paper and a pencil?'

'It just so happens I do, Sam,' Howard said. He fished a small spiral notebook from the pocket of an ill-fitting leather jacket and handed it to Astrid.

She wrote and handed it to Howard.

'You can have all the fresh stuff, like produce, that you want. It's all going to go bad. Ice cream is mostly gone, but there might be some Popsicles.' He glanced at Little Pete. 'You like the Popsicles, Pe-tard?'

'Get on with it,' Sam said.

'If you want canned stuff or, like, pasta or whatever, you have to get special permission from Caine or one of the sheriffs.'

'What are you talking about?' Astrid demanded.

'I'm talking about you can have lettuce and eggs and deli and milk because that's all going to expire soon, but we're saving up the stuff like canned soup or whatever that won't spoil.'

Astrid admitted, 'OK, that makes sense, I guess.'

'Likewise paper products. Everyone gets one roll of toilet paper. So make it last.' He glanced at the list again. 'Tampons? What size?'

'Shut up,' Sam said.

Howard laughed. 'Go ahead on in. But I'll check everything on the way out, and if it's not OK, I'll make you put it back.'

The store was a mess. Before Caine had posted a guard, it had been looted of almost all the snack foods. And the kids who had looted had not been neat or careful. There were broken jars of mayonnaise, displays turned over, shattered glass from smashed freezer doors.

There were flies everywhere. The place had begun to smell like garbage. Some of the overhead lights had burned out, leaving pockets of gloom. Brightly coloured posters still hung over their heads touting specials and price reductions.

Sam grabbed a cart and Astrid lifted Little Pete into the seat.

The flowers in the little florist's corner were all looking tired. A dozen Mylar balloons with 'Happy Birthday' or Thanksgiving messages on them still floated but were losing altitude.

'Maybe I should get a turkey,' Astrid said, looking at the display of Thanksgiving-related food: pumpkin pie mix, mincemeat, cranberry sauce, turkey basters, stuffing.

'You know how to cook a turkey?'

'I can find instructions online.' She sighed. 'Or not. Maybe they have a cookbook around.'

'I guess no cranberry sauce.'

'Nothing canned.'

Sam walked ahead into the produce section, then stopped, realising Astrid was still staring at the seasonal display. She was crying.

'Hey, what's the matter?'

Astrid brushed at her tears, but more came. 'Grocery shopping was always something the three of us did, my mom and Petey and me. It was a time every week when we could talk. You know, we'd shop kind of slowly and discuss what to eat and talk about other stuff, too. Just casually. I've never been in here without my mom before.'

'Me neither.'

'It feels weird. It looks the same, but it's not.'

'Nothing's the same any more,' Sam said. 'But people still need to eat.'

That earned a reluctant smile from Astrid. 'OK. Let's shop.'

They picked up lettuce and carrots and potatoes. Sam went behind the counter to lift a pair of steaks and wrap them up in paper. Flies were thick on some cuts of meat that had been left out when the butchers disappeared. But the meat from inside the case seemed untouched.

'Anything else, ma'am?' he asked.

'Well, since no one else is taking them, I might as well take that roast.'

Sam leaned down to look in the display. 'OK, I give up. Which one is a roast?'

'The big thing there.' She tapped the glass. 'I can put it in the freezer.'

'Of course. The roast.' Sam lifted it out and slapped it down on a sheet of waxed butcher's paper. 'You realise it's, like, twelve dollars a pound or whatever?'

'Put it on my tab.'

They moved on to the dairy case. And there was Panda, standing nervously and holding his bat at the ready.

'You again?' Sam snapped.

Panda didn't answer.

Astrid screamed.

Sam turned, saw just a flash of Drake Merwin before something hit the side of his head. He staggered into a shelf of Parmesan cheese, knocking the green bottles everywhere.

He saw a bat swinging, tried to block it, but his head was swimming and his eyes would not focus.

His knees collapsed and he hit the floor.

As if from far off he saw kids moving quickly, four or five, maybe. Two grabbed Astrid and held her hands behind her.

There was a girl's voice, one Sam didn't recognise until he heard Panda say, 'Diana.'

'Bag his hands,' Diana said.

Sam resisted but he didn't have control of his muscles.

MICHAEL GRANT

Something went over his left hand, then his right. Strong fingers held him securely.

When he could focus at last he stared stupidly at what had been done. His wrists were lashed together with a plastic tie. And around each hand was a deflated Mylar balloon, duct-taped in place.

Diana Ladris knelt down, bringing her face to his level. 'It's Mylar. It's a reflective surface. So I wouldn't try to turn on your mojo, Sam: you'd fry your own hands.'

'What are you doing?' Sam slurred.

'Your brother wants to have a nice conversation with you.'

That made no sense and Sam wasn't sure he'd heard right. The only person he ever called 'brother' was Quinn. 'Let Astrid go,' Sam said.

Drake moved past Diana and kicked Sam on to his back, legs twisted beneath him. Drake stood over him and pushed the end of his bat down against Sam's Adam's apple. The same move he had used on Orc the night before. 'If you're a good little boy, we'll be nice to your girlfriend and her retarded brother. If you cause trouble, I'll mess her up.'

Little Pete had begun his wind-up to a full howl.

'Shut that kid up or I'll shut him up for you,' Drake snapped at Astrid. Then, to Howard, Panda, and the others, he said, 'Grab the big hero here and throw him in a grocery cart.'

Sam was lifted and dropped into a cart.

Howard was the one pushing. 'Sammy, Sammy, Sammy. School Bus Sam is Grocery Cart Sam now, huh?'

Drake leaned over and the last thing Sam saw was a

strip of duct tape coming down over his eyes.

They pushed him down the highway in the grocery cart. They pushed him through town. He couldn't see but he could feel the bumps. And he could hear the laughter and taunts of Howard and Panda.

Sam tried to make sense of the route, tried to figure out where they were going. After what seemed like a long time he could feel that they were going uphill.

Howard began to complain. 'Man, somebody help me push this thing. Yo, Freddie, man, help me out.'

The cart accelerated for a while, then slowed again. Sam could hear heavy breathing.

'Get some of these people just standing around,' Freddie demanded.

'Yeah. Hey, you: come here and help me push this cart.'

'No, man. No way.'

Quinn. Sam's heart leaped. Quinn would help.

The cart came to a stop.

Howard said, 'What, you afraid your boy here will find out what you've been up to?'

'Shut up, man,' Quinn said.

'Sammy, who do you think gave us the heads-up you were going shopping with Astrid? Huh?'

'Shut up, Howard,' Quinn said, sounding desperate.

'Who do you think told us about your powers, Sam?'

'I didn't know they were going to do this,' Quinn said. 'I didn't know, brah.'

Sam found he wasn't even surprised. But still, Quinn's betrayal hurt more than anything Drake had done to him. He wanted to yell at Quinn. He wanted to call him a Judas. But yelling, shouting, crying would make him seem weak.

'I didn't know, brother, I'm telling you the truth,' Quinn said.

'Yeah. You thought maybe we just wanted to hold a meeting of the Sam Temple fan club,' Howard said, and laughed at his own wit. 'Now grab on and push.'

The cart started moving again.

Sam felt sick inside. Quinn had betrayed him. Astrid was with Drake and Diana. And there was nothing he could do.

It seemed to take forever. But finally they stopped.

Without warning the cart tipped over and Sam landed on pavement. He rolled over on to his hands and knees and tried to surreptitiously scrape the Mylar against the concrete.

The kick to his ribs knocked the wind out of him.

'Hey,' Quinn yelled. 'You don't have to be kicking him.'

Hands grabbed Sam by the arms and then he heard Orc's voice. 'You make any trouble, I'll beat you down.'

They marched him, stumbling, up a set of steps. There was a door, large from the sound of it. Then their feet echoed on polished linoleum.

They paused. Another door opened. Sam was marched through. Orc kicked him in the back of the knees and he fell face down.

Orc straddled his back, grabbed his hair, and pulled his head back sharply.

'Take the tape off,' a voice commanded.

Howard picked at the edge of the tape, got a hold, and ripped it off, taking part of Sam's eyebrows with it.

Sam recognised his surroundings immediately. The school gym.

He was on the polished wood floor with Caine standing calmly before him, arms crossed, gloating.

'Hey, Sam,' Caine said.

Sam swivelled his head to left and right. Orc, Panda, Howard, Freddie, and Chaz all armed with baseball bats. Quinn tried to shrink out of sight.

'You have a lot of guys, Caine. I must be dangerous.'

Caine nodded thoughtfully. 'I like to be careful. Of course, Drake has your girlfriend. So if I was you, I wouldn't try to cause any trouble. Drake is a violent, disturbed boy.'

Howard laughed.

'Let him up,' Caine ordered.

Orc climbed off Sam's back but not without digging a knee into his ribs first. Sam stood, shaky, but glad to be off the floor.

He studied Caine closely.

Caine studied him just as closely.

'What is it you want with me?' Sam asked.

Caine started to chew at his thumb, then put his hands down by his side so that he looked almost as if he were standing at attention. 'I wish there was some way we could be friends, Sam.'

'I can see you're dying to be my new homey.'

Caine laughed. 'See? You have a sense of humour. That wouldn't have come from your mother. She never seemed very funny to me. Maybe it came from your father?'

'I wouldn't know.'

'No? Why not?'

'You have my mother's laptop. You have all her personal papers. And you have Quinn answering questions about me. So I'm guessing you already know the answer.'

Caine nodded. 'Yes. Your father disappeared soon after you were born. I guess he wasn't too impressed with you, huh?' Caine laughed at his own joke, and some of his toadies joined in half-heartedly, not really getting it. 'Well, don't feel bad. As it happens, my biological father disappeared, too. And my mother.'

Sam didn't answer. His hands were numb from the plastic tie. He was scared but determined not to show it.

'You're not supposed to wear street shoes on the gym floor,' Sam said.

'So, your father disappears and you don't even want to know why?' Caine asked. 'Interesting. Me, I've always wanted to know who my real parents were.'

'Let me guess: you're secretly a wizard who was raised by muggles.'

Caine's smile was cold. He raised his hand, palm out. An invisible fist hit Sam in the face. He staggered back. He barely stopped himself from falling, but his head was reeling. Blood leaked from his nose.

'Yeah. Kind of,' Caine said.

He extended both hands and Sam felt himself rising off the floor.

Caine raised him about three feet, then laced his fingers together and Sam fell hard.

Sam picked himself up slowly. His left leg was wobbly. His ankle felt sprained.

'We have a system for measuring the power,' Caine said. 'Diana came up with it, actually. She can read people if she holds their hands, she can tell how much they have. She describes it as being like a cell phone signal. One bar, two bars, three bars. You know what I am?'

'Crazy?' Sam spat out the blood that ran down into his mouth.

'Four bars, Sam. I'm the only one she's ever read who has four bars. I could pick you up, fly you into the ceiling, or slam you against a wall.' He illustrated his point with hand motions that made it look as if he were doing a hula dance.

'You could get work with a circus,' Sam said brightly.

'Oooh, tough guy.' Caine seemed annoyed that Sam hadn't responded with awe.

'Look, Caine, my hands are tied, you've got five of your thugs standing around me with baseball bats, and I'm supposed to be terrified because you can do magic tricks?' Sam made the count 'five' rather than 'six'. He wasn't about to count Quinn as anything.

Caine registered the omission and shot a suspicious glance at Quinn. Quinn still looked like a kid who didn't know where to stand or what to do with himself.

'And one of those five,' Sam said, 'is a murderer. A murderer and a bunch of cowards. That's your posse, Caine.'

Caine's eyes went wide. He bared his teeth, furious, and suddenly Sam was flying across the room.

Flying like he'd been shot out of a catapult.

The gym spun around him.

He hit the basketball hoop hard, head smashing into the glass. He hung for a moment from the hoop and then fell on to his back.

He was dragged by unseen hands of terrifying strength, like he'd been swept back by a tornado. He came to rest at Caine's feet.

He was slow getting back up this time. The flow from his nose had been joined by a trickle of blood from his forehead.

'Several of us developed strange powers, starting a few months ago,' Caine said conversationally. 'We were like a secret club. Frederico, Andrew, Dekka, Brianna, some others. We worked together to develop them. Encouraged each other. See, that's the difference between Coates people and you townies. In a boarding school it's hard to keep secrets. But soon it became clear that my powers were of a whole different order. What I just did to you? No one else could do that.'

'Yeah, that was cool,' Sam said with shaky defiance. 'Can you do it again?'

'He's baiting you.' It was Diana coming into the room and obviously not happy with what she was seeing.

'He's trying to prove he's tough,' Caine snapped.

'Yes. And he's proved it. Move on.'

'Watch how you talk to me, Diana,' Caine grated.

Diana sauntered over to stand beside Caine. She crossed her arms over her chest and shook her head at Sam in mock dismay. 'Well, you look pretty bad, Sam.'

'He'll look worse,' Caine threatened.

Diana sighed. 'Here's the deal, Sam. Caine wants some answers from you.'

'Why not ask Quinn?'

'Because he doesn't know the answers, but you do, so here's the thing: if you don't answer Fearless Leader's questions, Drake is going to start beating on Astrid. And just so you know: Drake is sick in the head. I'm not saying that to scare you, I'm saying it because it's true. I'm a bad girl, Caine has delusions of grandeur, but Drake is flat-out sick in the head. He could kill her, Sam. And he's going to start up in five minutes unless I go back and tell him not to. So, tick-tock.'

Sam swallowed blood and bile. 'What questions?'

Diana rolled her eyes and turned to Caine. 'See how easy that was?'

Amazingly, Caine took it from Diana. No threats, no attack on her, just seething and resentment and acceptance.

He's in love with her, Sam realised with a shock. The times he had seen them together there had never been any outward sign of affection, but there was no other possible answer.

Caine said, 'Tell me about your father.'

Sam shrugged, a painful move that made him wince. 'He

wasn't a part of my life. All I know is, my mom didn't like talking about him.'

'Your mother. Nurse Temple.'

'Yeah.'

'The name on your birth certificate, where it has father's name? It says "Taegan Smith".'

'OK.'

'Taegan. A very unusual name. Very rare.'

'So what?'

'Whereas "Smith" is really common. It's a name a man might use who wanted to hide his real name.'

'Look, I'm answering your questions, let Astrid go.'

'Taegan,' Caine repeated. 'Right there on the birth certificate. Mother: Constance Temple. Father: Taegan Smith. Date of birth: November the twenty-second. Time of birth: ten twelve p.m. Sierra Vista Regional Medical.'

'So now you can do my horoscope.'

'You're not interested in any of this?'

Sam sighed. 'I'm interested in what's going on. Why the FAYZ happened. How we make it stop, or else how we escape from it. On the big list of things to worry about, my biological father, who I never knew, who wasn't anything to me, is way down that list.'

'You bug out in five days, Sam. Interested in that?'

'Let Astrid go.'

Diana said, 'Come on, Caine. Get on with it.'

Caine smirked. 'I'm very interested in the question of

disappearing. You know why? Because I don't want to die. And I don't want to suddenly find myself back in the world. I like it here in the FAYZ.'

'Is that what you think happens? We jump back into the world?'

'I'm asking the questions,' Caine snapped.

'Let Astrid go.'

'The point is,' Caine continued, 'you and I share something in common, Sam. We were born just three minutes apart.'

Sam felt a tingle go up his spine.

'Three minutes,' Caine said, moving closer. 'You go first. And then me.'

'No,' Sam said. 'It can't be.'

'It can,' Caine said. 'It is. And you are . . . brother.'

The door burst open. Drake Merwin barrelled into the room. He was looking for something. 'Is she here?'

'Who?' Diana demanded.

'Who do you think? The blonde and her retard brother.'

'You let her get away?' Caine demanded, forgetting Sam for the moment.

'I didn't let her get away. They were in the room with me. The girl was pissing me off so I smacked her. Then they disappeared. Gone.'

Caine shot a murderous look at Diana. Diana said, 'No. She was months away from turning fifteen. And, anyway, her little brother is four.'

'Then how?' Caine furrowed his brow. 'Can it be the power?'

Diana shook her head. 'I read Astrid again on the way here. She's barely at two bars. No way. Two people teleporting?'

The colour drained from Caine's face. 'The retard?'

'He's autistic, he's like in his own world,' Diana protested.

'Did you read him?'

'He's a little autistic kid, why would I read him?'

Caine turned to Sam. 'What do you know about this?' He raised his hand, a threat. His face inches from Sam's, he screamed, 'What do you know?'

'Well. I know that I enjoy seeing you scared, Caine.'

The invisible fist sent Sam sprawling on his back.

Diana, for the first time, looked worried. Her usual smirk was gone. 'The only time we saw teleporting was Taylor up at Coates. And she could only go across a room. She was a three. If this kid can teleport himself and his sister through walls . . .'

'He could be a four,' Caine said softly.

'Yes,' Diana said. 'He could be a four.' When she said the word 'four', she looked straight at Sam. 'He could be even more.'

Caine said, 'Orc, Howard: lock Sam up, tie him down so he can't get that Mylar off his hands, then get Freddie to help you. He's done plastering before, he knows what to do. Get whatever you need from the hardware store.' He grabbed Drake by the shoulder. 'Find Astrid and that kid.'

'How am I going to catch them if they can just zap out whenever they want?'

'I didn't say catch them,' Caine said. 'Take a gun, Drake. Shoot them both before they see you.'

Sam charged at Caine and ploughed into him before he could react. The momentum carried them both to the floor. Sam headbutted Caine in the nose. Caine was slow to recover, but Drake and Orc swarmed over Sam and kicked him off Caine.

Sam groaned in pain. 'You can't kill people, Caine. Are you crazy?'

'You hurt my nose,' Caine said.

'You're screwed up, Caine. You need help. You're insane.'

'Yeah,' Caine said, touching his nose and wincing at the pain. 'That's what they keep telling me. It's what Nurse Temple . . . Mom . . . told me. Just be glad I need to keep you around, Sam. I need to see you blink out, figure out how to keep it from happening to me. Orc, take this hero away. Drake, go.'

'If you hurt them, Drake, I'll hunt you down and kill you,' Sam shouted.

'Don't waste your breath,' Diana said to him. 'You don't know Drake. Your girlfriend's as good as dead.'

ASTRID WANTED TO scream at Drake and Diana, to denounce them, to demand to know what kind of worthless human beings used the FAYZ as an excuse for violence.

But she had to keep Little Pete calm. That was her top priority, her brother. Her blank-faced, helpless, unloving brother.

She resented him. He had turned her into a mother at age fourteen. It wasn't right. This should be her time to shine, to be bold. This was her time to use her intellect, that supposedly great gift. Instead, she was a babysitter.

Astrid and Little Pete were shown, with mock courtesy, into a classroom. It wasn't one of Astrid's classes but might as well have been. Everything was achingly familiar: books open on desks, walls festooned with student artwork and projects.

'Have a seat. Read a book, if you want,' Diana said. 'I know you like that kind of thing.'

Astrid hefted one of the books. 'Yes, fourth-grade math. I love that kind of thing.'

'You know, I really dislike you,' Diana said.

Drake leaned against a wall and smirked.

'Of course you dislike me,' Astrid said. 'I make you feel inferior.'

Diana's eyes flashed. 'I don't feel inferior to anyone.'

'Really? Because usually a person who does bad things recognises that there's something a little wrong with them. You know? Even if they suppress it, they know they're sick inside.'

'Yeah,' Diana said laconically. 'I feel bad about that. My evil heart and all. Give me your hand.'

'What?'

'I promise not to infect you with my badness. Give me your hand.'

'No.'

'Drake. Make her give me her hand.'

Drake came off the wall.

Astrid stuck out her hand. Diana took it in hers and held it.

'You read people,' Astrid said. 'I should have figured it out earlier. You have the power, don't you?' She looked at Diana like she was looking at a specimen in a laboratory.

'Yep,' Diana said, releasing her. 'I read people. But don't worry, I just read power levels, not your secret little thoughts about how much you want to make out with Sam Temple.'

Astrid flushed, despite herself. Diana laughed at her.

'Oh, please, that's obvious. He's cute. He's brave. He's smart, but not as smart as you. He's perfect.'

'He's a friend,' Astrid said.

'Uh-huh. Well, we're about to find out how good a friend he is. He knows we have you. If he doesn't tell Caine everything

Caine wants to know, and do whatever Caine tells him to do, Drake here is going to hurt you.'

Astrid's insides turned to jelly. 'What?'

Diana sighed. 'Well, that's why we keep Drake around. He enjoys hurting people. We don't keep him around for his conversational skills.'

Drake looked like he'd rather take a shot at Diana. His narrow lizard eyes narrowed further. Diana didn't miss his expression.

'Go ahead, raise a hand against me, Drake,' Diana taunted. 'Caine would kill you.' To Astrid, she said, 'Better behave yourself, he's all riled up now.'

Diana left.

Astrid felt Drake's eyes on her but she couldn't look at him. She kept her gaze down on the math book. Then glanced at her brother, who sat playing his stupid game, unable, unwilling, uncaring.

Astrid felt ashamed of her own fear. Ashamed that she couldn't look at the thug who leaned insouciantly against the wall.

She had no doubt that Sam would do his best to save her. But Caine might ask for something Sam couldn't give.

She needed to think. She needed to work out a plan. She was scared, she always had been scared of physical violence. She was scared of the emptiness she sensed in Drake Merwin.

She scooted her desk up beside Little Pete's and put a hand on his shoulder. No reaction. He knew she was there, but he showed nothing, absorbed in his game.

Still not looking at Drake, Astrid said, 'Doesn't it bother you that Diana treats you like some wild animal she keeps on a leash?'

Drake said, 'Doesn't it bother you going around with that retard? Having a little 'tard practically attached to you?'

'He's not retarded,' Astrid said evenly.

'Oh. Is that the wrong word? "Retard"?'

'He's autistic.'

'Retarded,' Drake insisted.

Astrid looked at him. She willed herself to meet his gaze. '"Retarded" is a word people don't use any more. When they did use it, they used it to signify an impairment of intelligence. Petey is not intellectually impaired in that way. He has at least normal IQ, and may have a higher than normal IQ. So the word doesn't apply.'

'Yeah? Huh. Because I like the word "retard". In fact, I'd like to hear you say it. Retard.'

Astrid felt dread sap her strength. There was not the slightest doubt in her mind that he meant to hurt her. She held his gaze for a while but then looked down.

'Retard,' Drake insisted. 'Say it.'

'No,' Astrid whispered.

Drake sauntered across the room. He was not carrying a weapon. He didn't need to. He placed his fists on her desk and leaned over her.

'Retard,' Drake said. 'Say, "My brother is a retard."'

Astrid didn't trust herself to speak. She was choking back

tears. She wanted to believe she was brave, but now, with the thug inches away from her, she knew that she was not.

'My. Brother. Come on, say it with me. My. Say it.'

The slap was so quick, she barely registered his hand moving. Her face burned.

'Say it. My . . .'

'My,' she whispered.

'Louder, I want the little retard to hear it. My brother is a retard.'

The second slap was so hard, she almost fell from the chair.

'You can say it while your face is still pretty, or you can say it after I've smashed it in – your choice. My brother is a retard.'

'My brother is a retard,' Astrid said, her voice shaking.

Drake laughed delightedly and crossed to Little Pete, who had looked up from his video game and seemed almost to register what was happening. Drake put his face into Little Pete's space and with one hand yanked Astrid by the hair so that her mouth was close to Little Pete's ear and said, 'One more time, nice and loud.' He pushed Astrid's face against the side of Little Pete's head and yelled, 'My brother is –'

And Astrid fell back on her bed.

Her bed. Her bedroom.

Little Pete was in the window seat, cross-legged on the bench, video game in his hand.

Astrid knew immediately what had happened. But it was still impossibly disorienting. One second in the school, the next in her room.

She couldn't look at him. Her face burned from the slaps, but even more from shame.

'Thanks, Petey,' she whispered.

Orc dragged Sam from the gym into the weight room.

Howard looked around, considering what he should do.

'Howard, man, you can't be down with this,' Sam pleaded. 'You can't be OK with Caine killing Astrid and Little Pete. Orc, even you can't be OK with this. You didn't mean to kill Bette. This is way over the line.'

'Yeah. It is over the line,' Howard admitted, preoccupied, his mouth twisted quizzically to one side.

'You have to help me. Let me go after Drake.'

'I don't think so, Sammy. See, I've seen what kind of stuff Drake can do. And we've both seen what kind of stuff Caine can do.' To Orc, Howard said, 'Let's put him here on this bench. Face-up. We'll tie his legs to the upright here.'

Orc lifted Sam and slammed him down on to the weight bench.

'Orc, this is going to be cold-blooded murder,' Sam said.

'Not me, man,' Orc said. 'I'm just tying you up.'

'Drake is going to murder Astrid. She helped you get through math. You can stop this, Orc.'

'She wasn't supposed to tell anyone about that,' Orc grumbled. 'Anyway, no more math class.'

They used rope to lash his ankles to the legs of the bench. They tied another rope around his waist.

'OK, now here's the good part,' Howard said. 'We load some weight on the bar. We tie Sam's hands to the bar and lower it down on the slide, right? He'll be busy keeping the bar up off his neck.'

Orc was slow to understand, so Howard showed him. Then Orc piled weight plates on to the bar.

'What can you bench-press, Sam?' Howard asked. 'I'd say put on two forty-fives on each end, right? With the bar, that makes it two hundred pounds.'

'No way he presses two hundred,' Orc opined.

'I think you're right, Orc. I think he's going to be busy just keeping that bar from choking him.'

'This isn't right, Howard,' Sam said. 'You know it isn't right. You don't do stuff like this, either of you. You're bullies, you're not cold-blooded killers.'

Howard sighed. 'Sammy, it's a whole different world, haven't you noticed? It's the FAYZ, man.'

Orc lowered the weight. The bar rested on Sam's bound wrists, which pressed down against his Adam's apple. He pushed upward with all his strength, but on his best day he couldn't lift two hundred pounds. All he could do was keep up enough upward pressure to keep breathing.

Orc laughed and said, 'Come on, man, we better get back to Caine before we miss more fun.'

Howard followed Orc but paused at the door. 'It's kind of weird, Sam. That first night, man, I thought, "Old School Bus Sam, he's going to be running things soon if we don't look out."

Everyone was looking to you. You know that. But no, you were too cool to play it that way. Off you go without a word to anyone, off with Astrid.' He laughed. 'Of course, she is hot, isn't she? And now Caine's running the FAYZ and Drake's going to take out your girlfriend.'

Sam struggled against the weight, but there was no way to lift it. Even if he'd had a good angle on it, he could not have hefted it.

But Howard, for all his cleverness, had overlooked one thing: in this position, Sam could reach the Mylar with his teeth.

He tried to rip at the fabric, but it was slow work and he had no time. He had no doubt that Little Pete had teleported himself and Astrid to their home. Drake would find them there.

Sam tried to get the Mylar between his teeth, but it was slippery and tough. And when he focused on that, he lost focus on keeping the weight off his neck.

The bar pressed his knuckles into his throat. He pushed upward, but already his arms were cramping. His muscles were weakening.

He could tear at the Mylar and free his hands, or he could keep the bar from choking him. It was impossible to do both.

And even if he did free his hands, so what? He wasn't like Caine. He didn't have control of his powers. He might tear the Mylar and then be unable to do anything.

The bar slipped lower.

He had the Mylar between his teeth.

He chewed it, trying to make a small hole he could enlarge.

By now, Drake would be out of the school and on the move. Would he have to stop somewhere first to retrieve the gun?

Astrid would know they were going to come after her. She would know it would be dangerous to stay in her house. Would she move fast enough?

And where could she go?

Sam felt the grind of tooth on tooth. He had made a hole.

But he was gasping for breath.

He barely noticed the door opening.

Quick steps on the carpet and the sound and feel of one of the weight plates sliding off the bar. Sam took a breath.

'Hang on, brah.'

Quinn slid the rest of the weights from the bar.

With quaking arms, Sam pushed the bar up off his neck.

'I didn't know they would do this, brah, I didn't know, man,' Quinn said. He was pale. Like he'd never ever seen the sun. 'You gotta believe me, Sam.' He was working at the ropes. Sam sat up.

Quinn was a wreck. He had been crying, and his eyes were red and puffy.

'Honest to God, I didn't know.'

'I have to get to Astrid before Drake does,' Sam said.

'I know. I know. This is messed up.'

With his legs free, Sam stood. 'Is this another trick? Are they going to follow me to Astrid?'

'No, man. They'll beat me up if they find out I let you go.' Quinn spread his hands, pleading. 'You have to take me with you.'

'How am I supposed to trust you, Quinn?'

'If you leave me here, what do you think Caine is going to do to me?'

Sam had no time for argument. He decided quickly. 'You'd better pray Astrid doesn't get hurt, Quinn. If you're doing this to sell me out, you better make sure I'm dead, too.'

Quinn licked his lips nervously. 'You don't have to threaten me, brah.'

'Don't call me brah,' Sam said. 'I'm not your brother.'

TWENTY THREE

ASTRID FELT A wave of relief followed by a far stronger wave of self-loathing. She had let Drake terrorise her. She had called Little Pete a retard.

Her hands were trembling. She had betrayed her brother. She hated him for being what he was, for being so needy, and she had betrayed him to spare herself. And now she was far more angry at herself than she had ever been at him.

But now she had to think. Quick. What to do?

Drake would catch her again. Surely Caine or that wicked creature Diana would figure out what had happened.

It would take only a few seconds for Drake to run to report to them. A few seconds more for Caine to realise what had happened. If Diana really could read the power in people, she would know it wasn't Astrid who had teleported them. She would know it was Little Pete.

She and Little Pete had to go. Now. But where?

Somewhere Drake wouldn't look. Somewhere Sam might look.

If he escaped.

If he was even alive.

Her brain was moving in slow motion, spinning in circles,

264

unable to focus. She kept seeing that terrible, sick face, feeling the sharp sting of his hand, the way the heat of it lingered and joined with the hot blush of shame.

'Think, you idiot,' she berated herself. 'Think. It's all you're good at.'

They couldn't go through town. They couldn't take a car – it was too late to start teaching herself to drive.

Her mind was an out-of-focus camera, turning and swirling and coming back again and again to the moment when the fear took over, when she couldn't resist any more, when she betrayed her brother. Over and over a loop in her head played the words 'My brother is a retard.'

Clifftop.

The room they had shared there that first night.

Yes. Sam would figure it out. But Quinn had been there, too. He might reach the same conclusion.

Astrid hesitated. No time for hesitation. Drake wouldn't hesitate. By now, he was already after them. He was already on his way.

She couldn't face him again.

'Petey, we have to go.' Astrid grabbed his hand and drew him after her. Down the stairs. No time to stop for anything. No time at all.

To the front door. No. Back door was better.

They walked – Little Pete could seldom be induced to run – across the backyard. The natural-wood fence was fairly low, but still it was exhausting and time-consuming getting Little

265

Pete to scale it. They ran through the neighbour's backyard.

'Stay off the streets,' she told herself.

They went as far as they could, backyard to backyard, then dodged into the street when their way was blocked, and then back to yards and alleyways again.

They saw no one. But there was no way to know if they were being watched.

They reached the hill that marked the edge of town and the beginning of the Clifftop grounds. They scrambled up through shrubbery clinging to sand. Astrid pulled Little Pete along, desperate to move quickly, but afraid to do anything to set him off.

Clifftop had not changed. The barrier was still there. The lobby was still clean, still bright, still empty.

Astrid had the electronic key they'd made on that first night. She found the suite, opened the door, and collapsed inside on to the bed.

She lay there, panting, staring up at the blank ceiling. The bed was soft. The air-conditioning hummed.

She could explain away the words Drake had put in her mouth. They were meaningless words. Just words. Little Pete didn't care.

But she could not explain away the fear. It shamed her.

She put a cold hand to her face, to see if it really was as hot as it was in her imagination.

'Where are we going, Sam?' Quinn asked anxiously. They

were moving at an easy lope, not an all-out run, but a jog they could sustain.

Sam was leading them straight through town, straight through the plaza, as if indifferent to pursuit.

'We're going to find Astrid before Drake does,' Sam said.

'Let's go check her house.'

'No. The good thing about a genius is, you don't have to wonder if she's doing the stupid thing. She'll know she has to get out of her house.'

'Where would she go?'

Sam thought for a moment. 'Power plant.'

'The power plant?'

'Yeah. So we're going to grab a boat and head up the coast.'

'OK. But, brah . . . I mean, dude, shouldn't we be a little more sneaky instead of just running right through town?'

Sam didn't answer him. Part of the reason he was going in a straight line rather than being sneaky was that he hoped to pick up Edilio at the fire station. The other was that he needed to know whether Quinn would betray him the first chance he got.

And there was a matter of tactics that Sam understood intuitively: Caine had more power, so Sam would need more speed. The longer he let the game go on, the more likely it was that Caine would win.

They reached the fire station. Edilio was sitting in the cab of the fire engine with the engine running. He spotted Sam and Quinn and leaned out of the window. 'Good timing, man, I'm going to try it out, take it on a . . .' He fell silent when he saw Sam's blood-streaked face.

'Edilio. Come on. We have to go.'

'OK, man, just let me get –'

'No. I mean right now. Drake's looking for Astrid. He's going to kill her.'

Edilio jumped down from the fire engine. 'Where to?'

'The marina. We're going to take a boat. I think Astrid will head for the power plant.'

The three of them jogged towards the marina. Sam knew that Orc and Howard were up at the school with Caine. Drake was on his way to Astrid's house. That would leave a few thugs still roaming loose, but Sam wasn't too worried about any of them.

They spotted Mallet and a Coates kid lounging on the steps of the town hall. Neither challenged them as they ran past.

The marina wasn't large, just forty slips, about half of them full. There was a dry dock, and the rattling, rusty, tin warehouse that had once been a cannery and now housed boat-repair shops. A lot of boats were up out of the water on blocks, looking ungainly and like a stiff breeze might topple them.

No one was there. No one was blocking their path.

'What do we take?' Sam wondered. He had reached his first goal, but he knew nothing about boats. He looked to Edilio and got a shrug.

'OK. Something that will carry five people. Motorboat. With a full tank of gas. Quinn, take the boats on the right, Edilio, left. I'll go to the end of the dock and work back. Go.'

They split up and started working their way along, jumping into each likely-looking boat, looking for keys, trying to figure out how to check the gas as time ticked away.

In his mind's eye Sam saw Drake searching Astrid's house. A gun in his hand. He would be slowed down a little by fear that Astrid and Little Pete would simply teleport again. Drake wouldn't know that Little Pete was not really in control of his powers, so he would try to be stealthy, he would be patient.

That was good. The more uncertainty Drake had, the slower he'd go.

Suddenly an engine roared to life. Sam jumped back on to the dock from the boat he'd been exploring. He raced back along the dock and found Quinn sitting proudly in a Boston Whaler, an open motorboat.

'She's gassed up,' Quinn said over the sluggish chugging of the engine.

'Good job, man,' Sam said. He jumped into the boat beside Quinn. 'Edilio, cast off.'

Edilio whipped the ropes off the cleats and jumped in. 'I gotta warn you, man: I get seasick.'

'Not our biggest problem, huh?' Sam said.

'I started it, but I don't know how to drive it,' Quinn said.

'Neither do I,' Sam admitted. 'But I guess I'm going to learn.'

'Hey. Hey.' It was Orc's booming voice. 'Don't you pull away.'

Orc, Howard, and Panda were at the end of the dock.

'Mallet,' Sam said. 'He saw us. He must have told them.'

The three bullies started running.

269

Sam looked frantically at the controls. The engine was chugging, the boat, unmoored, was drifting away from the dock, but too slowly. Even Orc could easily jump the gap.

'Throttle,' Edilio said, pointing at a red-tipped lever. 'That makes it go.'

'Yeah. Hang on.'

Sam moved the throttle up a notch. The boat surged forwards and slammed into a piling. Sam was knocked almost but not quite off his feet. Edilio snatched at the railing and held on tight. Quinn sat down hard in the bow.

The bow scraped past the piling and almost by accident ended up aimed towards open water.

'You might want to take it slow at first,' Edilio said.

'Stop! Stop that boat,' Orc yelled breathlessly, pounding down the dock. 'I'll beat your stupid head in.'

Sam steered – he hoped – in the right direction and chugged slowly away. There was no way Orc could clear the distance now.

'Caine will kill you,' Panda shouted.

'Quinn, you traitor,' Howard yelled.

'Tell them I made you do it,' Sam said.

'What?'

'Do it,' Sam hissed.

Quinn stood up, cupped his hands, and yelled, 'He made me do it.'

'Now tell them we're going to the power plant.'

'Dude.'

'Do it,' Sam insisted. 'And point.'

'We're heading to the power plant,' Quinn yelled. He pointed north.

Sam released the wheel, spun and landed a hard left hook into Quinn's face. Quinn sat down hard again.

'What the –'

'Had to make it look good,' Sam said. It was not an apology.

The boat was in the clear now. Sam raised his hand, middle finger extended, high above his head, moved the throttle up another notch, and turned north towards the power plant.

'What's the game?' Edilio asked, mystified. He stood well back from Sam, just in case Sam decided to punch him next.

'She won't be at the plant,' Sam said. 'She'll be at Clifftop. We're just going north as long as Orc is watching us.'

'You lied to me,' Quinn accused. He was playing with his chin, making sure his jaw was still attached.

'Yeah.'

'You didn't trust me.'

Orc, Howard, and Panda disappeared from view, presumably running back to town to report to Caine. As soon as he was sure they were gone, Sam spun the wheel, pushed the throttle all the way up, and headed south.

Drake lived in an empty house just off the plaza. It was less than a minute's walk away from the town hall. It once had belonged to a guy who lived alone. It was small, just two bedrooms, very neat, very organised, the way Drake liked things.

The guy, the homeowner, Drake forgot his name, had been a

gun owner. Three guns in all, a twenty-gauge over-under shotgun, a thirty-ought-six hunting rifle with a scope, and a nine-millimetre Glock semi-automatic pistol.

Drake kept all three guns loaded all the time. They were set out on the dining-room table, a display, something to be gazed at lovingly.

Now he hefted the rifle. The stock was as smooth as glass, polished to a high shine. It smelled of steel and oil. He was hesitant about taking the rifle because he'd never fired a long gun before. He had no real idea how to use the scope. But how hard could it be?

He slid into the leather strap and tested his shoulders for freedom of movement. The rifle was heavy, and a little long. The rubber-cushioned butt came down to the back of his thigh. But he could manage it.

Then he hefted the pistol. He squeezed the cross-hatched grip and wrapped his fingertip around the trigger. Drake loved the feel of this gun in his hand.

His father had taught him to shoot, using his service pistol. Drake still remembered the first time. The loading of shells into the clip. Sliding the clip into the butt of the gun. Ratcheting the slide to lift a round into place. Clicking the safety.

Click. Safe.

Click. Deadly.

He remembered the way his father had taught him to grip the butt firmly but not too tight. To rest his right hand in the palm of his left and sight carefully, to turn his body sideways to present a smaller target if someone was shooting back. His father had had to yell because they were both wearing ear protection.

'If you're target shooting, you centre the front sight in the notch of the rear sights. Raise it till your sights are sitting right under your target. Let your breath out slowly and squeeze.'

That first bang, the recoil, the way the gun jumped six inches, the smell of powder – it was all as clear in Drake's mind as any memory he had.

His first shot had completely missed the target.

Same with the second because after feeling the kick the first time, he had flinched in anticipation.

The third shot he had hit the target, catching just a piece of the lower corner.

He had shot up a box of ammo that first day and by the time he was done, he was hitting what he aimed at.

'What if I'm not shooting targets?' he'd asked his father. 'What if I'm shooting at a person?'

'Don't shoot a person,' his father had said. But then he relented, relieved no doubt to find something he could share with his disturbing son. 'Different people will tell you different techniques. But if it's me, say I'm doing a traffic stop and I think I see the citizen reaching for a weapon, and I'm thinking I may have to take a quick shot? I just point. Point like the barrel is a sixth finger. You point and if you have to fire, you shoot half the clip, bang, bang, bang, bang.'

'Why do you shoot so many times?'

'Because if you have to shoot, you shoot to kill. Situation like that, you're not aiming carefully for his head or his heart, you're pointing at the centre of mass and you're hoping you get a lucky shot, but if you don't, if all you're hitting is shoulder or belly, the sheer velocity of the rounds will still knock him down.'

Drake didn't think it would take six shots to kill Astrid.

He remembered with vivid, slow-motion detail the time he had shot Holden, the neighbour's kid who liked to come over and annoy him. That had been a bullet to the thigh, with a low-calibre gun, and still the kid had nearly died. That 'accident' had landed Drake at Coates.

He was holding a nine-millimetre Glock right now, less powerful than his father's forty-calibre Smith & Wesson, but a lot more gun than the target twenty-two he'd used on Holden.

One shot would do it. One for the snooty blonde, one for the retard. That would be cool. He would come back, give his report to Caine, and say, 'Two targets, two rounds.' That would wipe the smirk off Diana's face.

Astrid's house was not far. But the trick would be to get her before her little brother used the power to disappear again.

Drake hated the power. There was only one reason why Caine and not Drake was running the show: Caine's powers.

But Caine understood that the kids with powers had to be controlled. And once Caine and Diana had all the freaks under control, what was to stop Drake from using his own nine millimetres of magic to take it all for himself?

First things first.

He stared at Astrid's house from halfway down the block. Looking for any sign of which room she might be in.

He crept around to the back and up on to the back porch. The door was locked. Anyone who locked their back door locked their front door. But maybe not their windows. He hopped up on to the deck railing and leaned out to get a purchase on the window. It slid up easily. It was not an easy thing getting through the window without making a lot of noise.

It took him ten minutes to go through every room in the house, look in every closet, under every bed, behind every curtain, even look into the attic crawl spaces.

He felt a moment of panic then. Astrid could be anywhere. He would look like a fool if he didn't get her.

Where would she go?

He checked the garage. Nothing there. No cars, certainly no Astrid. But there was a lawnmower, and where there was a lawnmower, there would be . . . yes, a gas can.

He wondered what would happen if Astrid and the retard magicked their way into a burning building?

Drake opened the gas can, went to the kitchen, and began drizzling the gasoline across the counters, into the family room, a splash for the drapes, trailing into the dining room, across the table, and another splash for the front curtains.

He couldn't find a match. He tore a piece of paper towel and lit it on the stove. He tossed the burning twist of paper on to the dining-room table and left by the front door, not bothering to close it.

'That's one place she won't be able to hide,' he told himself.

He raced back to the plaza and up the stairs of the church. The church had a steeple. It wasn't very tall, but it would give him a pretty good perspective.

Up the circular stairs. He pushed a hinged hatch and climbed up into a cramped, dusty, cobwebbed space dominated by a bell. He carefully avoided touching the bell – the sound would carry.

The windows were shuttered, covered with angled vents that let airflow through and sound resonate out, but only allowed him to see down. He used the butt of the rifle to knock the first vent out. It tumbled to the ground below.

Kids in the plaza looked up. Let them. He smashed the other three vents out and they clattered down. Now he had an unrestricted view in every direction across the orange tile roofs of Perdido Beach.

He started from Astrid's house, which was already beginning to smoke. He worked his way methodically, a hunter, looking for any movement. Each time he spotted someone walking or running or biking, he would take a look at them through the rifle scope, line them up in the crosshairs.

He felt like God. All he had to do was squeeze the trigger.

But none of the moving shapes far below was Astrid. There was no way to miss that blonde hair. No. No Astrid.

Then, just as he was giving up, he spotted a flurry of activity down at the marina. He swivelled the scope, and suddenly Sam Temple was clear in the bright circle. For a moment the sights were on his chest. But then he was gone. He had jumped on to a boat.

Impossible. Caine had Sam up at the school. How had he gotten away?

Edilio and Quinn were on the boat too, pulling away. Drake could see the water churning from the motor.

Quinn. That's how Sam had gotten away. It had to be.

Drake would have to have a nice talk with Quinn.

On the dock he could make out Orc waving a bat, yelling, unable to do anything. The boat gathered speed and arced north, leaving a long white wake drawn like an arrow on the water.

There was no question Sam would try to find Astrid. And he was heading north.

The power plant. Had to be.

Drake cursed and, again, for just a moment, felt the almost desperate fear of failing Caine. He wasn't worried what Caine would do to him – after all, Caine needed him – but he knew if he failed to carry out Caine's orders, Diana would laugh.

Drake put down the rifle. How could he reach the power plant ahead of Sam?

There was no way. Even if he took a boat he would be playing catch-up. A car? Maybe. But he didn't know the way, and the trip by boat would be more direct. It would take him a while to get down to the marina and . . . but, wait. Wait a minute.

The motorboat was pulling a U-turn.

'Aren't you clever, Sam?' Drake whispered. 'But not clever enough.'

Through the scope he could just make out Sam's face as he stood at the wheel, wind in his face, having escaped from Caine, having outwitted Orc, and now all cocky and sure of himself as he sped south.

There was no way to take a shot from this distance. Drake knew that.

He traversed the gun sight south and stopped at the barrier. Sam wouldn't have far to go in that direction.

The beach at the bottom of the cliffs? If she was down there, Drake could never reach her before Sam got there in the motorboat. If she was down there, the game was over.

But if not . . . if she was, say, in the hotel, Clifftop? Then, he had a chance if he moved fast.

How great would it be to shoot her right where Sam Temple could watch?

ASTRID ALMOST MISSED spotting the boat. She had gone to the window only to draw the shades. But from the corner of her eye she saw the motorboat out there, the only thing on the water.

For a brief moment she'd wondered if it was adults, someone coming to rescue them from the FAYZ. But no, if rescue was coming from outside the FAYZ, it wouldn't be a single open boat.

And, anyway, Astrid was convinced, no one was coming. Not now. Probably not ever.

She squinted but could not tell who was on the boat. If only she had binoculars. It seemed like it might be three people. Maybe four. She couldn't tell. But the boat was speeding closer.

She knelt to see what was still available in the minibar refrigerator. During their last stay, she and Sam and Quinn had almost cleaned it out. All that was left to eat were some cashews.

She would need to feed Little Pete sooner rather than later. Before whoever was on the boat got here.

'Come on, Petey,' she said, and guided him up from the end of the bed. 'Come on, we're going to get some food. Munchy

279

munchy?' she said, using a trigger phrase that sometimes worked. 'Munchy munchy?'

They could head for the Clifftop restaurant and probably find something there, maybe cook a chicken sandwich or something, or at least find some yogurt or whatever. Or they could play it safe and just empty out the minibars in other rooms.

She opened the door. Looked out into the hallway. It was empty.

'Candy bars it is,' she said, realising she just didn't have the nerve to go down to the restaurant.

The room next door had a minibar but no key in the lock. She tried three more rooms before realising that she had just been lucky that first night. The refrigerators were all locked. But, wait, maybe all the keys were interchangeable.

'Come on, back to our room,' she said.

'Munchy munchy,' Little Pete protested.

'Munchy munchy,' Astrid confirmed. 'Come on, Petey.'

Out in the hallway again and then she heard the ding of an elevator. The smooth electric motors opening the door.

Was it Sam? She froze, poised between fear and hope.

Fear won.

The elevator was at the end of the hall and around a bend. She had seconds.

'Come on,' she hissed, and pushed Little Pete forwards. With fumbling fingers she slid the passcard into and out of the slot. Too fast. She had to do it slower. Again. Still no green light. One more time and now she could hear the elevator door closing.

It was him. Suddenly she knew it was Drake.

'Hail Mary, full of grace, the Lord is with thee.' It was the only prayer she could think of.

She tried the key again. The light blinked to green.

She turned the handle.

He was there. At the end of the hall. Standing there with a rifle over his shoulder and a gun in his hand.

Astrid almost collapsed.

Drake grinned.

He raised the handgun and took aim.

Astrid pushed Little Pete into the room and tumbled in after him.

Astrid slammed the door closed and threw the bolt. Then she added the security lock.

An impossibly loud noise.

The door had a hole in it the size of a dime, with the metal puckered out.

Another explosion and the door handle was hanging half off.

Little Pete could save them. He could. He had the power. But he was still calm, still oblivious.

Useless.

The balcony. It was the only way.

'Petey, come on!' she rasped.

'Munchy munchy,' he argued.

Drake slammed against the door, but it held. The dead bolt was still in place.

He fired again and again, frustrated, blasting away at the dead bolt.

He was frantic that she and Petey would teleport again.

She had to make him believe it had happened.

She dragged Little Pete to the balcony, slid open the door, looked down. The ground was too far. Way too far. But there was a balcony directly below them.

Astrid climbed over the railing, scared to death, shaking, but with no alternative.

How could she get Little Pete to follow? He was fixated on food now.

'Game Boy,' she hissed, and pushed the toy close to his face. 'Come on, Petey, come on, Game Boy.'

She guided her brother over, placed his hand on the rail, only one hand because now he was in his game again, lost in his stupid game, too calm to use his power, too unpredictable.

'Blessed art thou among women, and blessed is the fruit of thy womb, Jesus,' Astrid sobbed.

This wasn't going to work. She could make it, but how could she get her brother to do it?

He was small. She could swing him. She could hold on for the few seconds it'd take.

'Holy Mary, Mother of God . . .'

She gripped the railing with her left, grabbed Little Pete's wrist with her right, and yanked him away from the rail. He fell. She caught him, held on by her fingernails, and then he was falling. He slammed on to the porch chair below.

He had landed hard. He was stunned.

Astrid heard Drake slamming against the door again and heard a splintering sound as the dead bolt gave way. Now only the frail chain still held and he would be through that in a heartbeat.

'. . . pray for us sinners now . . .'

She swung herself down and landed almost on top of Little Pete. No time for the sharp pain in her leg, no time for the blood and the scraped flesh, only time to grab Little Pete, hug him, hold him close, and withdraw back against the sliding-glass door of the balcony.

'Window seat, window seat, baby, window seat,' she whispered, her mouth pressed to his ear.

She heard Drake in the room above.

She heard him slide open the door above and step out on to the balcony.

They were out of sight. Unless he leaned out far enough.

'Pray for us sinners now and at the hour of our death,' she finished the prayer silently and held on to her brother.

'Amen.'

She heard Drake curse in fury.

They had done it. He thought they had disappeared.

'Thank you, Lord,' Astrid prayed silently.

And then, Little Pete began to moan.

His game had fallen when she had dropped him to the balcony. The back was open. One of the batteries had rolled away. And now Little Pete was trying to make it work and it wouldn't.

Astrid almost sobbed out loud.

Drake stopped cursing.

She looked up and there he was, leaning far out over the railing. The shark grin was wide.

The gun was in his hand, but he couldn't quite get an angle on them, so he swung one leg over the railing, crouched just as Astrid had done, and now he could see them quite clearly.

He aimed.

He laughed.

And then he bellowed in pain and fell.

Astrid leaped to the railing. Drake was on the grass below, sprawled on his back, unconscious, lying on his rifle with the pistol beside him.

'Astrid,' Sam said.

He was above her, still holding the table lamp he'd used to smash Drake's hand, leaning out over the railing.

'Sam.'

'You OK?'

'As soon as I get Petey's battery I will be.' That sounded stupid, and she almost laughed.

'I have a boat down on the beach.'

'Where are we going?'

'How about not here?'

TWENTY FIVE

IT HAD BEEN two days since Lana had survived the coyotes. The *talking* coyotes. Two days since her life had been saved by a snake. A *flying* snake.

The world had gone crazy.

Lana had watered the lawn that morning, careful to keep a sharp eye out for coyotes and snakes. She paid close attention to Patrick's every bark, growl or twitch. He was her early warning system. They'd been owner and pet in the old days, or, maybe you could say, friends. But now they were a team. They were partners in a game of survival: Patrick's senses, her brain.

It was a stupid thing to do, watering the lawn, since she couldn't be sure there would be water enough for her. But the man who had owned this tumbledown desert abode had loved the few square metres of grass. It was an act of defiance against the desert. Defiance, even though he had chosen to live out here in the middle of absolutely nowhere.

Anyway, in a crazy world, why shouldn't she be crazy, too?

The man who owned the cabin was named Jim Brown. She found that out from papers inside his desk. Plain old Jim Brown. There was no picture of him, but he was only forty-

285

eight years old, a little too young, Lana thought, to leave civilisation behind and become a hermit.

The shed behind the cabin was stacked to the roof with survival rations. Not a single fresh thing to be found, but enough canned crackers, canned peanut butter, peaches, fruit cocktail, chilli, Spam, and military-style meals ready to eat to last Lana and Patrick at least a year. Maybe longer.

There was no phone. No TV or any electronics. No air-conditioning to soften the brutal afternoon heat. There was no electricity at all. The only mechanical things were the windmill that turned the pump that brought water up from the aquifer below, and a foot-powered grindstone used to hone picks and shovels and saw blades. There were more than a few picks, shovels, saws, and hammers.

There was evidence as well of a car or truck. Tyre marks led through the sand from a sort of carport that sagged against the side of the house. There were empty oil cans in the trash and two red, twenty-five-gallon steel tanks that smelled like they were full of gasoline.

Out back was a stack of railroad ties, neatly formed into a square pile. Beside this was smaller lumber, a lot of it used two-by-fours scarred by nails.

Hermit Jim, as Lana thought of him, must be out. Maybe he had left forever. Maybe what had happened to her grandfather had happened to him, and now she was the only person left alive in the whole world.

She didn't want to be there if he came back. There was no

way to know whether you could trust a man who lived in a searing-hot valley between dusty hills at the end of no road, and had a lawn as lush as a putting green.

Lana finished watering the grass and sprayed Patrick playfully with the hose before turning it off.

'Want some chilli, boy?' she asked the dog.

She led the way back inside. It was an oven in the cabin, so hot, she started sweating before she had cleared the threshold, but Lana did not think she would ever complain about something so minor. Not after what she had endured.

Heat? Big deal. She had water, she had food, and all her bones were unbroken, which was how she liked them.

The chilli came in a big number-ten can. With no refrigeration, they had to eat it before it could go bad, so it was chilli, meal after meal, till it was gone. But at least there was fruit cocktail for dessert. Tomorrow, maybe she'd open one of the number-ten cans of vanilla pudding and just eat pudding for a couple of days.

There was no oven, just a one-burner cooktop. No sink. There was a single chair and a table, and an uncomfortable cot against a wall. The one decorative feature was a ratty Persian rug in the centre of the only room. The best seat in the house was a smelly but comfortable La-Z-Boy that sat on that rug. It was stuck in the recline position, but that was fine with Lana. She was all about reclining and taking things easy.

The only thing to do was read. Hermit Jim had exactly thirty-eight books. She had inventoried them. There were fairly recent novels by Patrick O'Brian, Dan Simmons, Stephen King, and Dennis Lehane, and some books that she supposed were philosophy by writers like Thoreau. There were classics whose names seemed familiar to her: *Oliver Twist, The Sea Wolf, The Big Sleep, Ivanhoe.*

Nothing had exactly jumped out at her, there were no J. K. Rowling or Meg Cabot books, nothing for kids at all. But over the course of the first day she had read all of *Pride and Prejudice* and now she was starting *The Sea Wolf.* Neither was an easy book. But Lana had nothing but time on her hands.

'We can't stay here, Patrick,' Lana said as the dog attacked his bowl of chilli. 'Sooner or later we have to move on. My friends will be worried. Everyone will be. Even Mom and Dad. They must think we're dead.'

But even as she said it, Lana had her doubts. There wasn't much to do once she had inventoried the groceries, so she spent most of her time sitting on the wooden chair, reading, or just watching the desert landscape. She would pull the chair into the doorway where she could have some shade and look out across the lawn at the hills around. She had mastered the trick of reading a paragraph at a time, looking up to scan the area for danger, checking Patrick for warning signs, then sinking back into the book for another paragraph.

After a while the unending emptiness took a toll on her never-strong sense of optimism.

The barrier was still there. It was behind the cabin, not in her field of vision unless she stepped away from the cabin.

Lana carried a tin cup of water towards the door, intending to drink it while having another look at the lawn and suddenly there was Patrick, racing towards her. His fur was up. He shook his head like he was having a seizure.

'Get in!' Lana yelled.

She held the door open. Patrick barrelled in. She slammed the door and threw the bolt.

Patrick hit the rug, skidded, rolled over twice, and came up to a sitting position. Something was in his mouth. Something alive.

Lana approached cautiously. She bent down to see.

'A horny toad? That's what you have? You scared me half to death over a horned toad?' She felt her heart thud heavily as it restarted. 'Spit that thing out. Good grief, Patrick, I count on you and you freak out over a stupid horned toad?'

Patrick didn't want to give up his prize. Lana decided to let him have it. It was dead now, anyway, and she supposed Patrick was entitled to his own version of crazy.

'Take it outside and you can keep it,' she said. She headed for the door but knelt first to straighten the rug. Then she noticed the hatch in the floor.

Lana pulled the rug back farther, folding it up over the La-Z-Boy.

She hesitated, not sure if she wanted to see what was under those floorboards. Maybe Hermit Jim was Serial Killer Jim.

But it wasn't like she had anything else to do. She shoved the recliner aside and rolled up the rug. There was a recessed steel ring. She pulled it up.

Lying in the space below were neatly stacked metal bricks, each maybe six or eight inches long, half as wide, and a third as thick.

There was no question in Lana's mind what they were.

'Gold, Patrick. Gold.'

The gold bars were heavy, twenty pounds or more, but she lifted enough out to be able to see the extent of the pile. Her best estimate was that there were fourteen in all, each at least twenty pounds.

Lana had no idea what gold was worth, but she knew what a pair of gold hoop earrings cost.

'That is a lot of earrings,' she said.

Patrick looked into the hole with puzzlement.

'You know what this means, Patrick? All this gold here and all those picks and shovels outside? Hermit Jim is a gold miner.'

She ran outside to the lean-to where Hermit Jim had formerly parked his truck. Patrick bounded along, hoping for a game. Sometimes she tossed a broken axe handle for him to retrieve, but today Patrick was to be disappointed.

For the first time Lana carefully followed the tyre tracks. They were fading, but still visible. A hundred feet from the house, they split. Some tracks, older ones, it seemed, headed one direction, south-east, probably towards Perdido Beach. Somewhat fresher tracks headed towards the base of the ridge to the north.

Perdido Beach, she believed, could be fifteen, maybe twenty miles or so away, a very long walk in the heat. But if the mine was at the base of the ridge, it didn't look like even a tenth of that distance. Hermit Jim might be there. If he was, so was his truck. If he wasn't, his truck might still be there, anyway.

Lana felt a profound aversion to the idea of venturing into the wild again. She'd come very, very close to dying the last time. And the coyotes might still be out there, waiting patiently. But the mile to the mine? She could do that.

She filled a plastic jug with water. She filled herself with water and made sure Patrick was hydrated, too. She stuffed her pockets with MREs – meals ready to eat – and packed more into a towel she twisted to form a pouch. She smeared herself with sunscreen from an emergency medical kit.

'Let's go for a walk, Patrick.'

Edilio grinned as Astrid took her seat on the left side of the Boston Whaler. 'Thank God. Now at least we got one smart person on this boat.'

Edilio and Quinn pushed the boat off the sand, back into the gently lapping surf. They climbed aboard, then trailed their legs over the side to clean off clinging sand.

Sam headed the boat out to sea, out towards the barrier. He hoped Drake was dead or at least badly injured. But he wasn't sure and he wanted to get well away before the psychopath started shooting at them.

It occurred to Sam that never before in his life had he wished someone dead. Eight days had passed since the coming of the FAYZ. Eight days and he'd seen enough craziness to last him a lifetime. And now he was fantasising about a kid being dead.

Once he pushed the throttle forwards and was beyond the range of any bullet, he started to feel better. This was as close as Sam had come to surfing since the coming of the FAYZ. The waves were unimpressive short chop, but the Whaler landed on them with wonderful force that translated up through his legs, rattled his teeth, and brought a smile to his lips. Salt spray was flying, and for Sam it was hard to be grim when the spray was lashing his face.

'Thanks, Edilio. You too, Quinn,' Sam said. He was still furious at Quinn, but they were – literally – all in the same boat now.

'See how much you want to thank me when I hurl all over this boat,' Edilio said. He was looking a little green.

Sam reminded himself to keep a safe distance from the FAYZ barrier, but at the same time he wanted to keep it close. There was still the tantalising possibility of a gap, a gate, an opening through which they could all sail and say goodbye to this madness.

Far to the north he could see the cliffs that marked the inlet occupied by the power plant. Beyond that, just a smudge in the haze, the outline of the nearest of half a dozen small private islands.

Astrid had dug out the life jackets and was strapping one on to Little Pete. Edilio accepted one too, but Quinn refused.

Astrid also found a small cooler packed with warm sodas, a loaf of bread, and the rest of the makings of peanut butter and jelly sandwiches. 'We won't starve,' she said. 'At least not right away.'

The barrier was just to their left, a terrible, imposing, blank wall. The waves lapped against it, an impatient sound. The water wanted to escape, too.

Sam was a fish in an aquarium and the FAYZ wall was the side of the tank. It was the same semi-translucent mystery it was on land.

He skimmed along until he was far enough out that Clifftop was no bigger than a LEGO perched above a narrow ribbon of sand. Perdido Beach was like an oil painting, dots and splashes of colour that suggested a town without providing any detail.

'I'm going to try something,' he announced.

Sam killed the engine and let the boat wallow. The boat seemed to want to drift along the wall. There was a current, only slight, but definite. The current chased down the side of the wall heading away from land, following the long curve still farther out to sea.

'Do we have an anchor?' Sam asked.

The answer was a retching sound. Sam looked away as Edilio gave up his lunch.

'Never mind,' said Sam, 'I'll look.'

There was no anchor. But he noticed that Astrid was making peanut butter and jelly sandwiches. She handed one to Sam.

He had not realised he was hungry. He stuffed half the sandwich in his mouth. 'This is why they call you Astrid the Genius,' he mumbled through the peanut butter.

'Man, don't talk about food,' Edilio groaned.

Sam searched his little boat. No anchor anywhere, but there

were some plastic bumpers, which he hung over the side in case he brushed against the barrier. And there was a coil of blue-and-white nylon rope. He tied one end securely to a cleat and tied the other end around his ankle. He stripped off his shirt and kicked off his shoes, leaving him in shorts. Rummaging in one of the holds, he found a long screwdriver.

'What are you doing?' Quinn asked.

Sam ignored him. 'Edilio, man, you going to live?'

'I hope not,' Edilio said through gritted teeth.

'I'm going to dive down, see if I can get below the barrier.'

Astrid looked sceptical, worried, but Sam could see she was in her own head, preoccupied. Probably trying to come to grips with almost getting shot.

Quinn said, 'I'll haul you in if you get jammed up.'

Sam nodded, not ready to talk to Quinn. Not sure he would ever be ready to talk to Quinn. Then he dived off the side.

The water was a welcome friend. Cold, a shock, but welcome. He laughed at the taste of salt.

He took a couple of deep breaths, held the last one, and dived. He swam with powerful kicks and his free hand while the other hand held the screwdriver out to fend off the FAYZ wall. He had no desire to be pushed up against it. Touching with a finger had hurt. Laying a shoulder or thigh against it would not be pleasant.

Down and down he went. He wished he'd had the foresight to grab some scuba gear or at least a face mask and fins at the marina, but he'd been a bit preoccupied at the time. The water was pretty clear, but still, visibility was reduced in the shadow of the barrier.

When he reached the end of his air he stabbed towards the barrier. The screwdriver hit nothing, and he felt a momentary surge of excitement that disappeared when his next thrust stopped dead against solid resistance.

He shot to the surface and gasped for air.

The barrier extended at least twenty feet down below the surface. If there was a bottom to it, he'd have to find it using an air tank and flippers.

The boat was rocking against the barrier, fifty feet away. He heard the distinct snap and *pff* as Astrid popped open a Coke for Little Pete. Quinn sat on the bow tending the rope, and Edilio was still looking as if he might heave up a part of his liver.

Sam swam to the boat, taking his time, enjoying the water on his skin too much to feel disappointed that he hadn't found a way out of the FAYZ.

He heard the sound of the engine and the smack-on-wave impact long before he saw the boat. He kicked hard to lift his head above the water far enough to see. 'Hey,' he yelled.

Quinn had heard the engine at the same time. 'Boat coming. Fast,' Quinn yelled.

'Where?'

'From town,' Quinn reported.

'Fast,' he repeated.

SAM SWAM AT full speed and soon had his hand on the gunwale of the Boston Whaler. Quinn hauled him aboard. Up and over, falling and rolling on to the deck.

He was on his feet in a flash and saw the big speedboat, the kind they called a cigarette boat, bearing down on them, not a quarter of a mile away. The boat threw out a huge bow wave. At the wheel was a kid Sam couldn't recognize from this distance. Standing like they were holding on for dear life were Howard and Orc. No Drake.

'We can't outrun them,' Quinn said.

Adrenaline seemed to have steadied Edilio's stomach. 'Maybe, man, but we don't know till we try.'

'No, Quinn's right,' Sam said. 'Astrid, hold on to Little Pete.'

Edilio reeled up the slack in the rope, both hands flying. They couldn't leave it trailing in the water or it would foul the propeller.

As soon as the rope was aboard, Sam gunned the throttle and quickly picked up speed, running along the barrier. Orc's boat veered to follow.

Astrid, clutching her little brother, peeked over the side and yelled, 'He's chasing, not aiming to intercept us.'

It took Sam a second to understand what she meant. The cigarette boat could have set an intercept angle and easily cut them off. But the driver hadn't thought of that.

Almost too late, the speedboat's driver veered right, trying to drop in behind Sam, but the turn was sloppy and the speed too great. The cigarette boat slid sideways into the barrier with a surprisingly loud, bass-drum smack. Then, when the props bit again, the cigarette boat surged forwards and shot past the Whaler.

'Hold on,' Sam warned.

The wave from the cigarette boat's turn washed over the Whaler and slammed the smaller boat against the barrier. Sam rocked but held on, his bare feet fighting the crazily tilting deck for traction.

The Boston Whaler stayed upright and, as the propeller found water again, it gained speed. They shot to the right of the cigarette boat, close enough that Sam could have stuck his arm out and high-fived Howard.

Now the Whaler was going all out, bouncing from wave top to wave top with the barrier flying by on the left, heading farther from land.

But the speedboat was much faster, and now that the driver had recovered, he came roaring after Sam and was soon churning Sam's wake.

'Pull over, moron,' Orc bellowed at Sam.

Sam ignored the demand. His mind was racing. How could he get away? His boat was slower. It was more nimble, but it was definitely slower. And the speedboat was so much bigger, so much heavier, that it could run right over the Boston Whaler.

'Pull over or we'll run you down,' Orc shouted again.

'Don't be stupid, Sammy,' Howard yelled in a smaller voice, barely audible over the roar of engines and rush of water.

Astrid was suddenly at his side. 'Sam. Can you do anything?'

'Maybe. I have an idea.'

In a tight whisper she said, 'Are you talking about . . .'

'I don't know how to do that, Astrid, it just happens. And this isn't exactly the time for me to consult Yoda on how to use my power.'

Edilio was with them now. 'You got a plan, Sam?'

'Not a good one.'

Sam picked up the radio handset beside the throttle. He keyed the button. 'This is Sam, are you guys receiving? Over.'

Glancing back, he saw the surprise on Howard's face. Yes, they were receiving. Howard lifted his handset and frowned at it.

Sam keyed his radio. 'You hold down the button, Howard,' Sam said. 'Then when you're done, you say "over" and let go of the button. Over.'

'You have to pull over,' Howard said, his voice harshened by the tinny receiver. 'Oh, over.'

'I don't think we're going to do that, Howard. Drake tried to kill Astrid. You and Orc almost killed me. Over.'

That occupied Howard for a minute while he thought up a good lie. 'It's OK, Sammy, Caine changed his mind. He says if you behave yourselves, he'll let you all go free. Over.'

'Yeah. I absolutely believe you,' Sam said.

Sam edged his boat still closer to the barrier. It was so close now, he could have touched it.

He depressed the send button again. 'You try to run me down, you may run into the barrier,' Sam warned. 'Over.'

There was a silence. Then, a new voice, faint but audible. It had to be coming from a radio onshore. 'Get him,' the voice commanded. 'Get him or don't come back.'

Caine. He was using the radio he used to stay in contact with Drake and the day care and the fire station.

Howard said, 'Hey, Caine, they have Astrid and the retard, too. And Quinn.'

'What? Say again. Astrid is with them?'

It was Sam who answered him, relishing the moment, even though the triumph was likely to be short-lived. 'That's right, Caine. Your pet psycho failed you.'

'Get them all,' Caine ordered.

'What if they use the power?' Howard whined.

'If they could use the power, they'd already have done so,' Caine said with a smirk that carried across the airwaves. 'No excuses: take them down. Caine out.'

Astrid said, 'Sam, if you can do it, you need to do it.'

'Do what?' Edilio demanded. 'Oh. The thing?'

The radio crackled to life again. Howard said, 'You have till I count ten, Sammy. Then we hit it and run you down. Doesn't have to be like that, but we have no choice. So . . . ten.'

'Edilio, you and Astrid and Little Pete, down on the deck. Quinn, you with them.'

'Nine.'

Edilio pulled Astrid down beside him and lay flat on the deck with Little Pete between them.

'Eight.'

'This better be a good plan, brah,' Quinn said. But he went and crouched with Astrid.

'Seven. Six.'

The bow of the cigarette boat towered above the stern of the Whaler, a huge red cleaver, bouncing up and down, chopping its way towards them. The roar of all three engines bounced off the barrier, twisting and amplifying the sound.

'Five.'

He had a plan. But the plan was suicide.

'Four.'

'Everyone ready?'

'Ready for what?'

'Three.'

'He's going to hit us.'

'That's your plan?' Quinn shrilled.

'Two.'

'Pretty much,' Sam said.

'One.'

Sam heard the twin engines of the cigarette boat ramp up. The red meat cleaver bow leaped forwards. It was like someone had strapped a rocket to the back.

Sam shoved the throttle of the Whaler into neutral and steered to scrape the left side of the boat into the FAYZ wall.

The Whaler slowed very suddenly.

'Hang on!'

He dropped into a low crouch, kneeling on the wet deck, clutching the wheel with one hand and yanked it to the right, then steadied it. He covered his head with his free arm, shouting to keep his nerve up.

The Boston Whaler slowed.

The speedboat did not.

The tall, dagger-sharp prow ran up over the left half of the Boston Whaler's stern.

There was a screech of shattered fibreglass. The impact knocked Sam away from the wheel. The back end of the Whaler plunged, and the five of them and the entire boat were suddenly underwater. Sam was yelling into water, yelling and fighting to avoid being sucked up into the propellers that tornadoed the water a millimetre above his head.

The speedboat blocked out the sun, deep red and death white, a knife drawn across the smaller boat. The big twin outboard engines screamed.

But the cigarette boat didn't entirely crush the smaller boat. Instead, hitting the Whaler at an angle, the cigarette boat went airborne like a stunt car hitting a ramp. It rolled in mid-air and smashed its topside into the barrier, shattering its windshield and crumpling its railings.

The cigarette boat hit the water hard on its side twenty feet ahead of the Boston Whaler. It landed in a sideways bellyflop, ploughed so deep, Sam thought it might stay under, but then it wallowed back up like a surfacing submarine and righted itself.

The Whaler had taken a bad beating. The stern was crushed, the railings on the left side were gone, the black-cowled engine was askew but still attached. There was a big divot smashed out of the fibreglass on the bow. Two feet of water sloshed on the deck. The command console was bent forwards and to the side so that the steering wheel was askew and the throttle handle was out of its slot and hanging loose. The engine had been swamped and had sputtered out.

But Sam was not hurt.

'Astrid!' he yelled, terrified when he didn't see her immediately. Little Pete was alone, staring, almost as if this at least had really penetrated his consciousness.

Quinn and Edilio jumped up and leaned over the back. They had spotted Astrid's slender hand holding the railing. They pulled her aboard, half drowned and bleeding from a gash in her leg.

'Is she OK?'

Edilio nodded, too waterlogged to answer.

Sam turned the key and hoped. The big Mercury motor roared. The throttle was stiff, jammed, but by pushing with all his might he could shift it forwards. The crooked wheel still turned.

The cigarette boat was just ahead, stalled. Orc was in the water, yelling in fury. Howard scampered around, looking for a life jacket, while the driver tried to restart the engines. Unfortunately, the engines did not appear to be damaged.

It was now or never.

With frantic fingers Sam untied the rope from his ankle and

took the loose end in his teeth. He jumped into the water and ploughed through the few feet separating the Whaler from the speedboat.

'He's swimming over here. His boat is sinking,' the speedboat driver yelled, misunderstanding.

But Howard knew better. 'He's up to something.'

Sam dived down under the water. It had to be now, before the driver got the engines started. If those props started turning it would be too late, and there was a very good chance that Sam would lose his fingers or even a whole hand.

Fighting his own buoyancy, Sam stayed under, peering through the churn, fingers trying to make sense of . . . there. That was one propeller.

He looped the nylon rope around the rightward prop and twisted it as tight as he could. Then he jetted to his left, blowing out the last of his air so he could stay submerged.

He heard the ignition click, the key being turned over. One twist of the boat driver's fingers and . . .

The engine gave a start. Sam pushed back in panic.

Both props jerked and churned. Then the right prop seized and the left spun and stopped.

With the last of his strength Sam wound the rope around the left propeller, kicked off from the stern, and surfaced a few feet away for a quick gasp of air.

He heard the engines turn over again, and stall again.

The cigarette boat's driver now realised what had happened, and Howard was at the stern shouting angry threats.

Sam twisted and started swimming hard for the Whaler, which was bouncing against the barrier.

'Sam.' It was Astrid shouting. 'Behind you.'

The blow came out of nowhere.

Sam's head spun. His eyes wouldn't focus. The muscles in his limbs were all slack.

He'd been here before. It was just like when he'd fallen off his surfboard and it had come back and hit him. A corner of his mind knew what to do: avoid panic, take a few seconds to let his head clear.

Only this wasn't a surfboard. A second impact hit just beside him, missing his head and hitting his collarbone.

The sharp pain helped Sam focus.

He saw Howard raise the long aluminium boathook for a third blow, and now Sam avoided it easily. As the boathook slapped the water, Sam lunged, bringing all his weight on to it.

Howard lost his balance and Sam yanked. Howard let go of the boathook and slammed chest first on to one of the engines.

Again Sam turned towards the Whaler, but too late. Orc was on him now, and while one giant hand grabbed for a purchase on Sam's neck, the other pounded at him.

Orc's fist hit water before it hit Sam's nose, so it was slowed down, but still the impact was shocking.

Sam curled into a ball and drove both his legs as hard as he could into Orc's solar plexus. His blow, too, was slowed by the drag of the water, but it pushed Sam forwards and Orc back.

Sam was the better swimmer, but Orc was stronger. As Sam

tried to escape, Orc grabbed the waist of Sam's shorts and held him firmly.

Howard was on his feet now, shouting encouragement and praise for Orc. The fight was directly beneath the Whaler's crunched bow. Sam somersaulted backwards, slammed his bare feet against the hull, and pushed himself down under the water. He hoped when Orc's head submerged, he'd panic and let go. It worked, and Sam was free. Free but trapped in a tight corner between the FAYZ wall and the boat's bow.

Orc's face was a fright mask of rage. He came straight at Sam and Sam had no choice at all. He waited for Orc, grabbed his shirt as he came in range, twisted and, using Orc's own momentum, drove the bully face first into the FAYZ wall.

Orc screamed. He flailed madly and screamed again.

Sam kicked away, using Orc's body as a launchpad. The kick drove Orc sideways into the barrier and he bellowed like a dying bull.

Sam swam, snagged the starboard gunwale and held on.

'Edilio. Go.'

Edilio threw the throttle forwards as Sam, with a hand from Astrid and Quinn, pulled himself aboard.

Orc was yelling incoherent, half-drowned curses from the water. Howard was reaching down to him, and the boat's driver was shell-shocked, not sure what to do.

The rope was firmly tied to the deck cleat. The cleat would never hold, but a good sharp snap might finish off at least one of the jammed props.

Edilio turned the Whaler away from the barrier and said, 'Watch the rope, Sam.'

The warning was just in time, as the slack came off the rope and it shot up out of the water. The rope tightened, nearly snapping Sam's arm in the process.

The Whaler jerked from the impact. The cleat tore from the deck. But the cigarette boat's props were useless now.

'OK, that was crazy,' Edilio said with a laugh.

'I guess you're over the seasickness?'

The radio crackled to life, Howard's familiar voice, subdued and afraid now, whining. 'This is Howard. They got away.'

The faint voice from shore answered, 'Why am I not surprised?'

Then, Howard again. 'Our boat doesn't work.'

'Sam,' Caine said. 'If you can hear me, brother, you better know I'll kill you.'

'Brother? Why is he calling you brother?' Astrid asked.

'Long story.'

Sam smiled. Plenty of time to tell stories now. They'd done it. They had escaped. But it was a hollow victory.

They couldn't go home.

'OK,' Sam said. 'So it's escape or nothing.'

He set the tiller on a course that followed the long, curved barrier. Astrid found a cut-top bleach bottle and began the long job of bailing out the boat.

TWENTY SEVEN

IT TOOK LANA far longer than she had expected to reach the end of the tyre tracks. What had looked like a mile at most must have been three. And carrying the water and the food in the blazing heat had not made it easy.

It was afternoon by the time she dragged her weary feet around an outcropping from the ridge. There, before her amazed eyes, was what looked very much like an abandoned mining town. It must have been quite a camp once: there were a dozen buildings all jumbled together in the narrow, steep-walled crease of the ridge. The buildings were almost indistinguishable from one another now, mere collections of grey sticks, but there might once have been a sort of street, no more than half a block long.

It was a spooky place, silent, gloomy, with wrecked glassless windows like sad eyes staring down at her.

Behind the wreckage of the main street, out of sight of casual passers-by – although why anyone would ever come to this desolate, unlovely place Lana could not imagine – was a more sturdy structure. It was built of the same grey lumber, but was still upright and topped with a tin roof. This structure

307

was the size of a three-car garage. The tracks led there.

'Come on, boy,' Lana said.

Patrick ran ahead, sniffed at a weed near the shed's door, and came back, tail still high.

'So there's no one inside,' Lana reassured herself. 'Or else you would have barked.'

She threw the door open, not wanting to creep in like some girl in a horror movie.

Sunlight came through dozens of holes and seams in the tin roof and knotholes in the wood. Still, it was dark.

The truck was there. Newer than her grandfather's truck, with a longer bed.

'Hello? Hello?' She waited. Then, 'Hello?'

She checked the truck first. The tank was half full. The keys were nowhere to be found. She searched every square inch of the truck and nothing.

Frustrated, Lana began a search of the rest of the shack. It was mostly machinery. What looked like a rock crusher. Something that looked like a big vat with heat jets positioned beneath. A liquid petroleum gas tank that sat off in a corner.

'OK. We either find the keys and probably kill ourselves driving,' Lana summarised to an attentive Patrick. 'Or we walk however many miles through the heat to Perdido Beach and maybe die of thirst.'

Patrick barked.

'I agree. Let's keep looking for the keys.'

In addition to the tall double door on the front of the shed, there was a smaller door in the back. Through this Lana found a well-trodden path that wound through ugly piles of rock, past a graveyard of rusted-steel machines, and ended in a timber-framed opening in the ground. It looked like the mountain's surprised mouth, a crooked square of black with two broken support beams forming jagged buck teeth.

A narrow train track led into the mine.

'I don't think we want to go in there,' Lana said.

Patrick moved cautiously closer to the opening. His hackles went up and he growled.

But he wasn't growling at the opening.

Lana heard the rush of padded feet. Down the side of the mountain, like a silent avalanche, raced a pack of coyotes, maybe two dozen of them, maybe more.

They flowed down the mountain with shocking speed.

And as they came Lana could hear them whispering in strained, glottal voices, 'Food . . . food.'

'No,' Lana told herself.

No. She had to be imagining that.

Lana shot a panicked look over her shoulder back at the shack now far below her. The right wing of the pack was already racing to cut her off.

'Patrick,' she yelled, and bolted for the mine entrance.

The instant they were past the threshold of the mine the temperature dropped twenty degrees. Like stepping into air-conditioning. There was no light but that which came from outside, and Lana's eyes had no time to adjust.

There was a terrible smell. Something foul, sweet, and cloying.

Patrick turned back to face the coyotes and bristled. The coyotes boiled around the entrance to the mine, but stopped there.

Lana, half blind, felt around in the dark for something, anything. She found rocks as big as a man's fist. She began hurling, not aiming, just frantically flinging the rocks at the coyotes.

'Go away. Shoo. Get out of here.'

None of Lana's missiles connected with a target. The coyotes sidestepped them daintily, effortlessly, like they were playing a not very challenging game.

The pack split in two, forming a lane. One coyote, not the biggest, but by far the ugliest, walked with head high through the pack. One of his over-sized ears was half torn off, he had mange that left bare patches of skin showing on the side of his shrewd muzzle, and the teeth on the left side of his mouth were partly exposed by some long-ago injury that had given him a permanent sideways snarl.

The coyote leader growled at her.

She flinched but raised a large rock in threat.

'Stay back,' Lana warned.

'No human here.' The voice was slurred, like dragged boots on wet gravel, but high-pitched.

For several long seconds Lana just stared. It wasn't possible. But it sounded as if the voice had come from the coyote.

'What?'

'Go out,' the coyote said. This time it was unmistakable. She had seen his muzzle move, caught the struggle of his tongue behind sharp teeth.

'You can't talk,' Lana said. 'This isn't real.'

'Go out.'

'You'll kill me,' Lana said.

'Yes. Go out, die fast. Stay, die slow.'

'You can talk,' Lana said, feeling like she was crazy, really crazy now.

The coyote didn't respond.

Lana stalled. 'Why can't I stay in the mine?'

'No human here.'

'Why?'

'Go out.'

'Come on, Patrick,' Lana said in a shaky whisper. She began backing away from the coyote pack leader, deeper into the darkness.

Her foot hit something. She glanced down quickly and saw a leg sticking out of overalls caked with blood. She had found the source of the smell. Hermit Jim had been dead for a long time.

She hopped backwards over the body, putting it between herself and the coyote.

'You killed him,' Lana accused.

'Yes.'

'Why?' She spotted a lantern, just a big square flashlight, really. She bent quickly and picked it up.

'No human here.'

The coyote yapped a command to his pack and they rushed

into the cave and leaped over the body. Lana and Patrick turned and ran.

Lana fumbled with the light as she ran, trying to find a switch. The darkness was quickly total.

A sharp pain in her ankle almost brought her down, but she stumbled on. She found the switch and suddenly the mine shaft was bathed in eerie light that revealed only jagged rock and straining wooden beams. The shadows were like claw fingers closing around her.

The coyotes, startled by the light, fell back. Their eyes glittered. Their teeth were faint white grins.

And then they came for her.

A jaw-like vice closed around the muscle of her calf and she fell in a heap. The coyotes swarmed over her. Their stink was in her nose, their weight hammered her down.

She fought to get up on to her elbows. A second vice closed over her upper arm and she fell, knowing she would never get back up. She heard Patrick's terrified barking, so much deeper and louder than the coyotes' excited yip-yapping.

All at once the coyotes released her. They yelped in surprise and pranced and twisted their heads left and right.

Lana lay bleeding from a dozen bites in an eerie circle of light cast by the lantern.

The pack leader snarled and the coyotes calmed down at least a little, though it was clear that something had frightened them, and was still frightening them.

The coyotes stirred, nervous, jumpy. All ears pricked up and turned towards the deep shadows farther down the shaft. Like they were hearing something.

Lana strained to hear what they heard but the sobbing rasp of her own breathing was too loud. Her heart pounded like a pile-driver, like it would break her ribs with its pounding.

The coyotes no longer attacked her. Something had changed. Something in the air. Something in their unfathomable canine minds. She had gone from prey to prisoner.

The coyote pack leader approached slowly and nosed her. 'Walk, human.'

She bent low and laid her hand against the worst of the bite wounds. The pain ebbed as the healing began.

But she was still draining blood from a dozen small punctures as she stood and walked deeper into the cave, deeper, with Patrick staying close and the coyotes following behind.

Down and down they went. The train track ran out and they entered what looked like a new section of tunnel. Here the lumber used to shore up the roof was still green, the nail heads still bright. The floor of the shaft was less littered with crumbled rock and decades of dust.

This was where Hermit Jim had been working, digging down, following the seam of bright yellow metal.

As she walked Lana grew afraid in a new way. She had endured the panicky, choking fear of death. This was different. This new sensation turned her muscles to jelly, seemed to sap the heat from her blood and fill her arteries with ice water and her stomach with bile.

She was cold. Cold all the way through.

Her feet weighed a hundred pounds each, the muscles inadequate to lift them and shift them forwards.

Every corner of her brain was yammering, 'Run, run, run!' But she could not possibly run, could not physically do it. The only way was forwards as she felt herself now drawn deeper and deeper by some will that was no part of her.

Patrick could finally take it no longer. He turned tail and ran, shouldering his way past the contemptuous wild dogs.

She wanted to call him. But no sound came from her nerveless lips.

Deeper and deeper. Colder and colder.

The flashlight weakened and as it dimmed Lana became aware that the walls of the cave were glowing a faint green.

It was near now.

It.

Whatever it was, it was near.

The lantern fell from her numb fingers.

Her eyes rolled up into her head and she fell to her knees, indifferent to, unaware even of, the pain as her kneecaps landed on sharp rock.

On her knees, eyes blind, Lana waited.

A voice exploded inside her head. Her back arched in spasm and she fell on her side. Every nerve ending, every cell in her body screamed in pain. Pain like she was being boiled alive.

How long it lasted, she would never know.

The exact words she heard – if they had been words at all – she would never recall.

She would awake later, having been dragged from the cave by two of the coyotes.

They dragged her out of the cave into the night.

And there they waited patiently for her to live or die.

TWENTY EIGHT

SAM, EDILIO, QUINN, Astrid, and Little Pete followed the FAYZ wall out to sea. The curve of the barrier took them away from land, then back towards it.

There was no gap in the wall. There was no easy escape hatch.

The sun was setting as they travelled north of a handful of tiny private islands. One of those islands had a beautiful white yacht smashed into it. Sam considered detouring to take a closer look but decided against it. He was determined to survey the entire FAYZ wall. If he was to be trapped like a goldfish in a bowl, he wanted to see the whole bowl.

The FAYZ wall met the shore in the middle of Stefano Rey National Park, having inscribed a long semicircle on the face of the eerily placid sea.

The shoreline was impossible, a fortress of jagged rock and cliffs touched with the golden light of the setting sun.

'It's beautiful,' Astrid said.

'I'd rather have ugly and a place to land,' Sam said.

The surf was still tame, but it would take very little for the rocks to tear a hole in the hull of the already crippled Boston Whaler.

They headed south, creeping along, hoping for a place to put in before the gas tank ran empty and night fell.

Finally they spotted a minuscule spit of sand, a V shape, no more than twelve feet wide and half as deep. Sam figured he could, with luck, run the boat in there and beach it. But the boat would not survive for long, and they would be on foot, without a map, at the bottom of a seventy-foot cliff.

'How's the gas look, Edilio?'

Edilio stuck a stick down into the tank and pulled it back up. 'Not much. Maybe an inch.'

'OK. Well, I guess this is it, then. Tighten up your life jackets.'

Sam pushed the throttle forwards and aimed straight for the tiny beach. He had to keep up speed or the sluggish swell would shove him into the rocks that crowded in on both sides.

The boat ran up on the sand. The impact jolted Astrid, but Edilio caught her hand before she fell. The four of them quickly piled out. Little Pete could not be induced to get out, or even to acknowledge their existence. So Sam, fearful that at any moment Little Pete might freak out and choke him, or teleport him, or at least start howling, carried the boy ashore.

Edilio took with him the boat's emergency kit, which amounted to little more than a few Band-Aids, a book of matches, two emergency flares, and a tiny compass.

'How do we get Little Pete up this cliff?' Sam wondered aloud. 'It's not a really hard climb, but . . .'

'He can climb,' Astrid said. 'He climbs trees sometimes. When he wants to.'

Sam and Edilio wore identical expressions of doubt.

'He can,' Astrid said. 'I just need to remember the trigger words. Something about a cat.'

'OK.'

'He followed a cat up a tree once.'

'I don't know if we have tides any more,' Quinn said, 'but if we do, this beach is going to be underwater soon.'

'Charlie Tuna,' Astrid said.

The three boys stared at her.

'The cat,' she explained. 'His name was Charlie Tuna.' She crouched next to Little Pete. 'Petey. Charlie Tuna? Charlie Tuna? Remember?'

'This is not too crazy,' Quinn muttered under his breath.

Sam said, 'OK, how about Edilio, you go first, then Astrid so Little Pete will follow you. Quinn and I will come last in case L. P. slips.'

It turned out Astrid was right, Little Pete could climb. In fact, he almost passed Astrid on the way up. Nevertheless, it took them till dark to gain the top of the cliff. By the time they finally collapsed on a bed of grass and pine needles beneath towering trees, they needed every one of the Band-Aids Edilio had brought.

'I guess we sleep here,' Sam said.

'It's warm out,' Astrid said.

'It's dark,' Sam said.

'Let's light a fire,' Astrid said.

'Keep the bears away, huh?' Edilio agreed nervously.

'That's a myth, unfortunately,' Astrid said. 'Wild animals see fire all the time. They're not especially scared of it.'

Edilio shook his head ruefully. 'Sometimes, Astrid, you knowing everything isn't really helpful.'

'Understood,' Astrid said. 'What I meant to say was that bears, like all wild animals, are terrified of fire.'

'Yeah. Too late.' Edilio peered nervously into the blacker-than-black shadows beneath the trees.

Astrid and Edilio watched Little Pete while Sam and Quinn searched for firewood.

Quinn, nervous for more than one reason, said, 'This isn't me dogging you or anything, Sam, but brah, if you really do have some kind of magic, you need to be figuring out how to use it.'

'I know,' Sam said. 'Believe me, if I knew how to turn on a light, I would.'

'Yeah. You always have been scared of the dark.'

After a while Sam said, 'I didn't think you knew that.'

'It's no big thing. Everybody's scared of something,' Quinn said softly.

'What are you scared of?'

'Me?' Quinn paused, holding his few sticks of firewood, and considered. 'I guess I'm scared of being a nothing. A great big ... nothing.'

They collected enough wood and enough pine needles for kindling and soon they had a cheerful, if smoky, fire burning.

Edilio stared into the flames, 'That's better, even if it

doesn't scare any bears. Plus, I'm not on that boat any more. I like solid land.'

The warmth of the fire was unnecessary, but Sam enjoyed it anyway. The orange light reflected dully from tree trunks and branches and made the night even darker. But while the fire burned, they could pretend to be safe.

'Anyone know any ghost stories to tell?' Edilio asked, half joking.

'You know what I'd like?' Astrid asked. 'S'mores. I was at camp once. It was an old-fashioned camp with fishing and horseback riding and these awful sing-alongs by the fire. And s'mores. I didn't like them then, mostly because I didn't want to be at camp. But now . . .'

Sam peered at her through the flames. The starched white blouses of the pre-FAYZ had given way to T-shirts. And he wasn't completely intimidated by her any more, not now that he'd been through so much with her. But she was still so beautiful that sometimes he had to look away. And the fact that he had kissed her meant that now every thought of her came with a flood of overwhelming memories, scents, sensations, tastes.

He fidgeted and bit his lip, using the pain to keep him from thinking any more about Astrid and her shirt and her hair and skin. 'Not the time, not the place,' he muttered under his breath.

Little Pete sat, legs crossed, and stared into the fire. Sam wondered what was going on in his head. He wondered what power was concealed behind those innocent eyes.

'Hungry,' Little Pete said. 'Munchy munchy.'

Astrid gave him a hug. 'I know, little brother. We'll get food tomorrow.'

One by one they felt their eyelids grow heavy. One by one they stretched out, fell silent, slept. Sam was the last. The fire was dying. The darkness was moving in from every direction.

He sat cross-legged, criss-cross-applesauce they called it when he was in kindergarten, turned his hands around, palms up, and lay them on his knees.

How?

How did it happen? How had this happened to him?

How could he control it, make it happen on command?

He closed his eyes and tried to recall the panic he'd felt whenever he had created light. It wasn't hard to remember the emotion, but it was impossible to feel it.

As quietly as he could, he stole away from the fire. The darkness under the trees might conceal a thousand terrors. He walked towards his fear.

Pine needles crunched beneath his feet. He walked until he could only just make out the faint glow of the fire's embers behind him and could no longer smell the piney smoke.

He raised his hands, the way he'd seen Caine do, palms out, like he was signalling someone to stop, or else like he was a pastor blessing a congregation.

He dredged up the fear of that nightmare in his bedroom, the panic when Little Pete was choking him, the sudden reaction when the fire-starter tried to kill him.

Nothing. It wasn't going to work. He couldn't simulate fear, and trying to scare himself with a dark forest wasn't working, either.

He spun. A noise behind him.

'It's not working, is it?' Astrid said.

'It almost did, you almost scared me enough to make it happen,' Sam said.

Astrid came closer. 'I have a terrible thing I want to tell you.'

'A terrible thing?'

'I betrayed Petey. Drake. He wanted me to call him a name.'

She was twisting her fingers together so hard, it looked painful.

Sam took her hands in his. 'What did he do?'

'Nothing. Just . . .'

'Just what?'

'He slapped me a couple of times, it wasn't so bad, but –'

'He hit you?' It felt like he had swallowed acid. 'He hit you?'

Astrid nodded. She tried to explain, but her voice betrayed her. So she pointed at the side of her face, at the place where Drake's hand had hit her with enough force to jerk her head sideways. She steadied and tried again. 'No big deal. But I was scared. Sam, I was so scared.' She stepped closer, wanting maybe to have his arms around her.

Sam took a step back. 'I hope he's dead,' he said. 'I hope he's dead, because if he isn't, I'll kill him.'

'Sam.'

His fists were clenched. It felt like his brain was boiling inside his skull. His breath came shallow and harsh.

'Sam,' Astrid whispered. 'Try it now.'

He stared, uncomprehending.

'Now,' she yelled.

Sam raised his hands, palms out, aimed towards a tree.

'Aaaaahhhh!' he yelled, and bolts of brilliant, green-tinged light shot from his hands.

He dropped his hands to his side, panting, stunned by what he had done. The tree was burned through. It fell, slowly at first, then faster, and crashed heavily in a patch of thornbush.

Astrid came up behind him and slid her arms around him. He felt her tears on the back of his neck, her breath in his ear. 'I'm sorry, Sam.'

'Sorry?'

'You can't summon fear whenever you need it, Sam. But anger is fear aimed outward. Anger is easy.'

'You manipulated me?' He untwined her arms and turned to face her.

'It happened with Drake, just like I told you,' Astrid said. 'But I wasn't going to tell you until I saw you out here trying. You kept saying it was fear that made the power work. So, I thought . . .'

'Yeah.' He felt strangely defeated. He had just, for the first time, willed the light to come. But he felt sad, not elated. 'So, I have to be mad, not scared. I have to want to hurt people.'

'You'll learn to control it,' Astrid said. 'You'll get better at it, so that you can use the power without having to feel anything.'

'Well, won't that be a happy day?' Sam said with bitter

sarcasm. 'I'll be able to burn someone without feeling anything.'

'I'm sorry, Sam. I really am. Sorry for you, I mean, sorry this has to happen. You're right to be afraid of the power. But the truth is, we need you to have this power.'

They stood, distant from each other though only a foot apart. Sam's mind was far away, playing out memories from a time that seemed like a million years ago. A million years, or maybe just eight days.

'Sorry,' Astrid whispered again and threaded her arms beneath his to pull him against her.

He rested his chin on her head, looking past her, seeing the fire, seeing the darkness everywhere else, the darkness that had scared him ever since he was a baby.

'Sometimes you catch the wave. Sometimes the wave catches you,' he said at last.

'It's the FAYZ, Sam. It's not you, it's just the FAYZ.'

TWENTY NINE

LANA'S FOOT CAUGHT a root and she fell on to her hands and knees. Patrick bounded over to look at her, but kept his distance.

Nip, the coyote who was Lana's personal tormentor, snapped his jaws at her.

'I'm getting up, I'm getting up,' Lana muttered.

Her hands were scraped. Again.

Her knees were bloody. Again.

The pack was well out in front, weaving through sagebrush, leaping ditches, stopping to sniff at gopher holes, then moving on.

Lana could not keep up. No matter how fast she ran, the coyotes always outpaced her, and when she fell behind, Nip would snap at her heels, and occasionally draw blood.

Nip was a low-ranked coyote, anxious to prove himself to Pack Leader. But he wasn't vicious, not like some of them, so he wouldn't rip and tear at her with his teeth, he would only snarl and snap. But when she delayed the pack with her slow, clumsy human running, then Pack Leader would snarl at Nip and slash at him while Nip whimpered and abased himself.

Patrick was lowest of all in status, lower even than Lana. He was a big, strong dog, but he bounded along with his tail wagging, his tongue lolling, which the swift, efficient coyotes seemed to find contemptible.

The coyotes were solitary hunters, catching even the fastest rabbits or squirrels. Patrick was left to his own devices, and since he was much slower, he was going hungry.

Lana had been offered one of Pack Leader's kills – a half-eaten, still half-alive jackrabbit, but she wasn't that hungry. Yet.

She had almost forgotten that none of this was possible. Amazing how quickly she had come to accept a world defined by a giant barrier. Absurd that she knew she could heal with a touch. Ridiculous that she had accepted the fact that Pack Leader could speak. In words. In English, however garbled.

Madness.

Insanity.

But what had happened down in that mine, down where the seething darkness hid, far from the sun, far from the world of reason, had killed whatever doubt remained for Lana: the world had gone crazy.

She had gone crazy.

Lana's task now was to survive, not to analyse or understand, just to survive.

Her shoes were already beginning to fall apart. Her clothing was ripped in several places. She was filthy. She'd had to urinate and defecate in the open, like a dog.

Her legs and hands had been repeatedly torn by sharp rocks,

sliced by thorns, stabbed by mosquitoes. She had even been bitten by a cornered raccoon. But the wounds never lasted long. They hurt, each time they hurt, but Lana healed them.

They had run throughout the night, the coyotes, chasing the next meal.

It had been just twelve hours or so, but already it seemed like forever.

'I'm a human,' she told herself. 'I'm smarter than he is. I'm superior. I'm a human being.'

But here in the wild, in the dark desert night, she wasn't superior. She was slower and more clumsy and weaker.

To keep her spirits up, Lana talked to Patrick, or to her mother. That, too, was crazy.

'Really enjoying my time here, Mom,' Lana said. 'I'm losing a little weight. The coyote diet. Don't eat anything and run all the time.'

Lana fell into a hole and felt her ankle twist and break. The pain was excruciating. But the pain would last only a minute. The exhaustion was far deeper, the despair more painful.

Pack Leader appeared, looking down at her from a jutting rock.

'Run faster,' Pack Leader ordered.

'Why are you keeping me prisoner?' she demanded. 'Kill me or let me go.'

'The Darkness says no kill,' Pack Leader said in his tortured, high-pitched, inhuman voice.

She did not ask him what he meant by 'the Darkness'. She

had heard its voice in her head, down at the bottom of Hermit Jim's gold mine. It was a scar on her soul, a scar her healing power could not touch.

'I'm only slowing you down,' Lana sobbed. 'Leave me here. Why do you want me around?'

'Darkness say: you teach. Pack Leader learn.'

'Learn what?' she cried. 'What are you talking about?'

Pack Leader leaped at her, knocked her flat on her back, and stood over her with his teeth bare above her exposed throat. 'Learn to kill humans. Gather all packs. Pack Leader leader of all. Kill humans.'

'Kill all humans? Why?'

Pack Leader was salivating. A long string of slobber fell from his muzzle on to her cheek. 'Hate human. Human kill coyote.'

'Stay out of towns and no one kill coyote,' Lana argued.

'All for coyote. All for Pack Leader. No human.' With his strained, unworldly voice, Pack Leader couldn't really rant for long, but the fury and hatred came through in very few words. She didn't know what a sane coyote would sound like if it could talk, but there was no doubt in her mind that this was an insane coyote.

Animals didn't get grandiose ideas about obliterating a whole species. That thought had not come from Pack Leader. Animals thought about food and survival and procreation, if they thought at all.

The thing in the cave. The Darkness. Pack Leader was its victim, as well as its servant.

The Darkness had filled Pack Leader with this evil ambition. But it had not been able to teach Pack Leader the ways to take on the humans. When Lana appeared at the gold mine, the Darkness had seized the opportunity to use her.

There were limits to the power of the Darkness, no matter how terrifying it might be. It needed to use the coyotes – and Lana – to carry out its will. And there were limits to what the Darkness knew, as well.

She knew what she had to do.

'Go ahead, kill me,' Lana said. She arched her neck, presenting it for him, defiant. 'Go ahead.'

One quick bite and it would all be over. She would let the wound bleed. She wouldn't heal it but would let her arteries pump her life out on to the desert sand.

At that moment, part of Lana wasn't sure she was bluffing. The Darkness had opened a door in her mind, a door to something almost as frightening as the Darkness itself.

'Go ahead,' she challenged the coyote. 'Go ahead and kill me.'

The coyote leader faltered. He let loose an anxious, mewling sound. He had never caught helpless prey that did not struggle for life.

It was working. Lana pushed Pack Leader's wet muzzle away. She stood up, her ankle still painful.

'If you're going to kill me, kill me.'

Pack Leader's brown and yellow eyes burned holes in her, but she did not back down. 'I'm not afraid of you.'

Pack Leader flinched. But then his eyes went to Patrick, and back, with a sly sideways leer. 'Kill dog.'

It was Lana's turn to flinch. But she knew instinctively that she could not show weakness. 'Go ahead. Kill him. Then you'll have no way to threaten me.'

Again Pack Leader's scarred face showed confusion. The thought was complicated. It was a thought with more than one move, like trying to play chess and anticipate what would happen two or three moves further on.

Lana's heart leaped.

Yes, they were stronger and faster. But she was a human being, with a human brain.

The coyotes had changed in some ways from what they had been: some had muzzles and tongues that now allowed tortured speech, and they were bigger than they should have been, stronger than they should have been, even smarter than they had any right to be. But they were still coyotes, still simple, driven by hunger, by the desire for a mate, by a need for a place within the pack.

And the Darkness had not taught them how to lie or bluff.

'The Darkness says you teach,' Pack Leader said, falling back on familiar territory.

'Fine,' Lana said, her brain buzzing, trying to decide where to lead this conversation. Looking for the advantage. 'You leave my dog alone. And you get me some decent food. Some food that humans eat, not filthy half-chewed rabbits. And then I'll teach.'

'No human food here.'

That's right, you filthy, mangy animal, Lana thought as the next move fell into place. No human food here.

'I noticed,' she said, tamping down the triumph in her voice, keeping her face carefully neutral, giving nothing away. 'So take me to the place where the grass grows. You know what I'm talking about. The place where the patch of green grows in the desert. Take me there, or take me back to the Darkness and tell the Darkness you cannot control me.'

Pack Leader didn't like that, and he expressed his frustration not in human speech but in a series of angry yipping sounds that reduced the rest of the pack to anxious skulking.

He twisted away from her in a pantomime of frustration, unable to control or hide his simple emotions.

'See, Mom,' Lana whispered as she pressed healing hands on her ankle. 'Sometimes defiance is a good thing.'

Finally, without a word, Pack Leader trotted off towards the north-east. He moved, and the pack followed, but slowly, at a pace that Lana could match.

Patrick fell into step beside his master.

'They're smarter than you, boy,' Lana whispered to her dog. 'But they're not smarter than me.'

'Wake up, Jack.'

Computer Jack had fallen asleep at the keyboard. He was spending nights in the town hall, working to deliver on his promise of assembling a primitive cell phone system. It wasn't easy. But it was fun.

And it took his mind off other things.

It was Diana who had awakened him, shaking his shoulder.

'Oh, hi,' Computer Jack said.

'That computer keyboard face? It's not a great look for you.'

Jack felt his face and blushed. There were imprints of the square keys on his cheek.

'Big day today,' Diana said, moving across the room to the small refrigerator. She pulled out a soda, popped it open, raised the window shade, and drank while looking down at the plaza.

Computer Jack adjusted his glasses. One side was a little askew. 'It's a big day? Why?'

Diana laughed in her knowing way. 'We're going home for a visit.'

'Home?' It took Jack a few seconds to click. 'You mean to Coates?'

'Come on, Jack, say it like you're excited.'

'Why are we going to Coates?'

Diana came to him and put her hand against his cheek. 'So smart. And yet so slow sometimes. Don't you ever read that list Caine has you keep? You remember Andrew? It's his happy fifteenth. We have to get up there before the hour of doom.'

'Do I have to go? I have all this work to do . . .'

'Fearless Leader has a plan that includes you,' Diana said. She spread her hands, dramatic, like she was a magician revealing the payoff of an illusion. 'We're going to film the big moment.'

Jack was both frightened and excited by the idea. He loved anything involving technology, especially when it gave him an opportunity to show off his technical knowledge. But, like everyone, he'd heard what happened to the twins, Anna and Emma. He did not want to see anyone die, or disappear, or whatever it was they did.

Yet . . . it would be fascinating.

'The more cameras the better,' Jack mused aloud, already working on the problem, already picturing the layout. 'If it happens in a flash, we'll have to get lucky to get a shot at the precise second . . . Digital video, not stills. As expensive and high end as Drake can find. Each one has to have a tripod. And we'll need lots of light. It would be best if we had a simple background, you know, like a white wall or something. No, wait, maybe not white, maybe green, that way I can chroma-key. Also . . .' He stopped himself, embarrassed that he'd gotten carried away, and not liking what he was about to say.

'Also what?'

'Look, I don't want Andrew to get hurt.'

'Also what, Jack?' Diana pressed.

'Well, what if Andrew doesn't want to just stand there? What if he moves? Or tries to run away?'

Diana's expression was hard to read. 'You want him tied down, Jack?'

Jack looked away. He hadn't meant to say that. Not exactly. Andrew was nice enough . . . for a bully.

'I didn't say I want him tied down,' Jack said, emphasising the word 'want'. 'But if he moves out of frame, out of where the cameras are pointed . . .'

Diana said, 'You know, Jack, sometimes you worry me.'

Computer Jack felt a flush crawl up his neck. 'It's not my fault,' he said hotly. 'What am I supposed to do? And, anyway, who do you think you are? You do whatever Caine says, same as me.'

It was as angry as Jack had ever allowed himself to be in front of Diana. He flinched, waiting for her biting reply.

But she answered softly. 'I know what I am, Jack. I'm not a very nice person.' She pulled a rolling chair up and sat down close to him. Close enough that her nearness made him uncomfortable. Jack had only recently begun to really notice girls. And Diana was beautiful.

'Do you know why my father sent me to Coates?' Diana asked.

Jack shook his head.

'When I was ten years old, Jack, younger than you, I found out my father had a mistress. Do you know what a mistress is, Jack?'

He did. Or at least thought he did.

'So I told my mother about the mistress. I was mad at my father because he wouldn't get me a horse. My mom freaked out. Big scene between my mom and dad. Lots of screaming. My mom was going to get a divorce.'

'Did they get a divorce?'

'No. There wasn't time. Next day my mom slipped and fell down the big staircase we have. She didn't die, but she can't really do anything any more.' She pantomimed a person barely able to hold their head up. 'She has a nurse full-time, just has to lie there in her room.'

'I'm sorry,' he said.

'Yeah.' She clapped her hands together, signalling the end of sharing time. 'Come on, let's go. Pack up your little techie bag. Fearless Leader doesn't like hanging around.'

Jack obeyed. He began stuffing things – small tools, a thumb drive, a juice box – into his Hogwarts shoulder bag.

'It doesn't mean you're bad just because your mom got hurt in an accident,' Jack said.

Diana winked. 'I told the police my dad did it. I told them I saw him push her. They arrested him, it was all over the news. Messed up his business. The cops finally realised I was lying. Dad sent me to Coates Academy, the end.'

'I guess that's worse than what I did to get sent to Coates,' Jack conceded.

'And that's only part of the story. What I'm saying is that you don't seem like a bad person, Jack. And I have a feeling that later on, when you realise what's going on, you're going to feel bad about it. You know, guilty.'

He stopped packing, stood with a set of earbuds dangling. 'What do you mean? What do you mean about what's going on?'

'Come on, Jack. Your little PDA of doom? The list you keep for Caine? All the freaks? You know what that list is about. You know what's going to happen to the freaks.'

'I'm not doing anything, I'm just keeping the list for you and Caine.'

'But how will you feel then?' Diana asked.

'What do you mean?'

'Don't be deliberately obtuse, Jack. How will you feel when Caine starts going down that list?'

'It's not my fault,' Jack said desperately.

'You're a deep sleeper, Jack. Just now, while you were sleeping? I held your pudgy little hand. Probably as close as you'll ever get to holding hands with a girl. Assuming you even like girls.'

Jack knew what she was going to say next. She saw his fear and smirked triumphantly.

'So, what is it, Jack? What's your power?'

He shook his head, not trusting himself to talk.

'You haven't added your own name to the list, Jack. I wonder why? You know Caine uses freaks who are loyal to him. You know as long as you are completely loyal you'll be fine.' She leaned so close he was breathing her exhalation. 'You're a two bar, Jack. You used to be a nothing. Which means your powers are developing. Which means, surprise, that people can acquire the power late. Isn't that so?'

He nodded.

'And you didn't bother to tell us. I wonder what that means in terms of your loyalty?'

'I'm totally loyal,' Computer Jack blurted. 'I am totally loyal. You don't have to worry about me.'

'What is it you can do?'

Jack crossed the room on shaking legs. Without warning life

had turned suddenly dangerous. He opened the closet. He drew out a chair. The chair was steel, functional, no frills, but very solid. Except for the back of the chair, where the metal crossbar had been squeezed till it formed the perfect impression of fingers. As if it were made of clay, not steel.

He heard Diana's sudden, sharp gasp.

'I stubbed my toe,' Jack explained. 'It hurt a lot. I grabbed the chair while I was hopping around and yelling.'

Diana examined the metal, tracing the outline of his grip with her fingers. 'Well, well. You're stronger than you look, aren't you?'

'Don't tell Caine,' Jack pleaded.

'What do you think he would do to you?' Diana asked.

Jack was terrified now. Terrified of this impossible girl who never seemed to make sense. Suddenly he knew the answer. He had a way to push back.

'I know you did a reading on Sam Temple. I saw you,' he accused. 'You told Caine you didn't, but you did. He's a four bar, isn't he? Sam, I mean. Caine would lose it if he knew there was another four bar out there.'

Diana didn't even hesitate. 'Yes. Sam is a four bar. And Caine would freak. But, Jack: your word against mine? Who do you think Caine will believe?'

Jack had nothing else. No threat. His will crumbled. 'Don't let him hurt me,' he whispered.

Diana stopped. 'He will. He'll put you on the list. Unless I protect you. Are you asking me to protect you?'

Jack saw a ray of hope in his personal darkness. 'Yes. Yes.'

'Say it.'

'Please protect me.'

Diana's eyes seemed to melt, from ice cold to almost warm. She smiled. 'I'll protect you, Jack. But here's the thing. From now on you belong to me. Whenever I ask you to do something, Jack, you're going to do it. No questions asked. And you will not tell anyone else about your power, or about our deal.'

He nodded again.

'You belong to me, Jack. Not Caine. Not Drake. Me. My own little Hulk. And if I ever need you . . .'

'Whatever you want, I'll do it.'

Diana planted a butterfly kiss on Jack's cheek, sealing the deal. And she breathed into his ear, 'I know you will, Jack. Now, let's go.'

THIRTY

QUINN WAS SINGING a song. The lyrics were a sort of gloomy homage to surfing.

'That's perky,' Astrid commented drily.

Quinn said, 'It's Weezer. Me and Sam saw them down in Santa Barbara. Weezer. Jack Johnson. Insect Surfers. Awesome concert.'

'Never heard of any of them,' Astrid said.

'Surfer bands,' Sam said. 'Well, not Weezer so much, they're more ska-punk. But Jack Johnson, you'd probably like him.'

They were walking out of Stefano Rey National Park, downhill, down the dry side of the ridge. The trees were smaller and more sparse, mixing with tall, sere grasses.

That morning they had stumbled on a campground. The bears had gotten to a lot of the food there, but enough had survived for the five of them to eat a hearty breakfast. They now had backpacks and food and sleeping bags belonging to strangers. Edilio and Sam each had a good knife, and Quinn was charged with carrying the flashlights and batteries they had found.

The food had improved everyone's mood quite a bit. Little Pete had come very close to actually smiling.

They walked with the barrier on their left. It was an eerie

339

experience. Trees were often cut in half by the barrier, with branches extending into it and disappearing. Or else poking out of it. The branches that came out of the barrier did not fall, but they were clearly dying. The leaves were limp – cut off, it seemed, from nutrition.

From time to time Sam would check out some gully or peer behind a boulder, always looking for a place the barrier did not reach. But that soon came to seem pointless. The barrier reached into every ditch, every culvert. It wrapped itself around every rock, sliced through every bush.

It did not fail.

It did not end.

The workmanship of the barrier was, as Astrid had observed, impeccable.

'What kind of music do you like?' Sam asked.

'Let me guess,' Quinn interrupted. 'Classical. And jazz.' He stretched the word 'jazz' out to comic length.

'Actually –'

'Snake,' Edilio yelled. He danced backwards, tripped, and fell, bounced back up looking sheepish. Then, in a calmer tone, he said, 'There's a snake there.'

'Let me see,' Astrid said eagerly. She approached cautiously while Sam and Quinn stayed even more cautiously out of range.

'I don't like snakes,' Edilio admitted.

Sam grinned. 'Yeah, I kind of got that from the way you moved away so gracefully.' He brushed some clinging dirt and dry leaves off Edilio's back.

'You should look at this,' Astrid called urgently.

'You look at it,' Edilio said. 'I saw it once already. One look at a snake is all I need.'

'It's not a snake,' Astrid said. 'At least it's not just a snake. It should be fairly safe, he's down a hole.'

Sam approached reluctantly. He didn't really want to see the snake. But he also didn't want to look like a coward.

'Just don't startle it,' Astrid said. 'It may be capable of flight. At least short flights.'

Sam froze. 'Excuse me?'

'Just step lightly.'

Sam crept closer. And there it was. At first he just saw the triangular head peeking up from the bottom of a foot-deep hole padded with fallen leaves. 'Is that a rattlesnake?'

'Not any more,' Astrid said. 'Come around behind me.' When Sam was in position she said, 'Look. About six inches below his head.'

'What is that?' Flaps of leathery skin, not covered with scales, but grey and ribbed with what looked like pink veins, hung flat against the snake's body.

'They look like vestigial wings,' Astrid said.

'Snakes don't have wings,' Sam said.

'They didn't used to,' she said darkly.

The two of them drew slowly back. They rejoined Edilio, Quinn, and Little Pete, who was gazing up at the sky like he was expecting someone from that direction.

'What was it?' Quinn asked.

'A rattlesnake with wings,' Sam said.

'Ah. That's good, because I was thinking we didn't have quite enough to be worried about,' Quinn said.

'I'm not surprised,' Astrid said. When the others stared at her she explained. 'I mean, it's obvious that there's some sort of accelerated mutation at work in the FAYZ. In fact, given Petey and Sam and the others, the mutation must have preceded the FAYZ. But I suspect the FAYZ is accelerating the process. We saw the gull that had mutated. Then there was Albert's teleporting cat. Now this.'

'Let's get moving,' Sam said, mostly because there was no point standing around moping. Everyone walked more carefully now, eyes down, very aware of what they might step on.

They stopped for lunch when Little Pete started losing it and staged a sit-down strike. Sam helped make the food, then took his can of peaches and his Power Bar and sat alone at a distance from the others. He needed to think. They were all waiting for him to come up with a plan, he could feel it.

They were a little bit above the valley floor still, out in the open with no shade. The ground was rocky. The sun beat down. It didn't look like there was much in the way of shelter or shade ahead of them. Just the barrier extending on and on, forever and ever. From this height he should have been able to see over the top of it, but Astrid was right: no matter where you stood, the barrier seemed to be equally tall, equally impenetrable.

It glowed a little in the sunlight, but mostly the barrier never changed, day or night. It was always the same faintly shimmering grey. It was just reflective enough that sometimes you could almost believe you saw an opening, trees that extended beyond the barrier, or a feature of the land that seemed to pass through a hole in the barrier. But it was always an optical illusion, a trick of the light.

He felt rather than heard Astrid come up behind him.

'It's a sphere, isn't it?' he said. 'It goes all the way around us. All the way under us and all the way over us.'

'I think so,' she said.

'Why do we see the stars at night? Why can we see the sun?'

'I'm not sure we're seeing the sun,' Astrid said. 'It may be an illusion. It may be some kind of reflection. I don't know.' She stepped deliberately on a small twig and snapped it in half. 'I really don't know.'

'You hate saying "I don't know", don't you?'

Astrid laughed. 'You noticed.'

Sam sighed and hung his head. 'This is a waste of time, isn't it? I mean, trying to find a gate. Trying to find a way out.'

'There may not be an out,' Astrid confirmed.

'Is the world still there? I mean, on the other side of the barrier?'

She sat beside him, close enough to be companionable, but not touching. 'I've been thinking a lot about it. I liked your egg idea. But to tell you the truth, Sam, I don't think the barrier is just a wall. A wall doesn't explain what's happening to us. To you and Petey and the birds and Albert's cat and the snakes. And it doesn't explain why everyone over fourteen disappeared all at once. And keeps disappearing.'

'What would explain all that?' He held up a hand. 'Wait, I don't want to make you say it again: you don't know.'

'Remember when Quinn said "someone hacked the universe"?'

'You're getting your ideas from Quinn now? What happened to you being a genius?'

She ignored the gibe. 'The universe has certain rules. Like the operating-system software for a computer. None of what we're seeing can be happening under the software of our universe. The way Caine can move things with his mind. The way you can make light come from your hands. These aren't just mutations: they are violations of the laws of nature. At least the laws of nature as we understand them.'

'Yeah. So?'

'So.' She shook her head ruefully, disbelieving her own words as she said them. 'So I think it means . . . we're not in the old universe any more.'

Sam stared at her. 'There's only one universe.'

'The theory of multiple universes has been around for a long time,' Astrid said. 'But maybe something happened that began altering the rules of the old universe. Just a little, just in a small area. But the effect spread, and at some point it became impossible for the old universe to contain this new reality. A new universe was created. A very small universe.' She took a deep breath, a relieved sound, like she'd just set down a heavy load. 'But you know what, Sam? I'm smart, but I'm not exactly Stephen Hawking.'

'Like if someone installed a virus in the software of the old universe.'

'Right. It started small. Some changes in individuals. Petey. You. Caine. Kids more than adults because kids are less fully formed, they're easier to alter. Then, on that morning, something happened that tipped the balance. Or maybe several somethings.'

'How do we get through that barrier, Astrid?'

She laid her hand over his. 'Sam, I'm not sure there is a "through". When I say we're in a different universe, I mean we may not have any point of contact with the old universe. Maybe we're like soap bubbles that can drift together and join. But maybe we're like soap bubbles a billion miles apart.'

'Then what's on the other side of the barrier?'

'Nothing,' she said. 'There is no other side. The barrier may be the end of all that is here in this new universe.'

'You're depressing me,' he said, trying and failing to make it light-hearted.

She twined her fingers through his. 'I could be wrong.'

'I guess I'll find out in . . . what is today? In less than a week.'

Astrid had no answer for that. They sat together and gazed out over the desert. In the distance a lone coyote trotted along, nose down to catch a scent of prey. A pair of buzzards inscribed lazy circles against the sky.

After a while Sam turned towards Astrid and found her lips waiting. It felt easy and natural. As easy and natural as something could feel that made Sam's heart threaten to break out of his chest.

They drew apart, saying nothing. They leaned against each other, both revelling in that simple physical contact.

'You know what?' Sam said at last.

'What?'

'I can't spend the next four days in a permanent cringe,' Sam said.

Astrid nodded, a movement he felt rather than saw.

'You make me brave, you know?' Sam said.

'I was just thinking that I don't want you to be brave any more,' Astrid said. 'I want you to be with me. I want you to be safe and not go looking for trouble, just stay with me, stay close to me.'

'Too late,' he said with forced lightness. 'If I blink out, where does that leave you and Little Pete?'

'We can take care of ourselves,' she lied.

'You're very confusing, you know that?' Sam said.

'Well, you're not as smart as I am, so you're easy to confuse.'

He grinned. Then grew serious again. He stroked her hair with one hand. 'The thing is, Astrid, I can spend the time being afraid, trying to find a way to escape. Or I can spend the time standing up. Maybe then, if I do disappear, maybe at least you and Little Pete . . .'

'We could all just –' she began.

'Nah. We couldn't. We couldn't just hide out in the woods eating dehydrated camping food. We can't just hide.'

Astrid's lip trembled and she brushed at a tear just forming.

'We have to go back. At least, I do. I have to stand up.'

As if to illustrate the point, Sam stood up. He took Astrid's hand and drew her after him. Together they walked back to the others.

'Edilio. Quinn. I have made a lot of mistakes. And maybe I'm making one now, too. But I'm tired of avoiding a fight. And I'm tired of trying to run away. I'm very, very worried I'm going to get you all killed. So you guys all have to decide for yourselves whether you want to go with me. But I have to go back to Perdido Beach.'

'We're going to fight Caine?' Quinn asked in alarm.

'About time,' Edilio said.

'Welcome to McDonald's,' Albert said. 'How may I help you?'

'Hey, Albert,' Mary said. She looked up at the menu, which had a number of items covered over with taped-on black construction paper. Salads had disappeared quickly. Milkshakes were gone because the machine had broken down.

Albert waited patiently and smiled at the little girl with Mary. Mary noticed and said, 'Oh, I'm sorry, I should introduce you. This is Isabella. Isabella, this is Albert.'

'Welcome to McDonald's,' Albert said.

'Isabella is new. A search team just found her and brought her in.'

'My mom and dad are gone,' Isabella said.

'I know. My parents are gone, too,' Albert replied.

'I guess a Big Mac and a Biggie fries for me,' Mary said. 'And a kid's meal for Isabella.'

'Chicken nuggets or hamburger?'

'Nuggets.'

'And would you like that Big Mac with a bagel bun, an English muffin bun, or on a waffle?'

'Waffle?'

Albert shrugged. 'Sorry, Mary, but there's no fresh bread to be found anywhere. I'm using anything frozen I can get for buns. And of course there's no lettuce, but you know that.'

'Still have special sauce?'

'I have about fifty gallons of Big Mac sauce. And as far as pickles, I'm good forever. Let me get your order started. I'd go with the bagel bun, I was you.'

'Bagel, then.'

Albert dropped a fresh basket of fries into hot oil. Then an order of nuggets in a second basket. He punched both timers. He moved with ease to the grill and slapped three patties down.

He laid out the bagel, squirted on some sauce, sprinkled onions, placed two pickle chips in the centre of the bagel top.

He waited and watched Mary trying to cheer Isabella up in the dining area. The little girl was solemn and seemed on the edge of tears.

Albert flipped the burgers and settled the burger press in place to speed cooking.

The fry timer went off. He lifted the basket, shook it to throw off extra oil, and tossed the fries into the bin. A quick pass with the salt shaker. Then up came the nuggets.

Albert enjoyed the balletic moves he had practised and

perfected over the last – how many days had it been? Eight? Nine? Nine days running the McDonald's.

'Cool,' Albert said with quiet satisfaction.

Since the incident everyone now referred to as 'Albert's Cat', Albert had stayed in, or at least close to, the McDonald's. There were no supernatural, teleporting cats in the McDonald's.

He assembled the order on to two trays and carried them out to the only occupied table.

'Thanks,' Mary said gratefully.

'We ran out of our regular promo,' Albert said. 'But I got some toys, you know, little stuff from Ralph's or whatever. So there is a toy in the Happy Meal. Just not the regular one.'

Isabella pulled a tiny plastic doll with bright pink hair from her bag. She did not smile. But she did hold on to the doll.

'So, how long can you keep this place open?' Mary asked.

'Well, I have lots of burger patties. The day of the FAYZ there was a delivery truck coming through. You must have seen it ploughed into that old house up behind the garage, right? Anyway, when I got there the engine was still running, so the cooling unit was still on. I have my walk-in packed. Plus I have burgers stashed in freezers all over town.' He nodded in satisfaction. 'I have sixteen thousand, two hundred and eighty patties – including Quarter Pounders. I'm selling about two hundred and fifty a day. So I'm good for about two months, give or take. Fries will run out sooner.'

'Then what?'

Albert hesitated, like he wasn't sure if he should get into it, but then, glad to have someone to share his worries with, he said, 'Look, we can't live forever on the food we have. I mean, OK, we have all the food here, all the food at the grocery store, and a bunch of food in all the different houses, right?'

'That's a lot of food. Sit with us, Albert.'

He was uncomfortable doing so. 'It says in the manual we don't sit down with customers. But I guess I could take a break and sit at this next table.'

Mary smiled. 'You're into this.'

Albert nodded. 'When the FAYZ comes down I want the district manager to come here and say, "Wow, good job, Albert."'

'It's more than a good job. You make people think maybe there's some hope, you know?'

'Thanks, Mary, that's cool of you to say that.' He thought it was the nicest thing anyone had ever said to him and it gave him a nice glow. Lots of kids just came in and complained that he didn't have exactly what they wanted.

'But you're worried about what happens next?' Mary prompted.

'There's a lot of food now. But already there are shortages. You almost can't find a candy bar or chips any more. Sodas will run out before too much longer. And eventually we'll be out of everything.'

'How long is eventually?'

'I don't know. But pretty soon people will be fighting over food. We're using food up. We're not growing more food or making or creating new things.'

Mary had taken two bites of the Big Mac. 'Does Caine know this?'

'I've told him. But he's got his mind on other things.'

'This is kind of a major problem,' Mary said.

Albert didn't want to talk about sad things, not while someone was enjoying his food. But Mary was the one asking, and as far as Albert was concerned, Mary was a saint just like the ones in the church. He shrugged and said, 'I'm just trying to do my thing here.'

'Can we grow food?' Mary wondered aloud.

'I guess that's up to Caine or . . . whoever,' Albert said cautiously.

Mary nodded. 'You know what, Albert? I don't really care who is running things, but I have to look out for my kids.'

'And I have this place,' Albert agreed.

'And Dahra has the hospital,' Mary added. 'And Sam used to have the fire station.'

'Yeah.'

It was a weird moment for Albert. He admired Mary, he thought she was the most beautiful person he'd ever known aside from his mom, and he wanted to trust Mary. But he didn't know for sure that he could. He was troubled by what was going on in Perdido Beach. But what if Mary felt differently? What if she told Drake that Albert was complaining, maybe without even meaning to?

Drake could order him to shut down. And Albert didn't know what he would do with himself if he lost the restaurant.

351

The work had kept him from thinking much about what had happened. And for the first time in his life, Albert was an important person. At school he was just another kid. Now he was Albert Hillsborough: businessman.

All things considered, Albert would want Caine and Drake gone. But the only other person who might step up and run things was off somewhere, a hunted person.

'How's the burger?' he asked Mary.

'You know what?' She smiled and licked ketchup from her finger. 'I think I actually like it better with the bagel bun.'

THEY DROVE WITH maddening slowness from Perdido Beach to Coates. Panda at the wheel, even more nervous than usual, terrified, it seemed to Jack. It was dark, and Panda kept saying he had never driven in the dark. It had taken him five fumbling minutes just to find the lights and figure them out.

Caine sat beside him, chewing on his thumb, quiet, but preoccupied. He had cross-examined Jack repeatedly on the procedure for recording Andrew's big exit. Somehow what had started out as Caine's brainstorm had become Jack's responsibility. If it worked, then Caine would reclaim it as his own. But if it failed, Jack would no doubt take the blame.

Diana, who sat beside Jack, for once had little to say. Jack wondered if she dreaded the return to Coates as much as he did.

Jack was wedged in between Diana and Drake. Drake was holding a handgun, an automatic, more grey than black, in his lap.

Jack had never seen a gun up close. He had certainly never seen a gun in the hands of a boy he thought was probably crazy.

Drake could not leave the gun alone. He kept thumbing the

353

safety on and off. He rolled down the window and aimed it at stop signs as they passed, but did not fire it.

'You know how to shoot that thing? Or are you going to shoot yourself in the foot?' Diana finally asked.

'He's not going to shoot it,' Caine snapped before Drake could answer. 'It's just a prop. We want Andrew to behave. And you know how difficult he can be. The gun keeps people calmed down.'

'Yeah, I know, it makes me feel really calm,' Diana said.

'Shut up, Diana,' Drake said.

Diana laughed in her drawly way and fell silent again.

Jack was sweating, although it was a cool evening and Caine had the windows down. Jack felt like he might throw up. He'd considered saying he was too sick to go, but he knew Caine wouldn't let him stay home. He'd felt worse and worse all day as he raced to assemble the equipment they would need. He had spent the day with Drake, searching homes for cameras and tripods. Jack had already had enough of Drake Merwin to last him forever.

They neared the gate. It was an impressive thing, two sides of filigreed wrought iron, twenty feet high and hanging from pillars of stone that were even taller. The Coates motto, *Ad augusta, per angusta*, was on two gold-tinged plaques that came together when the gates were closed.

'Honk the horn. Whoever's on gate must be asleep,' Caine ordered.

Panda tapped the horn. When there was no response, he

leaned on it. The sound was flat, swallowed up by the trees.

'Drake,' Caine said.

Drake climbed out, gun in hand, and advanced to the gate. He swung it open and stepped through to the stone guardhouse. He emerged a few seconds later and climbed back into the car.

'No one in the guardhouse.'

Caine frowned in the rear-view mirror. 'That's not like Benno. Benno follows orders.'

Benno was the thug Caine had left in charge at Coates. Jack had never liked the boy – no one did – but Caine was right: Benno was the kind of bully who did what the bigger bullies told him to do. He didn't make his own judgements. And he wasn't stupid enough to think he could override Caine's orders.

'Something isn't right,' Panda said.

'Everything isn't right, Panda,' Diana said.

Panda pulled through the gate. It was another quarter-mile to the school. They drove in silence. Panda pulled the car up to the end of the driveway, to the turnaround in front of the main building.

Lights were on in every window. One of the second-floor windows had been blown out so that an entire classroom could be clearly seen.

Desks were piled against one wall. The chalkboard was cracked and scarred. All the drawings and posters and exhortations that had once adorned the classroom walls were charred, curled by heat. A massive slab of brick and lathe wall lay on the lawn.

'Well, that's not good,' Diana drawled.

'Who has the power to do that?' Caine demanded angrily.

'The kid we're here to see,' Diana said. 'Although that's a lot of damage for a three bar.'

'Benno's lost control up here,' Drake commented. 'I told you Benno was a wimp.'

'Come on,' Caine said, and stepped out on to gravel, followed by the rest of them. 'Go up the stairs, Panda, open the door. Let's see what's waiting for us.'

'No way,' Panda said, his voice shaky.

'Coward,' Caine said. He raised his hands, palms out, and suddenly Panda was flying through the air. He slammed into the door and fell in a heap. Panda rose slowly, then he fell down again. 'My leg is hurt. I can't move it.'

At that moment the front door opened, smacking Panda where he lay. Light spilled out from inside and Jack saw half a dozen shapes, shapes like apes walking on all fours, pushing their way out, crying, howling, terrified.

They tumbled down the steps. Each carrying a rough-hewn cement block that they dragged as they ran. But of course Jack knew they weren't carrying the blocks. Their hands were encased in cement.

Jack had tried not to think about it. He had tried to put it out of his mind, this crude, cruel solution to the problem of disloyal kids with powers. But since discovering his own power he had thought of little else.

They had discovered early on that the supernatural powers seemed to be focused through the hands.

No, Jack corrected himself harshly, *they* hadn't discovered it, *he* had discovered it. He had observed it. And he had told Caine about it. And Caine had ordered Drake to do this horrible thing.

'Remember who owns you,' Diana whispered in Jack's ear.

'Feed us! Feed us! We need food!' the concrete-blocked victims cried.

It was a chorus of weak, desperate voices, so raw with need that Jack panicked. He couldn't be here. He couldn't be with these people. He turned away, but Drake grabbed his shoulder and yanked him forwards.

No escape.

The freaks cried for food.

A girl named Taylor, her arms red and raw above the block, face streaked with filth, stinking of her own bodily fluids, collapsed at Jack's feet. 'Jack,' she croaked. 'They're starving us. Benno was feeding us, but he disappeared. We haven't eaten . . . Please, Jack.'

Jack doubled over and threw up in the gravel.

'Rather overdramatic, Jack,' Diana remarked.

Caine was walking up the steps now and Drake rushed to catch up.

Diana half lifted Jack and propelled him forwards, past the kids with the cinder-block hands.

Jack saw Caine silhouetted in the doorway, Drake rushing to move in front, good little dog that he was.

There was a boom, like the crack of a supersonic jet going overhead.

Drake fell back against Caine. The gun went flying from his hand. Caine kept his footing, but Drake clutched at his ears, on his knees, moaning.

Caine reached back over his shoulder with one hand, not even looking back. He spread his fingers, bared his palms.

The fallen portion of wall came apart, brick by brick. One by one, as though each brick had sprouted wings, they lifted off and flew.

The bricks hurtled past Caine's head and through the open door as fast as machine-gun bullets.

The door slammed shut. The bricks smashed through. Wood splintered with a sound like a jackhammmer. In seconds the door was a shattered mess.

Caine laughed, taunting whoever was on the other side of the door. 'Is that you, Andrew? Is that you, thinking you can fight me?'

Caine advanced, still directing the Gatling gun flow of bricks above his head.

'You've got your mojo working, Andrew,' Caine yelled. 'But you're still just second best.'

Caine stepped through the decimated doorway.

Diana, ducking beneath the brick stream, her expression wild with excitement, said, 'Come on, Jack. You don't want to miss the show.'

Inside was the grand hallway that Jack knew well. Three storeys high, dominated by a massive chandelier. Twin staircases led to the landing on the first floor.

The bricks had already hammered one of those staircases to splinters. The noise was like a chainsaw chewing on metal.

Andrew, a boy Jack had known as a fairly nice kid, not even really much of a bully until his powers had come, stood shell-shocked not ten feet from Caine. There was a wet stain in the crotch of his pants.

The barrage of bricks stopped as suddenly as it had begun.

Andrew made an abortive move for the second staircase.

'Don't make me destroy that staircase, too,' Caine warned. 'It would be very inconvenient.'

The fight went out of Andrew. He let his hands drop to his sides. He looked like a kid whose mother had just caught him doing something wrong. Guilty. Scared. Looking for a way to bargain.

'Caine. I didn't know it was you, dude. I thought we were, like, you know, being attacked by Frederico.' His voice shook. He tried to cover the telltale stain with his hands.

'Freddie? What has Frederico got to do with anything?'

'Man, Benno disappeared, right? And someone had to run things, right? Frederico tried to take over, even though Benno was more my friend than his and then –'

'I'll handle Freddie later,' Caine interrupted. 'Who do you think you are, trying to run things, Andrew?'

'What was I supposed to do, Caine?' Andrew wheedled. 'Benno poofed. Frederico was all, like, I'm taking over. But me, I was standing up for you, Caine.' The idea had obviously just occurred to Andrew. 'That's all I was doing, I was standing up for you. Frederico was, like, Caine sucks, forget Caine, I'm taking over.'

Caine tuned Andrew out and aimed a furious glare at Jack. 'How did we miss Benno's birthday?'

Jack had no answer. His insides turned to water. He shrugged, helpless. Then he began to fumble for his PDA, wanting to prove that Benno's birthday was not due yet.

Diana said, 'Caine, you think maybe sometimes the school records could be wrong? Like maybe some senile school secretary wrote down a one instead of a seven or whatever? Don't blame Jack. You know Jack is too anal to make a mistake with a number.'

Caine stared hard at Jack. Then he shrugged. 'Yeah, whatever. Besides, we still have Andrew getting ready for his big jump.'

Andrew licked his lips, then tried to laugh. 'I'm not going to vacate. I'm not taking the exit. See, Benno was asleep. He had powers, but the dude was asleep. So I don't think if you have powers you poof, not if you're awake and you're, you know, ready.'

Diana laughed out loud, a jarring sound.

Caine flinched. Then he said, 'That's an interesting theory, Andrew. We're going to put it to the test.'

'What's that mean?'

'We just want to watch,' Drake said.

'Just don't . . . you're not going to plaster me, right? I'm still your guy, Caine, I would never use my powers against you. If I knew it was you, I mean.'

Diana snapped, 'You're letting these freaks starve. I can see why you'd be worried about being plastered.'

'Hey, we're running out of food,' Andrew whined.

'Drake, shoot the creep,' Diana said.

Drake just laughed.

'I think we'll do this in the dining hall,' Caine said. 'Jack, do you have your gear?'

Jack jumped six inches, startled at being addressed again. 'No. No. I-I-I have to go back and get it.'

'Drake, take I-I-I and get the stuff,' Caine said. 'Diana, take Andrew's hand and lead him to the dining hall.'

It was a sound that was almost quaint when the sun was shining. But now, in the dark, the yip-yip-howl sent shivers down their spines.

'It's just a coyote,' Sam said. 'Don't worry about him.'

They could barely see where they were placing their feet, so they moved slowly, tentatively.

'Maybe we should have camped back in that gulch,' Edilio said.

'As soon as we find a fairly flat place to lay out our sleeping bags, I'm all for stopping,' Sam said.

Hours before, they had come to a deep, steep-sided gulch, impossible to bypass, and almost impossible to climb. Little Pete had gone into a complete meltdown while being hauled bodily up the far side of the gulch, and they had all been terrified he might do something.

'Hawaii,' Quinn began saying, as Little Pete howled. 'Hawaii.'

'Why you keep saying Hawaii, man?' Edilio had asked him.

'If he freaks and decides to take us on a Little Pete magical mystery tour, I want it to be Hawaii, not back to Astrid's house.'

Edilio thought that over for a while. 'I'm down with that. Hawaii, L. P., Hawaii.'

But Little Pete had not choked anyone, had not teleported anyone or otherwise violated the original laws of physics.

The barrier was farther and farther off to their left, all but invisible in the light of the rising moon. Sam was still determined to follow it, but no longer with any real hope of finding a gate, just because it was the only way he knew to find his way home. Sooner or later the barrier would curve back around to Perdido Beach.

There was a startlingly loud yip, yip, yip.

'Jeez, that was close,' Edilio said.

Sam nodded. 'That direction. Maybe we veer off a little, huh?'

'I thought coyotes were nothing,' Edilio grumbled.

'They are. Normally.'

'Tell me you're not thinking about coyotes growing wings,' Edilio said.

'I think we're getting more sand and less rock,' Astrid observed. 'Petey hasn't tripped in a while.'

'I can't see well enough to be sure,' Sam said. 'But let's pull up in five minutes, either way. Everyone start looking for firewood as you go.'

'If I can't see the ground how am I going to see firewood?' Quinn asked.

'Hey. Look.' Sam pointed. 'There's something over there. I think. Looks like . . . I don't know, a building or something.'

'I can't see a thing,' Quinn said.

'It's just darker than the regular darkness. I'm not seeing stars.'

They veered towards it. There might be food or water or shelter.

Suddenly Sam's feet landed on a springy surface that reminded him of the soft pine needle flooring of the forest. He bent down and felt what could only be grass.

'Guys, hold up.'

Sam was cautious about using the flashlights. They had a limited supply of batteries and an unlimited supply of darkness. 'Quinn. Give us some light here.'

There was no mistaking the green colour, even in the harsh white light.

Cautiously Quinn played the light around and illuminated a cabin. Beside it was a windmill.

They approached cautiously, the five of them bunched up around the doorway as Quinn shone the light on a door handle, and Sam touched it, gripped it, and froze.

He heard the sound of running, scuffling steps in the darkness behind them.

'Get inside, you idiots!' a voice, a girl's voice, screamed.

Quinn swivelled the light, a rush of motion, something pelting towards him.

Other things moving, like a sea of grey in the gloom.

The beam bounced from a bounding dog on to the terrified face of a ragged, filthy girl.

'Run! Run!' she screamed.

Sam grabbed the door handle and twisted it. But before he could throw it open the girl ploughed into Sam and bowled him over so that he sprawled on to the wooden floor and gathered a rug as he slid. A dog landed on his chest and bounced off.

Quinn shouted in pain and shock. He had lost the light. It was still shining across a planked floor and he scrambled after it. In the beam Sam saw Astrid's legs, Edilio falling.

There came a chorus of angry canine yipping and the girl who had run Sam down was fighting to stand up and a dog was barking and snarling and there were other snarls too as swift bodies came in a rush.

'The door! Get the door!' the girl screamed.

Something was on her, something quick and furious, snarling.

Sam lurched to his feet, grabbed the door, and tried to slam it closed, but a furry body was in the way. There was a canine protest, a snarl, and sudden pain in his leg. An iron jaw closed around his knee, bone-crushingly strong.

Sam fell against the door and it closed. He slipped and landed on his butt against the door and the animal, the wild, snarling thing, had its muzzle in his face. Teeth snapped an inch from his eyes.

He shoved his hands outward and encountered rough fur over writhing muscle.

There was a terrible, sharp pain in his shoulder, and he knew the beast's jaws had closed on his flesh, and now the animal was shaking him, tearing at his flesh, ripping it, digging deeper.

Sam cried out in fear and beat with nerveless fists against the beast. It was futile. The beast shifted its jaws with lightning speed from shoulder to Sam's neck. Blood sprayed down his chest.

Sam raised his hands, palms out, but the onslaught was too ferocious. His jugular was pumping his brain dry. His hands were no longer his. His entire body now seemed far away. He spiralled down and down into darkness.

A soft, heavy thud.

And the iron jaw loosed its hold.

Another heavy thud.

Sam's eyes rolled up in his head, but before he passed out, he caught a glimpse of the wild, ragged girl standing over him. The girl raised her hands, both together, over her head. All was in slow motion for Sam, and there were sparks in his eyes as the girl brought down something heavy and rectangular and yellow on the coyote's head.

LANA LIT ONE of Hermit Jim's lanterns and surveyed the scene. The cabin was just as she had left it. Only now there were two dead coyotes, three scared kids, a creepy, staring four-year-old, and one nearly dead boy on the floor.

She kicked Nip with her toe. No reflex. He was dead, his brain smashed by a solid gold bar. She'd pounded him again and again until her arms were tired.

The other coyote she didn't know well enough to name. But he had died the same way, too intent on his prey to realise his peril.

Patrick lay in a corner, abashed, confused, not knowing how to behave. One of the kids, a surfer-looking dude, seemed to mirror that confusion.

'Good boy,' Lana said, and Patrick thumped his tail weakly on the floor.

'Who are you?' Lana asked the surfer kid.

'Quinn. My name is Quinn.'

'How about you?' the pretty blonde girl asked.

Lana was inclined to dislike her at first sight: she looked like the kind of too-perfect girl who would blow off someone like

Lana. On the other hand, she was shielding the strange little boy, cradling him in her arms, so maybe she wasn't all bad.

A kid with a round face and dark crew cut knelt over the wounded kid. 'Guys, he's hurt bad.'

The blonde scrambled to him. She tore the wounded boy's shirt open. A river of blood ran down his chest.

'Oh, God, no,' the blonde cried.

Lana pushed her aside and laid a hand against the pumping wound. 'He'll live,' Lana said. 'I'll fix him.'

'What do you mean, you'll fix him?' the blonde demanded. 'We need stitches, we need a doctor. Look at how he's bleeding.'

Lana said, 'What's your name?'

'Astrid, what does it matter? He's . . .' She stopped talking then and leaned in close to see. 'The blood flow is slowing.'

'Yeah. I noticed that, too,' Lana said drily. 'Relax. He'll be fine. In fact . . .' She tilted her head to get a better look at him. 'In fact, I'll bet when he's not covered in blood, he's cute. Your boyfriend?'

'That's not what it's about,' Astrid snapped. Then, in a low voice, like she didn't want the others to hear, she said, 'Kind of.'

'Well, I know how crazy this sounds, but he'll be fine in a few minutes.' She pulled her hand away to reveal that the jagged wound was already closed. She covered the wound again. 'Don't ask me how.'

'No way,' the crew-cut kid breathed.

Outside, the coyote pack yipped madly and thudded against the door. But the latch held firm. Lana wedged the back of a chair under the handle and calculated her next move.

The door would not hold forever. But the pack would be aimless, unsure of what to do until Pack Leader came back from his private hunt.

'His name's Sam,' Astrid said. 'That's Edilio, this is my brother, Little Pete, and I'm Astrid. And I think you just saved our lives.'

Lana nodded. Better. The girl was showing Lana respect. 'My name's Lana. And listen, people, the coyotes aren't done with us. We need to make sure that door will hold.'

'I'm on it,' Edilio said.

The wounded boy woke with a start.

He stared at the dead coyotes. He reached for his neck. He stared at the blood on his hand.

'You'll live,' Lana said. 'And I'll fix the rest of it. Just let me keep my hand on it.'

He seemed dubious. He glanced at Astrid.

'She saved our lives,' Astrid said. 'And she just closed up a wound that was gushing blood a minute ago.'

Sam allowed her to place her hand against his neck.

'Who are you?' he asked in a croak of a voice.

'Lana. Lana Arwen Lazar,' she said.

'Thanks.'

'No problem. But don't be too grateful: your life may not stay saved.'

He nodded. He listened to the frenzy outside, and flinched when one of the coyotes threw himself against the door.

'Is that a gold bar Edilio is using as a hammer?' Edilio had broken down the bed and was hammering one of the rails over the door.

Lana laughed sardonically. 'Yeah. We have a lot of gold. Patrick and me, we're rich.'

She moved her hand down his neck to his shoulder. 'It works better if you take off your shirt,' she said.

He winced in pain. 'I don't think I can.'

Lana slid her hand under his shirt, feeling the gruesome mess of secondary wounds. 'It'll feel better in a few minutes.'

'How do you do that?' he asked.

'There are a lot of weird things going on.'

The boy nodded. 'Yeah. We noticed. Thanks for saving my life.'

'You're welcome, but like I said, it may be temporary. They're not really trying to get in yet. When Pack Leader gets here, that could change. They're strong, you know, and smart.'

'You're bleeding yourself,' he said.

'I'll fix that,' she said, almost indifferent. 'I've gotten kind of used to being cut up one way or another.'

She pressed her blood-covered hand against her leg.

'Who is this Pack Leader?' Sam asked.

'He's the head coyote. I tricked him into letting me come here. I hoped I'd be able to get away. Or at least have something to eat besides roadkill. Coyotes are smart, but they're still just smart dogs, basically. Are you guys hungry? I am.'

Sam nodded. Then he climbed stiffly to his feet, moving like an old man.

'As soon as I'm done with my leg, I'll do yours,' Lana said. 'We have a pretty good supply of food and plenty of water, at least for a while. The question is whether Pack Leader will be able to find a way in here.'

Astrid said, 'You're talking about this coyote like he's a person.'

Lana laughed. 'Not a person you'd want to hang out with.'

'Is he . . . is he just a coyote?' Astrid asked.

Lana stared at the girl. Now she could see the intelligence beneath the pretty-girl looks. 'What do you know about that?' Lana asked cautiously.

'I know some animals are changing. We've seen a seagull with talons. And we saw, well, a snake with what looked like little stub wings.'

Lana nodded. 'Yeah, I've seen those. Up close. They scare the coyotes half to death, I can tell you that. They can't quite fly, but the rattlers use the wings to get just a little more range than they used to have. They actually saved my butt once. And I saw them kill a coyote just a few hours ago. Pack Leader said –'

'"Said"?' Edilio echoed.

'I'll tell you all about it, but let's eat first. I've had nothing to eat. Although I was offered some raw squirrel. Canned pudding, that's what I want. I've been dreaming about it.'

She hauled out a can and feverishly worked the can opener. She didn't wait for a dish or spoon, but thrust her hand in and scooped some into her mouth. Then she stood transfixed, overwhelmed by the wonderful sweetness of it.

She was crying when she said, 'I'm sorry, I've forgotten how to be polite. I'll get you guys your own can.'

Sam hobbled over and scooped some pudding of his own, following her lead. 'I'm way past polite myself,' he said, although she could see he was a little appalled by her wolfish behaviour. She decided then that she liked him.

'Listen, Sam, and everyone, you need to know something so it won't freak you out: Pack Leader can speak. I mean, human words. Like Smart-Girl Barbie there was saying, he's some kind of mutant or whatever. I know you think I'm probably crazy.'

She had Hermit Jim's tin cup now and used it to scoop up another helping of wonderful, wonderful pudding. Blondie – Astrid – was opening a can of fruit cocktail.

'What do you know about the FAYZ?' Astrid asked.

Lana stopped eating and stared at her. 'The what?'

Astrid shrugged and looked embarrassed. 'That's what people are calling it. The Fallout Alley Youth Zone. FAYZ.'

'What does that mean?'

'Have you seen the barrier?'

She nodded. 'Oh, yeah. I've seen the barrier. I touched the barrier, which, by the way, is not a good idea.'

Sam said, 'As far as we can tell, it goes clear around in a big circle. Or maybe a sphere. We think the centre is the power plant. It seems like a ten-mile radius from there, you know, twenty miles across.'

'Circumference of 62.83 miles, with an area of 314.159 square miles,' Astrid said.

'Point 159,' Quinn echoed from his corner. 'That's important.'

'It's basically pi,' Astrid said. 'You know, 3.14159265 . . . OK, I'll stop.'

Lana hadn't stopped being hungry. She took a scoop of the fruit cocktail. 'Sam, you think the power plant caused it?'

Sam shrugged, and then he hesitated, surprised. Lana guessed that he felt no pain in his shoulder. 'No one knows. All of a sudden every single person over the age of fourteen disappears and there's this barrier and people . . . animals . . .'

Lana slowly absorbed this new information. 'You mean all the adults? They're gone?'

'Poof,' Quinn said. 'They ditched. They blinked out. They vacated. They took the off-ramp. They cut a hole. They emigrated. Adults and teenagers. Nothing left but kids.'

'I've done all I can to strengthen the door,' Edilio announced. 'But all I have is nails. Someone can break it in eventually.'

'Maybe they didn't all ditch,' Lana said. 'Maybe we did.'

Astrid said, 'That's definitely one of the possibilities, not that it makes any real difference. It's effectively the same thing.'

So the blonde was definitely a brain. Lana wondered about her brother. He was awfully quiet for a little kid.

'My grandfather disappeared while he was driving the truck,' Lana said, recalling that terrible day. 'The truck crashed. And I was dying. I mean, bones sticking out. Gangrene. Then, it was like I could just heal. My dog. Myself. And I don't know why.'

From beyond the wooden door came a sudden chorus of excited yelps.

'Pack Leader's here,' Lana said. She crossed to the sink and picked up Hermit Jim's kitchen knife. She turned to Sam, her expression fierce. 'I'll stab him in his heart if he comes in here.'

Sam and Edilio both drew their knives.

From outside the door, just inches away, came the strangled, snarling, high-pitched voice. 'Human. Come out.'

'No,' Lana yelled.

'Human. Come out.'

Lana said, 'Not by the hair of my chinny chin chin.'

Astrid smiled. 'Nice,' she whispered.

'Human. Come out. Human teach Pack Leader. Human say.'

'Lesson number one, you filthy, ugly, nasty, mangy animal: never trust a human.'

That resulted in a protracted silence.

'The Darkness,' Pack Leader growled.

Lana felt fear contract her heart. 'Go ahead. Go tell your master in the mine all about it.' She started to say that she wasn't afraid of the Darkness. But those words would have sounded false.

'What's this about a mine?' Sam asked.

'Nothing.'

'Then why is that coyote out there talking about it? What's this darkness thing?'

Lana shook her head. 'I don't know. They took me there. It's an old gold mine. That's all.'

Sam said, 'Look, you saved our lives. But we still want to know what's going on.'

Lana twined her fingers together around the knife hilt to keep herself from shaking. 'I don't know what's going on, Sam. There's something down in that mine. That's all I know. The coyotes listen to it, they're scared of it, and they do what it says.'

'Did you see it?'

'I don't know. I don't remember. I don't really want to remember.'

There was a loud thump at the door and it rattled on its hinges.

'Edilio, let's find more nails,' Sam said.

The dining hall of Coates Academy had always seemed like a strange, unfriendly place to Jack. In terms of design and decor, it was an attempt to be airy and colourful. The windows were tall, the ceiling lofty; the doors were high arches decorated with bright ornamental Spanish tiles.

The long, heavy, dark wood tables of Jack's first year at Coates, tables that had accommodated sixty students each, had just this last year been replaced by two dozen smaller, less formal round tables decorated with papier-mâché centrepieces made by students.

At the farthest end of the dining hall a mosaic had been created of individually painted construction paper squares. The theme was 'Forwards Together'. The squares had been arranged to form a giant arrow pointing from the floor to the ceiling.

But the more they tried to brighten the room, the less friendly it seemed to grow, as if the little touches of colour and whimsy just accented the crushing size, age, and irreducible formality of the room.

Panda, his leg not broken but badly sprained, slumped into a chair and looked mournful and resentful. Diana stood to one side, not liking what she was about to witness, and not keeping that feeling a secret.

'Get up on the table, Andrew,' Caine ordered, pointing to one of the large round tables in front of the arrow mosaic.

'What do you mean, get up on the table?' Andrew demanded.

Some kids poked their heads into the dining hall. Drake said, 'Shoo.' And they disappeared.

'Andrew, you can climb up on the table or I can levitate you up there,' Caine said.

'Get up, moron,' Drake snapped.

Andrew climbed on to a chair, then on to the table. 'I don't see what . . .'

'Tie him up. Computer Jack? Start setting up.'

Drake pulled rope from the bag he'd retrieved from the car. He tied one end around a table leg, measured out about six feet, cut the rope, then tied the end around Andrew's leg.

'Man, what is this?' Andrew said. 'What are you doing?'

'It's an experiment, Andrew.'

Jack began setting up lights and tripods for cameras.

'This is bogus, man. This isn't right, Caine. It's not right.'

'Andrew, you're lucky I'm giving you a chance to survive the big blink,' Caine said. 'Now stop snivelling.'

Drake tied Andrew's second leg and then hopped on to the table to tie Andrew's hands firmly behind him.

'Dude, I need my hands free for the power.'

Drake looked at Caine, who nodded. Drake untied Andrew's hands and glanced at the chandelier above. He tossed the rope end up over the chandelier, an ornate, heavy iron thing that Coates kids joked was the tenth Nazgul.

Drake cinched the rope up around Andrew's chest, pulled it up under his armpits, and hauled him up till his feet barely touched the table top.

'Make sure his hands can't aim in this direction,' Caine said. 'I don't want that shock-wave thing of his knocking cameras over.'

So Drake suspended each hand by the wrist, leaving Andrew looking like a boy who was trying to surrender.

Jack watched the LED viewfinder of one of the cameras. Andrew would still be able to move out of frame by swaying one way or the other. Jack didn't want to say anything, he felt sorry for Andrew, but if the video got messed up . . .

'Um. He could still move left or right a little.'

Drake then ran ropes from Andrew's neck, four of them leading to tables on four sides. Andrew could move no more than a foot in any direction.

'What's the time, Jack?' Caine asked.

Jack checked his PDA. 'Ten minutes.'

Jack busied himself with the cameras, four of them on tripods, three video and one a motorised still camera. He had two lights on poles shining down on Andrew.

Andrew was lit up like he was some kind of movie star.

'I don't want to die,' Andrew said.

'Me neither,' Caine agreed. 'That's why I really hope you can beat the poof.'

'I would be, like, the first, huh?' Andrew said. He sniffed. Tears were starting to flow.

'First and only,' Caine said.

'This isn't fair,' Andrew said.

Jack adjusted the lens to encompass Andrew's entire body.

'Five minutes,' Jack said. 'I'm going to go ahead and start the video running.'

'Do what you have to do, Jack, don't announce it,' Caine said.

'Can't you help me out, Caine?' Andrew pleaded. 'You're a four bar. Maybe you and me, if we both used our power at the same time, right?'

No one answered him.

'I'm scared, OK?' Andrew moaned, and now the tears were flowing freely. 'I don't know what's going to happen.'

'Maybe you wake up outside the FAYZ,' Panda said, speaking for the first time.

'Maybe you wake up in hell,' Diana said. 'Where you belong.'

'I should pray,' Andrew said.

'God forgive me for being a creep who starves people?' Diana suggested.

'One minute,' Jack said softly. He was nervous about when to start the still camera. No one figured Andrew's birth certificate was exact to the minute – Benno's had been off by weeks. He could disappear early.

'Jesus, forgive me for all the bad stuff I did and take me to my mom I miss her so bad and please let me live I'm just a kid so let me live OK? In Jesus' name, amen.'

Jack switched on the still camera.

'Ten seconds.'

The room erupted with a sonic explosion from Andrew's upraised hands. Waves of shattering sound began to crack the plaster ceiling.

Jack covered his ears and stared in fascination and horror.

'Time,' Jack remembered to yell over the barrage of noise. Chunks of plaster were falling from the ceiling like hail. The bulbs in the chandelier all shattered, sending down a snowfall of glass dust.

'Plus ten,' Jack yelled.

Andrew was still there, hands high, crying, sobbing, beginning to hope maybe, beginning to hope.

'Plus twenty,' Jack said.

'Keep it up, Andrew,' Caine yelled. He was on his feet now, eager, hoping it was true that the blink could be beaten.

The ceiling was cracking more deeply, and Jack wondered if it would fall.

The sonic blast ended.

Andrew stood, exhausted, but still there. Still standing.

'Oh, God,' he said. 'Oh, thank –'

And he was gone.

The ropes fell, suddenly released.

No one said a word.

Jack pushed rewind on one of his high-speed video cameras. He backed it up ten seconds. Then he hit play and watched it on the tiny LCD screen, frame by frame.

'Well,' Diana was saying, 'so much for the theory that you don't ditch if you have powers.'

'He stopped blasting,' Caine said. 'Then he blinked out.'

'He stopped blasting and then ten seconds later, he ditched,' Diana said. 'Birth certificate records are never going to be a hundred per cent, precisely accurate. Some nurse writes down the time, maybe it's five minutes one way or the other. Some are probably off by a half-hour.'

'Did you get anything, Jack?' Caine asked. He sounded disheartened.

Jack was advancing, frame by frame. He saw Andrew projecting sonic blasts. He saw him stop, worn out from the effort. He saw the nervous half-smile, the moment when he opened his mouth, each syllable, and then . . .

'We need to play this on a bigger monitor,' Jack said.

They carried the cameras to the computer centre and left the tripods and lights behind. There they found a twenty-six-inch monitor, crystal clear. Jack didn't waste time downloading, just hooked up the leads and started playing. Caine, Drake, and Diana crowded around over his shoulder, eager faces lit with blue light. Panda limped over to a chair and slumped down.

'Look,' Jack explained. 'Right here. Watch what happens.'

He advanced the file frame by frame.

'What is that?' Diana asked.

'He's smiling. See?' Jack said. 'And he's looking at something. And what's weird is that it's not possible because this frame is, like, a thirtieth of a second but he's got time to go from this expression . . .' He backed it up a frame. 'To this expression. To this, see here where he's moved his head again. And right here, the ropes are slipping away, his hands are free. Move it ahead just three frames and he's completely gone.'

'What does it mean, Jack?' Caine almost implored.

'Let me look at the other cameras,' Jack stalled.

Of the two remaining video cameras only one had a shot of the actual moment. This one, too, showed a blurry picture of Andrew moving in a sudden jerk from one posture to another. In this one too, the ropes were loose and his arms were extended.

'He's reaching out for a hug,' Diana said.

The still camera was unlikely to yield anything useful, Jack knew, but he attached it and fast-forwarded to the right time signature. When the photo loaded up there was a collective gasp.

Andrew was clearly visible, smiling, happy, transformed, with arms outstretched. The thing he was reaching towards looked like a light flare, a reflection of something, except that it was an almost fluorescent green and all the lights had been white.

'Zoom in on that green blob,' Caine said.

'It's a depth-of-field problem,' Jack said. 'Let me try to enhance it.' It took a few seconds for the image to focus into the green cloud. It took several layers of enhancement before they could see what looked like a hole ringed by needle-sharp teeth.

'What is that thing?' Drake wondered aloud.

'It looks like . . . I don't know,' Jack said. 'But it doesn't look like something you'd be reaching out for.'

'He was seeing something different,' Diana said.

'It altered time somehow, accelerated Andrew's time,' Jack said, thinking out loud. 'So for Andrew, it was all lasting a lot longer than it was for us. For him it may have been ten seconds, or even ten minutes, although for us it was less than the blink of an eye. It was just sheer luck we caught any of it.'

Caine surprised him then and actually patted him on the back. 'Don't sell yourself short, Jack.'

Diana said, 'He didn't just poof. He saw something. He reached out to it. That green thing, what looks like some kind of a monster to us, must have looked like something else to Andrew.'

'What, though?'

'Whatever he wanted it to be,' Diana said. 'Whatever he wanted so badly at that moment that he reached for it. If I had to guess, I'd say Andrew saw his mommy.'

Drake spoke for the first time in a while. 'So this big blink thing isn't just something that happens.'

'No, there is deception involved,' Caine said. 'A trick. A lie.'

'A seduction,' Diana said. 'Like one of those carnivorous plants that attracts the bug with perfume and bright colours and then . . .' She closed her hand around an imaginary bug.

Caine seemed mesmerised by the frozen image. In a dreamy voice he said, 'Is it possible to say no? That's the question. Can we say no to the bright flower? Can we say no . . . and survive?'

'OK, I get the mommy thing. But I got another question,' Drake said harshly. 'What's that thing with the teeth?'

THIRTY THREE

ALL THROUGH THE night the coyotes slammed against the door, trying to break it down. But Sam and Quinn and Edilio had stripped the cabin of everything that could be used to strengthen the door, and it would hold. Sam was confident of that.

For a while, at least.

'They're locked out,' Sam said.

'And we're locked in,' Lana agreed.

'Can you do it?' Astrid asked Sam.

'I don't know,' Sam admitted. 'I guess. But I have to go out there to do it. If it works, OK. Maybe. If it doesn't . . .'

'More pudding, anyone?' Quinn, trying to lighten the mood.

'Better to stay in here,' Astrid opined. 'They'll have to come through the door. That means one or two at a time. Wouldn't that be easier, Sam?'

'Yeah. It'll be a party.' He held out his tin cup. 'Quinn, pudding me.'

After several long hours the coyotes tired of slamming against the door. The trapped kids grabbed a few hours of sleep each, two at a time, always making sure two were awake.

The sky began to lighten to pearl grey, not enough to see clearly, but enough for Edilio to find a knothole that gave him a dim view of the front yard.

'There's got to be, maybe, a hundred of them out there,' he reported.

Lana got up from repairing her clothing with a needle and thread and looked for herself. 'That's more than one pack,' she said.

'You can tell that?' Astrid asked, yawning and rubbing sleep from her eyes.

'I know a little about coyotes now,' Lana said. 'If we see this many, it means there's at least twice as many around here. Some have to be out hunting. Coyotes hunt day and night.'

She sat back down and picked up her sewing. 'They're waiting for something.'

'What?'

'I didn't see Pack Leader. Maybe he left. Maybe they're waiting for him to come back.'

'Sooner or later they'll lose interest, won't they?' Astrid asked.

Lana shook her head. 'Normal coyotes, sure. But these aren't normal coyotes.'

They waited and every hour or so Sam or Edilio would check the view, and every time they saw coyotes.

Suddenly there came the sound of a hundred canine voices raised in excited yips.

Patrick stood up, bristling.

Sam ran to the peephole. Lana shone the flashlight on him.

'They have fire,' Sam said.

Lana pushed past him and climbed up to see for herself. 'It's Pack Leader,' she confirmed. 'He has a burning branch.'

'It's not just a burning branch, it's a torch,' Sam said. 'It's not just something he found. It's only burning at one end, a branch wouldn't do that. Someone with hands has to have made it. Someone gave it to him.'

'The Darkness,' Lana whispered.

'This cabin will burn like a match,' Sam said.

'No. I don't want to burn,' Lana cried. 'We have to get out, make some kind of a deal with Pack Leader.'

'You said he'd kill us,' Astrid said. She had her hands over Little Pete's ears.

'They want me alive. They want me to teach them human ways, that's what the Darkness said. He can't kill me, he needs me.'

'Try,' Sam said.

'Pack Leader,' Lana shouted. 'Pack Leader.'

'He doesn't hear you.'

'He's a coyote, he can hear a mouse in its hole from fifty feet away,' Lana snapped. Raising her voice to a scream then, 'Pack Leader. Pack Leader. I'll do whatever you want.'

Sam was back at the spy hole. 'He's right outside,' he whispered.

'Pack Leader, don't,' Lana begged.

'They're all backing away.'

'Oh, God.'

'Smoke,' Edilio said, and pointed a flashlight beam at the door's threshold.

Lana hefted a gold brick and began beating at the boards they had nailed over the door. Edilio grabbed her arms.

'You want to burn alive?' Lana demanded.

Edilio released her.

'We're coming out,' Lana shouted as she banged at the boards. 'We're coming out.'

But the boards were no easier to remove than they had been to put up. A yellow tongue licked beneath the door.

Sam pulled back suddenly from the spy hole. 'Fire.'

'I don't want to burn,' Lana wailed.

'It's the smoke that kills you,' Sam whispered, looking at Astrid. 'There's got to be a way out.'

Astrid said, 'You know the way out.'

From the back wall now, smoke snuck in through cracks and seams.

Lana hammered at the boards. Smoke was gathering under the rafters. The cabin was burning quickly. Already the heat was becoming intolerable.

'Help me,' Lana cried. 'We have to get out.'

Edilio sprang into action, helping to pull boards away.

Sam leaned over Little Pete's head and kissed Astrid on the mouth. 'Don't let me turn into Caine,' he said.

'I'll keep an eye on you,' she said.

'OK. Everyone get back from the door,' Sam said, but too quietly for it to register above the panic sounds.

He grabbed Lana's hand as she swung with a gold brick. 'What are you doing?' she cried.

'You saved my life with your power,' Sam said. 'My turn.'

Lana and Edilio and Quinn shrank back from the doorway.

Sam closed his eyes. It was easy to find the anger. He was angry at so many things.

But for some reason, when he tried to focus on the outrage of this attack, his mind's eye did not call up pictures of the coyote leader, or even of Caine. The picture in his mind was of his own mother.

Stupid. Wrong. Unfair of him, even cruel.

But still, when he reached for his anger, it was his mother he saw.

'It wasn't my fault,' he whispered to that image.

He raised his hands. Fingers splayed wide.

But at that moment the half-burned door burst open.

Flames and smoke were everywhere, a torrent of choking smoke.

And through the inferno leaped a coyote as big as a Great Dane.

That, Sam thought, made it easier.

A flash of green-white light erupted from his upraised hands and the coyote dropped to the floor. An eight-inch hole was burned clear through his body.

A second flash, like a thousand light bulbs, and the front of the cabin blew apart.

The sudden vacuum swallowed some of the flames, not all,

just a pause in the inferno, and Sam was moving, dragging Astrid by the arm, Astrid dragging Little Pete in turn. The others shook off their shock and followed.

They advanced through the hole in the cabin and the coyotes surged forwards, a mass of dangerous teeth beneath cold, focused eyes.

Sam let go of Astrid, raised his hands and the light exploded again. A dozen coyotes caught fire and fell or writhed or ran screeching into the night like mad sparklers in the retreating gloom.

'Pack Leader,' Lana warned in a voice reduced to a croak by the smoke that swirled around them. She was leaning on Edilio's arm, the two of them safely out of the cabin but far from safe on the lawn.

The cabin fell with a crash behind them and burned like a bonfire. The orange light revealed a hundred staring, uncomprehending canine faces. Their eyes and teeth shone.

Pack Leader stood out from his pack, facing Sam, bristling, fearless.

Pack Leader barked a command and the entire pack moved as one, a wave of snarling fury.

Sam held his hands high and beams of purest green-white light fired. The first wave of coyotes caught fire instantly. They turned in terror and raced back through their brothers and sisters, setting off complete panic.

The pack turned tail and ran into the night. And Pack Leader was no longer fearless, no longer leading, but following, racing to keep up with his beaten army. Some burned as they ran and set alight dry shrubbery.

Sam lowered his hands to his sides.

Astrid was beside him.

'Dude,' Quinn said in an awestruck voice.

'I don't think they'll come back,' Sam said.

'Where to now, man?' Edilio asked him.

Sam stood gazing out at empty desert, so dark still that it swallowed all the light of the burning cabin. He wanted to cry. He hadn't known he had that much anger inside. It made him sick. His mother had done her best, she wasn't to blame. He wanted to throw up.

Astrid saw that Sam was in no condition to talk, so she said, 'We'll head back to Perdido Beach. We'll go back, and we'll make things right.'

'And Caine will just step aside,' Quinn said. 'No problem, la di da.'

Astrid flared. 'I'm not saying it will be easy. It will be a test for us.'

Edilio shook his head. 'Isn't going to be a test. It's going to be a war.'

'Sun will be up soon. We'll be able to see something,' Drake said.

'See what?' Panda whined. 'There's nothing but desert out there.'

'Caine says he's probably staying close to the barrier, to find his way back.'

Panda sounded nervous when he said, 'Caine thinks Sam is coming back?'

Panda was still sulking about his sprained ankle and almost useless, so Drake had grabbed two other Coates kids. The first was a fat Chinese-American kid called Chunk. Chunk was a low-level bully, not someone Drake would normally have hung out with. Plus, he would not shut up but chattered away, mostly bragging about what bands he'd seen in concert and what movie stars he'd met. Chunk's father was a talent agent in Hollywood.

If there still was a Hollywood.

The other kid was a skinny little black girl named Louise, one of the drivers. With Panda semi-useless, Drake needed a driver.

After the Andrew poof, Caine and Diana, along with the creepy little nerd, Jack, had gone to deal with Frederico and try to get things back under control at Coates. Caine had sent Drake off with orders to see if he could find Sam.

Drake didn't like having to follow this order. He was sleepy and, as he pointed out to Caine, there was a lot of emptiness out there, let alone at night, so how was he supposed to find Sam, even if he was still following the barrier?

'There's a road goes up Piggyback Mountain,' Caine said. 'Remember? The field trip? You can see for miles.'

So despite it still being dark, and despite the fact that Louise was a much crazier driver than cautious Panda, and despite Panda's whining and Chunk's babble, they had driven up Piggyback Mountain and after a time found the lookout.

They had been there for a while, listening to coyote howls from down in the valley, Drake threatening to punch Chunk if he didn't shut up about how he had met Christina Aguilera one time.

Drake was steaming, unhappy to be up here in the middle of nowhere, with no food or sodas or anything, just a bottle of water and these idiots.

'So what happened with Andrew?' Louise asked during one of Chunk's rare silences.

'He ditched, man. He cut a hole,' Panda said.

'I still got more than a year, I'm only thirteen,' Louise said, like anyone cared. 'Someone will come rescue us in a year, right?'

'Sooner would be better,' Drake drawled, 'what with me having a month.'

'I got till June,' Chunk said. 'You know what that makes me? I'm a Cancer.'

'Got that right,' Drake muttered.

'Sign of the crab,' Chunk added.

'I have to go,' Drake said. He climbed down out of the SUV they were in and walked to the edge of the lookout, up to the railing. He started peeing over the side and that's when he saw it. It looked like a match being carried through the night. Impossible to tell distances.

'Chunk! Get the binoculars.'

Chunk came hustling up a few seconds later. Drake had watched as the tiny, flickering light went racing in zigzags far below.

Chunk said, 'This is like being up in the Hollywood Hills, you know? Up on Mulholland Drive, which is where all these famous actors and stuff live. One time I went to this guy's house, he was, like, a director that my dad reps, right? And –'

Drake yanked the binoculars from Chunk's hands and tried to capture the spark in his field of vision. Almost impossible. He would catch it and then lose it. Even when he managed to follow it for a few seconds, he couldn't make anything out, it was just an orange flame wandering through a featureless void. But it was almost surely moving too fast to be carried by a person, even a fast person.

Then the spark stopped moving. And gradually Drake realised the flame was growing.

He peered intently and thought he could make out some kind of structure, like a house or something in the spreading glow.

Panda had limped over to join them. Drake handed him the binoculars. 'What do you think that is?'

Panda peered through the binoculars and at that moment there was a flash of light and he tore the binoculars away and yelled.

The second flash was even clearer, and now there were sparklers making light trails through the darkness of early morning.

Panda looked again. 'There's some kind of house . . . and a tower or something. And there's, like . . . like dogs or something.'

A third blinding light and now even more of the number of crazily weaving sparklers.

'I don't know, man,' Panda said.

'I think maybe we just found what we were looking for,' Drake said.

Chunk, scared, said, 'You think that's this kid you're trying to catch? Dude's got the power, man. Like in that movie –'

Drake yanked the gun from his belt and said, 'No, Chunk, this is the power. And I've got it.'

That shut Chunk up for a few seconds.

'The fire is spreading,' Louise pointed out. 'It's probably all dry down there and bushes and stuff catching fire.'

Drake had noticed the same thing. He glanced back in the direction they'd come from, tried to make sense of the topography. 'Coates is back that way. The barrier is over that way.' He pointed. 'There's no wind, so the fire is going to climb the hill. Which means they'll be coming this way, towards Coates. They'll pass down below us.'

'What are you going to do, shoot them when they walk past?' Chunk asked, eager and afraid.

'Yeah, that's right, three thousand feet down this hill and I'm going to shoot them with a handgun,' Drake said sarcastically. 'Moron.'

'So what do we do?' Panda asked. 'No wonder Caine's scared of this guy. Dude can do all that?'

'That's a four bar, right there, I bet,' Chunk opined. 'I seen all kinds of stuff at Coates with Benno and Andrew and Frederico, none of them could do that kind of stuff. You think he can take Caine down?'

Drake spun and smacked Chunk in the mouth with the back

of his free hand. When Chunk staggered back, Drake moved in and kicked him in the groin.

Chunk grabbed himself and fell to his knees. He whimpered, 'Why'd you do that, man?'

'Because I'm sick of listening to you,' Drake snapped. 'I'm sick of all this powers crap. You saw what we did to freaks at Coates? Who do you think it was that took care of that? All these kids with their stupid so-called powers. Starting fires and moving stuff around and reading your mind and all? Who do you think it was grabbed them one by one in their sleep and beat them down and when they woke up their hands were setting up in a block of cement?'

'It was you, Drake,' Panda said, placating him. 'You got them all.'

'That's right. And I didn't even have a gun then. It's not about who's got powers, morons. It's about who's not afraid. And who's going to do what has to be done.'

Chunk was climbing to his feet now with a hand from Panda.

'It's not Sam Temple or even Caine you little worms need to worry about, it's me,' Drake said. 'Mr Laser Hands down there isn't going to make it to where he can fight Caine. I'm going to take him down long before that.'

THEY WERE SIX now. Sam, Edilio, Quinn, Lana, Astrid, and Little Pete. All plans for following the FAYZ wall home were abandoned for now. The fire, a patchwork of brilliant yellow and orange, was climbing the hills to the north, cutting them off. They could only keep moving south.

Dawn came at last, an unsatisfying grey that bleached the colour from everything, even the fire.

They could see where they were placing their feet, now, but that didn't stop them from tripping and stumbling. They were lead-footed from exhaustion.

Little Pete silently collapsed and was left behind until Astrid noticed. After that Edilio and Sam took turns carrying him on their backs, which made their progress even slower and more treacherous.

Little Pete slept that way for a while, maybe two hours, then, when the boys couldn't manage another step, he woke up and set off on his own, and now they were all following him, too tired to argue or try to redirect him, since he was going mostly in the right direction.

'We gotta stop, man,' Edilio said. 'The girls are tired.'

'I'm fine,' Lana said. 'I've been running with coyotes. Walking with you guys is like standing still.'

'I've had it,' Sam agreed, and stopped right where he was, which happened to be beside something that was either a very big bush or a small tree.

'Petey,' Astrid shouted. 'Come back. We're stopping.'

Little Pete had stopped walking, but he would not come back. Astrid wearily trudged to him, every sore footstep communicating the pain she was in.

'Sam,' Astrid yelled. 'Quick.'

Sam thought he was too far gone to respond, but he somehow started his feet moving again and went up to where Little Pete was standing and Astrid kneeling.

There was a girl lying in the dirt. Her clothing was a mess, her black hair ratty. She was Asian, pretty without being beautiful, and little more than skin and bones. But the first thing they noticed was that her forearms ended in a solid concrete block.

Astrid made a quick sign of the cross and pressed two fingers against the girl's neck. 'Lana,' Astrid cried.

Lana sized up the situation quickly. 'I don't see any injuries. I think maybe she's starving or else sick in some other way.'

'What's she doing out here?' Edilio wondered. 'Oh, man, what did someone do to her hands?'

'I can't heal hunger,' Lana said. 'I tried it on myself when I was with the pack. Didn't work.'

Edilio untwisted the cap from his water bottle, knelt, and

carefully drizzled water across the girl's cheek so that a few drops curled into her mouth.

'Look, she's swallowing.'

Edilio broke a tiny bite from one of the PowerBars and placed it gently into the girl's mouth. After a second the girl's mouth began to move, to chew.

'There's a road over there,' Sam said. 'I think so, anyway. A dirt road, I think.'

'Someone drove by and dumped her here,' Astrid agreed.

Sam pointed at the dirt. 'You can see how she dragged that block.'

'Some sick stuff going on,' Edilio muttered angrily. 'Who would do something like this?'

Little Pete stood staring down at the girl. Astrid noticed. 'He doesn't usually stare at people that way.'

'I guess he's never seen what some creeps can do,' Edilio said.

'No,' Astrid said thoughtfully. 'Petey doesn't relate to people usually. They're not totally real to him. I cut my hand once, really badly with a kitchen knife, I was bleeding all over and he didn't even blink. And I'm the person he's closest to in the whole world.'

Lana said, 'Sam, can you, you know, like burn that concrete off her hands?'

'No. I can't aim that precisely.'

'I don't even know what can be done,' Edilio said as he fed the girl another microscopic bite of food. 'You try and break that stuff off with a sledge hammer or something, or even a hammer and a chisel, it's going to really hurt. Probably break every bone in her hands, man.'

'Who would have done this to her?' Lana wondered.

'That's a Coates Academy uniform,' Astrid answered. 'We're probably not far from there.'

'Shh,' Lana hissed. 'I hear something.'

Everyone instinctively ducked down. In the silence they could clearly hear a car engine. It was being driven erratically, revving one minute, slowing the next.

'Come on, let's find out who it is,' Sam said.

'How we going to move this girl?' Edilio asked. 'I can maybe carry her, but I can't carry her and that block, man.'

'I'll grab her, you grab the block,' Sam said.

'This thing is really heavy,' Edilio said. 'I better not even meet the *pendejo* who did this. Do this to a person? What kind of animal does something like that?'

The car turned out to be an SUV. It was driven, as far as Sam could tell, by a lone boy.

'I know him,' Astrid said. She waved. The SUV lurched to a halt. Astrid leaned against the open window. 'Computer Jack?'

Sam had seen the techie wizard around town but had never really spoken to him.

'Hi,' the boy said. 'Oh, good. You found Taylor. I was looking for her.'

'You were looking for her?'

'Yeah. She's sick. You know, like in the head. She wandered away from school, and so I was looking for her and –'

Right at that moment, Sam knew it was a trap. A split second too late.

Drake rose up from behind the third row of seats. He had a gun pointed at Astrid's head, but he was looking straight at Sam. 'Don't even think about it. However fast you think you are, all I have to do is squeeze the trigger.'

'I'm not moving,' Sam said. He raised his hands in surrender.

'Ah ah ah, no no no, Sam boy. I know all about the power. Keep your hands by your side.'

'I have to help carry this girl,' Sam said.

'No one's carrying her anywhere. She's done for.'

'We're not leaving her here,' Astrid said.

'The guy holding the gun makes the decisions,' Drake said, and grinned. 'And if I were you, Astrid, I wouldn't push me. Caine wants to try to take you and your little brother alive. But if you two try and do your disappearing act, I'll shoot Sam.'

'You're a psychopath, Drake,' Astrid said.

'Wow. Such a big word. I guess that's why you're Astrid the Genius, huh? You know what else is a good word? Retard.'

Astrid flinched like he had hit her.

'My brother is a retard,' Drake mimicked. 'I wish I had recorded it. OK. We're going to climb in the truck here one by one. Nice and slow.'

'Not without the girl,' Sam said flatly.

'That's right,' Edilio agreed.

Drake sighed theatrically. 'OK. Pick her up. Throw her in the front seat next to Jack.'

Doing that took some effort. The girl was alive, but not really conscious and was too weak to move.

Quinn had gone rigid with fear and indecision. Sam could see the conflict on his face. Should he stick with Sam or try and ingratiate himself with Drake?

Sam wondered what he would decide. For now, his friend was staring wide-eyed, blank, mouth trembling, eyes darting, looking for an answer.

'It'll be all right, Quinn,' Sam whispered.

Quinn didn't even hear him.

Astrid climbed in. She sat directly behind Jack. 'I really thought there might be some hope for you, Jack.'

'Nah,' Drake said. 'Jack's like a screwdriver or a pair of pliers. He's just a tool. He does what we tell him to do.'

Little Pete and Lana shared the middle bench with Astrid. Edilio and Sam were in the back row. Drake pressed the gun to the back of Edilio's head.

'Your problem's with me, Drake,' Sam said.

'You might take a chance if it's only your own life on the line,' Drake said. 'But you won't risk me shooting your pet Mexican here, or your girlfriend.'

They drove in jerks and starts, Jack frequently weaving off the road on to the shoulder. But they didn't crash, which was Sam's only hope. They pulled up outside Coates Academy.

Sam had been once before, brought there to see where his mother worked. The gloomy old building looked like it had been shelled. One entire room upstairs was exposed. The main door had been blown apart.

'Looks like a war zone,' Edilio commented.

'The FAYZ *is* a war zone,' Drake said darkly.

The sight of the place brought Sam a wave of sad memories. His mother had done her best to portray her job as something she was excited about, and Coates as a place where she was going to love working. But even then Sam had known that she was only here because he had broken up his mother's marriage.

He felt within him the residue of his rage at his mother. It was childish. Shameful, really. Wrong. And it was the wrong time to be thinking about all that, now, where he was, with what was happening, what was likely to happen.

What was that phrase of Edilio's? *Cabeza de turco?* Scapegoat? He needed someone to blame, and his anger had been building at his mother since long before the FAYZ.

But as mad as I am, Sam thought, it must be worse for Caine. I was the son she kept. He was the one she gave away.

When they pulled up, Panda and a couple of kids Sam didn't know were waiting. They were armed with baseball bats.

'I want to see Caine,' Sam said as they climbed out.

'No doubt,' Drake said. 'But first we have things to take care of. Line up. Walk single file around the building.'

'Tell Caine his brother is here,' Sam insisted.

'You're not dealing with Caine, Sammy, you're dealing with me,' Drake said. 'I'd just as soon shoot you. I'd just as soon shoot all of you. So don't piss me off.'

They did as ordered. They turned the corner and came to the commons area behind the main building. There was a small performance stage made to look like a gazebo.

More than two dozen kids lined a low railing around the gazebo. They were all tied to it by a rope leash that gave them no more than a few feet of movement. Neck to rail, like tethered horses. Each of the kids was weighed down by a concrete block that encased their hands. Their eyes were hollow, their cheeks caved in.

Astrid used a word that Sam had never imagined coming from her.

'Nice language,' Drake said with a smirk. 'And in front of the Pe-tard, too.'

A cafeteria tray had been placed in front of each of the prisoners. It must have been a very recent delivery because some were still licking their trays, hunched over, faces down, tongues out, licking like dogs.

'It's the circle of freaks,' Drake said proudly, waving a hand like a showman.

In a crusty old wheelbarrow to one side, three kids were using a short-handled shovel to mix cement. It made a heavy sloshing sound. They dumped a shovelful of gravel into the mix and stirred it like lumpy gravy.

'Oh, no,' Lana said, backing away, but one of the Coates kids smashed her behind the knee with his baseball bat, and she crumpled.

'Gotta do something with unhelpful freaks,' Drake said.

'Can't have you people running around loose.' He must have seen Sam start to react because he stuck his gun against Astrid's head. 'Your call, Sam. You so much as flinch and we'll get to see what a genius brain really looks like.'

'Hey, I got no powers, man,' Quinn said.

'This is sick, Drake. Like you're sick,' Astrid said. 'I can't even reason with you because you're just too damaged, too hopelessly messed up.'

'Shut up,' Drake snapped. 'OK, Sam. You first. It's easy to do. You just stick your hands in and then, presto, no more powers.'

Quinn pleaded. 'Sam's a freak, I'm not, man, I have no powers. I am just a normal person.'

Sam walked with shaky steps to the wheelbarrow. The kids mixing the concrete looked very unhappy about what they were doing, but Sam didn't kid himself: they would do what they were told.

There was a hole dug in the dirt, about a foot long, half as wide, and maybe eight inches deep.

The cement mixers sloshed a shovelful of concrete into the hole, filling it a third of the way.

'Stick your hands in, Sam,' Drake ordered. 'Do it or pop-goes-the-genius.'

Sam plunged his hands into the cement. The kid with the shovel dumped a load of wet, heavy cement into the hole and used a trowel to poke it down. Then half a shovelful and the boy used the trowel to smooth it over and return the excess to the wheelbarrow.

Sam knelt there, hands encased, his brain crazed with desperate plans and wild calculations. If he moved, Astrid would die. If he did nothing, they would be slaves.

'OK, Astrid, your turn,' Drake said.

Another hole and the same process. Astrid was crying, saying, 'It'll be OK, Petey, it'll be OK,' through her tears.

One of the mixers got busy digging a third hole. He did it with quick, practised moves, slicing the turf with a trowel.

'Takes about ten minutes is all, Sam,' Drake said. 'If you're going to do something brave, you've got about eight minutes. Tick-tock.'

'This is how you have to deal with freaks,' Quinn said. 'No choice, Drake.'

Sam could feel the concrete hardening. Already if he tried to move his fingers, he found they were imprisoned. Astrid was more upset than Sam had ever seen her. She was crying openly. Her fear fed his. He couldn't bear it. For himself it was bad enough, but seeing her this way . . .

And yet, Astrid wasn't returning his gaze, she was focused entirely on Little Pete. Almost as if she was crying for his benefit, communicating her terror to him.

Of course she was. But it wasn't working. Little Pete was in his game, in another world.

'I think time's about up for you, Sam,' Drake said with a laugh. 'Try pulling your hands out. Can't do it, can you?'

Drake stepped up behind him and swatted him on the back of his head.

'Come on, Sam. Even Caine's scared of you, so you must be tough. Come on, show me what you've got.' He hit Sam again, this time with the barrel of the gun. Sam collapsed face down in the dirt.

Sam raised himself up. He tugged as hard as he could, but his hands were imprisoned. His flesh itched. He fought against a tide of panic. He wanted to scream curses, but that would only entertain Drake.

'Yeah, take it like a man,' Drake crowed. 'After all, you're fourteen, right? So how long till you vacate? It's all just a passing phase here in the FAYZ, right?'

The mixers dug the concrete block out of the dirt, and now, as he tried to stand, Sam felt the terrible weight of the thing. He could stand, but not without struggling.

Drake got up close to him. 'So who's the man here? Who brought you and the rest of these freaks down? Me. And me without any powers at all.'

Sam heard a door slam. He craned his head and saw Caine and Diana coming across the lawn.

Caine walked at a languid pace across the lawn, smiling more broadly the closer he got.

'Well, if it isn't the defiant Sam Temple,' he said. 'Let me shake your hand. Oh, sorry, my bad.' He laughed, a sound that seemed more a release of tension than anything else.

'I got him,' Drake announced. 'I got them all.'

'Yes, you did,' Caine said. 'Good work, Drake. Very good work. And I see Sam's little friends are likewise caught.'

'Why don't you give Drake a little scratch behind the ears, Caine, he's been such a good dog,' Diana said.

The mixers had dug Astrid's hands out of the dirt. She was crying hysterically, unable to stand all the way up. Little Pete went to her, walking like he was in a dream, head down over his Game Boy.

Astrid bumped her concrete block into Little Pete.

And suddenly Sam knew what she was doing. He had to provide distraction. He had to keep the focus away from Astrid and Little Pete.

'You don't want to mess with this girl, her name is Lana,' Sam said, jerking his chin towards her. 'She's a healer.'

Caine's eyebrows shot up. 'A what? A healer?'

'She can heal anything, any kind of injury,' Sam said. Astrid, barely able to move, was slowly, rhythmically swinging her block back and forth in a narrow arc, bumping it against Little Pete's Game Boy.

'She healed me,' Sam said. 'Coyote bit me. Want to see?'

Caine said, 'I have a better idea. Drake, give the girl something to heal.'

Drake laughed out loud, a gleeful sound. He pressed the muzzle of his pistol against Sam's knee.

'No,' Diana yelled.

The explosion was shocking. The pain, at first, didn't register, but Sam collapsed. He fell on his side like a felled tree. The leg, blown half off, buckled and twisted beneath him.

And then came the pain.

Drake smiled hugely and yelled an exultant, 'Yeah!'

Astrid, startled, slammed the concrete block so hard against Little Pete that she knocked the Game Boy from his hands and knocked him back a step.

Diana frowned, alarmed. For the first time she really registered Little Pete's presence.

Through a red mist of pain Sam saw her eyes fly open, her finger stab towards Little Pete.

'Drake, you idiot, the kid. The kid.'

Astrid dropped to her knees, slammed the concrete block down on the Game Boy.

There was no flash of light. No sound.

But suddenly the concrete encasing Astrid's hands was gone. Simply gone.

So was the concrete block on Sam's hands.

And every one of the other children.

Astrid was on her hands and knees, knuckles pressed into the soft dirt.

The concrete blocks were gone like they had never existed, though the hands of those who had been trapped longest were masses of pale, dead, sloughing skin.

Caine was quick. He backed away, turned, and ran for the building. Diana seemed torn, uncertain; then she bolted after Caine.

Little Pete picked up his game. The block had disappeared a split second before smashing down on the game. It was dirty and had a piece of grass sticking out of it now, but it still worked.

Drake stood rooted. The gun was still in his hand, smoking from the bullet he had fired into Sam's knee.

He blinked.

He raised the gun and fired at Little Pete. But his aim was wild. His aim was off because of the blinding flash of greenish-white light.

Drake's arm, the entire arm holding the gun, burst into flame.

Drake screamed. The gun fell from his melting fingers.

The flesh burned black. The smoke was brown.

Drake screamed and stared in stark horror as the fire ate away at his arm. He broke and ran, the wind fanning the flames.

'Good shot, Sam,' Edilio said.

'I was aiming at his head,' Sam said, gritting his teeth through the pain.

Lana knelt beside Sam and laid her hands on the bloody mess of his knee.

'We have to get out of here,' Sam managed to say. 'Forget me, we have to run. Back to . . . Caine will . . .'

But that was the last of his strength. It felt as if a black hole was swallowing him up. He swirled down and down into unconsciousness.

THIRTY FIVE

'**WHERE** ARE WE?' Sam woke up all at once and was embarrassed to find that he was being half dragged down the road by Edilio and a kid he didn't know.

Edilio stopped. 'Can you stand?'

Sam tested his legs. Lana's healing of his leg had been complete. 'Yeah. I'm fine. Feel OK, actually.'

He looked back and realised they had been leading a sort of ragtag parade. Astrid and Little Pete, Lana holding a boy's hand while her dog bounded into the woods to chase a squirrel. Quinn walked by himself along the shoulder of the road, shunned and ashamed. And there were almost two dozen kids, the liberated freaks from Coates.

Edilio saw the look on his face. 'You got yourself a crowd of followers, Sam.'

'Caine hasn't come after us?'

'Not yet.'

The group of them was straggling down the road, bunched here and there, spread out elsewhere, wandering, undisciplined.

Sam winced when he saw the hands of the Coates kids. The concrete had leeched all the moisture from their skin, which was

409

white and loose, hanging in tatters in some cases, like the tattered bandages of some horror-movie mummy. Their wrists revealed red circles where the concrete had rubbed the flesh bloody. They were filthy.

'Yeah,' Edilio said, knowing what he was seeing. 'Lana's going through them one at a time. Healing them. She's amazing.'

Sam thought he heard something extra in Edilio's voice. 'She's cute too, huh, Edilio?'

Edilio's eyes went wide and he started blushing. 'She's just . . . you know . . .'

Sam slapped his shoulder. 'Good luck with that.'

'You think she . . . I mean, you know me, I'm just . . .' Edilio stammered his way to a stop.

'Dude, let's see if we can stay alive. Then you can ask her out or whatever.'

Sam surveyed the scene. They were on the Coates road, passing the iron gate, still many miles from Perdido Beach.

Astrid noticed that he was awake and hurried her pace. 'About time you woke up,' she said.

'Well,' he played along with her bantering tone, 'usually after I get shot and then fire lasers out of my hands, I like to enjoy a brief nap.' He caught Lana's eye and mouthed the word 'thanks'.

Lana shrugged as if to say 'no biggie'.

'Caine won't let this stand,' Astrid said, turning serious.

'No. He'll come after us,' Sam said. 'But not just yet. Not until he's come up with a plan. He's lost Drake. And he's gotta be worried that we have all these kids with powers who hate his guts.'

'What makes you think he won't just come after us?'

'Think about when he first came rolling into Perdido Beach,' Sam said. 'He had a plan. He trained his people and rehearsed.'

'So we go back to Perdido Beach?' Astrid asked.

'Orc is still there, and a few others. There may be trouble with them.'

'We need to get some food for these kids,' Edilio said. 'That's first.'

'Three or four miles to Ralph's,' Sam mused. 'Can they make it?'

'I guess they have to,' Edilio said. 'But they're scared, too. I mean, you got some messed-up kids here. What they been through and all.'

'We're all scared, there's not much we can do about it,' Sam said. But he didn't like the sound of that. It was glib. It was meaningless: sure, they were all scared, but there was something they could do about it.

In fact, they had to do something about it.

Sam stopped in the middle of the road and waited for the others to catch up.

'Listen,' he said. He raised his hands to get their attention, calm them down, but they had seen what happened when Sam raised his hands. They flinched and seemed about ready to dart off the road and into the woods.

Sam dropped his hands hastily. 'Sorry. Let me start over: could I have everyone's attention?' he said, using a gentler voice. He kept his hands by his sides. He waited patiently until he was sure everyone was listening. Quinn still hung back.

'Some bad stuff has happened to all of us,' Sam said. 'Some very bad stuff. We're beat up, we're tired. We don't know what's going on. The whole world has gone bizarre on us. Our own bodies and minds have changed in ways that are even weirder than puberty.'

That earned a few smiles and one grudging laugh.

'Yeah. I know we're all shook up. We're all scared. I know I am,' he admitted with a rueful smile. 'So, let's not try and play like it isn't scary. It is. But sometimes the worst thing is the fear. You know?' His gaze travelling over the faces, he realised anew that they had another concern, greater even than fear. 'Although hunger's no joke, either. We're a few miles from a grocery store. We'll get you all fed there. I know some of you have been in hell since this happened. Well, I would like to tell you it's over, but it's not.'

Grim looks on every face.

Sam had said all he had really planned to say, but they still needed something more. He shot a glance at Astrid. She was as solemn as anyone, but she gave him a nod, encouraging him to say more.

'OK. OK,' he said so softly that some had to move closer to hear him. 'Here's the thing. We're not going to give in. We're going to fight.'

'Got that right,' a voice cried out.

'First thing we need to have clear: there's no line between freak and normal here. If you have the power, we'll need you. If you don't, we'll need you.'

Heads were nodding. Looks were being exchanged.

'Coates kids, Perdido Beach kids, we're together now. We're together. Maybe you did things to survive. Maybe you weren't always brave. Maybe you gave up hope.'

A girl sobbed suddenly.

'Well, that's all over now,' Sam said gently. 'It all starts fresh. Right here, right now. We're brothers and sisters now. Doesn't matter we don't know each other's names, we are brothers and sisters and we're going to survive, and we're going to win, and we're going to find our way to some kind of happiness again.'

There was a long, deep silence.

'So,' Sam said, 'my name is Sam. I'm in this with you. All the way.' He turned to Astrid.

'I'm Astrid, I'm in this with you, too.'

'My name is Edilio. What they said. Brothers and sisters. *Hermanos.*'

'Thuan Vong,' said a thin boy with as-yet-unhealed hands like dead fish. 'I'm in.'

'Dekka,' said a strong, solidly built girl with cornrows and a nose ring. 'I'm in. And I have game.'

'Me too,' called a skinny girl with reddish pigtails. 'My name's Brianna. I . . . well, I can go real fast.'

One by one they declared their determination. The voices started out soft and gained strength. Each voice louder, firmer, more determined than the one before.

Only Quinn remained silent. He hung his head and tears rolled down his cheeks.

'Quinn,' Sam called to him.

Quinn didn't respond, just looked down at the ground.

'Quinn,' Sam said again. 'It starts fresh right now. Nothing before counts. Nothing. Brothers, man?'

Quinn struggled with the lump in his throat. But then, in a low voice, he said, 'Yeah. Brothers.'

'OK. Now let's get everyone some food,' Sam said.

When they started out again, they no longer spread in every direction. They didn't march like an army, but they came as close as a bunch of traumatised kids could. They walked with their heads a little higher.

Someone actually laughed. It was a good sound.

In a low voice Astrid said, 'Nothing to fear but fear itself.'

'I don't think I said it quite that well.'

Edilio slapped him on the back. 'You said it well enough, man.'

'Sam's back.'

'What?'

'Sam. He's back. He's coming down the highway.'

Howard's chest tightened. He was halfway down the steps of the town hall, on his way to McDonald's for one of Albert's waffle-burgers.

It was Elwood, Dahra Baidoo's boyfriend, who had delivered the news. He sounded relieved, there was no denying it. He sounded glad. Howard made a mental note that Elwood was disloyal, but he realised at the same time that he might have bigger issues to worry about than Elwood's loyalty.

'If Sam's coming back, it's on the end of a leash held by Drake Merwin,' Howard blustered.

But Elwood was off to tell Dahra and was no longer listening.

Howard looked around, feeling a little lost, not quite sure what to do. He spotted Mary Terrafino pushing a shopping cart loaded with juice boxes, A&D ointment, and some bruised apples across the plaza towards the day care. Howard trotted down the steps and caught up with her.

'T'sup, Mary?' he asked.

'Um, your time?' Mary said, and laughed at her own wit.

'Yeah, you think? My time's up?'

'Sam's on his way.'

'You saw him?'

'I had three different people tell me he's coming down the highway. You better rush out and stop him, Howard,' Mary crowed.

'He's one guy, we'll kick his butt.'

'Good luck with that,' Mary said.

Howard wished Orc was here. With Orc at his side, he didn't have to put up with any of Mary's lip. But one-on-one was a different story.

'You want me telling Caine you're on Sam's side?' Howard demanded.

'I didn't say I was on anyone's side. I'm on the side of the prees I take care of. But here's what I notice, Howard: I notice you hear Sam's name and all of a sudden you're ready to wet yourself. So, you know what? Maybe it's you who is disloyal.

After all, if Caine is so great, why would you be scared of Sam? Right?' She leaned against her basket and got it rolling again.

Howard swallowed hard and argued with his own fear. 'It's no big thing,' he told himself. 'We have Caine and Drake and Orc. We're cool. We're cool.'

He believed that for a good twenty seconds before he broke and ran for Orc.

Orc was in the house he had taken over and now shared with Howard, just across the street from where Drake lived. It was on a short street, the closest place to the town hall that you could live. Kids called it Bully Row.

Orc was asleep on the couch with a DVD of a kung fu movie playing at blasting volume on the TV. Orc had taken to staying up through the night and sleeping days.

It was a lousy house, in Howard's opinion, badly decorated and smelling of garlic, but Orc hadn't cared. He wanted to stay close to the action in town. And he wanted to stay close enough to keep an eye on Drake across the street.

Howard searched for the remote and shut off the TV. There were empty beer cans on the glass-topped coffee table and cigarettes in an ashtray. Orc was now drinking a couple of beers a day.

Since Bette. That's when the drinking had started in earnest. Howard was worried about Orc. Not that he exactly liked him, but Howard's fate was bound up with Orc's and he didn't like the picture of what his world would be if Orc dumped him.

'Orc, get up, man.'

No response.

'Orc. Get up. We have trouble.' Howard poked him in his shoulder.

Orc opened one slit eye. 'Why are you bothering me?'

'Sam Temple is coming back.'

It took Orc a while to process that. Then he sat up quite suddenly and grabbed his forehead. 'Oh, man. Headache.'

'It's called a hangover,' Howard snapped. Then, when Orc shot him a murderous look, he softened and said, 'I have some Tylenol in the kitchen.' He filled a glass of water and tapped two pills into his palm and brought them back for Orc.

'What's the big deal?' Orc asked. He'd never been exactly quick, but now Orc's thick-headedness was really irritating Howard.

'The big deal? Sam is coming back. That's the big deal.'

'So?'

'Come on, Orc. Think about it. You figure Sam is cruising into town and he doesn't have some kind of plan? Caine isn't here, man, he's up the hill. Drake, too. Which means it's you and me in charge.'

Orc reached for one of the beer cans, rattled it, sighed contentedly when he heard an inch of beer sloshing. He poured it down his throat.

'So we have to go kick Sam's butt?' Orc asked.

Howard hadn't thought that far ahead. If Sam was back, that wasn't good. Sam was back and Caine wasn't? It was hard to figure that out.

'We go spy him out, man. We see what he's up to.'

Orc squinted. 'If I see him, I'll kick his butt.'

'We have to at least figure out what he's after,' Howard cautioned. 'We should get whoever is around at the town hall. Mallet, maybe. Chaz. Whoever we can find.'

Orc stood up, belched and said, 'I gotta pee. Then we'll get the Hummer. Go kick some butt.'

Howard shook his head. 'Orc. Listen to me. I know you don't want to hear this, but backing Caine may not be the winning move.'

Orc stared his blank, stupid stare.

'Orc, man, what if Sam wins this? I mean, what if Sam gets over on Caine? Where does that leave us?'

Orc didn't answer for so long, Howard was sure he hadn't heard him. Then Orc heaved up a sigh that was almost a sob. He grabbed Howard's arm, something he never did.

'Howard, I killed Bette.'

Howard said, 'You didn't mean to, Orc.'

'You're the smart one,' Orc said sadly. 'But sometimes you're dumber than me, you know that?'

'OK.'

'I killed someone who didn't do me any harm. Astrid ain't ever going to even look at me again unless she's hating me.'

'No, no, no,' Howard argued. 'Sam is going to need help. He's going to need someone tough. If we go to him now, eat crow, you know, say, "Yeah, you're the man, Sammy."'

'You kill somebody, you burn in hell,' Orc said. 'My mom told me that. Once my dad was beating on me, we was in the garage, so I grabbed up a hammer.' Orc now pantomimed the scene. Grabbing the hammer, looking at it, raising it. Then he let it drop. 'She said, "You kill your father, you'll burn in hell."'

'What happened then?'

Orc held up his left hand. He pushed it close to Howard's face. There was a scar, almost perfectly round, no more than a quarter-inch across.

'What's that?' Howard asked.

'Power drill. Three-sixteenths bit.' Orc laughed ruefully. 'Guess I'm lucky it wasn't the three-quarter-inch, huh?'

'That's messed up, man,' Howard said. He'd always known that Orc came from a tough home. But a power drill was off the hook. He himself came from a fairly average home, neither of his parents was a drunk or violent or anything. Howard did what he had to do to survive, being small and weak and not popular. He liked being in charge, having people scared of him, so being Orc's friend had worked out for him.

But now Howard was starting to see that though Orc was stupid, he wasn't wrong. Orc and School Bus Sam, the big hero, were never going to get along.

And now Howard was as trapped as Orc.

Trapped.

'OK, then,' Howard said. 'We go to Caine.'

Orc belched loudly. 'Caine's mad at us.'

'Yeah,' Howard said. 'But he still needs us.'

'**HOLD** HIM DOWN,' Diana yelled.

The sound of her voice was far off. Drake Merwin heard it bubbling up through a red scream that filled his brain.

Screaming, screaming, screaming everywhere, all through his brain, from a million mouths, rising and falling, gasping for breath.

'I can hold him,' a voice said. Caine. 'Back away on three. One . . . two . . .'

Drake flailed madly, unbound, shrieking, thrashing, hurting himself but unable to stop. The pain . . . he had never felt anything like it, never imagined anything could be like it.

A force pressed down on him like a thousand hands holding him with firm pressure.

'You have the saw?' Diana's voice asked. Not smug now, not smug at all, but raw and horrified.

Drake struggled against the invisible force, but Caine had him pinned down with his telekinetic power. Drake could only scream and curse, and could barely move his facial muscles enough for that.

'I am not doing this,' Panda said, weeping. 'I'm not sawing

off his arm, man.'

The words sent a shock of terror to join the pain. His arm? They were . . .

'He'll kill me if I do it,' Panda said.

'I'm not doing it,' various voices chimed in. 'No way.'

'I'll do it,' Diana said, disgusted. 'You're all such big tough guys. Give me the saw.'

'No, no, no!' Drake screeched.

'It's the only way to stop the pain,' Caine said, almost showing some emotion, some pity. 'The arm is done for, Drake-man.'

'The girl . . . the freak . . .' Drake gasped. 'She could fix it.'

'She's not here,' Caine said bitterly. 'She's gone with Sam and the rest of them.'

'Don't cut off my arm,' Drake cried. 'Let me die. Just let me die. Shoot me.'

'Sorry,' Caine said. 'But I still need you, Drake. Even one-handed.'

There was the sound of someone bursting into the room. 'All I could find was Tylenol and Advil,' Computer Jack said.

'Let's get this over with,' Diana snapped.

Impatient to maim him. Looking forwards to it.

'You do this, he's going to kill you,' Panda warned.

'Oh, Drake's already decided he wants to do that,' Diana said. 'Tighten the tourniquet.'

'He's going to bleed to death,' Jack warned. 'There must be big arteries in his arm.'

'He's right,' Caine said. 'We need a way to seal the stump.'

'It's already cauterised,' Diana said. 'I just need to cut below the burn.'

'Yeah, OK,' Caine agreed.

'I can't reach him through your force field,' Diana said. 'Can you pull it back to keep his left side paralysed, and maybe Panda and some of these other supposedly tough guys can grab on to his stump?'

'Let me get a towel, at least. I don't want to touch that,' Panda said with revulsion.

'Nobody cuts my arm,' Drake rasped. 'I'll kill anyone who touches me.'

'Let him up, Caine,' Diana snapped.

The elephant was off Drake's chest, he could move again. But now Diana's face was inches from his, her dark hair hanging down on his tear-streaked face.

'Listen, you stupid thug,' Diana said. 'We're cutting off the pain. As long as that burned stump is there, you'll be like this. You'll be screaming and crying and wetting your pants. Yeah, you've peed yourself, Drake.'

Somehow that fact shocked Drake into silence.

'You have one hope. Just one. That we cut off the dead part of your arm and do it without starting the bleeding again.'

'Anyone cuts me dies,' Drake said.

Diana pulled back, out of Drake's view.

Caine said, 'Do it. Panda. Chunk. Grab that stump.'

The pressure was on Drake again, immobilising him. He

didn't feel the towel that was wrapped around his arm or the grip of hands. That part of his arm was naked bone, all flesh melted away, nerves burned off, dead. The pain started higher up, where just enough nerve endings still survived to slam his fevered brain with wave upon wave of agony.

'It's not Diana or Panda or Chunk or even me,' Caine said. 'It's none of us, Drake. It's Sam. It's Sam who did this to you, Drake. You want him to get away with it? Or do you want to live long enough to make him suffer?'

Drake heard a shimmery, metallic sound. The saw was too big for Diana to handle easily. The blade wobbled a little as she lined it up.

'OK,' Diana said. 'Hold on to him. I'll be as quick as I can be.'

Drake lost consciousness, but his dreams were as pain-racked as his waking. He weaved in and out, awake and screaming, asleep and crying.

He heard a distant thump as his arm dropped to the floor.

And then a sudden frenzy of running and yelling, shouted orders and confusion, a flash of Diana threading a needle with bloody fingers. Hands all over him, the pressure squeezing the air from his lungs.

Staring up from the bottom of a deep well, Drake saw lunatic faces looking down at him, eyes wild, bloody faces like monsters.

'He'll live, I think,' a voice said.

'God help us if he lives,' a voice said.

'No. God help Sam Temple.'

And then nothing.

423

*

'Astrid, I need you to start talking to these kids,' Sam said. 'Find out their powers. Find out how much control they have. We're looking for anyone who might be able to help in a fight.'

Astrid looked uncomfortable. 'Me? Shouldn't Edilio be doing that?'

'I have a different job for Edilio.'

They were in the plaza, sitting wearily on the steps of the town hall, Sam, Astrid, Little Pete, and Edilio. Quinn was gone, no one knew where. The liberated Coates kids – the Coates Freaks, as they now proudly called themselves – had been fed at Ralph's and were being fed again by Albert, who was walking among them handing out burgers. Some of the kids had eaten too much all at once and had thrown up. But most still had room for a hamburger – even if it was on a toasted chocolate chip waffle.

Lana was just about finished healing the hands of the refugees. She was staggering from exhaustion and finally, as Sam watched, her legs folded under her and she fell to the grass. Before he could even get up to help, some of the Coates kids stretched her out with gentleness bordering on reverence. They rolled jackets to make her a pillow and borrowed a blanket from a tattered pup tent to spread over her.

'OK, I'll talk to them,' Astrid said. But she still looked reluctant. 'I can't read people like Diana does.'

'That's what's bothering you? You're not my Diana. And hopefully I'm not Caine.'

'I guess I was hoping this would all kind of be over. At least for a while.'

'I think it will be over. For a while. But first we have to plan and make sure we're ready when Caine comes back.'

'You're right.' She smiled wanly. 'Anyway, it's not like I was dreaming of a big meal, a hot shower, and hours and hours of sleep.'

'Yeah. You wouldn't want to start getting soft now, would you?' Something else occurred to him. 'But hey, keep L. P. happy, huh? I don't want you disappearing suddenly.'

'That would be a shame, wouldn't it?' she said drily. 'Maybe I'll try Quinn's trick: Hawaii, Petey, Hawaii.'

Astrid rounded up her brother, made sure he was OK, then plunged into the crowd.

Sam motioned Edilio closer. 'Edilio. I have something I need you to do.'

'Whatever you want.'

'It involves driving. And it involves keeping a secret.'

'The secret is no problem. Driving?' He gulped theatrically, like a cartoon character doing a double take.

'I need you to get a truck and go to the power plant.' He explained what he wanted, and Edilio's expression grew darker with each word. When he was done, Sam asked, 'Can you handle that? You'll need to take at least one other guy with you.'

'I can do it,' Edilio said. 'I'm not happy about it, but you know that.'

'Who will you take with you?'

'Elwood, I guess, if Dahra will let me borrow him.'

'OK. Go take an hour or two to figure out how to drive.'

'A day or two more like it,' Edilio said. But then he executed a mock salute and said, 'No problem, General.'

Sam sat alone now, shoulders hunched, head buzzing from lack of sleep and the after-effects of pain and fear. He needed to think, he told himself, needed to prepare. Caine would be planning.

Caine. His brother.

His brother.

How long did he have? Three days.

In three days he would . . . disappear.

And so would Caine.

Maybe die. Maybe be changed in some way. Maybe just pop neatly back into the old universe with lots of incredible stories to tell.

And leave Astrid behind.

If Caine had been a normal, well-adjusted person, he might spend his last days preparing for whatever the poof meant – death, disappearance, escape. But Sam doubted Caine would do that. Caine would need to triumph over Sam. That need would be even greater than the need to be ready for the end.

'I never have liked birthdays,' Sam muttered.

Albert Hillsborough had finished handing out burgers to grateful Coates kids. He climbed the steps to Sam.

'Glad you're back, man,' Albert said.

For some reason, Sam felt compelled to stand and offer his hand to the kid. Albert shook it solemnly.

'It's cool what you've done, keeping the Mickey D's open.'

Albert looked faintly annoyed. 'We don't call it Mickey D's. It's McDonald's. It will always be McDonald's. Although,' he allowed, 'I've strayed pretty far from the standard operating manual.'

'I saw the waffle-burgers.'

There was something on Albert's mind. Whatever it was, Sam didn't have the time or the energy, but Albert was becoming an important person, someone not to blow off. 'What's up, Albert?'

'Well, I've done inventory at Ralph's, and I think if I had a lot of help, I could put together an OK Thanksgiving dinner.'

Sam stared at him. He blinked. 'What?'

'Thanksgiving. It's next week.'

'Uh-huh.'

'There are ovens at Ralph's, big ones. And no one has taken the frozen turkeys. Figure two hundred and fifty kids if pretty much everyone from Perdido Beach shows up, right? One turkey will feed maybe eight people, so we need thirty-one, thirty-two turkeys. No problem there, because there are forty-six turkeys at Ralph's.'

'Thirty-one turkeys?'

'Cranberry sauce will be no problem, stuffing is no problem, no one has taken much stuffing yet, although I'll have to figure out how to mix, like, seven different brands and styles together, see how it tastes.'

'Stuffing,' Sam echoed solemnly.

'We don't have enough canned yams, we'll have to do fresh

along with some baked potatoes. The big problem is going to be whipped cream and ice cream for the pies.'

Sam wanted to burst out laughing, but at the same time he found it touching and reassuring that Albert had put so much thought into the question.

'I imagine the ice cream is pretty much gone,' Sam said.

'Yeah. We're very low on ice cream. And kids have been taking the canned whipped cream, too.'

'But we can have pie?'

'We have some frozen. And we have some pie shells we can bake up ourselves.'

'That would be nice,' Sam said.

'I'll need to start three days before. I'll need, like, at least ten people to help. I can haul the tables out of the church basement and set up in the plaza. I think I can do it.'

'I'll bet you can, Albert,' Sam said with feeling.

'Mother Mary's going to have the prees make centrepieces.'

'Listen, Albert –'

Albert raised a hand, cutting Sam off. 'I know. I mean, I know we may have some great big fight before that. And I heard you have your fifteenth coming up. All kinds of bad stuff may happen. But, Sam –'

This time, Sam cut him off. 'Albert? Get moving on planning the big meal.'

'Yeah?'

'Yeah. It will give people something to look forward to.'

Albert left, and Sam fought down a yawn. He noticed Astrid

deep in conversation with three of the Coates kids. Astrid had been through all kinds of horror, he thought, but somehow, even with her blouse filthy, her blonde hair hanging lank and greasy, her face smudged, she looked beautiful.

When he raised his gaze he could see across the plaza, across the buildings at the far end, clear out to the ocean, the too-placid ocean.

Birthday. Thanksgiving. Poof. And a showdown with Caine. Not to mention just daily life if they somehow all survived. Not to mention finding a way to escape or end the FAYZ. And all he wanted to do was take Astrid's hand and lead her down to the beach, stretch a blanket out on the hot sand, lie down beside her and sleep for about a month.

'Right after the big Thanksgiving dinner,' Sam promised himself. 'Right after pie.'

THIRTY SEVEN

COOKIE ROLLED OVER and stood up. His legs were still weak and shaky. He had to hold himself up by leaning on the table.

But he steadied himself with the arm that had been utterly shattered.

Dahra Baidoo was there, and Elwood, both staring like they were witnessing a miracle.

'I suppose they are,' Lana said to herself.

'It doesn't hurt,' Cookie said.

He laughed. It was an incredulous, disbelieving sound. He rotated his arm, all the way forwards, all the way up. He squeezed his fingers into a fist.

'It doesn't hurt.'

'OK, I never thought I'd see that,' Elwood said, shaking his head slowly.

Tears came to Cookie's bloodshot eyes. He whispered to himself, 'It doesn't hurt. It doesn't hurt at all.'

He took a tentative step. Then another. He had lost a lot of weight. He was pale, and more than pale, almost green. He was shaky, a bear walking on its hind legs and about to topple over. He looked like what he was: a kid who'd taken a round trip to hell.

'Thank you,' he whispered to Lana. 'Thank you.'

'It's not my doing,' Lana said. 'It's just . . . I don't know what it is.'

She was tired. Healing Cookie had taken a long time. She'd been in the hospital since eight o'clock that morning, having been awakened by Cookie's cries of agony.

His injury was even worse than her own broken arm had been. It had taken her more than six hours, and now whatever benefit she'd gained from sleeping in the park was wasted, and she was weary again. Outside, she was pretty sure the sun was shining, but all she wanted now was a bed.

'It's a thing I can do,' Lana said, fighting a yawn and stretching to get the kinks out of her back. 'Just a . . . a thing.'

Cookie nodded. Then he did something no one expected. He got down on his knees before a shocked Dahra.

'You took care of me.'

Dahra shrugged and looked mightily uncomfortable. 'It's OK, Cookie.'

'No.' He took her hand awkwardly and leaned his forehead into her. 'Anything you ever want. Anything. Any time. Ever.' Tears choked his voice. 'Anything.'

Dahra pulled him back to his feet. He had been as big and as heavy as Orc. He was still big enough to tower over Dahra. 'You need to start eating,' she said.

'Yeah, eat,' Cookie said. 'Then what do I do?'

Dahra looked a little exasperated. She said, 'I don't know, Cookie.'

Lana had an idea. 'Go find Sam. There's a fight coming.'

'I can fight,' Cookie confirmed. 'As soon as I get some food down and, you know, kind of get my strength back.'

'McDonald's is open,' Dahra said. 'Try the French-toast-burger. It's better than it sounds.'

Cookie left. Dahra said, 'Lana, I know it's mostly about Cookie, but I feel like you saved my life, too. I've been losing my mind taking care of him.'

Lana was uncomfortable with gratitude. She always had been, even in small things. Now the idea that people were thanking her for performing near-miracles, that was preposterous. She said, 'Do you know any place I could sleep? Like, in a bed?'

Elwood guided her and Patrick to his house. It was half a mile from the plaza and Lana was practically sleepwalking by the time they reached it.

'Come on in,' Elwood said. 'You want something to eat?'

Lana shook her head. 'Just a place to . . . that couch.'

'You could use one of the bedrooms upstairs.'

Lana was already face down on the couch. And a split second later, she was asleep.

Night had fallen by the time she woke. It took a while to figure out where she was.

Elwood had thoughtfully fed Patrick. There was a clean-licked plate on the kitchen tiles. Patrick was curled up before a gas fireplace, though there was no fire.

Lana was ravenously hungry. She searched the kitchen, feeling like a burglar. The refrigerator had been emptied of everything but lemon juice, soy sauce, a carton of very expired half-and-half, and some very, very old lettuce.

The freezer was better. There were frozen buffalo wings, something in a Tupperware container, and a microwavable pepperoni pizza.

'Oh, yes,' Lana said. 'Oh, definitely.'

She popped the pizza in the microwave and punched the numbers. It was fascinating watching it rotate. Her mouth watered. It was all she could do to wait till the microwave dinged.

She ate the pizza by ripping it with her bare hands, folding up the gooey slices and scooping up whatever dripped on the counter.

'Oh, you want some, too?' she asked when Patrick showed up, wagging his tail and looking eager. She tossed him a piece, which he caught in the air.

'Well. We've been through it, huh, boy?'

Lana found the master-bedroom shower upstairs and spent half an hour in the stream of hot water. The water ran red and black down the drain.

Then she invited Patrick in, shampooed him up, rinsed him off, and kicked him out to shake like crazy and spray dog water all over the bathroom.

She wrapped herself in a towel and went exploring through the house for clothing. Elwood didn't seem to have any sisters, but his mother was petite, so with some cinching and tying-off Lana managed to put together an outfit.

She picked her old clothes up and almost fainted from the stench.

'Oh, my God, Patrick, that's what I've been smelling like? I have to burn these things.'

But she contented herself with stuffing the bloodstained, dirt-crusted, sweat-stinking, torn, and shredded clothing into a trash bag. Unfortunately she was stuck with her old shoes: Elwood's mother's shoes were two sizes too large.

She trotted down the stairs, feeling better than she had in a very long time. Then she spotted the phone and could not resist the urge to pick it up. Call her mom. Tell her mom . . . well, something. She knew what everyone had told her about the FAYZ. But, still . . .

'No dial tone, Patrick.'

Patrick was not interested.

'You know what, Patrick? I'm just going to sit down and cry for a while.'

But the tears wouldn't come. So after a while she sighed and carried a warm Diet Pepsi out on to the porch.

It was the middle of the night. The street was quiet. She was in a town she had grown up in but had been away from for years. She'd run into some kids she'd known back in the day, but most of them hadn't recognised her beneath her coating of filth. Now maybe at least people would know her. Although it occurred to her that Sam and Astrid and Edilio probably wouldn't recognise her now that she was clean.

'I feel like going somewhere, Patrick,' she said. 'But I don't know where.'

A car turned on to the street. It was moving slowly. Whoever was behind the wheel was clearly not an experienced driver.

Lana stiffened, preparing to rush back inside and lock the door. She raised a cautious wave, but she couldn't see the driver and the driver didn't seem to want to stop and chat. The car continued on down the street and turned off.

'Some kind of patrol,' Lana said to Patrick.

She stayed a while longer on the porch before heading back inside.

She instantly recognised the boy standing in the kitchen.

Patrick growled and raised his hackles.

'Hello, freak,' Drake said.

Lana backed away, but too late. Drake levelled his gun at her.

'I'm right-handed. Least I used to be. But I can still hit you from this distance.'

'What do you want?'

Drake motioned towards the stump of his right arm. It was gone from just above the elbow. 'What do you think I want?'

The one time she'd seen Drake Merwin, he had made her think of Pack Leader: strong, hyper alert, dangerous. Now, the lean physique looked gaunt, the shark's grin was a tight grimace, his eyes were red-rimmed. His stare, once languidly menacing, was now intense, burning hot. He looked like someone who had been tortured beyond endurance.

'I'll try,' Lana said.

'You'll do more than try,' he said. He convulsed in pain, face scrunched. A low, eerie moan escaped his throat.

'I don't know if I can grow a whole arm back,' Lana said. 'Let me touch it.'

'Not here,' he hissed. He motioned with his gun. 'Through the back door.'

'If you shoot me, I can't help you,' Lana argued.

'Can you heal dogs? How about if I blow his brains out? Can you heal that, freak?'

The car Lana had seen driving by was parked, engine running, in the alley behind the house. The boy called Panda was at the wheel.

'Don't make me do this,' Lana pleaded. 'I would help you no matter what. You don't have to do this.'

But there was no point in arguing. If Drake had ever owned a conscience, it had died along with his arm.

They drove off through the sleeping town.

Out into the night.

Howard had seen with his own eyes the small army Sam had assembled. He'd seen them descending on Ralph's. The grocery store was unguarded, which meant the other sheriffs had decided to get out of the way and make themselves scarce.

'There's too many,' Howard had concluded.

So he and Orc had stolen a car and made their way towards Coates Academy. But they had taken a wrong turn somewhere along the road and ended up on a dirt track leading into the desert as night fell.

They had turned around, retracing their way to the main road, but that hadn't worked, either. Finally, they ran out of gas.

'This was your stupid idea,' Orc muttered.

'What did you want to do? Stay in town with Sam? He had, like, twenty kids with him.'

'I could kick his butt.'

'Orc, don't be a moron,' Howard snapped in frustration. 'If Caine's not there, and Drake's not there, and Sammy is marching back into town like a big deal, what do you think that means? I mean, come on, Orc, do the math.'

Orc's pig eyes had narrowed to slits. 'Don't call me stupid. If I have to, I'll kick your teeth in.'

Howard wasted twenty minutes ameliorating Orc's hurt feelings. Which still left them sitting in a dead car in the middle of nowhere.

'I see a light,' Orc said.

'Hey, yeah.' Howard jumped from the car and started running. Orc lumbered after him.

The twin beams of a car moved at an intercept angle to them. If they slowed down, the car would miss them, never see them.

'Hurry up,' Howard yelled.

'Catch them.' Orc urged Howard on as he gave up the race and slowed to a heavy-footed slog.

'OK,' Howard yelled. His foot caught on something and he

sprawled into the dirt. He picked himself up and only then felt the sharp pain in his ankle.

'What the – ?' He froze. There was something there in the darkness. Not Orc, something that smelled rank and panted like a dog.

Howard was up and running in a heartbeat. 'Something is after me,' he yelled.

The car lights were vectoring towards him. He could make it. He could make it. If he didn't fall again. If the monster didn't get him first.

Howard's feet hit blacktop and he was illuminated, brilliant white. The car screeched. It came to a stop.

The monster was nowhere in sight.

'Howard?'

Howard recognised the voice. Panda was leaning out of the window.

'Panda? Man, am I glad to see you. We've been –'

Something dark and swift leaped and caught Panda's arm. He let out a shriek.

From inside the car, a dog barked frantically.

Something whacked Howard in the back and he hit the pavement on his hands and knees.

The car lurched forwards. The bumper stopped six inches from Howard's head.

There came a scream, a male voice. Orc. Orc back in the darkness somewhere.

There were dogs everywhere, swarming around Howard.

No, not dogs, he thought, wolves. Coyotes.

The car door opened and Panda fell out, wrapped half around a coyote.

A loud bang and a stab of orange light.

But the coyotes didn't stop.

Another shot and one of the coyotes yelped in pain. Drake staggered into view, looking like a scarecrow in the headlights.

The coyotes retreated, out of the light but by no means gone. Howard got slowly to his feet.

Drake pointed the gun at Howard's face. 'Did you set these dogs on me?'

'They chewed on me too, man,' Howard protested. Then he yelled out at the desert, 'Orc. Orc, man. Orc.'

A voice like wet gravel, but with an eerie high-pitched tone, said, 'Give us female.'

Howard peered into the night, trying to make sense of it. It wasn't Orc. Where was Orc?

'What female?' Drake demanded. 'Who are you?'

Slowly, on every side, all around the car the desert moved. Shadows crept closer. Howard shrank back, but Drake stood firm.

'Who's out there?' Drake demanded.

A mange-eaten coyote with a scarred muzzle that gave him a sinister grin stepped into the circle of light. Howard almost fell down when he realised it was this coyote who spoke.

'Give us female.'

'No,' Drake said, recovering quickly from the shock. 'She's

mine. I need her to heal my arm. She has the power and I want my arm back.'

'You are nothing,' the coyote snarled.

'I'm the kid with the gun,' Drake said.

The two of them, two of a kind, it seemed to Howard, stared holes in each other.

'What do you want with her?' Drake demanded.

'Darkness say: bring female.'

'Darkness? What's that supposed to mean?'

'Give us female,' Pack Leader said, returning to his single-minded point. 'Or we kill all.'

'I'll kill plenty of you.'

'You die,' Pack Leader said stubbornly.

Howard felt it was time to speak up. 'Guys. Guys. We have a standoff here. So why don't we see if we can figure out an arrangement?'

'What are you talking about?'

'OK, look, Drake, you said something about the female healing your arm?'

'She has the power. I want my arm back.'

'And Mr, um . . . coyote . . . you're supposed to take her to some other dog called Darkness?'

Pack Leader eyed Howard in a way that suggested he was considering how to butcher and eat him.

'OK,' Howard said shakily. 'I think we can work a deal.'

THIRTY EIGHT

'ASTRID,' EDILIO SAID. 'I'm so sorry about your house.'

Astrid squeezed Edilio's hand. 'Yeah. I have to admit, it was hard for me to see.'

'You could stay over at the firehouse with me and Sam and Quinn,' Edilio offered.

'It's OK. Petey and I are going to room with Mother Mary and Brother John for a while. They're hardly ever home. And when they are, well, you know, it's good to have people around.'

The three of them, Edilio, Astrid, and Little Pete, were in the office that had once belonged to the mayor of Perdido Beach and most recently had been occupied by Caine Soren. Sam had resisted the idea of taking the office, feeling it made him seem self-important. But Astrid had argued that symbols were important and kids wanted to think that someone was in charge.

She settled Little Pete into a chair and handed him a Baggie full of Rice Chex. Little Pete liked to eat them plain, no milk.

'Where's Sam?' Astrid asked. 'And why are we here?'

Edilio looked uncomfortable. 'We have something to show you.'

Sam opened the door. He did not smile at Astrid. He

441

looked warily at Little Pete. He said hello, then, 'Astrid, there's something you need to see. And I'm thinking Little Pete shouldn't see.'

'I don't understand.'

Sam flopped into the chair last occupied by Caine. Astrid was struck by how alike the two boys looked superficially. And by how different a reaction she had to their similar features. Where Caine hid his arrogance and cruelty beneath a smooth, controlled surface, Sam let his emotions play out on his face. Right now he was sad and weary and concerned.

'I wonder if L. P. could sit with Edilio in the other room.'

'That sounds ominous,' Astrid said. The expression on Sam's face did not contradict her.

She managed to get Little Pete to move, though not without a struggle. Edilio stayed with him.

Sam had a DVD in his hand. He said, 'Yesterday I sent Edilio to the power plant to get two things. First, a cache of automatic weapons from the guardhouse.'

'Machine guns?'

'Yeah. Not just for us to have, but to make sure the other side doesn't get them.'

'Now we have an arms race,' Astrid said.

Her tone seemed to irritate Sam. 'You want me to leave them for Caine?'

'I wasn't criticising, just . . . you know. Ninth-graders with machine guns: it's hard to make that a happy story.'

Sam relented. He even grinned. 'Yeah. The phrase "ninth-graders with machine guns" isn't exactly followed by "have a nice day".'

'No wonder you looked so grim.' As soon as she said it, she knew she was wrong. He had something else to tell her. Something worse. The DVD.

'I've been wondering, like you, why the FAYZ seems to be centred on the power plant. Ten miles in every direction. Why? So Edilio went through some of the security videos at the plant.'

Astrid stood up so suddenly, she surprised herself. 'I really shouldn't leave Petey alone.'

'You know what this DVD will show, don't you?' It wasn't a question. 'You guessed it that first night. I remember, we were looking at the video map. You put your arm around Little Pete and you gave me a very weird look. At the time, I didn't know what to make of that look.'

'I didn't know you then,' Astrid said. 'I didn't know if I could trust you.'

Sam slid the DVD into the player and switched on the TV. 'The sound quality is pretty bad.'

Astrid saw the control room of the power plant from a high vantage point with a wide angle.

The camera showed the control room. Five adults, three men and two women. One of them was Astrid's father. The image brought a lump to her throat. There he was, her father, rocking in his chair, joking with the woman at the next station, leaning forward to fill out some paperwork.

And sitting in a chair against the far wall, his face lit by the glow of his omnipresent Game Boy, was Little Pete.

The only sound was muddy, unintelligible conversation.

'Here it comes,' Sam said.

Suddenly a klaxon sounded, harsh and distorted on the audio.

Everyone in the control room jumped. People rushed to the monitors, to the instrument readouts. Astrid's father shot a worried glance at his son, but then leaned into his monitor, staring.

Other people swept into the room and moved with practised efficiency to the untended monitors.

Panicky instructions were shouted back and forth.

A second alarm went off, more shrill than the first.

A strobe warning light was flashing.

Fear on every face.

And Little Pete was rocking frantically, his hands pressed over his ears. He had a look of pain on his innocent face.

The ten adults now in the room were a terrifying pantomime of controlled desperation. Keyboards were punched, switches thrown. Her father grabbed a thick manual and began snapping through the pages, and all the while people shouted and the alarms blared and Little Pete was screaming, screaming, hands over his ears.

'I don't want to see this,' Astrid said, but she couldn't look away.

Little Pete jumped to his feet.

He ran to his father, but his father, frantic, pushed him away. Little Pete went sprawling against a chair. He ended up flung against the long table, staring at a monitor that flashed, flashed, flashed a warning in bright red.

The number fourteen.

'Code one-four,' Astrid said dully. 'I heard my dad say that one time. It's the code for a core meltdown. He would make a joke out of it. Code one-one, that was minor trouble, code one-two, you worry, code one-three, you call the governor, code one-four, you pray. The next stage, code one-five, is . . . obliteration.'

On the tape, Little Pete pulled his hands from his ears.

The klaxon was relentless.

There was a flash that blanked out the tape. Several seconds of static.

When the picture stabilised, the warning alarm was silent.

And Little Pete was alone.

'Astrid, you'll notice that the time signature on the tape says November tenth, ten eighteen a.m. The exact time when every person over the age of fourteen disappeared.'

On the tape, Little Pete stopped crying.

He didn't even look around, he just walked back to the chair where he had been sitting, retrieved his game, and resumed play.

'Little Pete caused the FAYZ,' Sam said flatly.

Astrid covered her face with her hands. She was surprised by the tears she felt rising, and their force. She struggled to keep from sobbing. It was a few minutes before she could speak. Sam waited patiently.

'He didn't know he was doing it,' Astrid said in a low, unsteady voice. 'He doesn't know what he's doing. Not the way we do. Not like, if I do "this", then "that" will happen.'

'I know that.'

'You can't blame him.' Astrid looked up, eyes blazing defiantly.

'Blame him?' Sam moved to sit beside her on the couch. Close enough that their legs were touching. 'Astrid, I can't believe I'm saying this to you, but I think you overlooked something.'

She turned her tear-stained face to him, searching.

'Astrid, they were having a meltdown. They didn't seem to be getting it under control. They all looked pretty scared.'

Astrid gasped. Sam was right: she had missed it. 'He stopped the meltdown. A meltdown might have killed everyone in Perdido Beach.'

'Yeah. I'm not crazy about the way he did it, but he may have saved everyone's life.'

'He stopped the meltdown,' Astrid said, still not grasping it fully.

Sam grinned. He even laughed.

'What's funny?' she demanded.

'I figured something out before Astrid the Genius. I am totally enjoying that. I'm just going to gloat here for a minute.'

'Enjoy it, it may never happen again,' Astrid said.

'Oh, believe me, I know that.' He took her hand, and she was very glad to feel his touch. 'He saved us. But he also created this whole weird thing.'

'Not the whole thing,' Astrid said, shaking her head. 'The mutations prefigure the FAYZ. Indeed, the mutations were the

446

sine qua non of the FAYZ. The thing without which the FAYZ could not have occurred.'

Sam refused to be impressed. 'You can hammer me all you want with your "indeeds" and your "prefigures" and your "sine qua nons", I am still gloating here.'

She raised his hand to her lips and kissed his fingers.

Then she released him, stood up, paced across the room and back, stopped, and said, 'Diana. She talks about it being like cell phone bars. Two bars, three bars. Caine is a four bar. You are, too, I would guess. Petey . . . I guess he's a five or a seven.'

'Or a ten,' Sam agreed.

'But Diana thinks it's like reception. Like some of us can get better reception. If that's true, then we aren't generating the power, just using it, focusing it.'

'So?'

'So where's it coming from? To extend the analogy: where's the cell phone tower? What is generating the power?'

Sam rose with a sigh. 'One thing for sure: this never gets out. Edilio knows, I know, and you know. No one else can ever know.'

Astrid nodded. 'People would hate him. Or try to use him.'

Sam nodded. 'I wish . . .'

'No,' Astrid said, and shrugged helplessly. 'There's no way to get him to undo it.'

'That's a pity,' Sam said, making a wry smile that did not reach his eyes. 'Because tick-tock, tick-tock.'

*

Lana stumbled through the night.

Back with the coyotes. A nightmare revisited.

And now, adding to the misery, Drake and Howard stumbled along with her.

Drake with his gun. Drake cursing his pain.

And Howard calling, 'Orc, Orc,' into the night.

Greater than any misery, the dread of that mine shaft and what lay at the bottom.

She had disobeyed the Darkness.

What would the seething monster do to her?

'Let's stop and I'll try to fix Drake's arm, OK?' she pleaded.

'No stop,' Pack Leader snarled.

'Let me try, at least.'

Pack Leader ignored her, and they ran and tripped and picked themselves up and ran some more.

No escape now. No possibility of escape.

Unless.

She manoeuvred closer to Drake. 'What if he won't let me heal you?'

'Don't try to play me,' Drake said tersely. 'Anyway, now I want to see this thing that has you so terrified.'

'No, you don't,' Lana promised.

'What is it?' Howard asked, nervous, almost as scared as Lana herself.

Lana had no answer to that question.

Each step was harder than the one before, and several times Pack Leader nipped at her to move her along. When he didn't,

Drake did, waving his gun at her, threatening her with word and gesture and look.

They reached the abandoned mining camp after the moon had set and as the stars were just fading before the promise of dawn.

She had never felt such dread. It was as if her blood had all been drained and replaced with a cold sludge. She could barely move. Her heart beat in loud, shuddering thumps in her chest. She wanted to pet Patrick, to take some tiny measure of comfort from him, but she couldn't make herself bend, couldn't bring herself to speak. She held herself tightly contained, silent, rigid.

I'm going to die here, Lana thought.

'Human light,' Pack Leader slurred. He indicated a flashlight lying wedged between the rocks. Howard leaped at it and switched it on. His hand shook so badly, the light danced across rock walls, sending shadows flying like swift-moving ghosts.

Now even Drake seemed leery, frightened of something he couldn't quite explain. He was asking questions, ever more agitated as they stepped into the icebox chill of the mine.

'Someone needs to tell me what we're going to see,' Drake insisted.

'I need to know what we're up to,' Drake said.

'Maybe we better talk about our deal,' Drake said.

'How much farther?' Drake said.

But all the while, they moved down the shaft.

Lana had to force each breath. Had to remind herself: breathe, breathe.

Patrick was gone. He'd abandoned them at the mouth of the mine.

'Man, I . . . I can't do this,' Howard said. 'I gotta . . . I . . .' He was gasping for breath.

'Shut up,' Drake snapped, glad to have someone to take out his frustrations on.

Howard turned suddenly and bolted, taking the flashlight with him.

Pack Leader yipped a command and two coyotes went in pursuit.

With the flashlight gone, Lana could see the faint green glow from the walls. Darkness behind. The Darkness ahead.

'Let him go,' Drake said.

'Howard's not important,' Drake said.

'I'm important,' Drake said. His voice was small.

Lana closed her eyes tight, but somehow the green glow penetrated her eyelids, as though it could shine right through her flesh, right through the bone of her skull.

She could go no farther. She sank to her knees.

Close enough. It was there, just ahead, just around that last bend, a moving, sliding, grinding pile of glowing rock.

The soundless voice was a cudgel slamming her head. The Darkness thrust invisible fingers of ice into her mind, and Lana knew that she herself was speaking its words.

'The healer,' she cried in a tortured, manic parody of her own voice.

She kept her eyes shut but could feel Drake kneeling beside her.

'Why do you come to me?' Lana cried, a puppet, nothing but a tool for the Darkness to use.

'The coyote . . .' Drake managed.

'Faithful Pack Leader,' the Darkness said through Lana. 'Obedient, but not yet equal to a human.'

Open your eyes, Lana told herself. Be brave. Be brave. See it, face it, fight it. But the darkness was in her skull, pushing and prodding, peeking inside her secrets, laughing at her pathetic resistance.

And yet she opened her eyes. A lifelong habit of defiance gave her the strength. But she kept her eyes cast down, strong enough to force them open, too terrified to look on the face of the thing itself.

The rocks under her knees glowed.

She was touching it, touching the hem of it.

Pack Leader grovelled, lowering himself to the floor of the cave beside Lana, crawling on his belly.

Suddenly, Lana felt an electric shock of terrifying force. Her back arched, her head went back, her arms flew wide.

A pain like an icicle stabbing her eye and searing her brain.

She tried to scream, but no sound would come out.

Then it was gone and she fell on to her back, legs folded beneath her. She gasped like a landed fish, unable to fill her lungs.

'Defiance,' she croaked in a voice not her own.

'She's supposed to fix my arm,' Drake said. 'If you kill her, she can't help me.'

'You are bold to make demands,' the Darkness said through Lana.

'I'm not . . . it's . . . I want my arm back,' Drake shouted raggedly.

Lana found she could breathe again. She sucked in oxygen. She pushed out against the floor, scooted inch by inch away from the Darkness.

Drake shrieked in agony. Lana saw him as she had been, like he'd grabbed a power line. His body jerked like a marionette.

The Darkness released him.

'Ah,' the Darkness said, and twisted Lana's mouth into a rictus. 'I have found a much better teacher for you, Pack Leader.'

Pack Leader had dared to stand up. He kept his tail and head aligned in a submissive posture. He glanced at Drake, who had now been released and was doubled over, clutching his arm in pain.

'This human will teach you to kill humans,' Lana said.

Drake spoke as though each syllable was an effort. 'Yes. But . . . my arm.'

'Give me the arm,' Lana said, and, unwilling, crawled to Drake.

Drake stood up, shaky but determined. He extended the burned, sawed-off stump.

'I will give you an arm such as no human ever had,' the Darkness said through Lana. 'You have no magic within you, human, but the girl will serve.'

Drake moved with surprising speed. He pivoted and

yanked Lana up by her hair. 'Take my arm,' he hissed.

She placed her trembling hand against the melted flesh, feeling the fresh-cut bone beneath it, wanting to throw up.

The glow deepened. Lana felt her entire body filled with it, not hot but cold, as cold as ice.

Drake's flesh was growing.

She could feel it moving beneath her fingers. But it wasn't human flesh.

Not human flesh at all.

'No,' she whispered.

'Yes,' Drake breathed. 'Yes.'

THIRTY NINE

36 HOURS 37 MINUTES

'And sometimes when you lie to me
Sometimes I'll lie to you
And there isn't a thing you could possibly do
All these half-destroyed lives
Aren't as bad as they seem
But now I see blood and I hear people scream
Then I wake up
And it's just another bad dream . . .'

SAM SANG ALONG to the Agent Orange tune on his iPod, feeling as if the familiar lyrics had crossed the line from being just another self-consciously disturbing song to being too close to describing his life.

He was in the fire station not exactly enjoying a lonely lunch. Quinn was . . . well, he never seemed to know where Quinn was any more. His friend – was that word even appropriate? His friend Quinn was a shadow who came and went, sometimes joking like his old self, sometimes sitting sullen and watching DVDs he'd seen a million times before.

In any case, he wasn't there for lunch at the fire station,

454

despite the fact that Sam had made enough soup for extra mouths.

Edilio materialised silently in the doorway. He looked discouraged. Sam realised he'd been singing aloud and, embarrassed, dialled down the music and pulled out the earbuds.

'What did you find, Edilio?'

'If she's anywhere in Perdido Beach, she's doing a good job of hiding, Sam,' Edilio said. 'We've looked. We've talked to everyone. Lana's gone. Her dog is gone. She was in Elwood's house, then she was gone.'

Sam tossed his music player on to the table. 'I have soup. Want some?'

Edilio sagged into a chair. 'What's the song?'

'What? Oh. It's called "A Cry for Help in a World Gone Mad".'

They shared a mordant laugh.

'Next I'll dial up that old song, what's it called?' Sam searched his memory. 'Yeah. REM. "It's the End of the World as We Know It".'

'It is that,' Edilio commented. 'I been searching for a girl who can heal people with magic, and taking some time to learn how to shoot a machine gun.'

'How'd that go, by the way?'

'I got four boys can more or less handle it, counting Quinn. But, man, we aren't exactly the marines, you know? Kid named Tom starts shooting and he almost shoots me. I had to dive into a pile of dog poop.'

Sam tried not to laugh, but neither of them could stop once it started.

'Yeah, you think it's funny. Wait till it's you,' Edilio said.

Sam was serious again. 'I don't know what's holding Caine back. It's been two days. What's keeping him?'

'What's the hurry? The more time we have, the more we're prepared.'

'Dude, tomorrow night I'm out of here,' Sam said.

'You don't know that for sure, man,' Edilio said, embarrassed.

'I just wish I knew what was going on up at Coates.'

Edilio caught on immediately. 'You talking about spying them out?'

Sam pushed his soup away. 'I don't know what I'm talking about, man. I'm halfway thinking we should take it to them, you know? Go up there and do this.'

'We have guns. We have guys who can drive. We got, in addition to you, four other mutants with powers that might be useful. You know, powers you can fight with, not like this one girl where she can disappear but only if she's really embarrassed.'

Sam smiled despite himself. 'You're kidding.'

'No man, she's really bashful and all, so you say something like, "you have nice hair", and suddenly she's invisible. But she's still there. You touch her, but you can't see her.'

'That's not exactly going to stop Caine.'

'Taylor is working on her teleporting. She can go a couple of blocks now.' Edilio shrugged. 'But in terms of useful, we got that kid, he's nine, he can do like you do with the light, but not as much.'

'Nine. We can't make a nine-year-old hurt someone,' Sam protested.

'How about an eleven-year-old who can move so fast, you can barely see her?'

'That girl Brianna?'

'She calls herself the Breeze now. Like, as fast as the breeze.'

'The Breeze? Like a superhero name?' He shook his head ruefully. 'Great. That's all we need', Sam said. It was one of his mother's favourite phrases, 'that's all we need'. He felt a sharp pang in his chest, but it passed quickly. 'What do we have the Breeze do when she's zipping around?'

Edilio looked uncomfortable. 'I guess we give her a gun. She shoots and zooms away and shoots again.'

'Oh, God.' Sam hung his head. 'Eleven years old and we're giving her a gun? To shoot at people? At human beings? It's sick.'

Edilio didn't have anything to say to that.

'Sorry, man, I'm not laying this off on you, Edilio. It's just . . . I mean, this is nuts. It's wrong. Bad enough kids our age, but fourth-graders and fifth-graders?'

There came the clattering of feet on the stairs, and both Sam and Edilio leaped to their feet, expecting the worst.

Dekka, one of the Coates refugees, came barrelling into the room and skidded on the waxed floor. Her forehead had been injured, a two-inch gash, and she had refused to let Lana heal it.

'I got that from Drake's shoe when he kicked me,' she had

said. 'Heal up my hands from the plastering, but leave my head. I want something to remember it by.'

Sam reflected that that was only the second-most interesting thing about Dekka. Number one would probably be the fact that she seemed to have the power to suspend the force of gravity within a small area.

'What is it, Dekka?' Sam asked.

'That guy Orc. He just walked into town, all raggedy-looking.'

'Orc? Just Orc? No Howard?'

Dekka shrugged. 'I didn't see anyone else. He just walked on in, and that guy Quinn told me I better go tell you. He said he was going to follow Orc home.'

That would be the house Orc had shared with Howard. It wasn't a long walk.

'Maybe I should bring a gun,' Edilio said darkly.

'I think I can handle Orc now,' Sam said. His own confidence surprised him. He'd never before in his life thought he could handle Orc.

Quinn was waiting outside the house. Sam thanked Quinn almost formally. 'I appreciate you sending Dekka to me and keeping an eye on things.'

'I do what I can,' Quinn said, more bitterly than he had probably intended.

Sam and Edilio stood by as Quinn knocked on the door. The bully's all-too-familiar voice yelled, 'Come in, morons.'

Orc was popping the top of a can of beer.

'Let me drink this,' Orc muttered. 'Then you can kill me or whatever.'

Orc had lived a bad couple of days. He was scratched, bruised, battered. One eye was swollen and black. His pants were torn and filthy. His shirt was barely recognisable as a shirt. It had been ripped to tatters, then knotted crudely back together.

He was still big, but he looked less threatening than they'd ever seen him before.

'Where's Howard?' Sam demanded.

'With them,' Orc said.

'With who?'

'Drake. That girl, what's her name, Lana. And a talking dog.' Orc smirked. 'Yeah. I'm crazy. Talking dog. Was the dogs that took me down. Ripped a hole out of my guts. Ate my thigh.'

'What are you talking about, Orc?'

He drank deep. He sighed. 'Man, that's good.'

'Talk sense, Orc,' Sam snapped.

Orc belched loudly. He stood up slowly. He set down his beer. With stiff arms he pulled his ragged shirt up and over his head.

Edilio gasped. Quinn turned away. Sam just stared.

Great patches of Orc's chest and belly were covered by gravel. The individual rocks were the colour of muddy water, green-grey. As Orc breathed, the gravel rose and fell.

'It's spreading,' Orc said. He seemed bemused by it. He touched it with his finger. 'It's warm.'

'Orc . . . how did this happen?' Sam asked.

'I told you. The dogs ate out my leg and my guts and some other parts I ain't telling you about. Then this stuff kind of filled it in.'

He shrugged, and Sam heard a faint sound like footsteps on a wet gravel driveway.

'It doesn't hurt,' Orc said. 'It did. But it doesn't hurt now. Itches, though.'

'Mother of God,' Edilio said softly.

'Anyway,' Orc said. 'I know you all hate me. So either kill me or get out. I'm thirsty and hungry.'

They left him.

Outside, Quinn walked quickly down the street, stopped suddenly, and threw up into a bush.

Sam and Edilio caught up with him. Sam put his hand on Quinn's shoulder.

'Sorry,' Quinn said. 'I guess I'm just weak.'

'Worse is coming,' Sam said darkly. 'But all of a sudden a nice easy blink doesn't seem like the worst thing that could happen, does it?'

'Drake's been gone for two days,' Diana said. 'We need to look at what we have here.'

'I'm busy,' Caine snapped.

They were standing on the front lawn of Coates. Caine was supervising an effort to repair the hole caused by the earlier power struggle. He teleported bricks, a few at a time, up to where Mallet and Chaz were attempting to cement them in place.

It had all collapsed twice already. It was one thing to pour concrete into a mould in the ground. It was a lot harder to mortar bricks into place.

'We need to make some kind of deal with . . . with the townies,' Diana said.

'Townies. Carefully avoiding having to say "Sam". Or "your brother".'

'OK. You caught me,' Diana said. 'We have to make some kind of deal with your brother, Sam. They still have food. We are running out.'

Caine made a show of being distracted as he levitated another stack of bricks out through the front door of the school and up to the first floor, where Mallet and Chaz dodged the arriving load.

'I'm getting better at this,' Caine said. 'I'm gaining control. Precision.'

'Goody for you.'

Caine's shoulders sagged. 'You know, you could occasionally show some support. You know how I feel about you. But all you ever do is bust me.'

'What do you want to do, get married?'

Caine reddened, and Diana erupted in an unusually loud laugh. 'You get that we're fourteen, right? I mean, I know you think you're the Napoleon of the FAYZ, but we're still kids.'

'Age is relative. I'm one of the two oldest people in the FAYZ. And the most powerful.'

Diana bit her tongue. She had a smart-ass answer ready, but

she had tweaked Caine enough for one day. She had bigger issues to deal with than Caine's puppy love. And that's all it was. Caine wasn't capable of real love, the deep kind, the kind that would grow over time.

'Of course, neither am I,' Diana muttered.

'What?'

'Nothing.' She watched Caine as he worked. Not what he was doing, but the boy himself. He was the most charismatic person she'd ever known. He could have been a rock star. And clearly he thought he was in love with her. It was the reason he tolerated her impertinence.

She supposed she liked him. They had been attracted to each other almost from the start. They had been friends . . . no, that wasn't quite the word. Accomplices. Yes, that would do: accomplices. They had been accomplices since Caine had discovered his powers.

She had been the first person he showed. He had knocked a book off the table from across the room.

She'd been the one who encouraged him to work at it, develop it, practise it in secret. Each time he reached some new level, he would show it off for her. And when she showed even the slightest kindness towards him, a word of praise, an admiring nod, even, he would puff up and seem to shine with some reflected light.

It took so little to manipulate him. It didn't require real affection, just the hint of it.

Diana would task Caine to use his power to trip some snob

she didn't like, or humiliate some teacher who had come down on her. And when she reported to Caine that the science teacher had cornered her in an empty lab and tried to feel her up, Caine sent him sprawling down a set of steps and into the hospital.

Diana enjoyed that time. She had a protector who would do her bidding and ask nothing in return. Caine, despite his oversized ego, his looks, his charm, was terribly awkward with girls. He had never even tried to kiss her.

But then he had attracted the attention of Drake Merwin, who had already acquired a reputation as the most dangerous bully in a school with plenty of bullies to go around. And from that point on, Caine had played them off against each other, doing a little for Diana when she asked, and a little with Drake.

As Caine's powers grew, both relationships changed.

And then the school nurse, Sam's mother – Caine's mother too, though none of them knew that then – started to figure out that something was very, very strange about her long-lost little boy.

The bricks collapsed suddenly, a series of thuds as they hit the lawn, and a series of groans and curses from Chaz and Mallet.

Caine seemed almost not to notice. 'What do you think it was, Diana?' he said, almost as if he'd read her thoughts.

'I think they didn't set them straight enough,' she replied, knowing that wasn't what he meant.

'Not that. Her. Nurse Temple.' He repeated the name, drawing it out to get the feel of it. 'Nurse. Connie. Temple.'

Diana sighed. This was not a conversation she wanted to have. 'I didn't really know the woman.'

'She has two sons. One she keeps. The other she gives up for adoption. I was a baby.'

'I'm not a shrink,' Diana said.

'I always had the feeling, you know? That my family wasn't my real family. They never said I was adopted, but my mother – well, the woman I thought was my mother, I don't know what to call her now. Anyway, her, she never talked about having me. You know, you hear moms talking about going into labour and all. She never talked about that.'

'Too bad Dr Phil's not around. You could tell him all about it.'

'I think she must have been pretty cold. Nurse Temple. My so-called mother.' He was looking at Diana now, head cocked, frowning, sceptical. 'Kind of like you, Diana.'

Diana made a rude sound. 'Don't try to get deep, Caine. She was probably just a screwed-up teenager at the time. Maybe she figured she could handle one kid but not two. Or maybe she tried to adopt both of you out, but no one would take Sam.'

Caine was taken aback. 'Are you sucking up to me with that?'

'I'm trying to get you to move on. Who cares about your mommy issues? We have enough food for two, maybe three weeks. Then we're down to beans.'

'See what I mean? I'll bet she was just like you, Diana. Cold and selfish.'

Diana was about to answer when she heard a rushing sound

behind her. She spun and saw a wave, a swarm of rough, shaggy yellow beasts. The coyotes seemed to come from everywhere at once, a disciplined, purposeful invasion that would quickly overwhelm her and Caine.

Caine raised his hands, palms out, armed and ready.

'No,' a voice yelled. 'Don't hurt them, they're friends.'

It was Howard, marching up towards them, waving his hands. Behind him came the healer girl, Lana, looking shell-shocked.

And behind them, Drake.

Diana cursed. He was still alive.

And then she saw Drake's arm.

The burned stump, the remains of the arm she had sawed off while Drake screamed and cried and threatened, had been altered.

It was stretched, like it had been turned into dark, blood-red taffy. It wrapped twice around his body.

No.

Impossible.

Howard came rushing up first. 'Has Orc shown up here?' But neither Caine nor Diana answered. Both were staring at Drake, who sauntered towards them, all his cockiness restored, no longer the ragged scarecrow who had wept when he saw the melted stump of his hand lying on the tile floor.

'Drake,' Caine said. 'We thought you were dead.'

'I'm back,' Drake said. 'And better than ever.'

The red tentacle unwrapped itself from around his waist, like a python releasing its victim.

'Like it, Diana?' Drake asked.

The arm, that impossible blood-red snake, coiled above Drake's head, swirled, writhed. And then, so fast that the human eye could barely register the movement, it snapped like a bullwhip.

The sound was a loud crack. A mini sonic boom.

Diana cried out in pain. Stunned, she stared at the cut in her blouse and the trickle of red from her shoulder.

'Sorry,' Drake said with no attempt at sincerity. 'I'm still working on my aim.'

'Drake,' Caine said, and, despite the blood, despite Diana's wound, he grinned. 'Welcome back.'

'I brought some help,' Drake said. He extended his left hand, and Caine shook it awkwardly with his right. 'So. When do we go take down Sam Temple?'

FORTY

'**THEY'LL** COME TOMORROW evening,' Sam said. 'I believe Caine needs to defeat me. I think it's an ego thing with him.'

They held the final council of war in the church. The same church where Caine had carried out his smooth takeover. The cross had been propped back up against the wall. It wasn't where it was supposed to be, but at least it wasn't on the floor any more.

From the Perdido Beach kids there were Sam, Astrid, Little Pete, Edilio, Dahra, Elwood, and Mother Mary. Albert had been invited, but he was focusing on his plan for Thanksgiving, and on experimenting with the tortilla-burger. Representing the Coates refugees were three girls: Dekka, little Brianna the Breeze, and Taylor.

'Caine's a guy who needs to win. He needs to win before he poofs. Or he needs to win before I poof. The point is, he's not going to just accept us freeing all these kids from Coates and taking over Perdido Beach,' Sam said. 'So we need to be ready. And we need to be ready for something else, too: tomorrow is my birthday.' He made a wry face. 'Not a birthday I'm exactly looking forward to. But, anyway, we need to decide who takes over for me if . . . when . . . I step outside.'

Several of the kids made sympathetic or encouraging noises about how Sam maybe wasn't going to blink out, or maybe it would be a good thing, an escape from the FAYZ. But Sam hushed them all.

'Look, the good thing is, when I go, so does Caine. The bad thing is, that still leaves Drake, probably, and Diana and other bullies. Orc . . . well, we don't exactly know what's going on with him, but Howard's not with him. And Lana . . . we don't know what happened to her, whether she left or what.'

The loss of Lana was a serious blow. Every one of the Coates refugees adored her for the way she had healed their hands. And it was reassuring to think that she could heal anyone who was injured.

Astrid said, 'I nominate Edilio to take over if . . . you know. Anyway, we need a number two, a vice president or vice mayor or whatever.'

Edilio did a double take, like Astrid must be talking about some other Edilio. Then he said, 'No way. Astrid's the smartest person here.'

'I have Little Pete to look after. Mary has to care for the prees and keep them out of harm's way. Dahra has responsibility for treating anyone who gets hurt. Elwood has been so busy in the hospital with Dahra, he hasn't dealt with Caine or Drake or any of the Coates faction. Edilio's been up against Orc and Drake. And he's always been brave and smart and able.' She winked at Edilio, acknowledging his discomfort.

'Right,' Sam said. 'So unless someone has an objection, that's the way it is. If I get hurt or I ditch, Edilio's in charge.'

'Respect to Edilio,' Dekka said, 'but he doesn't even have powers.'

'He has the power to earn trust and to come through when he has to,' Astrid said.

No one objected further.

'OK, then,' Sam said. 'We have our people in position and Edilio tells them when to go. Taylor, I know it's going to be boring for you, and a little scary, too. Pick out a friend to go with you, trade off on sleep, but make sure one of you is awake the whole time. And keep practising. Breeze, your role is critical: you're our communications system once it starts. Dekka? As soon as we hear from Taylor, you and I move out.'

'Cool,' Dekka said.

'We're going to win this,' Sam said.

They all got up to leave. Astrid stayed behind. Sam tapped Edilio's shoulder. 'Listen, man, if you can find something useful for Quinn to do . . .'

'I'm on it. He's not a bad shot. I have him on top of the day care with one of the machine pistols.'

Sam nodded, patted Edilio on the back, and watched him leave.

'Quinn with a machine gun,' Sam said. 'I'm asking my friend to shoot people.'

'You're asking him to defend himself and defend the prees,' Astrid said.

'Yeah, that changes everything,' Sam said sarcastically.

'What do you want me to do?' Astrid asked. 'You haven't given me a job.'

'I want you to find a safe place and hide there till it's all over. That's what I want.'

'But –'

'But . . . as of tomorrow afternoon, I need you up there.' He pointed upward.

'In heaven?' Astrid asked with a grin.

'Follow me.' He led Astrid and her brother to the steeple. The lattice panels were still knocked out, just as Drake had left them. The lights of Perdido Beach looked eerily normal from up here. Many houses still had lights on. The sparse street lights were lit. The yellow McDonald's sign was brilliant. A breeze stirred, carrying the smell of French fries and pine needles, salt spray and seaweed.

Two sleeping bags had been laid out in the snug enclosure. A pair of binoculars and a kid's walkie-talkie lay next to a paper grocery bag.

'I packed you some food and batteries for L. P.'s game in that bag. I don't think the walkie-talkie works very well, but I have the other one. You can see almost everything from up here.'

It was a tight space. Little Pete immediately sat down in a dusty corner. Astrid and Sam stood awkwardly close together, crowded by the bell.

'Did you leave me a gun?'

He shook his head. 'No.'

'You're asking everyone else to do terrible things. You're just asking me to watch.'

'There's a difference.'

'Is there? What?'

'Well . . . I need you for your brains. I need you to observe.'

'That's lame,' she said.

He nodded. 'Yeah. Well. You haven't been trained to shoot. You'd probably end up shooting yourself in the foot.'

'Ah,' she said, not convinced.

'Listen, I know this is crazy, but maybe you should think about Quinn's idea, you know, of getting L. P. to zap you to Hawaii. Or whatever. He has the power. In case things don't work out . . .'

'I don't want him to zap me away somewhere,' Astrid said. 'I don't really think it would work, for one. And for two . . .'

'Yeah?'

'And for two, I don't want to leave you.'

He laid his palm gently against her cheek, and she closed her eyes and leaned into him. 'Astrid, I'm the one who's going to be leaving. You know that.'

'No. I don't know that. I've prayed for it not to happen. I've asked Mary to intercede.'

'Mary Terrafino?'

'No, duh.' Astrid laughed. 'You are such a heathen. Mary. The Virgin Mary.'

'Oh. Her.'

'I know you don't really believe in God much, but I do. I

471

think He knows we're here. I think He hears our prayers.'

'You think this is all some master plan of God's? The FAYZ and all?'

'No. I believe in free will. I think we make our own decisions and carry out our own actions. And our actions have consequences. The world is what we make it. But I think sometimes we can ask God to help us and He will. Sometimes I think He looks down and says, "Wow, look what those idiots are up to now. I guess I better help them along a little."'

'I'll gladly accept the help,' Sam said.

'Just the same, I wish I had a gun.'

Sam shook his head. 'I hurt my stepfather. I hurt Drake. I may have killed Drake. I don't know. And I don't know what's going to happen next. But here's what I do know: when I hurt someone it makes a mark on me. Like a scar or something. It's like . . .' He searched for words, and she wrapped her arms tight around him. 'It's like my knee, where Drake shot me? That's all healed up, thanks to Lana, like it never happened. But me burning Drake? That's inside me, in my head, and Lana didn't heal that.'

'If there's a fight, others will feel that hurt.'

'You're not others.'

'No?'

'No.'

'Why?'

'Because I love you.'

Astrid was silent for so long, Sam thought he must have upset her. Yet she never loosened her hold on him, never pulled away but kept her face buried in his neck. He felt her warm tears on his skin. And at last she said, 'I love you, too.'

He sighed with relief. 'Well, we got past that.'

But she didn't join in the nervous laughter. 'I have something to tell you, Sam.'

'A secret?'

'I wasn't sure of it, so I didn't say anything. It's hard to separate it from IQ. Intuition is usually just the name we give to heightened but normal perception that takes place below the level of conscious thought.'

'Uh-huh,' he said, using his dumb-guy voice.

'For a long time I wasn't sure it was anything other than normal intuition.'

'The power,' he said. 'I was wondering if you knew. Diana said you were a two bar. I kind of didn't want to, you know, force you to think about it.'

'I suspected. But it's weird. I touch a person's hand and I sometimes see what looks in my mind like a streak of fire across the sky.'

He held her out at arm's length, the better to see her face. 'A streak?'

She shrugged. 'Weird, huh? I see it as bright or dim, long or short. I don't know what it means, I don't have any control over it and I haven't really tried exploring it yet. But it feels like I'm seeing some measure of, I don't know, significance or something? It's like I'm seeing a person's soul or maybe their fate, but in highly metaphorical terms.'

'Highly metaphorical,' he echoed. 'Your power is the power of metaphor?'

That at last earned him a smile and a shove. 'Smart-ass. The point is, I've known from the start that you were important in some way. You're a shooting star across the sky, trailing sparks.'

'Do I shoot right into a brick wall tomorrow?'

'I don't know,' she admitted. 'But I know you're the brightest shooting star in the sky.'

Computer Jack woke and felt her soft hand over his mouth. It was dark outside, but the room was bathed in the blue glow of a computer screen. He could see the outline of her face, her dark hair. Her eyes glittered.

'Shh,' she cautioned, and put a finger to her lips.

His heart was already pounding. Something was wrong, no question.

'Get up, Jack.'

'What's happening?'

'You remember our deal? You remember your promise?'

He didn't want to say yes. He didn't want to. He had always known that whatever Diana wanted, it would be dangerous. And Jack was more terrified than ever.

Drake was back. Drake was a monster.

Diana stroked his cheek with her fingertips. He felt a shiver go up his spine. Then, just ever so softly, she slapped his cheek.

'I asked if you remembered your promise.'

He was mute. Too confused to be able to find his voice, too

aware of her beside him, too terrified of what she might want.

He nodded.

'Get dressed. Just your clothes. Nothing else.'

'What time is it?' he temporised.

'Time to do the right thing.' Her soft mouth twitched a wry smile. 'Even if it is for the wrong reason.'

Jack climbed out of bed, very, very glad that he had found a pair of pyjama bottoms to wear. He made her turn away and dressed quickly.

'Where are we going?'

'You're going for a drive.'

'I only drove once and I almost ran into a ditch.'

'You're a very smart boy, Jack. You'll figure it out.'

They crept from the room into the darkened hallway. Down the stairs, careful, careful. Diana inched the outside door open and looked at the courtyard. Jack wondered if Diana had an excuse ready if someone stopped them.

The sound of sneakers on the gravel of the driveway was amplified in the foggy night air. It was as if they were trying to make noise. Like each step was delivered with a sledgehammer.

Diana led him to an SUV parked haphazardly on the grass. 'The keys are in it. Get in. The driver's seat.'

'Where are we going?'

'Drive to Perdido Beach. And it's not we. Just you.'

Jack was alarmed. 'Me? Just me? No, no, no! If I go, Caine will think it was all my idea. He'll send Drake after me.'

'Jack, either obey me or I'll stand here and scream. They'll come and I'll say I caught you trying to escape.'

Jack felt his resistance crumble. It was all too plausible. She would do it, and Caine would believe her. And then . . . Drake. He shuddered.

'Why?' Jack pleaded.

'Find Sam Temple. Tell him you escaped.'

Jack gulped and bobbed his head.

'Better yet, find that girl, Astrid.' Diana recovered some of her mocking attitude. 'Astrid the Genius. She'll be desperate to save Sam.'

'OK. OK.' He steeled himself. 'I better go.'

Diana touched his arm. 'Tell them about Andrew.'

Jack froze with his hand on the key. 'That's what you want me to do?'

'Jack, if Sam blinks out, Drake will turn on me, and Caine won't be able to stop him. Drake is stronger than before. I need Sam alive. I need someone for Drake to hate. I need balance. Tell Sam about the temptation. Warn him that he'll be tempted to surrender to the big jump, but maybe, maybe, if he says no . . .' She sighed. It was not a hopeful sound. 'Now: go.'

She spun on her heel and marched back to the school.

Jack followed her with his eyes till she reached the door. Now was her chance to escape, too. She could get away from Caine and Drake and all they represented. But she was staying.

Was it possible that Diana really did love Caine?

He drew a deep, steadying breath and turned the key. The engine roared. He'd given it too much gas. Too much noise.

'Shh, shh,' he said.

He moved the gear to 'D', for drive.

He pushed the gas pedal down. Nothing happened. He almost panicked. Then he remembered: the emergency brake. He released the brake pull and tried the gas pedal again. The SUV crunched across the gravel at a creeping pace.

'Hey. Where are you going?'

Howard. What was he doing out here in the middle of the night?

Of course: still looking for his bully friend Orc. Always looking out for Orc.

Howard's expression went quickly from puzzled to questioning to alarmed.

'Hey, man, stop. Stop.'

Jack drove past him.

In the rear-view mirror he saw Howard racing back into the school.

He should drive faster. But driving was terrifying for Computer Jack. Too many decisions to make, too much attention demanded, too dangerous, too deadly.

He came to a stop at the iron gate. It was closed. He jumped out and quickly swung the gate open.

He stood still for a moment and listened. The sounds of the woods. Condensation dripping from leaves and tiny animals

477

rustling and a faint breeze that barely pushed the leaves. Then the sound of a car's engine.

Back to the SUV. Into gear and a lurch forwards through the gate.

Leave it open and go. It's not like the gate would slow anyone down. But it had slowed him down. They were already after him. Panda would be driving, no doubt, he was the most experienced driver, much more experienced than Jack.

Panda. With Drake beside him. Drake and that monstrous arm of his.

Jack felt the fear rising within him. He squeezed the steering wheel. Too tight. The top of it broke off in his hands.

He threw the six-inch arc of plastic away and whinnied in fear. He forced himself to hold the wheel more carefully, control the panic, focus on the driving. Focus on the road as it wound down the mountain, from dense woods to more open terrain and round the spur.

Lights in the rear-view mirror.

Oh, God. Oh, God.

They would kill him. Drake would use that whip hand on him.

'Think, Jack,' he screamed with sudden, shocking vehemence. 'Think.'

This was not a programming issue. It wasn't technological. It was more primitive. It was force and force, violence and violence, hate and fear.

Or was it?

Maybe it was just about clearance. The SUV sat high off the

road. The car now rapidly closing the distance was low to the ground.

Sport-utility vehicle. Four-wheel drive.

Jack peered at the roadside. A deep ditch all along the right side. A steep dirt and rock wall to his left.

The car was coming up with such speed. No more than a few hundred feet back.

There. A dirt road to the right. It might go nowhere. It might go twenty feet and stop. No choice. Jack yanked the wheel to his right and even at low speed, he felt he might tip over.

But the SUV righted itself and bounced on to the dirt road. Headlights illuminated a bright, featureless circle of dirt and scrub in the inky, moonless blackness. No way to see . . . no way to know . . . He was driving on faith, in the hope that the dirt road didn't suddenly end in a cliff.

It was hard to hold on to the steering wheel as it bounced violently. But he couldn't grip it too hard or the wheel would come apart in his powerful hands, and then he would really be finished.

Behind him the lights of the sedan were crazy, up and down, veering wildly. The dirt road was harder for the car. As bad as it was for the SUV, it was impossible for the car.

Slowly, Jack pulled away from the car. Finally, the headlights dwindled away behind him and it became clear that the car had stopped.

Jack slowed his own pace, making it easier for him to control the SUV.

He had left pursuit behind. But how would he get to Perdido Beach? The only way he knew was the main road. Would this dirt track lead somewhere?

The one thing he knew for sure was that he could not ever turn back.

FORTY ONE

03 HOURS 15 MINUTES

THE DAYLIGHT HOURS passed quietly.

Sam knew it would begin soon.

And in just a few hours, it would end.

Sam kept people on watch at the outskirts of town but otherwise advised people to sleep, eat, try to relax. Caine would come in the night. Sam was sure of that.

He had tried to take his own advice, but sleep had been impossible.

He was changing clothes and thinking about the need to eat something despite feeling sick to his stomach, when Taylor suddenly appeared in the firehouse. Sam was wearing boxers.

'They're coming,' Taylor said without preamble. 'Hey, nice abs.'

'Talk to me.'

'Six cars coming down the highway from the direction of Coates. They'll be at Ralph's in about a minute. They're moving slowly.'

'Did you see any faces? Caine or Drake?'

'No.'

Sam went into the bunkroom, shook Edilio's bed, kicked Quinn's bed, and yelled, 'Guys. Get up.'

481

'What?' Quinn said, sounding bleary and confused. 'I thought we were supposed to get some sleep.'

'You got some. Taylor says they're on the move.'

'I'm up.' Edilio rolled out of bed fully dressed. He unslung the sinister-looking machine pistol from the bed railing.

Sam slipped into his jeans and hunted for his shoes.

'What do you want me to do now?' Taylor asked.

'Bounce back and see if they go into Ralph's or split off into groups,' Sam said.

'You might want to keep your clothes on,' Taylor warned. 'I could be right back.'

'When you bounce back, go to the plaza. I'm heading straight there,' Sam said.

Taylor vanished.

'You ready?' Sam asked Edilio.

'No. You?'

Sam shook his head. 'Let's make it work, anyway.'

Quinn rolled out of his bunk. 'Is it time?'

'Yeah. Evening. Like we figured,' Sam said. 'You know where you're going, right?'

'Straight to hell?' Quinn muttered.

Sam and Edilio dropped down the fireman's pole and landed in the garage. The walkie-talkie in Sam's belt crackled, very loud. Astrid's voice, staticky and strained.

'Sam. I see them.'

Sam keyed the volume down a little and pressed the button. 'Taylor just told me,' Sam said. 'You and L. P. OK?'

'I'm fine. I see six cars. They're past Ralph's. I think they may be turning towards the school.'

'Why that direction?'

'I don't know.'

Sam bit his lip and considered. 'Keep your head down, Astrid.'

'Sam . . .' she began.

'I know,' he said. 'Me too.'

He started walking fast, not running. Running would look like panic. To Edilio, he said, 'I figured they'd come in the same way they did the first time. It's the clearest path into the centre of town.'

'I thought they might take over Ralph's and make us come after them,' Edilio said.

'I don't get it,' Sam admitted. They reached the plaza and Edilio ran ahead to the town hall to check on his troops.

Taylor appeared a dozen feet away, looking in the wrong direction.

'Taylor. Here.'

'Oh. They're going towards the school. And Caine is definitely with them. Caine and Diana. I didn't see Drake. Maybe he's dead.' She said that last part with unmistakable relish. Then, just in case Sam had missed it, she added, 'I hope he's dead, that evil piece of –'

'Did they see you?'

'No. They can't touch me, anyway. I'm too good at this now. I could bounce right into the school, see what they're up to.'

Sam pointed a finger at her. 'Don't get cocky. I don't want to lose you. Keep your distance. Go.'

Taylor winked and blinked out.

Astrid on the walkie-talkie. 'They're getting out of their cars, going into the school.'

Sam looked up at the steeple. She was right up there, so close, he could yell up to her, but her gaze was drawn to the school, not down at him. Sam spotted Quinn running by with his machine gun over his shoulder.

'Good luck, brah,' Sam said.

Quinn stopped dead. 'Thanks. Look, Sam . . . I . . .'

'No time for that now,' Sam said firmly, but gently.

Sam stood alone in the plaza, leg propped on the edge of the fountain. The school. Why? And why come in daylight, why not wait till night fell?

Albert came trotting out of the McDonald's. He handed Sam a bag. 'Some nuggets, man. In case you're hungry.'

'Thanks, dude.'

'We have faith in you, Sam.' Albert took off.

Sam munched a nugget and tried to think. The move to the school was unexpected. Was it an opportunity? If Caine was out of the car, on foot, in a school building that Sam knew a lot better than he did . . .

He keyed the walkie-talkie. 'Is there any sign they're leaving the school?'

'No. They have one guy standing outside as a guard. I think it's Panda. I definitely did not see Drake.'

He could end this, maybe. Right now, one-on-one with Caine. It would mean none of these kids would have to be involved. It would mean no one would have to pull a trigger.

Dekka was running towards him. 'Sam. Sorry, I couldn't find you.'

Maybe just the two of them, Sam and Dekka. It would double his chances. It would be right: one from Perdido Beach, one from Coates, side by side.

'Caine's at the school,' Sam said. 'I'm thinking maybe we take it to them.'

'Is Drake there?' Dekka asked.

'No one has seen him. He may be . . . he may be not showing up.'

'Good,' Dekka said bluntly.

'We haven't had much time to get to know each other,' Sam said. 'And now, well, I don't have much time, period. How much control do you have over your power?'

Dekka blew out some air and considered this question. She looked at her hands as if they would give her the answer. 'I have to be pretty close. I can rattle a wall pretty good, or send someone flying, but only from a few feet away.'

'Yeah?'

'I'm up for it,' she said.

Taylor popped in. 'They're all inside the school. One guard, as far as I can see. And definitely no Drake.'

'OK,' Sam said. 'Here's what we do. Dekka and I are going after them. Taylor, I need you to go tell Edilio. Then I need you to climb up the steeple, up where Astrid is. If Dekka and I get in trouble, we may need a distraction.'

'Dude. I don't climb. I pop. And I'm on it.' Taylor disappeared.

'I'll probably get used to her doing that some day,' Sam muttered.

He took a deep, shaky breath. It was his first big tactical decision of the coming battle. He hoped it wasn't a mistake.

Jack had kept the SUV hidden in a patch of trees all through the day. He had slept fitfully, crunched in the driver's seat, all the doors locked, too scared to think about stretching out more comfortably in the back.

Jack didn't care how big a hurry Diana was in for him to reach Sam, he wasn't going to die for her.

Only when the sun set at last did he turn the key and creep from his shady hiding place.

Down dirt roads with no signposts, lights off, moving at a crawl. Around blind corners, up, down, left, right. The SUV had a compass built into the rear-view mirror, but the directions never seemed to make sense. One second it would read south and the next minute east even though he hadn't turned.

It was impossible to know where he was going. He could drive with the lights on and see the road, but then others could see him as well. So he drove in the dark at little more than walking speed. Even at such low speed, the SUV bounced and lurched so badly that Jack felt like he'd been beaten up.

That he absolutely had to get to Sam was clearer than ever. Caine would never forgive Jack for this betrayal. His only salvation lay with Sam. But only if Sam survived the poof. If Sam stepped outside, Caine would win. And then the FAYZ would be too small a place for Jack to hide from Caine and Drake.

Jack checked the dashboard clock. He knew the day and hour of Sam's poof. Just over two hours left.

The moon rose and the road straightened so that he motored along at a somewhat higher speed than before, anxious to reach safety. A rabbit darted in front of him. Jack jerked the wheel and missed the rabbit but bounced off the road into a field.

He yanked the wheel hard and swerved back on to the road just as a pickup truck shot by coming from the other direction.

Jack cursed and turned in his seat to look back. Brake lights flared and the pickup screeched to a stop.

Jack stepped on the gas. The SUV leaped forwards. But now the truck was turning around and coming up fast.

In the darkness it was impossible to see who was driving the truck, but in Jack's mind it could be only one person: Drake.

Weeping, Jack accelerated. The gas tank needle edged closer to empty. But still the pickup truck came on.

The only escape would be to drive into the field where the truck might not be able to follow. Jack slowed just slightly and steered into the fallow field. The ground was ploughed up, soft, and the SUV bounced madly across the rows.

The truck kept pace.

In the field ahead of him, powerful headlights snapped on. A tractor was moving with surprising speed to cut him off. Beyond the tractor a dark, dilapidated farmhouse was set far back from the road.

Jack was sick inside. They had him. Somehow, impossibly, they had him trapped.

Jack never saw the dry creek bed. The SUV went airborne for a few feet, he felt weirdly weightless, and then it hit the far bank of the creek and stopped hard. There was a loud bang, the airbag deploying, and a sickening crunch, and Jack found himself lying flat on his back in the dirt, not hurt but too stunned to move.

The SUV's headlights illuminated the field where he lay. Two kids, a boy and a girl, were silhouetted by the glare. Neither of them was Drake Merwin.

Jack dared to breathe. He didn't dare stand up.

'We saw you driving around out here with your lights off,' the girl said accusingly.

Jack wondered how she could have seen him on a pitch-black night. He didn't ask, but she provided the answer, anyway.

'Even if you have your headlights off, your brake lights still come on. I guess you didn't think of that.'

'I'm not very experienced at driving,' Jack said.

'Who are you?' the boy, who looked to be Jack's age, asked.

'Me? I'm . . . Jack. People call me Computer Jack.'

The girl had a shotgun in her hands. She aimed the barrel at Jack's face.

'Don't shoot me,' he begged.

'You're on our land, and we protect our land,' the girl said. 'Why shouldn't we shoot you?'

'I have to . . . if I don't . . . Listen, if I don't get to Perdido Beach, something awful is going to happen.'

The girl had an odd combination of pigtails and a hard face made even harder by the harsh white light from the SUV. She seemed unimpressed. She was maybe eleven or twelve and it occurred to Jack that there was so much resemblance that the boy had to be her brother.

The boy said, 'He doesn't look dangerous.' To Jack, he said, 'How come they call you Computer Jack?'

'Because I know a lot about computers.'

The boy thought a while and said, 'Can you fix a Wii?'

Jack nodded violently, digging dirt into his hair. 'I could try. But really, really, I have to get to Perdido Beach. It's really important.'

'Well, my Wii is important to me. So if you fix my Wii, I won't let Emily shoot you. I guess not getting shot would be as important as you getting to Perdido Beach, huh?'

'Hi, Mary,' Quinn said. She met him at the door of the day-care classroom. 'I'm heading up top.'

Mary closed the door quickly behind her. 'I don't want the kids to see the guns,' she said. She herself was staring at the weapon.

'Mary, I don't want to see it my own self,' Quinn said.

'Are you scared?'

'Pee-less.'

'Me too.' She touched Quinn's arm. 'God bless you.'

'Yeah. Let's hope so, huh?' He wanted to stay and talk to her. Anything to avoid climbing up on the roof with a machine gun. But Mary had her duty, and he had his. He was ashamed to realise that he yearned to go into that day-care room and just hide in there with Mary.

He went through the day care to the alleyway in back. He slung the machine pistol carefully and climbed the rickety aluminium ladder.

The day care and the hardware shared a roof. It was flat, gravel and tar, adorned only by several vertical pipes and two ancient air-conditioning units. The roof was encircled by a parapet, a three-foot-high wall topped with cracked Spanish tiles.

Quinn went to the corner facing the church and the town hall. He watched as Sam and Dekka marched off.

'Don't screw up today,' Quinn told himself. 'Just don't screw up.'

The ladder rattled and something blurred over on to the roof. Quinn swung his gun around. The blur resolved itself into the figure of Brianna.

'You have got to stop doing that, Brianna,' Quinn said.

Brianna smiled and said, 'The Breeze. My name is the Breeze.'

'You are way too into this,' Quinn grumbled. 'I mean, what are you, ten?'

'I'm eleven. I'll be twelve in a month.' Brianna pulled a claw hammer from her belt and brandished it. 'Caine and Drake had me starving to death with a cinder block on each hand. I wasn't too young for Caine and Drake to almost kill me.'

'Yeah.' Quinn wished she would go away and leave him in peace, but it was her assignment to move between Quinn and Edilio and Sam and anyone else, carrying messages. 'So. How fast can you go, Brianna?'

'I don't know. Fast enough that people almost can't see me.'

'Doesn't it kind of wear you out?'

'Not really. But it kind of tears up my shoes.' She raised one foot to show him a worn sole on her sneakers. 'And I have to keep my hair in pigtails or it whips around and stings my eyes.' She gave her braided pigtails a toss.

'Must be weird. Having powers.'

'You don't have any?'

He shook his head. 'No. Nothing. I'm just . . . me.'

'You know Sam real well, right?'

He nodded. It was a question he got a lot from Coates kids.

'Do you think he'll win?' she asked.

'Guess we better hope so, huh?'

Brianna looked at her hands, the hands that had been imprisoned in concrete. 'That's why it doesn't matter that I'm just eleven: we have to win.'

Sam fought a sense of doom as he walked with Dekka towards the school. He wasn't afraid of getting hurt, mostly; after all, he expected to end the day by poofing, and then . . . well, he didn't know what.

The dread was fear of failure. Whatever happened to him, he had Astrid to think about. And Little Pete, because Astrid would be shattered if anything happened to Little Pete. Not to mention the fact that Little Pete might be the only one in all of existence who could end the FAYZ.

He had to beat Caine for her. For them. For all of them, all the kids. And that weighed him down like he was carrying an elephant on his back.

He had to win. Had to make sure Astrid was safe. Then he could blink out if that had to be.

But the closer he got, the more he doubted his decision. He was deviating from the plan, which meant no one would really know what role they were supposed to play. Caine going to the school had thrown everything off.

They stopped a block from the edge of the school grounds. Sam keyed the walkie-talkie.

'Has anything changed?'

'No,' Astrid said. 'The cars are parked. Panda is by the front door. The light's fading fast, so I can't be totally sure. Sam?'

'Yeah?'

'I think Panda has a gun.'

'OK.'

'Be careful.'

'Uh-huh.' He signed off. He wanted to tell her one more time that he loved her, but that seemed almost like tempting fate. He was already thinking too much about Astrid and not enough about Caine.

'OK, Dekka, there's no way to sneak up. I have to be within sight before I take Panda down.'

Dekka nodded. Her mouth was tight, like she couldn't open it at all. She was breathing hard, tense. Scared.

'I'm going to count to three. On three we go. All out. As soon as I can, I try to nail Panda. You do your thing when we get to the door. Ready?'

She didn't answer. For what felt like a very long minute she just stared at emptiness. Then at last she croaked, 'I'm ready.'

'One. Two. Three.'

They burst from cover and started running, flat out. They closed the distance to the edge of the school grounds and were pounding across the turf before Panda spotted them and yelped.

'Don't do it, Panda,' Sam warned, yelling as loud as he could while running.

Panda hesitated, hefting the gun, not quite raising it to fire.

'I don't want to hurt you,' Sam shouted.

Fifty feet away.

Panda aimed and fired.

The bullet flew wide.

Panda gaped at the weapon like he was seeing it for the first time.

'No,' Sam yelled.

Thirty feet.

Panda raised the gun again. His face was a fright mask of fear and indecision.

Sam dropped to the ground, rolled, and came up in a squatting position as Panda fired again.

Sam extended his arm, fingers splayed. The green-white light missed Panda and burned a hole in the brick beside his head.

Panda threw down the gun, turned, and ran.

Ten feet.

'Dekka, get the door.'

Dekka raised her hands high and gravity beneath the door was suspended. The whole wall, including the door frame, lurched suddenly, as if struck by a truck from the other side. The door swung slowly open. Loose dirt and fallen mortar shot straight up towards the sky.

Dekka dropped her hands and the dirt fell back to earth, the bricks slumped and cracked, the door jamb sagged and splintered.

Sam fired into the dark interior through the open door. He and Dekka barrelled through and slammed back against opposite walls, panting and ready. Paper signs and once-colourful posters on the walls burned and curled from Sam's blast.

There was no sound.

Sam glanced at Dekka. She looked as scared as he felt.

They edged along the hallway, nerves taut, eyes searching each doorway.

The office was on the right side, fronted by a reinforced glass wall. Sam crept closer. Peered inside. Nothing. Lights still on from the day of the FAYZ.

Should he move on without checking the office thoroughly?

If one of Caine's people was in there, Sam and Dekka could end up surrounded. Sam made a motion to Dekka: go in.

Dekka shook her head violently.

'OK,' Sam said. 'I got it.'

He crossed the hallway quickly and opened the door himself. Something large flew at him, he ducked instinctively, but he'd been hit, smacked a glancing blow that spun him around.

A boy with dark hair was crouched atop the school secretary's desk. He held a wooden club, short and thick, in one hand. The boy grinned. Then he leaped again, fast as a jungle cat.

Sam was caught off guard and landed hard, banging his head on the floor. He saw stars.

He rolled over, but the move was sluggish. The boy had jumped away to safety and was gathering himself for another assault.

Suddenly the boy, the papers, and mementoes on the desk, and the desk itself lifted off the floor, flew straight up and smashed into the low ceiling.

The boy had just long enough to register surprise and pain before Dekka restored gravity and he dropped like a rock. Sam reached him before he could recover, knelt with one knee on his chest, and grabbed his head with both his hands.

'Twitch and your head's a cinder,' Sam said.

The boy went limp.

'Good decision,' Sam said. 'Dekka, get his club. Find some duct tape.' To the boy he said, 'Who are you? And where's Caine?'

'I'm Frederico. Don't burn me up.'

'Where's Caine?'

'Not here. They all went out the back as soon as we got here. They left me and Panda.'

Sam's insides twisted. 'They left?'

Frederico read the fear in Sam's eyes. 'You can't beat Caine. Him and Drake, they have it all scoped.'

'I found tape,' Dekka said. 'You want me to tie him up?'

'It's a diversion,' Sam said. He punched Frederico in the nose, hard enough to distract him. Frederico roared in pain.

'Now tape him up. Fast.' He keyed the walkie-talkie. 'Astrid.'

Her voice was barely audible. 'Sam. Oh, my God.'

'What's happening?'

Her answer was too garbled to understand. But in snatches of static, he heard fear.

'I screwed up,' Sam said. 'It was all a trick.'

FORTY TWO

'**QUINN. QUINN.**'

'Is someone yelling my name?' Quinn wondered.

Brianna pointed at the steeple. Quinn squinted and saw Astrid in dark silhouette waving her arms like a crazy person, pointing, gesticulating, yelling something.

'I'll go see what she wants,' Brianna volunteered. She blurred, then she stopped suddenly, having just reached the top of the ladder. 'Oh, my God, look.'

Racing through the street, coming up from the south, pouring down the alley, came a swarm of rough, yellow canines. They threaded through parked cars, bounded over fire hydrants, paused briefly to sniff at garbage, but overall moved with shocking speed.

They were going straight for the day care.

Brianna began pulling the ladder up. Quinn jumped to help her. They slid it up and out of the way as the first coyotes passed beneath.

'What do I do?' Quinn cried.

'Shoot them,' Brianna said.

'Coyotes? Shoot coyotes?'

497

'They're not here by accident,' Brianna yelled.

One coyote, hearing them, glanced up.

'Quiet,' Quinn hissed. He crouched behind the wall and clutched the machine pistol to his chest.

'Quinn, they're going after the littles,' Brianna said.

'I don't know what to do.'

'Yes, you do.'

Quinn shook his head violently. 'No. No one told me to shoot coyotes.'

Brianna peeked over the side and sat back down very suddenly. 'It's him. Drake. And he's . . . there's something wrong with him.'

Quinn didn't want to look, didn't want to, but Brianna's ashen face made looking the less terrifying option. He rose just enough to get a view of the alleyway.

Swaggering along behind the coyotes came Drake Merwin.

He held in his hand a long, thick red whip.

Only he wasn't holding it in his hand. The whip was his hand.

'Shoot him,' Brianna urged. 'Do it.'

Quinn unlimbered the gun. He laid the short barrel on the Spanish tiles and aimed. Drake wasn't running, he wasn't moving furtively, he was right in the middle of the alleyway in plain view.

'I can't get a shot at him,' Quinn said.

'You're lying,' Brianna accused.

Quinn licked his lips. He aimed. He wrapped his finger around the trigger.

Impossible to miss from here. Drake was no more than thirty feet away. Quinn had practised firing the machine pistol. He had fired it at a tree trunk and seen the way it chewed through wood.

Squeeze the trigger, and the bullets would chew through Drake the same way.

Squeeze the trigger.

Drake passed directly below.

'He's gone,' Quinn whispered.

'I couldn't . . .' he said.

From the day care below there came the screams of terrified children.

Mary Terrafino had had a very bad day. That morning she'd had a major pig-out, a real gorge-a-thon, as she called it. She had found a carton of snack-sized Doritos. She'd sat and torn through twenty-four snack packs.

Then she had vomited it all back up. But even that didn't seem like enough to cleanse her of the offending food, so she had taken a strong laxative. The laxative kept her running back and forth to the bathroom all day.

Now she was sick to her stomach, wrung out, seething with anger at herself, ashamed.

Mary usually popped her pills in the morning, her Prozac and vitamins. But she was so frazzled as the day wore on that she had also popped a Diazepam she had found in her mother's bathroom medicine cabinet. The Diazepam spread a gentle mellowness over her mind, like molasses poured into gears. On the drug everything was slow, frustrating, fuzzy. To counteract the Diazepam she poured herself a cup of coffee in a covered safety cup, stirred in sugar, and carried it with her into the classroom.

That's when Quinn had walked through carrying a machine gun. She had shielded the kids from seeing him, but there was something deeply disturbing about the sight of a machine gun in the real world, not on TV or in a video game, but right there in front of her.

Now she sat cross-legged in circle time. A dozen kids paid varying degrees of attention as she read *Mama Cat Has Three Kittens* and *The Buffalo Storm*. She had read all the books so many times she could do them by heart.

Other kids were in various other corners playing with dress-up costumes, or painting, or stacking blocks.

Her brother, John, was doing diaper check on 'the tinies', as they now called the prees who were still in diapers.

One of Mary's helpers, a girl named Manuela, was bouncing a little boy on her knee while trying to get a marker stain out of her blouse. She muttered under her breath as she worked.

Isabella, who had become Mary's shadow since being brought to the day care, sat cross-legged and looked over her shoulder. Mary followed the words with her finger, word by word, thinking maybe she was teaching Isabella to read a little and feeling vaguely good about that.

She heard the sound of the back door opening. Probably Quinn wandering back through.

A scream.

Mary twisted around to see.

Screams, and a torrent of dirty yellow shapes piled into the room.

Screams as the coyotes brushed children aside, knocked them down, overturned easels and chairs.

Screams from little throats, screams and little faces filled with terror, eyes pleading.

Isabella bolted, panicked. A coyote was on her in a flash, knocked her to the ground, and stood over her, teeth bared, growling. His slavering muzzle was six inches from her throat.

Mary didn't scream or cry, she roared. She leaped to her feet bellowing a word she would never have wanted the prees to hear. She beat the coyote's shoulders with her fists.

'Get off her!' Mary cried. 'Get off her, you filthy animal!'

John tried to run to her aid and let loose a strangling cry. A coyote had the back of his hoodie in its jaws and was worrying it, shaking it like a frenzied dog with a chew toy, choking John with each twist.

Manuela stood frozen in a corner, hands over her mouth, rigid with fear.

The coyotes, excited and wild and agitated, yipped and jumped and snapped at everyone around them. A little boy named Jackson yelled at one of the coyotes, 'Bad dog, bad dog!'

The animal snapped and made contact, leaving a bloody scrape on Jackson's ankle.

Jackson wailed in pain and terror.

'Mary,' he cried. 'Mary.'

Then an aged, mangy coyote snarled and the animals calmed a little. But the children were all crying and wailing and John was shaking and Manuela was clutching two of the prees to her and trying to look brave.

And then Drake stepped into the room.

'You,' Mary raged. 'How dare you scare these children this way!'

Drake snapped his snake-like arm. The tip of it left a red welt across Mary's cheek.

'Shut up, Mary.'

The whip-crack had silenced some of the children. They stared with appalled amazement as the girl they had come to think of as their guardian touched the wound on her face.

'Caine won't like this,' Mary warned. 'He always said he'd keep the children safe.'

'You'll be safe,' Drake said. 'As long as you keep your mouths shut and do what I say.'

'Get these animals out of here,' Mary said. 'It's almost bedtime.' Bedtime, like that would mean anything to the dogs, or to the monster before her.

This time, the whip snapped and wrapped itself tight around Mary's throat. She felt blood pounding in her head, tried and failed to draw breath. She dug her fingernails into the scaly flesh of the whip but couldn't budge it.

'Which part of "shut up" do you have a problem understanding?' Drake yanked her close. 'You're getting all red in the face, Mary.'

She struggled, but it was no use. The living whip was as strong as a python.

'Now, you need to understand something, Mary: these dogs, as far as they're concerned, all these little kids are just so many hamburgers. They'll eat them just like they eat rabbits.'

He unwrapped his tentacle from her throat. She sank to the floor, sucking air through a throat that felt as narrow as a straw.

'What do you want?' Mary rasped. 'Drake, you have to get these coyotes out of here. You can have me as a hostage. But the children don't know what's happening and they are scared.'

Drake laughed cruelly. 'Hey, Pack Leader. You guys won't eat the kids, will you?'

To Mary's astonishment, the large, mangy coyote spoke. 'Pack Leader agreed. No kill. No eat.'

'Until . . .' Drake prompted.

'Until Whip Hand say.'

Drake beamed. 'Whip Hand. That's their affectionate name for me.'

Isabella, who had shrunk back into a corner, came forwards with her hand extended, like she wanted to pet Pack Leader. 'He can talk,' Isabella said.

'Stay back,' Mary hissed.

But Isabella ignored her. She laid her hand on Pack Leader's neck. The coyote bristled and made a low rumbling noise. But he did not snap at her.

Isabella stroked his harsh ruff. 'Good doggie,' she said.

'Just don't get too close,' Drake said coldly. 'Good doggie may get hungry.'

'He took the bait,' Panda reported. 'He's got some girl with him, too. She has some kind of mad powers, like . . . like I don't know what to call it. She kind of makes stuff fly off the ground.'

Diana Ladris said, 'It must be Dekka. We predicted she would be a problem. She and Brianna. Maybe Taylor, if she's improved her skills.'

They were in a home belonging to no one any of them knew. Just a house on a back street a block from the school. The shades were drawn, the lights were left just as they had been. No one came or went through the front door.

'Right now my brother is rushing towards the day care,' Caine said. He could barely contain his glee. 'He fell for it. He absolutely fell for it. See, the thing is, I knew he'd try to play hero and come after me.'

'Yes, you're brilliant,' Diana said drily. 'You're the master of all you survey.'

'Even you can't get on my nerves. That's how happy I am,' Caine smirked.

'Where's Jack?' Diana asked. When Caine scowled, she said, 'See? I still know how to get on your nerves.'

Diana knew that Jack had been driven from the highway into the desert. Panda and Drake had reported that. But she didn't know what had happened after that. If Caine got his hands on Computer Jack, Diana had no doubt that the techie wizard would give her up. What would Caine do then?

In the meantime, Diana had to play it smart by pretending to be concerned by Jack's escape or defection or whatever it should be called. It would throw Caine and Drake off the scent.

Unless they captured Jack.

She fought down a wave of fear and hid it by pouring herself a glass of water at the kitchen sink.

In the safe house, in addition to Diana and Caine, were Howard, Chunk, Mallet and Panda. Panda was badly shaken by his run-in with Sam and Dekka. He would occasionally mutter something like 'a hole blown right through the wall, could have been my head'.

Chunk had tried entertaining them with the same Hollywood stories they'd all heard a million times before. Caine had threatened to turn him over to Drake if he didn't shut up.

Howard was no less irritating. He sat and stewed and whined from time to time about going to look for Orc. 'Orc is a soldier, man, if he made it back here, he'll be over at the house we used to live in. It's not that far. I could sneak over there. He'd be good to have around.'

'Orc's dead in the desert,' Panda said harshly. 'You know those coyotes got him.'

'Shut up, Panda!' Howard yelled.

The other person in the little house was Lana. Ever since Lana had demonstrated her healing powers, Caine had insisted on keeping her close. To Diana, she remained a disturbing mystery. Her eyes seemed always to be looking at something far away. She rebuffed attempts at conversation. Not angrily, not like she was upset by any of them, more like she was in a completely different place, worrying, reflecting, seeing something completely different.

There was a shadow over Lana. A hollowness in her eyes.

Caine paced back and forth, from the open kitchen area into the family room, back and forth, back and forth. He had started biting his thumb again in that stupid way he had. He stopped and threw up his hands and asked Diana, 'Where is he? Where is Bug?'

Bug was one of the freaks who had signed up with Caine right at the start. Long before the FAYZ, back when Caine was first discovering his powers, learning to control them and learning to recognise others like himself. In those days it was all about getting control of the school environment: Coates had never been a nice place. Half the kids in the school were one kind of bully or another. Caine had just been determined to be the head bully, the bully who could not be bullied himself.

Bug had always been a little creep in Diana's eyes. He didn't rise to the level of a true bully, he was closer to being a Howard-like creature, a bootlick, a toady. He was just ten years old, a nose-picking gross-out artist. But then his power manifested one day when Frederico threatened to kick his butt. Bug, in terror, had disappeared.

Only he didn't really disappear, it was more that he seemed to blend in, like a chameleon. You could still see him if you knew he was there. But his skin and even his clothes would take on the protective coloration of whatever was behind him, like a mirror that reflected his background. The result could be pretty creepy. Bug standing in front of a cactus would seem to be green with needles poking out.

'You know Bug,' Diana said. 'He'll show up to get his strokes. Unless Sam or one of his people spotted him.'

At that moment the front door opened and closed. Something moved that was hard to see, hard to make sense of, like a wave in the wallpaper.

'Here's Bug now,' Diana announced.

Caine leaped at him. 'What did you see?'

Bug shut down the camouflage and emerged clearly, a short, brown-haired, buck-toothed kid with a freckled nose. 'I saw a lot. Sam is in town, right across from the day care. He doesn't look like he's doing anything.'

'What do you mean he's not doing anything?'

'I mean, he's standing there eating Mickey D's.'

Caine stared. 'What?'

'He's eating. Fries. I guess he's hungry.'

'Does he know Drake and Pack Leader have the littles?'

Bug shrugged. 'I guess so.'

'And he's just standing there?'

'What did you expect him to do?' Diana demanded. 'He knows we've got the kids. He's waiting to hear what we want.'

Caine bit savagely at his thumb. 'He's up to something. He probably figures we have a way to watch him. So he's making sure we see him. Meanwhile, he's up to something.'

'What can he do? Drake and the coyotes are in there with the kids. He has no choice. He has to do whatever you tell him to do.'

Caine wasn't convinced. 'He's up to something.'

Lana stirred herself, looked at Caine, seeming to hear him for the first time.

'What?' Diana asked her.

'Nothing,' Lana said. She patted her omnipresent dog. 'Nothing at all.'

'I need to go do this now,' Caine said.

'The plan was to wait till we were close to the birthday hour. That way he loses no matter what.'

'You think he can take me, don't you?'

'I think he's had a couple of days to prepare,' Diana said. 'And he's got more people. And some of his people, especially the freaks from Coates, really, really want you dead.' She stepped closer to him, right up in his face. 'Every step of the way, Caine, you listen to me, then you do exactly what I've told you not to do. I told you to let the freaks go who didn't want to play along. But no, you had to listen to Drake's paranoid advice. I told you to go into Perdido Beach and make a quick deal for food. You have to go try and take over. Now you're going to do whatever you want, and you'll probably end up screwing things up.'

'Your faith in me is touching,' Caine said.

'You're smart. You're charming. You have all this power. But your ego is out of control.'

He might have lashed out, but instead, he spread his arms

wide in a gesture of helplessness. 'What was I supposed to do? Coates? That's it? How do you not see what an opportunity this is? We're in a whole new world. I'm the most powerful person in that whole new world. No adults. No parents or teachers or cops. It's perfect. Perfect for me. All I have to do is take care of Sam and a few others, and I'll have complete control.' He was making fists by the conclusion of his rant.

'You'll never have complete control, Caine. This world is changing all the time. Animals. People. Who knows what's next? We didn't make this world, we're just the poor fools who are living in it.'

'You're wrong. I'm not a fool. This is going to be my world.' He slapped his chest. 'Me. I'm going to run the FAYZ, the FAYZ is not going to run me.'

'It's not too late to walk away.'

He grinned, a dark echo of his once-charming smile. 'You're wrong. It's time to win. It's time to send Bug to Sam with my terms.'

'I'll go,' Diana volunteered. It was foolish. She knew what he would say. And she could see the light of suspicion in his eyes.

'Bug. You know what to say. Go.' He pushed Bug away, and the chameleon blended into the background. The door opened and closed.

Caine took Diana's hand. She wanted to pull it away, but she didn't. 'Everyone out of here,' Caine said.

Howard got heavily to his feet. Lana as well. When it was just the two of them, Caine and Diana, he drew her close into an awkward embrace.

'What are you doing?' she demanded stiffly.

'I'm probably going to die tonight.'

'That's kind of melodramatic, isn't it? One minute you're invincible and the next –'

He interrupted her with a rushed, lunging kiss. She let him for a few seconds. Then she pushed him back, though not with enough force to free herself from his embrace.

'What was that for?' she asked.

'It's the least you owe me, isn't it?' Caine said. He sounded childish, needy.

'I owe you?'

'You owe me. Besides, I thought you . . . you know.' His cockiness had given way to petulance and now his petulance was dissolving into embarrassment and confusion.

'You're not very good at this, are you?' Diana mocked.

'What am I supposed to say? You're hot, all right?'

Diana threw her head back and laughed. 'I'm hot? That's what you want to tell me? One minute you're master of the FAYZ and the next minute you're like a pathetic little kid going for his first kiss.'

His face went dark and she knew immediately she had gone too far. His hand, fingers splayed, was in her face. She tensed, awaiting the blast of energy.

For a long time they stood that way, frozen. Diana barely breathed.

'You're scared of me after all, Diana,' Caine whispered. 'All your attitude, and underneath it, you're scared. I can see it in your eyes.'

She said nothing. He was still dangerous. At this range he had the power to kill her with a thought.

'Well, I don't want to seem like a pathetic little kid going for his first kiss,' Caine said. 'So how about you just give me what I want? How about from now on you just do what I say?'

'You're threatening me?'

Caine nodded. 'Like you said, Diana, we didn't make the FAYZ, we just live here. Here in the FAYZ it's all about power. I have it. You don't.'

'I guess we'll see if you're as powerful as you think, Caine,' Diana said, cautious but unbowed. 'I guess we'll see.'

FORTY THREE

THE DAY CARE had no window facing the plaza. Sam had snuck around into the alley to peek in one of the high-on-the-wall windows. He had seen the coyotes. He had recoiled from the sight of Drake.

The coyotes had instantly noted his presence. It was all but impossible to sneak up on them. Drake, looking him right in the eye, had uncoiled his whip hand and languidly drawn the shade.

The kids were huddled together, practically on top of one another, solemn and terrified and half watching *The Little Mermaid* on the TV.

Sam returned to the plaza. Neither Drake nor the coyotes could see him there. But he felt eyes on him just the same. He only slowly became aware of the kid standing beside him.

'Who are you? And how did you get there?'

'They call me Bug. I'm good at sneaking up on people.'

'I guess you are.'

'I have a message for you.'

'Yeah? What does my brother want?'

'Caine says it's you or him.'

'I figured that.'

'He says if you don't do what he says, he'll turn Drake and the coyotes loose on the prees.'

Sam stifled the urge to punch the little monster for the smug way in which he had delivered his vicious threat. 'OK.'

'OK. So, everyone has to come out in the open. All your people. Out in the open, out in the plaza where we can see them. If anyone stays in hiding, you know what happens.'

'What else?'

'Your people all set their guns or whatever on the steps of the town hall. All your freaks go into the church.'

'He's asking me to surrender before we even fight,' Sam said.

Bug shrugged. 'He said if you argue, Drake is going to start turning the coyotes loose on one kid at a time. You have to do all this and then Caine and you go mano a mano. If you win, no problem, Drake lets the littles go. All your side goes free. Caine goes back to Coates.'

'Why are you doing this, Bug? You're OK with this? Threatening little kids?'

Bug shrugged. 'Man, I'm not going to mess with Caine or Drake.'

Sam nodded. His mind was already elsewhere, trying to find a way, trying to find a path. 'Tell Caine I'll answer him in an hour.'

Bug grinned. 'He said you'd say that. See? He's smart. He said you have to send your answer back with me. Yes or no, with no extras or anything.'

Sam glanced at the steeple. He wished Astrid was here. She might have an answer.

513

The terms were impossible. He was absolutely sure, sure beyond any reasonable doubt, that even if he won, even if somehow Caine admitted defeat, Drake would never just walk away.

One way or the other, he had to beat Drake as well as Caine.

There were a thousand thoughts in his head, a thousand fears, yammering at him, crowding one another, demanding attention as Bug stared at him, impatient to be on his way. There was no time to make sense of it all. No time to plan. Just as Caine had intended.

Sam's shoulders slumped. 'Tell Caine I accept.'

'OK,' Bug said, no more concerned than he would have been by an announcement that he was having chicken for dinner.

The chameleon blended into the background, all but disappearing. Sam watched him trotting off, a warping of light and image. He soon became impossible to make out.

Sam keyed the walkie-talkie. 'Astrid. Now.' Edilio had been watching from his post in the hardware store. He came trotting out.

Sam steadied his breathing, kept a careful poker face. There were too many eyes on him. Too many people needing to believe in him.

On that school bus so long ago, no one had even realised there was a problem before Sam was up and taking charge. It was harder being bold when the whole world seemed to be watching your every move.

With Astrid and Edilio beside him, Sam quickly related

Caine's terms. 'We have very little time. Caine will send that chameleon back to spy, right after he reports to Caine. Caine will move fast, he won't want to give us any time to prepare.'

'Do you have a plan?' Astrid asked.

'Kind of. A piece of a plan, anyway. We need to stall a little. Bug sees Caine, Bug comes back, that's probably five minutes minimum wherever Caine is, probably a little more. Then Bug has to see whether we are doing what we've been told to do. He's going to see people out in the open and he's going to see our Coates friends heading into the church. Then he'll report that back. Caine will say, "Make sure they're all in."'

'More time.' Astrid nodded agreement. 'We don't hurry. In fact, maybe we have to force some of the kids, maybe they're arguing. You're right, Caine won't show up till he's sure.'

'If we're lucky, we have a half-hour,' Edilio said. He glanced at his watch, not easy to read in the swiftly falling night.

'Yeah. OK. All I've done so far is screw up. So if this is crazy, someone tell me.'

'You're our guy, Sam,' Edilio said.

Astrid squeezed his hand.

'Then here's what we do.'

Mary read.

She sang.

She did everything short of tap-dance. But there was no distracting the children from the horror before them. With

515

solemn, fearful expressions they followed Drake's every move. The whip hand filled every eye.

Some of the coyotes had gone to sleep. Others, though, eyed the children with a look that could only be described as hungry.

Mary wished she had another Diazepam or maybe three or maybe ten. Her hands shook. Her insides churned. She needed to go to the bathroom, but she needed to stay with the children, too.

Her brother, John, was changing a diaper, no different from usual, except that John's mouth was an upside-down 'U' of trembling lips.

Mary read, 'I would not eat green eggs and ham. I do not like them, Sam-I-am.'

And in her head, going around and around like a crazed merry-go-round she could not stop, was the question: what do I do? What do I do if . . . What do I do when . . . What do I do?

A boy named Jackson raised his hand. 'Mother Mary? The dogs stink.'

Mary kept reading. 'I will not eat them in the rain. I will not eat them on a train . . .'

It was true, the coyotes did stink. The smell of them was suffocating, the heavy scent of musk and dead animals. They urinated freely against crib legs and tables and chose the corner with the dress-up clothes to defecate.

But the coyotes were not at ease, far from it. They were jumpy, nervous, unused to being in an enclosed space, not used to being around humans. Pack Leader maintained order with

GONE

snarls and yips, but even he was jumpy and unsettled.

Only Drake seemed at ease. He lounged in the glider that Mary used to rock the tinies to sleep at night or feed them a bottle. He was endlessly fascinated by his whip hand, kept holding it up for inspection, coiling and uncoiling it, revelling in it.

Save the kids? Save John? Could she save anyone? Could she save herself?

What do I do?

What do I do when the killing starts?

Suddenly a girl was there. Taylor. Just there in the middle of the room.

'Hi. I brought food,' she announced. She held a plastic McDonald's tray. It was piled high with uncooked hamburgers.

Every coyote head snapped around. Drake was too slow to react, caught off guard.

Taylor flung the tray against the common wall shared by the day care and the hardware store. Meat slid down the gaily painted cinder blocks.

Drake's whip hand cracked.

But Taylor was gone.

The coyotes hesitated only a moment. Then they lunged towards the meat. In a flash they were snarling and snapping at one another, pushing, jostling, climbing over one another in a feeding frenzy.

Drake jumped to his feet and yelled, 'Pack Leader, get a grip on them.' But Pack Leader had joined the frenzy, laying about him viciously to establish his dominance and his share of the sudden bounty.

Two things happened at almost the same instant. The wall shuddered and cracked and the coyotes nearest to it suddenly floated upward, their paws scrabbling in mid-air.

'Dekka,' Drake snarled.

There was a blinding flash of green-white light and, like a butane torch cutting through tissue paper, a hole two feet across appeared in the cinder block. The hole was high up on the wall, well above the heads of the children but right about where the suddenly weightless coyotes were floating. One of the coyotes caught a straight blast. The beam of light cut it in two. The segments floated, spraying weightless globules of red.

The children screamed and John screamed and Drake backed away from the wall, away from the zone of weightlessness.

Edilio's head appeared in the hole. 'Mary. Down on the floor.'

'Everyone get down!' Mary screamed, and John threw himself on to a runaway toddler.

Edilio yelled, 'Sam, go!'

A new hole burned lower down, chest level, and this time the beams of light scoured the room, blasting walls covered in faded art projects, burning through coyotes, setting them alight to float like flaming Macy's parade balloons.

'OK, Dekka,' Edilio yelled.

The coyotes hit the ground hard, some dead, some alive, but none with any desire for a fight. The door flew open, yanked by some unseen hand, and the animals ran over one another trying to escape.

'Pack Leader!' Drake bellowed. 'You coward!'

The annihilating beam of light swung towards him. He hit the floor, cursing, and rolled out towards the door.

Quinn felt as well as heard the wall between the day care and the hardware store rumble and crack.

A few seconds later he saw the coyotes pouring in a panicked jumble into the alley and racing off this way and that.

And then Drake appeared.

Quinn shrank down behind the parapet. Brianna rushed boldly to look over.

'It's Drake. Now's your chance.'

'Get down, you idiot,' Quinn hissed.

She rounded on him, furious. 'Give me the gun, you wimp.'

'You don't even know how to shoot it,' Quinn whined. 'Besides, he's probably already gone. He was running.'

Brianna looked again. 'He's hiding. He's behind the Dumpster.'

Quinn nerved himself to look, just a peek, just enough to see. Brianna was right: Drake was behind the Dumpster, waiting.

The back door of the hardware store opened and Sam emerged alone. He looked left and right, but was unable to spot Drake.

Brianna yelled, 'Sam, behind the Dumpster.'

Sam whirled, but Drake was too quick. He snapped his whip,

slashed Sam's defensive arm, and ran straight at and over Sam.

Sam landed on his back and rolled over quickly, but not quickly enough. With inhuman speed, the whip hand sliced the air and cut a bright stripe across Sam's back, right through his shirt.

Sam cried out.

Brianna began hauling the aluminium ladder to the edge, but her speed betrayed her. She lost control of the ladder and it clattered down into the alley.

Drake had his whip around Sam's throat now, choking, squeezing. Killing.

Quinn could see Sam's face turning red. Sam thrust his hands back over his shoulders and fired blind.

The beams singed Drake's face but did not stop him. He threw Sam hard against the alley wall. Quinn heard the sickening crunch of skull on brick. Sam slumped, barely conscious.

'Forget Caine,' Drake crowed, 'I'm taking you down myself.'

He raised his whip hand, ready to lower it with enough force to lay Sam open from hip to neck.

Quinn fired.

The kick of the gun in his hands surprised him. It had happened without conscious thought. He hadn't aimed, hadn't carefully squeezed the trigger like he'd learned to do, he'd just fired on instinct.

The bullets left pockmarks in the brick.

Drake whirled, and Quinn rose shakily to his feet, standing now in full view.

'You,' Drake said.

'I don't want to have to kill anyone,' Quinn said in a shaky voice that barely carried.

'You'll die for this, Quinn.'

Quinn swallowed hard and this time took careful aim.

That was too much for Drake. With a furious snarl he ran from the alley.

Sam was slow getting up. To Quinn, he looked like an old man standing up after slipping on the ice. But he looked up at Quinn and performed a sort of salute.

'I owe you, Quinn.'

'I'm sorry I didn't get him,' Quinn answered.

Sam shook his head. 'Man, don't ever be sorry you don't want to kill someone.' Then, spotting Brianna, he shook off his weariness and said, 'Breeze? With me. Quinn, anyone comes back towards the day care, you don't have to shoot them, all right? But fire into the air so we know.'

'I can do that,' Quinn said.

Sam ran towards the plaza, confident that Brianna would catch up quickly. She was with him in seconds.

'What's up?' she asked.

'Everyone's putting on a show of complying with Caine's terms. If we're lucky, Bug will report back that we're obeying before Drake gets back to tell Caine that we've retaken the day care.'

'You want me to go after Drake?'

'Use those fast feet. Find him if you can, but don't try to fight him, just tell me.'

She was gone before he could add, 'Be careful.'

Sam broke into a trot that seemed painfully slow compared with the way Brianna moved. The kids, the normals, more than a hundred of them, all who could be rounded up on short notice, were milling around at one end of the plaza. Sam was counting on Caine not knowing exactly how many kids were in Perdido Beach, or how many were in town as opposed to hiding in their homes. He needed to make it look convincing, but Caine's demand left room for some few to still be hidden away with Edilio.

Astrid and Little Pete, Dekka and Taylor and the rest of the Coates Freaks were entering the church, protesting loudly, making a show of it.

Sam strode to the fountain and jumped up on the side. 'OK, Bug, I know you're watching. Go tell Caine we've done what he asked. Tell him I'm waiting. Tell him, if he's not a coward, to come here and face me like a man.'

He jumped down, ignoring the stares of the hundred or more kids huddled scared and vulnerable in the plaza.

Had Bug seen what went down in the day care? He had certainly heard the shots. Hopefully he would interpret them as coming from Drake himself, or as target practice.

And, just as dangerous, would Drake be able to warn Caine? He should find out soon. Either way, Sam doubted that Caine could resist a face-to-face confrontation. His ego demanded it.

Sam's walkie-talkie crackled. He had the volume turned down low and had to hold it to his ear to hear Astrid.

'Sam.'

'Are you OK in the church, Astrid?'

'We're both OK. We're all OK. The day care?'

'Safe.'

'Thank God.'

'Listen, get everyone in there to lie down. Get them under the pews – that may give them some protection.'

'I feel useless here.'

'Just keep Little Pete calm. He's the wild card. He's like a stick of dynamite. We don't know what he might do.'

'I think a vial of nitroglycerin would be a more apt analogy. Dynamite is actually quite stable.'

Sam smiled. 'You know it always gets me hot when you say "apt analogy".'

'Why do you think I do it?'

Knowing that she was right there, just fifty feet away, smiling sadly, scared but trying to be brave, sent a wave of longing and worry through him that almost brought tears to his eyes.

He wished Quinn had been able to eliminate Drake. But he suspected his friend would not have survived with his soul intact if he had. Some people could do things like that. Some couldn't. That second group were probably the luckier ones.

'Come on, Caine,' Sam whispered to himself. 'Let's do this.'

Brianna blurred up next to him. 'Drake went to his house. You know, the place where he was staying.'

'Is Caine there?'

'I don't think so.'

'Good job, Breeze. Now go into the church. Go slowly so Bug can see you if he's watching.'

'I want to help.'

'That's what I need you to do, Brianna.'

She trudged off, making a show of it. Sam was alone. The normals huddled at the far end of the plaza as Caine had ordered. The freaks – Sam hated using the word, but it was hard not to – were in the church.

And now it came down to him and Caine.

Would Caine come?

Would he come alone?

Sam glanced at his watch. In just a little over an hour, it wouldn't matter.

From not far enough away, he heard a coyote howl.

FORTY FOUR

'**THEY'RE** DOING IT,' Bug yelled as he burst through the door.

'All right,' Caine said. 'Showtime. Everyone load up. Into the cars.'

There was a scramble for the door. Chaz, Chunk, Mallet, and a much-abashed Frederico, who had finally freed himself from duct-tape bondage, all raced for the station wagon in the garage. Diana, oozing suppressed rage from every pore, followed. Panda grabbed Lana by the arm and pushed her towards the door.

Only then did Caine realise someone was missing. 'Where's Howard?'

'I . . . I don't know,' Panda admitted. 'I didn't see him leave.'

'Useless worm. Without Orc, he's dead weight,' Caine said. 'Forget him.'

The second car in the garage was a luxury car, an Audi with a sunroof. Panda jumped behind the wheel and Diana rode shotgun. Caine took the back seat for himself.

Panda pushed the automatic garage door remote control. Both doors rose.

The cars lurched forwards. The Subaru wagon promptly crunched into the side of the Audi.

Chaz was driving the wagon. He rolled down his window. 'Sorry.'

'Great start,' Diana said.

'Go,' Caine ordered tersely.

Panda accelerated into the street, keeping his speed to a prudent twenty-five miles per hour. The wagon stayed a block back.

'Bada bum bada bum bada bum bum bum.' Diana began humming the *William Tell Overture*.

'Knock it off,' Caine snapped.

They had gone two blocks when Panda slammed on the brakes.

A dozen coyotes streaked across the street.

Caine rose up through the sunroof and yelled, 'What are you doing? Where are you going?'

Pack Leader stopped and glared with yellow eyes. 'Whip Hand gone,' he snarled.

'What? What happened at the day care?'

'Whip Hand go. Pack Leader go,' the coyote said.

'No way,' Caine said. To Diana, he said, 'They've got the day care. What do I do?'

'You tell me, Fearless Leader.'

Caine slammed his fist down on the roof of the car. 'OK, Pack Leader, unless you're a coward, follow me.'

'Pack Leader follows the Darkness. All others follow Pack Leader. Pack is hungry. Pack must eat.'

'I've got food for you,' Caine said. 'There's a plaza full of kids.'

Pack Leader hesitated.

'It's easy,' Caine said. 'You can come with me and take as many kids as you want. Get every one of your coyotes. Bring them all. It's a buffet.'

Pack Leader yipped a command to his pack. The coyotes circled back towards him.

'Follow us,' Caine cried, caught up in it now, eyes wild and excited. 'We go straight towards the plaza. You go straight at the kids there. It will work perfectly.'

'The fire fist is there?'

Caine frowned. 'Who? Oh. Sam. Fire fist, huh? Yes, he'll be there, but I'll take care of him.'

Pack Leader seemed dubious.

'If Pack Leader is frightened, maybe someone else should be pack leader.'

'Pack Leader no fear.'

'Then let's kick,' Caine said.

'Oh, man,' Howard said. 'Oh, God. Oh, God, what happened to you, Orc?'

He had slipped out of Caine's hideout and made his way to the house he had once shared with Orc. He found his protector there, sitting on a couch that had broken beneath Orc's weight, collapsed in the middle. Empty beer bottles were everywhere.

Orc held up a game controller. 'My fingers are too big to work this thing.'

'Orc, man, how did this . . . I mean, man, what happened to you?'

Orc's face was still half his own. His left eye, his left ear and the hair above it, and all of his mouth were still recognisably Orc. But the rest of him was like some slumping statue made of gravel. He was at least a head taller than he had been. His legs were as big around as tree trunks, his arms as thick as fire hydrants. He had burst through his clothing, which now hung from him and provided the barest degree of modesty.

When he shifted in his seat, he made a sound like wet stones.

'How did this happen, dude?'

'It's a judgment on me,' Orc said flatly.

'What's that mean, man?'

'For hitting Bette. It's God, Howard. It's His judgment on me.'

Howard fought the urge to turn and run screaming. He tried to look at Orc's one human eye but he found himself looking into the other eye, a yellow oyster beneath a brow of stone.

'Can you move? Can you stand up?'

Orc grunted and stood much more easily than Howard expected.

'Yeah. I still have to be able to get up to pee,' Orc said.

'What happens when it spreads to your mouth?'

'I think it's done spreading. It stopped a few hours ago, maybe.'

'Does it hurt?'

'Nah. But it itches when it's spreading.' As if to illustrate, he used one of his sausage-sized stone fingers to scratch the line between his gravel nose and his human cheek.

'Heavy as you are, man, you must be pretty strong just to stand up.'

'Yeah.' Orc dipped his hand into the cooler by his feet and came up with a can of beer. He tilted his head back and opened his mouth. He squeezed the top of the can and it blew out an eruption of liquid and foam. Orc swallowed what landed in his mouth. The rest dribbled down his face on to his rocky chest. 'Only way I can open 'em now. My fingers are too big to pull the tab.'

'What are you doing, man? You just been sitting here drinking beer?'

'What else am I gonna do?' He shrugged his slag-heap shoulders. His human eye was either crying or teared up. 'Thing is, I'm almost out of beer.'

'Man, you have to get back in the game. There's a war coming. You need to be in on it, making your statement, you know?'

'I just want to get some more beer.'

'OK, then. That's what we'll do, Orc. We'll get some more beer.'

Stars filled the sky.

The moon glinted off the steeple.

A coyote howled, a wild ululation, a ghostly cry of despair.

In his mind Sam saw the mutants in the church. He saw Edilio concealed with a handful of trusted kids in the smoked-out ruins of the apartment building. He saw Quinn on the roof with the machine gun he might use or not. He saw the kids milling and lost and scared at the south end of the plaza. And Mary and the little kids still in the day care. And Dahra in the church basement awaiting casualties.

Drake had retreated. For now.

What would Orc do?

Where was Caine?

And what would happen in one hour when the clock ticked and marked exactly fifteen years since Sam had been born, linked though he hadn't known it to a brother named Caine?

Could he beat Caine?

He had to beat Caine.

And somehow he had to destroy Drake as well. If – when – Sam stepped outside, took the big jump, poofed, he didn't want to leave Astrid to Drake's mercy.

He knew he should be scared of the end. Scared of the mysterious process that would, it seemed, simply subtract Sam Temple from the FAYZ. But he wasn't as worried for himself as he was for Astrid.

Less than two weeks ago she had been an abstraction, an ideal, a girl he could check out furtively, but without ever revealing his own interest. And now she was almost all he thought about as his own personal clock ticked down towards a sudden and possibly fatal disappearance.

How would Caine play it, that's what the rest of his mind turned over and over. Would Caine walk into town like a gunslinger in some ancient cowboy movie?

Would they stand at thirty paces and draw?

Which would be more powerful? The twin with the power of light or the twin with the power to move matter?

It was dark.

Sam hated the dark. He had always known that when the end came for him it would be in the dark.

Dark and alone.

Where was Caine?

Was Bug watching him even now?

Would Edilio do what Quinn could not?

What surprise would Caine have up his sleeve?

Taylor appeared standing a few feet away. She looked like she'd just come from an interview with a demon. Her face was white, her eyes wide, glittering in the light of street lamps. 'They're coming,' she said.

Sam nodded, braced his shoulders, consciously slowed the sudden sprint of his heart. 'Good,' he said.

'No, not him,' Taylor said. 'The coyotes.'

'What? Where?'

Taylor pointed over his shoulder.

Sam spun. They came at a run, full out from two directions, racing straight for the unprotected crowd of children.

It was like some classroom nature film. Like watching as a lion pride attacked a herd of antelope. Only this herd was human. This herd had no reservoir of lightning speed.

Helpless.

Panic swept them. They surged towards the middle, kids at the edges seeing their doom approach on swift paws.

Sam broke into a run, raised his one good hand, looked for a target, yelled. But then, the loud roar of a car engine.

He skidded to a halt, spun again. Headlights raced down the street past the church. A dusty SUV. It slammed into the kerb surrounding the plaza, jumped the sidewalk, and came to a shuddering stop that sent up clods of damp dirt.

Behind it other cars, racing.

Screams as the coyotes neared the human herd.

Sam stretched out his hand and green fire lanced towards the left-side swarm of coyotes.

He couldn't fire at the other column, they were blocked by panicky, running children, all now racing towards Sam for protection and so making it impossible for him to beam.

'Get down, get down, get down,' he yelled. 'On the ground!' But it was useless.

'Save me!' said Computer Jack, falling from the SUV.

An Audi skidded to a stop in front of the church. Someone was standing up in the sunroof.

A scream of sheer terror and pain. Someone was down, struggling against a coyote twice his size.

'Edilio! Now!' Sam roared.

'Having a bad night, brother?' Caine shouted, exultant. 'It's going to get worse.'

Caine raised his hands, aimed not at Sam, not at Sam at all. Instead, he directed the impossible energy of his telekinesis at the church. It was as if an invisible giant, a creature the size of a dinosaur, had leaned against the ancient limestone. The stone cracked. The stained-glass window shattered. The door of the church, the weak point, blew inward, knocked clear off its hinges.

'Astrid!' Sam cried.

Screams, panicked screams from the plaza, mixed with snarls and wild yelps as the coyotes fell on the children.

Suddenly the impossibly loud clatter of a machine gun. Fire blasted from the roof of the day care.

Edilio running from the burned building, three others behind him, charging the coyotes.

Caine blasted again and this time the invisible monster, the beast of energy, pushed hard, hard against the front of the church.

The side windows, all the ancient stained glass and the new, exploded in a sparkling shower. The steeple swayed.

'How you going to save them, Sam?' Caine exulted. 'One more push and it collapses.'

Jack at Sam's feet, clutching him, tripping him, strangely strong.

Sam fired blindly at Caine as he fell.

'I can save you! Save me!' Jack pleaded. 'The poof, I can save you.'

Sam fell hard, kicked at Jack's grasping hands, wiggled free, and stood up in time to see the front wall of the church sag and collapse slowly, slowly inward.

The roof shuddered and slumped. The steeple teetered but did not fall. But tons of limestone and plaster and massive wooden beams fell in with a crash like the end of the world.

'Astrid!' Sam cried again, helpless.

He ran straight at Caine, ignoring the massacre behind him, blocking the screams and the ravening growls and the staccato of machine guns.

He aimed and fired.

The beam hit the front of Caine's car. The sheet metal blistered and Caine climbed awkwardly out through the sunroof, while others Sam didn't care enough to identify bolted through the doors.

Sam fired and Caine dodged.

A blast hit Sam, stopped him as dead as if he'd run into a wall. He searched wildly for Caine. Where? Where?

Muffled screams from inside the church joined the background roar, a noise out of a child's hell, high-pitched cries for mother, agonised cries, desperate, pleading.

A flash of movement and Sam fired.

Caine fired back and the statue on the fountain was blown off its pedestal and fell with a splash in the fetid water.

Sam was up and running. He had to find Caine, had to find him, kill him, kill him.

More machine guns firing and Edilio's voice yelling, 'No, no, no, stop firing, you're hitting kids!'

Sam rounded the burning Audi. Caine running ahead, leaping a fire hydrant.

Sam fired and the ground under Caine's feet burst into flames and oily black smoke. The pavement itself was burning. Caine went sprawling on to the street, rolled quickly, got to one knee, and Sam took a massive blow that laid him flat on his back, stunned, blood coming from his mouth and ears, limbs all askew, unable to . . . unable . . .

Caine, a wild, bloody, screaming face.

Sam felt hatred burn through him and erupt from his hands.

Caine jumped aside, too slow, and the scourging light seared his side. Shirt burning, Caine screamed and beat at the flame.

Sam tried to stand, but his head was swimming.

Caine bolted into the burned-out apartment building, through the same door Sam had entered to try and save the little fire-starter.

Sam wobbled but ran after him.

Up the stairs and to the scorched hallway, still stinking of smoke. The top floor was a wreckage of burned timbers and asphalt-tiled slopes of roof like children's slides, and fragments of walls and incongruous jutting pipes.

A blast and Sam could actually see the half-wall beside him ripple from the impact.

'Caine, let's finish this,' Sam rasped.

'Come get me, brother,' Caine cried in a pain-squeezed voice. 'I'll bring this place down on us both.'

Sam located the sound of his voice and ran down the hallway, ran beneath the stars, firing the deadly light from his hands.

No Caine.

A creaking door, still hanging from hinges though the wall around it was gone, swung slowly.

Sam kicked it, spun, and fired into the room.

A charred wooden beam flew through the air. Sam ducked under it. The next one hit his left arm, shattering the elbow. More debris, a torrent of it, drove Sam back.

Suddenly, there was Caine, not ten feet from him.

Caine's hands were raised over his head, fingers splayed, palms out. Sam clutched his shattered left elbow with his right hand.

'Game over, Sam,' Caine said.

Something blurred behind Caine and he reeled. He clutched his skull.

Brianna stood over him, brandishing her hammer.

'Run, Breeze!' Sam yelled, but too late. Even as he staggered backwards, Caine fired at point-blank range and Brianna flew backwards into the wall, through the wall.

Caine jumped after her through the opening.

Sam fired into the wall, burned a hole. Through it he could see Caine blowing away the next wall.

Sam felt the floor buckle beneath him.

The building was collapsing.

He turned and ran, but all at once the floor was gone and he was running in mid-air, falling, and the building with him, all around him.

He fell and the world fell on him.

FORTY FIVE

14 MINUTES

QUINN WATCHED IN frozen horror as the coyotes attacked the children.

He saw Sam fire and miss.

He saw Sam agonise for a terrible moment as Caine attacked the church.

Sam ran towards the church.

Quinn shouted, 'No!'

He aimed.

'Don't hit the kids, don't the kids,' he sobbed, and squeezed the trigger. Aiming at the mass of coyotes. So many more than before.

The coyotes barely noticed him.

One fell, twisting, like it had tripped, and didn't get up.

Then he could shoot no more, the beasts were in with the kids. He ran for the ladder and slid and fell and landed hard in the alley.

Run away, his brain screamed, run from it. He took three panicked steps away, towards the beach, running towards the beach, but then, as though some invisible force had taken hold of him, he stopped.

'Can't run away, Quinn,' he told himself.

'Can't.'

And even as he said the words, he was running back, into the day care, pushing past Mary shielding a child in her arms, past her out to the plaza, wielding the gun as a club now, running and screaming his head off like a lunatic, swinging the gun butt to a sickening crunch on a coyote's skull.

Edilio was there and kids were shooting and Edilio was shouting, 'No, no, no,' and then blood was in Quinn's eyes and blood was in his brain and blood was everywhere and he lost his mind, lost his mind swinging and screaming and hitting, hitting, hitting.

Mary clutched Isabella to her and huddled with John, and the kids cried, hearing the madness outside, the screams and snarls and guns.

'Jesus, save us, Jesus, save us,' someone was repeating in a racked, sobbing voice, and Mary knew in some distant way that it was her.

Drake heard the coyote howl in the night and knew in his black heart what it meant.

Enough of licking his wounds.

The battle was joined.

'Time,' he said. 'Time to show them all.'

He kicked his own front door open and marched towards the plaza, shouting, shouting, wishing he could bay at the moon like the coyotes.

He heard guns firing and pulled his pistol from his belt and uncoiled his whip hand and snapped it, loving the crack it made.

Ahead, two figures were moving away from him, also heading for the sound of battle, two figures. One seemed impossibly small. But no, it was the other that was impossibly big. Sumo big. A shuffling, slumping, thick-limbed creature.

The two mismatched ones moved into a pool of light cast by a street lamp. Drake recognised the smaller one.

'Howard, you traitor,' Drake shouted.

Howard stopped. The beast beside him kept walking.

'You don't want any of this, Drake,' Howard warned.

Drake whipped him across the chest, tore Howard's shirt open, left a trail of blood that was black in the harsh light.

'You better be on your way to help take down Sam,' Drake warned.

The rough beast stopped. It turned slowly and came back.

'What is that?' Drake demanded sharply.

'You,' the beast muttered.

'Orc?' Drake cried, half thrilled, half terrified.

'It's your fault I did it,' Orc said dully.

'Get out of my way,' Drake ordered. 'There's a fight. Come with me or die right now.'

'He just wants some beer, Drake,' Howard said placatingly, clutching the wound in his chest, hunched over in pain, but still trying to manipulate, still trying to be clever.

'God's judgement on me,' Orc slurred.

'You stupid lump,' Drake said, and whirled his whip hand and brought it down full force on Orc's shoulder.

'AAHHH!' Orc bellowed in pain.

'Get moving, you moron,' Drake ordered.

Orc got moving. But not towards the plaza.

'You want a piece of Whip Hand, freak?' Drake demanded. 'I'll cut you up.'

Astrid felt a crushing weight on her lower back and legs. She was face down, lying on top of Little Pete. She was stunned, but had enough presence of mind to understand that she was stunned.

She took a deep breath.

She whispered, 'Petey.' She heard the sound through her bones. Her ears were ringing, muffling sound.

Little Pete wasn't moving.

She tried to draw her legs up, but they wouldn't move.

'Petey, Petey,' she cried.

She wiped something out of her eyes, dust, dirt, sweat, and blinked to focus on her brother. She had shielded most of his body from the falling wall, but a chunk of plaster the size of a backpack lay on his head.

She bit back a sob. She pressed two fingers against his neck and felt a pulse. She could feel his shallow breathing, the rise and fall of his chest, beneath her.

'Help,' she croaked, unsure if she was shouting or whispering, unable to hear for the ringing.

'Someone help us. Someone help us.'

'Save my brother.'

'Save him,' she pleaded, and the plea became a prayer. 'Save Sam. Save us all.'

She began to recite from memory a prayer she'd heard once long ago. Her voice was far away, someone else's voice.

'St Michael the Archangel, defend us in battle. Be our defence against the wickedness and snares of the devil.' She could feel more than hear her own sobbing, a racking shudder that twisted the words in her throat.

As if in mocking answer to her plea for mercy, a shower of glass and plaster fragments fell around her.

'May God rebuke him, we humbly pray. And do you, O prince of the heavenly host, by the power of God . . .'

Little Pete stirred and groaned. He moved his head and she could see the deep gash, pushed inward, a cleaver-mark in his head.

'. . . cast into Hell Satan and all the evil spirits who prowl about the world seeking the ruin of souls.'

Someone stood on the rubble above her. She twisted her neck and saw, silhouetted against the high ceiling in a sudden flash of green lightning, a dark face.

'Amen.'

'I'm not exactly an angel, let alone an archangel,' Dekka said in a voice Astrid could only just make out. 'But I can get this stuff off you.'

Caine leaped from the wreckage of the building.

He had done it.

He had done it.

Sam was under the tangled debris, buried. Beaten.

But Caine could scarcely enjoy the moment. The pain from the damaged left side of his body was shocking. The dangerous green-white light had fused his shirt to his flesh and the result was beyond any agony he had ever imagined.

He staggered towards the ruined church, trying to make sense of the chaos around him. There was no more gunfire, but there were still screams and cries and snarls. And something else, a series of tiny sonic booms, the crack of a bullwhip. Below that, a bass drum keeping a random beat.

Caine stopped, stared, momentarily forgetting his pain.

On the steps of the town hall a titanic battle raged between Drake and some rough-hewn monster.

Drake cracked his whip hand and fired his pistol.

The monster lunged with clumsy blows that missed again and again as Drake danced around, whipping and whipping and yet not even backing the beast up.

The beast swung and missed Drake by inches. The stony fist slammed one of the limestone pillars in front of the town hall. The pillar cracked and almost shattered. Little stone chips flew.

Caine's gaze was drawn downwards by a snarling, slurring, high-pitched voice.

'Female say Pack Leader stop,' Pack Leader said angrily.

'What?' Caine could make no sense of it till he saw Diana striding up, dark hair flying, eyes furious.

'I told this filthy beast to stop,' Diana said, barely controlled.

'Stop what?' Caine demanded.

'They're still attacking the kids,' Diana said. 'We've won. Sam is dead. Call them off, Caine.'

Caine turned his attention back to the battle between Drake and the monster. 'They're coyotes,' Caine said coldly.

Diana flew at him. 'You've lost your mind, Caine. This has to stop. You've won. This has to stop.'

'Or what, Diana? Or what?' Caine demanded. 'Go get Lana. I'm hurt. Pack Leader, do what you want.'

'Maybe this is why your mother abandoned you,' Diana said savagely. 'Maybe she could see that you weren't just bad, you were twisted and sick and evil.'

Caine reacted with sudden violence, forgetting his powers and slapping her hard across the face.

Diana tripped backwards from the blow and sat down hard on the stone steps.

Caine could see her face with sudden, terrible clarity by the glow of a brilliant column of blinding, green-white light.

That light could have only one source.

The light was like a spear aimed at the sky. It arced upwards from the midst of the rubble of the apartment building.

'No,' Caine said.

But the light burned, burned away rubble and debris, all the crushing weight of the collapsed apartment building.

'No,' Caine said, and the light died, snapped off.

Behind him, Drake and Orc carried on their quick-and-slow,

nimble-and-heavy, sharp-and-dull battle, but all Caine could see was the blackened, soot-covered, bright-eyed figure who now walked towards him from the rubble.

Caine aimed his hands at the shattered wood and plaster of the church front. He threw his hands towards Sam and a truckload of debris went flying.

Sam raised his hands. Green fire exploded chunks of brick and heavy wooden beams. They burned in mid-air, turning to cinders before they could hit him.

Dekka raised the debris off Astrid and Little Pete.

But it was no easy thing. Her ability to suspend gravity suspended it under Astrid as well, and she and Little Pete floated up in a spinning galaxy of broken lumber and plaster.

Dekka darted a hand in and yanked Astrid out of the suspension zone. Astrid hit the floor along with Little Pete.

Dekka released her hold on the debris and it slammed down, scarily loud.

'Thanks,' Astrid said.

'There's a lot of other people trapped in here,' Dekka said, wasting no time in moving off to help others.

Astrid bent down and tried to lift Little Pete. He was limp, just a dead weight. She got her arms around his chest and hugged him close like a too-large baby. She hugged him to her and staggered awkwardly from the church, half dragging him, stumbling across rubble.

Lana could heal him, but Lana was gone. All she could think

of was to get him to Dahra down in the basement. But what could Dahra do? Was it even possible to reach the so-called hospital, or had the entrance been blocked by falling debris?

For the first time she realised that the front wall of the church was simply gone. She could see night sky and stars. But she could also see a terrible green-tinged lightning.

Her hearing was returning as the ringing subsided. She could make out animal growls and the sharp crack of a whip and too many voices crying.

Suddenly the debris piled around her began to fly.

Astrid dropped to the ground, shielding Little Pete again, still, always protecting Little Pete. Chunks of wall and shards of wood panelling and odd steel-and-wood joints rose like jets taking off from an airport and accelerated crazily, flying in a stream out through the broken church front.

The green lightning flashed and there came a sound of explosions, a roar of explosions and a brighter light still.

The debris stream stopped.

Astrid climbed up again, hauling Little Pete with her.

Someone ran towards her from the street. He stopped, panting, staring, a frightened animal at bay.

'Caine,' Astrid spat.

He did not speak. She could see that he was hurt. In pain. His face was streaked with sweat and dirt. He stared at her like he was seeing a ghost.

A dangerous light dawned in his clouded eyes.

'Perfect,' he whispered.

Astrid felt herself lifted off her feet. She clung desperately to Little Pete, but he slipped from her hands, escaped her clawing fingers, and fell to the floor.

'Come out and play, brother,' Caine shouted. 'I have a friend of yours.'

Astrid floated, powerless, helpless, and Caine strode behind her, using her as a shield. Out through the church front, out on to the steps, looking across a nightmare scene of mad dogs and raging battles.

Sam was there at the bottom of the steps. He was bloodied and bruised, and one arm hung limp.

'Come on, Sam, burn me now,' Caine shrieked. 'Come on, brother, show me what you've got.'

'Hiding behind a girl, Caine?' Sam asked.

'You think you can taunt me?' Caine said. 'All that matters is winning. So save it.'

'I'll kill you, Caine.'

'No. No, you won't. Not without killing your girlfriend.'

'We're both going to blink out of here in about a minute, Caine. It's over for both of us,' Sam said.

'Maybe for you, Sam. Not for me. I know the way. I know the way to stay.' He laughed in wild triumph.

Astrid said, 'Sam, you have to do it. Destroy him.'

Diana was mounting the stairs.

'Yeah, Sam, destroy me,' Caine mocked. 'You have the power. Just burn a hole right through her and you'll get me, too.'

Diana said, 'Caine, put her down. Be a man, for once.'

'Put her down, Caine,' Sam said. 'It's the end. Fifteen and out. I don't know what it is, but it may be death, and you don't want to die with more blood on your hands.'

Caine laughed mirthlessly. 'You know nothing about me. You didn't grow up not knowing who you were. You didn't have to create yourself out of your own imagination, out of your own will.'

'I grew up with no father at all,' Sam said. 'And no explanation. And no truth. Same as you.'

Caine glanced at his watch. 'I think time is up for you, Sam. You go first, remember? And here's what I want you to know before you go: I'm going to survive, Sam. I'm going to be here still. Me and your lovely Astrid and all of the FAYZ. All of it mine.'

Diana said, 'Sam, the way you beat the poof is –'

Caine rounded on her, raised his hand, and blasted her in mid-sentence. She flew through the air, somersaulted backwards and landed across the street on the grass of the plaza.

The effort had distracted Caine. He dropped Astrid.

Sam extended his hand, palm out.

A CLEAR SHOT.

With a thought, he could kill Caine.

But the world around him faded. Astrid, lying in a heap, seemed bleached, colourless, almost translucent. Caine himself, a ghost.

No sound. The screams of children were muted. The battle between Drake and Orc moved in slow motion, the attacks by the coyotes, all of it frame by frame, human and beast and monster.

Sam's body was numb, as if it had died and left only his brain still whirring away inside his skull.

It's time, a voice said.

He knew that voice and the sound of it was a knife in his guts.

His mother stood before him. She was as beautiful as she had always been to him. Her hair stirred in a breeze he did not feel. Her blue eyes were the only true colour.

'Happy birthday,' she said.

'No,' he whispered, though his lips did not move.

'You really are the man now,' she said, and her mouth made a wry smile.

'My little man,' she said.

'No.'

She stretched out her hand to him. 'Come.'

'I can't,' he said.

'Sam, I'm your mother. I love you. Come with me.'

'Mom . . .'

'Just reach out to me. I'm safe. I can carry you away, out of this place.'

Sam shook his head slowly, slowly, like he was drowning in molasses. Something was happening to time. Astrid wasn't breathing. Nothing was moving. The whole world was frozen.

'It will be like it was,' his mother said.

'It was never . . .' he began. 'You lied to me. You never told me . . .'

'I never lied,' she said, and frowned at him, disappointed.

'You never told me I had a brother. You never told –'

'Just come with me,' she said, impatient now, jerking her hand a little like she would when he was a kid and refused to take her hand to cross the street. 'Come with me now, Sam. You'll be safe and out of this place.'

He reacted instinctively, the little boy again, reacted to the 'mommy' voice, the 'obey me' voice. He reached for her, stretched his hand out to her.

And pulled it back.

'I can't,' Sam whispered. 'I have someone I have to stay here for.'

Anger flashed in his mother's eyes, a green light, surreal, before she blinked and it was gone.

And then, out of the bleached, unreal world, Caine stepped into the eerie light.

Sam's mother smiled at Caine, and he stared at her wonderingly. 'Nurse Temple,' Caine said.

'Mom,' she corrected. 'It's time for both my boys to join me, to come away with me. Out of this place.'

Caine seemed spellbound, unable to tear his gaze away from the gentle, smiling face, the piercing blue eyes.

'Why?' Caine asked in a small child's voice.

Their mother said nothing. Once again, for just a heartbeat, her blue eyes glowed a toxic green before returning to cool, icy blue.

'Why him and not me?' Caine asked.

'It's time to come with me now,' their mother insisted. 'We'll be a family. Far from here.'

'You first, Sam,' Caine said. 'Go with your mother.'

'No,' Sam said.

Caine's face darkened with rage. 'Go, Sam. Go. Go. Go with her.' He was shouting now. He seemed to want to grab Sam physically, push him towards the mother they had not quite shared, but his movements were odd, disjointed, a jerky stick figure in a dream.

Caine gave up trying. 'Jack told you,' he said dully.

'No one told me anything,' Sam said. 'I have things I have to do here.'

Their mother extended her arms to them, angry, demanding to be heeded. 'Come to me. Come to me.'

Caine shook his head slowly. 'No.'

'But you're the man of the house now, Sam,' his mother wheedled. 'My little man. Mine.'

'No,' Sam said. 'I'm my own man.'

'And I was never yours,' Caine sneered. 'Too late now, Mother.'

The face of their mother wavered. The tender flesh seemed to break apart in jigsaw-puzzle pieces. The gently smiling, pleading mouth melted, collapsed inwards. In its place a mouth ringed with needle-sharp teeth. Eyes filled with green fire.

'I'll have you yet,' the monster raged with sudden violence.

Caine stared in horror. 'What are you?'

'What am I?' the monster mocked him savagely. 'I'm your future. You'll come to me on your own in the dark place, Caine. You will come willingly to me.'

'No,' Caine protested.

The monster laughed, a cruel sound from that piranha's mouth.

Slowly the monster faded. Colour bled back into the world around Sam and Caine. Orc and Drake accelerated back to normal speed. The air smelled of gunpowder again. Astrid drew breath.

Sam and Caine stood facing each other.

The world was the world. Their world. The FAYZ. Diana stared. Astrid gasped and opened her eyes.

Caine was quick. He raised his hands, palms out.

But Sam was quicker. He leaped towards Caine, stepped inside his reach, and grabbed his brother's head with his good hand.

Sam's palm was flat against Caine's temple, his fingers curved into his hair.

'Don't make me do this,' Sam warned.

Caine didn't try to back away. His eyes were wild with defiance. 'Go ahead, Sam,' Caine whispered.

Sam shook his head. 'No.'

'Pity?' Caine sneered.

'You have to leave, Caine,' Sam said softly. 'I don't want to kill you. But you can't be here.'

Brianna zoomed up, screeched to a halt, and levelled a gun at Caine. 'If Sam doesn't get you, I will. You sure aren't faster than the Breeze.'

Caine ignored her contemptuously. But he would never get the chance to attack Sam now. Brianna was too fast to defy.

'It's a mistake to let me live, Sam,' Caine warned. 'You know I'll be back.'

'Don't. Don't come back. Next time . . .'

'Next time one of us will kill the other,' Caine said.

'Walk away. Stay away.'

'Never,' Caine said with some of his old bravado. 'Diana?'

'She can stay here,' Astrid said.

'Can you, Diana?' Caine asked her.

'Astrid the Genius,' Diana said in her mocking way. 'So intelligent. So clueless.'

Diana stepped close to Sam, cupped his cheek with her hand, and planted a light kiss on the corner of his mouth. 'Sorry, Sam. The bad girl ends up with the bad boy. It's the way the world works. Especially this world.'

She went to Caine. She did not take his extended hand, did not even look at him, but walked beside him as he descended the steps.

The battle between Drake and Orc had staggered to an exhausted draw. Drake was raising his whip hand once more to bring it down on Orc's pylon shoulders, but his movements were slow, leaden.

'Knock it off, Drake,' Diana said. 'Don't you know when the fight is over?'

'Never,' Drake gasped.

Caine raised his hand and almost casually pulled the struggling, cursing Drake after him.

The coyotes, those still alive, followed them out of town.

Edilio raised his gun and took aim at the retreating beasts, human and not. His eyes locked with Brianna's, the two of them ready.

Sam said, 'No, man. War's over.'

Edilio lowered the gun reluctantly.

'Put it down, Breeze. Let it go,' Sam said.

Brianna obeyed, more relieved than anything.

Quinn climbed the steps to stand with Edilio. He was spattered with blood. He threw his own gun down on the ground. He sent Sam a bleak, infinitely sad look.

Patrick bounded up excitedly, and with him, Lana. 'Sam, let me see that arm,' she said.

'No,' Sam said. 'I'm fine. Go to the others. Save them, Lana.

I couldn't. Maybe you can. Start with Little Pete. He's . . . he's very important.'

Astrid had gone back into the church to find her brother. She reappeared, holding him under the arms, dragging him. 'Help me,' Astrid begged, and Lana ran to her.

Sam wanted to go to Astrid. He needed to. But utter weariness rooted him to the spot. He leaned his good hand on Edilio's strong shoulder.

'I guess we won,' Sam said.

'Yeah,' Edilio agreed. 'I'll get the backhoe. Got a lot of holes to dig.'

FINAL

THE FOOD SEEMED almost to crush the tables. Turkey and dressing, and the biggest collection of pies Sam had ever seen.

The tables were set up first at the south end of the plaza. But then Albert realised that people didn't want to be away from the rows of graves at the north end, they wanted to stay near them. The dead were to be included in this Thanksgiving.

They ate off paper plates and used plastic forks, sat on the few chairs or on the grass.

There was laughter.

There were sniffles, and tears as well, as people remembered Thanksgivings past.

There was music from a stereo system rigged up by Computer Jack.

Lana had worked around the clock for days to heal everyone who could be healed. Dahra had been at her side, organising, prioritising the worst cases, handing out support and pain pills to those who had to wait. Cookie had missed the fight entirely, but had become Dahra's faithful nurse, using his size and strength to lift the injured.

Mary brought the prees out for the big feast. She and her

brother, John, prepared plates for them, spoon-fed some of them, and changed diapers on blankets spread on the grass.

Orc sat with Howard in a corner by themselves. Orc had fought Drake to a standstill. But no one – least of all Orc – had forgotten Bette.

The plaza was a disaster. The burned apartment building was a wreck. The church had only three walls now, and the steeple would probably topple over if there was ever a storm.

They had burned the dead coyotes. Their ashes and bones filled several large trash cans.

Sam watched it all, standing a little apart, balancing a plate of food and trying not to spill the dressing.

'Astrid, tell me if this is crazy: I'm thinking if there are any leftovers, we could send them up to Coates,' Sam said. 'You know, a peace offering.'

'No. Not crazy,' she said. Astrid put her arm around his waist.

'You know, I've had this plan in mind for a while,' Sam said.

'What plan?'

'It involved you and me just sitting on the beach.'

'Just sitting?'

'Well . . .'

'He says, allowing his elliptical tone to imply any number of things.'

Sam smiled. 'I'm all about elliptical implications.'

'Are you going to tell me what happened during the big blink?'

'I am. I will. Maybe not today.' He nodded towards Little

Pete, who hunched over a plate of food and rocked back and forth. 'I'm glad he's OK.'

'Yeah,' Astrid said shortly. Then, 'I think the injury, the blow to his head . . . oh, never mind. Let's not talk about Petey for once. Give your speech and then let's go and see if you even know what "elliptical" means.'

'My speech?'

'Everyone's waiting,' she said.

Sure enough, he realised, there were expectant glances in his direction and a feeling of unfinished business in the air.

'Got any more good quotes I can rip off?'

She thought for a moment. 'OK, here's one. "With malice towards none, with charity for all, with firmness in the right, as God gives us to see the right, let us strive on to finish the work we are in, to bind up the nation's wounds . . ." President Lincoln.'

Sam said, 'Yeah, that's totally going to happen, I'm going to give a speech that sounds like that.'

'They're all still scared,' she said. Then she corrected herself. 'We're all still scared.'

'It's not over,' Sam said. 'You know that.'

'It's over for today.'

'We have pie,' he agreed. Then, with a sigh, he climbed up on to the edge of the fountain. 'Um, people.'

It wasn't hard to get their attention. They gathered around. Even the littlest ones toned down their giggling, at least a bit.

'First of all, thanks to Albert and his helpers for this meal. Let's give it up for the true Mac Daddy.'

A round of hearty applause and some laughter, and Albert waved sheepishly. He frowned a little too, obviously conflicted about the use of the 'Mac' prefix in a way that was not approved in the McDonald's manual.

'And we have to mention Lana and Dahra, because without them, there would be a lot fewer of us here.'

Now the applause was almost reverential.

'Our first Thanksgiving in the FAYZ,' Sam said when the applause died down.

'Hope it's our last,' someone shouted.

'Yeah. You got that right,' Sam agreed. 'But we're here. We're here in this place we never wanted to be. And we're scared. And I'm not going to lie and tell you that from here on, it will all be easy. It won't be. It will be hard. And we'll be scared some more, I guess. And sad. And lonely. Some terrible things have happened. Some terrible things . . .' For a moment, he lost his way. But then he stood up straighter again. 'But, still, we are grateful, and we give thanks to God, if you believe in Him, or to fate, or to just ourselves, all of us here.'

'To you, Sam,' someone shouted.

'No, no, no.' He waved that off. 'No. We give thanks to the nineteen kids who are buried right there.' He pointed at the six rows of three, plus the one who started a seventh row. Neat hand-painted wooden tombstones bore the names of Bette and too many others.

'And we give thanks to the heroes who are standing around here right now, eating turkey. Too many names to mention, and they'd just be embarrassed, anyway, but we all know them.'

There was a wave of loud, sustained applause, and many faces turned towards Edilio and Dekka, Taylor and Brianna, and some towards Quinn.

'We all hope this will end. We all hope we'll soon be back in the world with people we love. But right now, we're here. We're in the FAYZ. And what we're going to do is work together, and look out for each other, and help each other.'

People nodded, some high-fived.

'Most of us are from Perdido Beach. Some are from Coates. Some of us are . . . well, a little strange.' A few titters. 'And some of us are not. But we're all here now, we're all in it together. We're going to survive. If this is our world now . . . I mean, it is our world now. It is our world. So, let's make it a good one.'

He stepped down in silence.

Then someone started clapping rhythmically and saying, 'Sam, Sam, Sam.' Others joined in, and soon every person in the plaza, even some of the prees, was chanting his name.

Quinn was there, and Edilio and Lana.

Sam said to Quinn, 'Would you do me a favour and keep an eye on Little Pete?'

'No prob, brah.'

'Where are you going?' Edilio asked.

'We're going to the beach.' Sam took Astrid's hand.

'You want us to come?' Edilio asked.

559

Lana put her arm through his and said, 'No, Edilio, they don't.'

The boy walked stiffly, favouring the half-healed burn on his side. The coyote walked just ahead, leading the way through the desert. The sun set to the west, sending long shadows from boulders and brush, painting the mountain's face an eerie orange.

'How much farther?' Caine asked.

'Soon,' Pack Leader said. 'The Darkness is near.'

WWW.MICHAELGRANTBOOKS.CO.UK

WWW.THEFAYZ.CO.UK

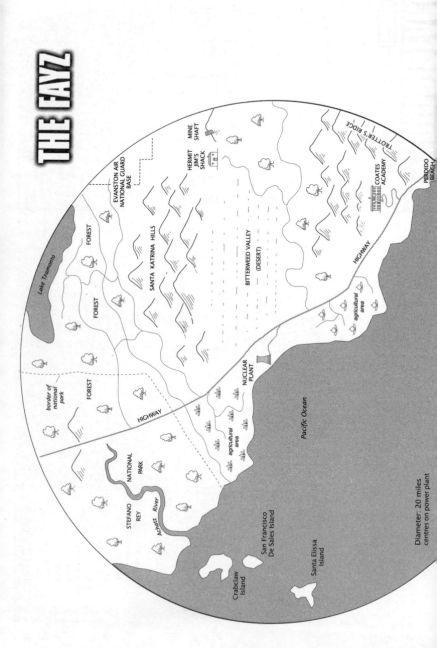

THE FAYZ

Lake Tramonto

FOREST

FOREST

FOREST

border of national park

STEFANO REY NATIONAL PARK

Achatz River

HIGHWAY

agricultural area

Crabclaw Island

San Francisco De Sales Island

Santa Elissa Island

Pacific Ocean

Diameter: 20 miles
centres on power plant

NUCLEAR PLANT

EVANSTON AIR NATIONAL GUARD BASE

SANTA KATRINA HILLS

BITTERWEED VALLEY
(DESERT)

HERMIT JIM'S SHACK

MINE SHAFT

TROTTER'S RIDGE

COATES ACADEMY

HIGHWAY

agricultural area

PERDIDO BEACH

PERDIDO BEACH
CALIFORNIA

ridge

FAYZ wall

various businesses

bluff

Golf Course Road

Clifftop forest

Clifftop road

cliff

Clifftop Resort

Eyeteeth Rocks

highway

gas station

Ralph's grocery

access road

Eastern Avenue

Fourth Avenue

Third Avenue

Second Avenue

Alameda Avenue

First Avenue

Pacific Boulevard

Sunset Street

Ocean Boulevard

San Pablo Avenue

Golding Street

Sheridan Avenue

Sherman Avenue

Grant Street

Chesney Road

Pacific Boulevard

Brace Road

breakwater

Town Beach

Town Plaza

apartment complex

old cannery

marina

parking lot

A
B
C
D
E
F
G
H
I
J
K

N W S E

Legend

A — hardware and day care
B — burned apartment building
C — church
D — town hall
E — Quinn's square
F — Astrid's house
G — Sam's house
H — McDonald's
I — Bully Row
J — firehouse
K — school

THE STORY CONTINUES IN

HUNGER

Read the exclusive preview . . .

ONE

SAM TEMPLE WAS on his board. And there were waves. Honest to God swooping, crashing, salt-smelling, white-foam waves.

And there he was about two hundred metres out, the perfect place to catch a wave, lying face down, almost numb from cold, while his wetsuit-encased, sun-baked back was steaming.

Sam woke suddenly, choking on dust.

He blinked and looked around at the dry landscape. Instinctively he glanced towards the ocean. Couldn't see it from here. And there hadn't been a wave in a long time.

Sam believed he'd sell his soul to ride just one more real wave.

The heat, the sound of the engine and the rhythmic jerking of the Jeep as it laboured down the dusty road conspired to force his eyelids closed again. He squeezed them shut, then opened them wide, willing himself to stay awake.

Three months after the coming of the FAYZ, Sam had still not learned to drive a car, so Edilio drove and Sam rode shotgun. In the back seat Albert Hillsborough sat stiff and quiet. Beside him was a kid named EZ, singing along to his iPod.

Sam pushed his fingers through his hair, which was way too long. His hand came back dirty, clotted with dust. Fortunately the electricity was still on in Perdido Beach, which meant light and hot water. He could at least look forward to a long, hot shower after they all got back.

And a meal. Well, not a meal, no. A can of something slimy was not a meal. His hurried breakfast had been a can of collard greens.

It was amazing what you could gag down when you got hungry enough. And Sam, like everyone else in the FAYZ, was hungry.

Edilio picked up speed.

There wasn't much to the left or right of the road, just bare dirt, fallow fields, and patches of colourless grass broken up by the occasional lonely stand of trees. But up ahead was green, lots of it.

Sam turned in his seat to get Albert's attention. 'So what is that up there, again?'

'Cabbage,' Albert said. Albert was an eighth-grader who no one had paid much attention to before, just one of a handful of African-American students at the Perdido Beach school. But no one ignored Albert any more: he had reopened and run the town's McDonald's. At least he had until the burgers ran out.

The mere memory of hamburgers made Sam's stomach growl. 'Cabbage?' he repeated.

'It makes you fart,' Edilio said with a wink. 'But we can't be too choosy.'

'I guess it wouldn't be so bad if we had coleslaw,' Sam said.

Sam stood up in the Jeep and stretched before jumping to the ground. He was naturally athletic. He had brown hair with glints of gold, blue eyes and a tan that reached all the way down to his bones.

Sam Temple was one of the two oldest people in the FAYZ. He was fifteen.

'Hey. That looks like lettuce,' EZ said.

'If only,' Sam said gloomily. 'So far we have avocados and cantaloupes, which is excellent news. But we are finding way too much broccoli and artichokes. Now cabbage.'

'We may get the oranges back,' Edilio said. 'It was just the fruit was ripe and didn't get picked so they rotted.'

EZ said, 'Hey, I'm going to grab one of those cabbages. I'm starving.'

The cabbages were a foot or so apart within their rows, and each row was two feet from the next. Not much different from other fields Sam had seen during this farm tour.

No, Sam corrected himself, there is something different. He couldn't quite figure out what it was. Sam frowned and tried to work through the feeling, tried to decide why he felt something was . . . off.

It was quieter, maybe.

'I don't even want to think about how many farts this all translates to,' EZ yelled over his shoulder as he marched purposefully into the field.

EZ was a sixth-grader but seemed older. He was tall for his

age, a little chubby. Thin, dishwater hair hung down to his shoulders. EZ was a good name for him: he was easy to get along with, would banter easily, laugh easily, easily find whatever fun there was to be found. He stopped about two dozen rows into the field and said, 'This looks like the cabbage for me.'

'How can you tell?' Edilio called back.

'I'm tired of walking. This must be the right cabbage.'

'Where are the birds?' Sam asked, finally figuring out what was bothering him.

'What birds?' Edilio said. Then he nodded. 'You're right, man, there've been seagulls all over the other fields.'

'They must not like cabbage.' Albert sighed. 'I don't know anyone who does.'

EZ squatted before the cabbage and began to work his hands down beneath the leaves. Then he fell back on his rear end.

'Ow! Ah! Ah!' EZ jumped to his feet. He was holding his right hand with his left and starting hard at his hand. 'No, no, no.'

Sam's mind was elsewhere, scanning for the missing birds, but the terror in EZ's voice snapped his head around. 'What's the matter?'

'Something bit me!' EZ cried. 'Oh, oh, it hurts. It hurts. It . . .' He let loose a scream of agony. The scream started low and went higher, into hysteria.

Sam saw what looked like a black question mark on EZ's pants leg.

'Snake!' Sam said to Edilio.

EZ's arm went into a spasm. It shook violently. It was as if some invisible giant had hold of it and was yanking his arm as hard and as fast as he could.

EZ screamed and began a lunatic dance. 'They're in my feet!' he cried.

Sam stood paralysed for a few seconds, just a few seconds, but later in memory it would seem so long. Too long.

He leapt forward, rushing towards EZ. He was brought down hard by a flying tackle from Edilio.

'What are you doing?' Sam demanded and struggled to free himself.

'Man, look. Look!' Edilio hissed.

Sam's face was mere feet from the first row of cabbages. The soil was alive. Worms. Worms as big as garter snakes were seething up from beneath the dirt. Dozens. Maybe hundreds. All heading towards EZ, who screamed again and again in agony mixed with confusion.

Sam rose to his feet but went no closer to the edge of the cabbage field. The worms did not move beyond the first row of turned soil. There might as well have been a wall, the worms all on one side.

EZ came staggering wildly towards Sam, jerking, flailing like some crazy puppet with half its strings cut.

Three, four feet away, Sam saw the worm erupt from the skin of EZ's throat.

And then another just in front of his ear.

EZ, no longer screaming, sagged to the ground, just sat there limp, cross-legged.

'Help me,' EZ whispered. 'Sam . . .'

EZ's eyes were on Sam. Pleading. Fading. Then just staring, blank.

The only sounds now came from the worms. Their hundreds of mouths seemed to make a single sound, one big mouth chewing wetly.

A worm spilled from EZ's mouth.

Sam raised his hands, palms out.

'Sam, no!' Albert yelled. Then in a quieter voice, 'He's already dead.'

'Albert's right, man. Don't burn them, they're staying in the field, don't give them a reason to come after us,' Edilio hissed.

The black worms swarmed over and through EZ's body. Like ants swarming a dead beetle.

It felt like a very long time before the worms slithered away and tunnelled back into the earth.

What they left behind was no longer recognisable as a human being.